CLARE LITTLEMORE

Drift

Contents

Dedication

To Marc, my hero.

Brit Alert!

If you are reading this book and not from the UK, a brief warning that I am a British author and use British spellings throughout the book. In The Beck, characters wear overalls of different 'colours' (not 'colors'), might run towards (not toward) each other and may even, on occasion, have to apologise (rather than apologize).

Happy reading!

Chapter One

I couldn't cry any more. My face felt taut and stretched, and if I stuck out my tongue, I could taste the salt water which had long dried on my skin. Lying slumped against the side of the boat, I tried in vain to concentrate on what was happening around me. The continuous swaying movement sent my stomach churning.

I drifted in and out of consciousness. Each time I came to, horrific memories of our escape invaded, and I allowed myself to sink back into the comforting blackness of sleep. Often, my head was filled with panicked shouting, distorted images, and shadowy, threatening figures which both taunted and confused me. At other times, some kind of survival instinct kicked in and allowed me to doze more peacefully, but all too soon I would wake and begin to relive the nightmare.

Eventually, it was my heaving stomach which forced me into action. Knowing I was facing the inevitable, I forced myself to a standing position and staggered to the front of the boat where only Rogers, steady as ever at the wheel, was present. Positioning myself with my back to the wheelhouse which he stood under, I leaned over the side of the rolling craft and heaved. It was all I could do to cling to the rail which ran around the side of the boat as I emptied the contents of my stomach into the waters below.

Once I regained control, I straightened up, wiping my face with my sleeve. I felt better, for the moment at least. Turning my attention to Rogers, I noticed that he was staring at me, a look of concern on his grizzled face.

"Ok?"

I managed to nod, stumbling over to him.

He peered through the windshield at the horizon ahead, a frown crossing his features as a thickening mist crept over the water towards us. The land we had been travelling closer to all night was all but hidden from view, and I could see that he was worried. I wondered how he had become so adept at sailing. Most Beck citizens had a distinct lack of experience with the water. It surrounded our community, imprisoning or protecting it depending on your viewpoint, yet we were completely unaware of the issues associated with traversing it. Since we had left the Beck, Rogers had seemed to steer the boat with complete confidence. Until now.

"How long," I breathed deeply, desperate to wrest control of my body back from my stomach, "til we're there?"

"Still a couple more hours. But we're making good time. You slept most of the way. I'm just... just trying to keep us a safe distance from the shoreline," He jerked his head over his shoulder, changing the subject, "How do you think we're doing?"

I turned to survey the people behind me, scattered in small groups all over the deck. The rescued. Honestly, I wasn't sure. Our escape had been a success, for the most part. We were free, on board a large boat with a motor, and we had rescued a good number of Beck citizens. But we had left people behind. Lost one friend for good.

I gazed at the blanketed figure at the rear of the deck. The rest of the citizens on board had left a wide berth around it, as though death was contagious. Except for Mason. Reeling from his loss, he knelt beside Davis' body, a hand resting on the blanket, his eyes staring out to sea.

We had all known an attempted escape was dangerous, that we were risking everything by attempting to leave. A society which treated its citizens as commodities was never going to allow such an exodus. When Shadow Patrol caught us, the consequences for some had been devastating. Davis, caught by a bullet as he loosened the rope which tethered us to our previous home. He had been dead before we left the harbour. Jackson, left behind, injured as she attempted to bring the new Patrol recruits safely to the boat. They had made it while she had not. I was terrified her injury would land her in Clearance, and was certain that Mason shared my fear.

I became aware of Rogers' eyes on me and realised I had yet to answer his question.

"We'll need a little time to adjust. And to get to know one another, I suppose." I gestured to the other occupants on the deck. "There are a lot of different groups here. And we left in a hurry, no time to properly explain, so..."

He hauled on the wheel and I felt the boat begin to turn, "There'll be time when we get there. I'm hoping we can create quite a community, now. There'll be more than twenty of us."

I fell silent. This had been my hope too, but a distant, future one. I had planned to stay behind, to continue the Resistance in The Beck, with Cam. The last-minute panic had landed me on the boat, setting off for the unknown, without his reassuring presence. Meanwhile there were other, newer issues to deal with. I found myself actually nervous about coping without the continuous sustenance and routines provided by the Beck which, however frustrating, were all I had ever known.

The sound of footsteps brought me back to the present and I turned to see Tyler striding in our direction. Taking a deep breath, I forced a smile that I hoped looked more confident than I felt. Ever since she had discovered the budding relationship between Cam and I, she had treated us coolly, and I worried that the tentative friendship we had started to develop was lost forever.

Ignoring me, she directed her gaze at Rogers. "How long?"

"Few hours yet. Better to get some sleep."

She snorted. "Not likely."

He shrugged and turned his attention to the wheel again. The fog now swirled thickly in all directions and I had no idea how he knew which direction he was travelling. He consulted an instrument to one side of the dashboard, and squinted again into the distance. Moving the wheel again, he adjusted our course for the second time in as many minutes, completely unaware of our presence now.

Left standing next to Tyler, I found myself staring awkwardly into the water with no idea what to say. My companion seemed to share my discomfort and, after a moment, gestured to the cupboards at the side of the deck.

"Everyone's starving, Quin. Want to see if you can find something to eat in there?"

Glad of something useful to do, and realising that my stomach was now far calmer than earlier, I followed her instructions. Opening the locker, I found several packages wrapped in a pale coloured cloth. I looked up at Tyler, but she had anticipated my question.

"Provisions for Shadow Patrol."

I remembered that the Clearance boats were also used for fishing. The first of the packages contained the standard-issue oatcakes. They were a little hard, but edible. I shut the locker and straightened up, the package clasped in my hands.

"Do we need to ration these?"

She nodded approvingly. "We should be ok to eat one package for now. A single cake each. We need to keep up strength and morale for the rest of the journey." She glanced at our captain, whose concentration was still fixed on the waters ahead. "Rogers has assured me there'll be food when we get there." She took two cakes from the stack in my hands and gestured to the rest of the boat, "Go on. I'll keep him company."

I moved away, happy that Tyler was at least able to converse with me about matters of importance. We had to be able to function as part of a team, and she knew that. Tyler's strength had always been her ability to remain calm in a crisis and put aside her own concerns for the benefit of others. It was what had made her such a good Patrol Super.

I made slow progress across the constantly rolling deck, heading for the Clearance citizens first, since they were the group who needed the sustenance most urgently. When I reached my friend Harper, I was rewarded with a smile. As I returned it, I heard a strange sound coming from my left as something struck the side of the boat.

"Get down!"

The scream came from Rogers, who was frantically spinning the wheel of the boat again. As the people around me began to stir, struggling to their knees before dropping onto the deck in response to Rogers' command, I focused my attention on the place the projectile had hit. A long, thin arrow jutted out

5

from between two of the planks to my left. At the same time, something barrelled into me, knocking me sideways. I fell, hitting the hard wood below me. A body lay on top of mine, pressing me into the deck.

Struggling to turn so that I could see who had assaulted me, I found myself staring into Mason's face. His eyes were blazing.

"When someone says 'Get down!' Quin, you get down."

As I attempted a reply, a second arrow shot through the air and bit into another section of the deck.

"What the–?"

Satisfied that I was now out of the immediate range of the arrows, Mason shuffled to the edge of the boat and peered through a crack in the hull. I followed him, knowing the curved edge would provide more of a shield than the open deck. The fog had cleared a little, and I was surprised at how close our boat now seemed to the land ahead.

"That mountain range." Mason shifted to the side to allow me access to the gap. "I think there are buildings, which means people, and weapons, clearly."

I turned to Rogers. Whilst I had been a little concerned about setting off for somewhere totally new, I had always anticipated that Rogers was leading us to a place where we would be better off than we had been back in The Beck. Yet here we were nearing land to find its inhabitants attacking us. Rogers still stood at the helm, the concentration on his face demonstrating the effort he was putting into steering the boat away from the shoreline, which had clearly been hidden by the fog.

Others on the boat had also begun to recover from their shock and take more practical action. Tyler was emptying the lockers of guns and passing them out. Hand to hand, they were circulated around the deck. Mason took one and lined it up at the crack in the boat's hull. I noticed that the new Patrol recruits seemed to have their share of the guns, and most of them were wriggling on their stomachs into fairly evenly-spaced positions around the deck. Blythe crouched as close to the edge of the boat as she could, her arms closed protectively around the tiny bundle that was her baby daughter Perry, and Barnes had positioned his bulky frame directly in front of her.

Having passed out the weapons, Tyler turned back to Rogers.

"Don't shoot!" he hissed, his voice was taut with tension. "Not yet, and only if we have to. We've limited ammo. Better to take evasive action." He gestured out to sea. "And I have a better line of sight now the mist is clearing."

The message passed silently between us. Hide, head away from the shore and save the bullets, only firing if it was absolutely necessary. The centre of the deck was empty now, and the only person visible above the ship's rail was Rogers.

There was a sharp gasp from the rear of the boat as another arrow flew through the air. It sailed just over the wheel, missing Rogers by inches. Tyler crawled on her stomach to the front of the boat and used the butt of her gun to smash off the door to the largest locker. Lying with her back to the boat side closest to shore, she held the length of wood upright at the rear of the wheelhouse, attempting to shield the man who was risking his life for us.

Rogers turned the boat even more sharply out to sea, desperately trying to avoid the piercing darts which still flew regularly in our direction. Perceptive as always, Tyler took note of the movement and adjusted the angle of the makeshift shield accordingly. I strained to scan the shore through the cracks in the wood next to me, but could see only sections

7

of it through the scattered mist. We seemed to have been sailing alongside a pebbled shelf of land which sloped down to the shore. Around the edges were some scrubby bushes and I thought I spotted a couple of tall, slender sheds, like sentry posts. I wondered if the people firing at us were hidden inside or in the bushes to the side of the beach. There were no obvious signs of life.

As I glanced back at Rogers, another arrow slammed into the door which Tyler shielded him with. She strained to keep the wood in place, bracing herself against the side of the boat as she took the impact. The arrow remained, piercing the door at head height. Rogers' hands tightened on the wheel, his knuckles turning white, as he steered us away from our attackers.

I shifted closer to Mason as the onslaught continued. Clearly, Rogers' friends were not the only ones out here in this new world. The thought made my hand tremble on the barrel of the gun.

Chapter Two

Our group was silent as the boat headed further out to sea, the arrows continuing to zip through the air around us for a while, ceasing as our attackers realised they could no longer hit us. Once we were out of range, Rogers slowed the boat again and we continued to pass the land which housed such defensive inhabitants at a slower pace. The fog had almost cleared now, a pale sun had appeared between the thinning clouds, and an eerie light was cast over the surrounding hillside. We studied the passing land with growing concern. The Clearance citizens began to whisper in low, worried voices, but the new Patrol trainees were muttering in unmistakable anger. Their complaints grew in volume until one of them, a wiry man with a thin face, stood up and faced Rogers, his fists clenched in fury.

"What was that?"

Rogers pointed at Tyler, who took the wheel. All eyes were fixed on our boat's captain, waiting for some kind of explanation of the unexpected assault that had just occurred. He looked sheepish as he turned to face us.

"Look, the island we're heading for is actually that one," he pointed into the distance, at a smaller rise of land a little further ahead. "But there are others... I mean other people living close by. Those were the people we just encountered. I was hoping we might escape their notice, trying to sail past at a distance, but... what with the weather, it was difficult, and their guards are pretty vigilant."

"Clearly." The recruit did not sound any calmer, "Look, we came with you because we were told our lives were in danger if we didn't. Jackson told us we'd be going somewhere safer! We're prepared for hard work, but not for fighting off enemies and getting killed before we even get there."

He thrust an angry finger at Rogers, taking a rapid single step towards him. Rogers didn't flinch, but held up his hands helplessly.

"Look, I told some of you here about how we lost one of the citizens we brought with us on the way here, remember?"

From her position at the helm, Tyler called back, "Lee."

"Lee, yes." Rogers looked even more disturbed at the mention of his friend's name, "Well I didn't exactly tell you how we lost him."

"Lost him?" The wiry man sneered, "Sounds like you're always careless with other people's lives."

Pain flickered momentarily across Rogers' face, and he seemed to take a deep breath before continuing. "We had a rough journey over here from The Beck. Far worse than this one, and we had a much smaller craft as well. By the time we reached this point we'd already suffered some damage to the boat. It took us far longer to get here than we'd anticipated. We were travelling in high winds and had to fight to keep any kind of control. When we saw land," he glanced behind us, sadness clouding his features, "we were just grateful to have made it. Once we were close enough, we looked for a suitable bay to steer into and moor up. We were within about a hundred metres from shore when it happened."

"When what happened?"

"They attacked so suddenly. We never saw them, but they were armed. And heavily. They shot at us from the shore under cover of the bushes, not arrows, like just now, but bullets. We had to make an immediate retreat. As we moved away from the shore, the boat we were in suffered some damage, and Lee was shot in the chest." His voice cracked a little as he finished his sentence, but he fought to continue. "We limped the boat to the next available piece of land, bailing out water all the way. By the time we reached safety and landed, the boat was useless. We staggered to shore, dragging Lee with us, but it was too late for him."

"And why would you not tell us that before now?" I asked, suspecting the answer before it was given.

"Because," he sighed heavily, "I didn't want to give anyone a reason not to come. I thought..." he ran a hand through his beard roughly, "I thought we might... on the way over to The Beck they didn't notice me... so I hoped that..."

The angry recruit took another step closer to Rogers, "You *hoped*? You seriously thought we'd get a boat this size past a heavily armed guard without them taking any kind of action?"

I had never seen Rogers look so uneasy. "I'm sorry. I was wrong. I should have told you, but... well there wasn't time, with the escape happening so fast, and–"

"You lied!"

"No. I omitted the truth." Rogers seemed to regain some confidence. "And that was from Tyler... Quin... but not from you. Jackson gave you the information she had, and you chose to come."

"But we didn't have all the information!" His voice was

11

rising steadily in volume, "We could be in more danger here than we were in The Beck!"

It was now Rogers who took a step closer to the recruit, "Believe me, you're not. We saved you−"

"Saved us!" the recruit's voice tore across the deck. "Saved us!" he called back to his fellow recruits with a bitter laugh, his fists clenched at his sides.

"Thomas," It was Cass who spoke, her tone more soothing than I was used to, but she was clearly trying to calm the situation. I hoped the fact that she knew him better than we did would help. "Calm down. Rogers didn't mean for anyone to get hurt."

"Calm down?" He spat the words at her and she recoiled at their venom. "I want the truth." He closed the gap between himself and Rogers, glaring into his face with unbridled fury.

"Look, Thomas is it?" Rogers held his ground. "I will tell you everything, I promise, but I think it's more important that we get to safety first."

As if she could sense the hostility, Perry began to cry, a plaintive, growing mewling stopped the man in his tracks and diverted his attention elsewhere. For a moment I was glad of the distraction, hoping that it would diffuse the situation, but the recruit's face only grew darker. He searched for the cause of the sound, which Blythe seemed unable to stem, despite cradling her daughter closer.

The tirade was no less venomous, just directed elsewhere. "And another thing. The baby. Why bring it with us? It's surely not sensible to bring along a helpless child? Not to mention the Clearance citizens." He gestured at one of Harper's weaker-looking friends.

Rogers looked increasingly frustrated, but attempted a rational explanation. "Look, you're right. Ideally, we wouldn't have brought weaker citizens along on a journey which might prove dangerous."

Thomas look was triumphant, as though he had scored a point against Rogers. Out of the corner of my eye I saw Tyler cut the engine, letting the boat idle. She was clearly concerned about the direction the conversation was taking. Rogers didn't seem to notice, and simply raised an eyebrow at Thomas' hostility as he continued.

"But this was a rescue mission, and we set out to save those Beck citizens who we felt were most in need of help. We saved you all, which you don't need to thank us for, but you have to respect the fact that we saved others who were in need. This is our boat, and I'm afraid you're in no position to criticise our decisions."

"But a baby, an old woman—seriously? And you keep saying that you saved us. How do we know that for sure?"

Rogers pressed on. "Look, Jackson explained the situation to you, didn't she? She told you what they were going to do to you? In the Dev Sector?"

I watched his face as he remembered what he had been told by Jackson. My friend was honest and calm in the face of danger, and I knew that she would have conveyed the urgency with which the recruits needed to be rescued. The truth—that Montgomery from the Development Sector, where they experimented with chemical mixtures all the time, had been planning to inject Cass' entire pod with a serum intended to make them into fearless soldiers prepared to do anything for the cause—was truly frightening. It had been enough to persuade more than half of Cass' pod to leave The Beck for the complete unknown.

This man had chosen to go with Jackson, so he must have believed her. I could only hope that remembering the plight they had been saved from would make him more sympathetic to the situations of others, which were equally as dire. As he continued, my heart sank.

"She explained, yes. And I get it. But I thought we were leaving with some kind of plan—a place we could retreat to which offered better options. We're all strong, able-bodied, willing to work hard to achieve something more. I s'pose even the Clearance citizens are capable of some kind of work. But how can a baby do anything other than drain resources and be a burden we have to protect?"

His voice had grown in volume, and I could see that Blythe was listening to the conversation. She continued to rock the baby, whispering words of comfort I couldn't hear into Perry's ear, all the time glancing fearfully at the group of recruits.

Out of the corner of my eye, I saw Barnes push himself to his feet, his fists clenched. "Why's it any of your business?"

"It's everyone's business if it puts us at risk!" The man's tone grew even more strident. "You say you've rescued people who needed saving. But Beck babies are well protected. Precious. Well cared for. How did she *need* saving?"

Rogers seemed at a loss for a moment, clearly wondering what else he could say to defend the decision. In truth, Perry hadn't been in any danger, but her mother Blythe had not been coping well with their separation. Clearly Tyler and Cam had thought she wouldn't survive the journey to a new place and her current depression would only worsen if she were without her daughter. Rogers had been persuaded that Perry should be brought along to help Blythe more than anything. But I knew this explanation would make little difference to Thomas.

He hadn't finished. "You can't justify it, can you? So, as well as being lied to, we're saddled with a useless child."

He was now shouting. As he completed his sentence, the figure of Barnes came flying at him. Clearly appointing himself as Perry's protector, he seemed to have lost all lost patience with Thomas and now began pummelling the recruit. I leapt forward alongside Tyler and Rogers, attempting to stop the assault. Barnes, realising that he couldn't continue to strike the recruit without hitting one of us, paused, panting hard. Thomas lay on the deck, cradling a hand over one of his cheeks. I sat back on my heels and made an attempt to calm things down.

"Look, can't you just accept that we had to bring her along, and leave it at that for now?" I glared at Barnes, and then turned back to the first man. "We have to try and find a way to coexist peacefully—our new lives depend on it. Like Rogers said, we can talk more about the challenges later. I'm sure there'll be more than one. But we have to try and stick together, don't we?"

Tyler removed a hand from Barnes' arm cautiously. "Quin's right. Shelve the fighting for now and let's get to dry land. We're all exhausted, but it won't be long now." She gestured at the land which was now coming into view ahead of us.

The men glared at one another, but Barnes slunk back to his original guard post next to Blythe and Thomas relaxed against the side of the boat. Rogers looked relieved, and I heaved an inward sigh of relief, satisfied that at least we had managed to soothe the conflicts for the time being. Hopefully once we arrived there would be opportunities to rebuild, and we would be able to separate those who did not get along. The deck of a boat was a cramped place for hot tempers and difficult conversations.

"Look, going back to those people," Tyler lowered her voice so the others couldn't hear, "we need to be aware that they pose a threat, right?"

Rogers straightened up and returned to the wheel. "Unfortunately, yes. They've left us alone until now, probably because there were only four of us and we weren't a threat. When I returned to The Beck last time I did it at night, and in a small vessel. I rowed past slowly and quietly and managed not to alert the lookouts. But he's right, with a boat this size..." His voice trailed off hopelessly.

I shuddered at his words. While he had told us of Lee's death, he had been deliberately vague about it, and our meeting had been interrupted by news that Reed and some Shadow Patrol were nearby. We had scattered, believing that we would have far more time to discuss the situation with Rogers before leaving, but fate had intervened and we had fled with no time to quiz him about life over the water. I could understand why he had not told us the truth, but others clearly didn't see it that way. And I had a feeling that Thomas would not remain silent for long.

Chapter Three

As we returned to our positions on the deck following the argument, an air of tension hung over the entire boat. The recruits were still muttering among themselves. At the helm, Rogers guided us ever closer to land, his back ramrod straight, and the Clearance citizens sat in ominous silence. Blythe was now trying to feed a bottle to her hungry daughter, and cradling her even more protectively. I noticed Harper and Marley observing them curiously, their expressions far warmer than those of the recruits. In them, perhaps, the tiny infant had a few supporters.

I watched her myself for a few moments. Having had no experience with babies other than my one trip to Meds, I knew little of their ways. She was so young, but her face was capable of reflecting a myriad of different expressions. I smiled, despite myself. Perry, perhaps sensing she was under scrutiny, or unfamiliar with a mother she had not known since she was a few weeks old, was fussing over taking the milk. I silently thanked Tyler for her Meds experience, which had shown her the necessary supplies we would need to feed and care for Perry. I didn't like to think about what would happen when they ran out.

In an attempt to soothe frayed tempers, I distributed the

oatcakes I had abandoned earlier. Most citizens accepted them gratefully, and they seemed to ease the strained atmosphere somewhat. When I had finished, Cass caught hold of my arm and pulled me to one side. I followed her to the front of the boat, away from her fellow recruits but still out of Rogers' hearing as long as we kept our voices low.

"Sorry about Thomas. He's always been opinionated."

I grimaced. "He certainly seems that way."

She sighed.

"You ok, Cass?"

She managed a small smile, looking more vulnerable now we were away from the rest of the recruits, "I suppose so."

Cass certainly didn't look her usual self. I thought back to the awkwardness of her movement the last time I had seen her before the escape. I knew that she had been subject to interrogation by Carter, the fearsome Governance Superintendent, but had never had the chance to ask her about it.

"Are your injuries healing?" I hesitated before continuing. "I can't imagine being questioned by Carter. Was it terrible?"

"Yes." She shuddered at my mention of the name. "Look Quin, I... there's something I should tell you before we..." She gestured at the island ahead. "Something that–"

She stopped, looking stricken, and I wondered what it was that haunted her. I wondered if Carter's torture had left her with permanent scars. When she didn't continue, I decided perhaps she wasn't ready to talk about it, and attempted to comfort her instead.

"Cass, I know it seems impossible, but we did manage to escape. We're almost there now, and once we are there'll be food and shelter. Things aren't so bad."

She didn't look convinced, and again it was a while before

her quiet reply came, "I hope you're right." A heavy sigh escaped her lips, "Aren't you frightened, Quin?"

I took a moment before responding, knowing the answer but unsure whether I should admit it. I decided that, as one of my oldest friends, I had to tell her the truth. "Honestly Cass, I'm terrified. But I wanted change. And now I've got what I wanted, I need to stay positive."

"What about..." she hesitated, "the man... the one who rescued us from the wall that night? Cam, is it?"

I closed my eyes briefly at the stab of pain which shot through my chest at his name. "Yes?"

"He's not on the boat. What was his part in the rescue?"

I didn't answer, for a moment the words too painful to contemplate.

"You're not telling me he didn't have some kind of involvement in this? Surely he was supposed to be here as well." She put a cool hand on my arm at my continued silence, "Didn't he make it?"

"He was on the beach, bringing someone along to be rescued," I forced my breathing to slow as I managed to get each word out, one after another. "He wasn't supposed to be on the boat though."

She looked puzzled and I continued, unsure of how she would react to what I was about to say.

"I was supposed to be staying behind, with him. I ended up on board by accident... when the Shadow Patrol started firing, we set off so quickly..."

Her face clouded with disappointment as she took in my words. "You weren't coming with us?" She glanced across at Harper, who was deep in conversation with the Clearance citizens around her. "I thought... I thought the three of us..."

She trailed off, a sadness haunting her face.

I tried to reassure her. "I was coming. In the future. When we had managed to work out a way of getting more people out."

Her eyes glistened with tears, and she looked away, blinking hard. Harper appeared to be totally wrapped up in the lives of her new friends, and I wasn't even supposed to be here. Never one to manage her emotions well, I knew she had taken my revelation as rejection. And it only added to whatever mental agony she was already going through. Moving closer, I put my arms around her. She allowed me to hold her, but didn't reciprocate. After a moment, I gave up and let her go. We stood side by side watching the island ahead loom larger. I wondered what lay in store for us in our new home.

The remainder of the journey passed quickly, and soon Rogers was guiding the boat towards land. Cautiously, I pushed myself into a standing position and found that I no longer felt queasy. We had reached the smaller island and were pulling into a cove which was sheltered, but rocky and bare. There was a sliver of land in sight, backed by a couple of fairly steep cliffs. A narrow path led away from the cove, disappearing between the two rock faces. Our boat had come to a standstill, floating in the water but still some way from land. Rogers glanced worriedly at the rocks on either side and the rest of the citizens watched him anxiously.

"What's the plan?" I whispered to Blythe, who was peering anxiously down into the water, still clutching Perry close to her chest.

"Not sure," she grimaced, gesturing to the baby. "It's not like we can all swim."

I turned my attention to our makeshift captain. "Rogers,

what's the best way to get to shore?"

He beckoned me over. "Look, in the past I've just sailed up close and waded in. But that was with a much smaller vessel. This boat," he tapped a hand on the wheel helplessly, "is much bigger. I'm worried we might damage the bottom if we go in too close, but the water's deep here. We'd have to swim."

"What about the canoes?" The voice came from further back on the deck. I turned to see one of the Patrol recruits from Cassidy's group, a sandy haired man with sallow features.

"Canoes?"

The man gestured to two small slender boats which were strapped inside the hull at the rear of the boat, "They should take two people each. We'll have to ferry people in gradually, but it should work. How close do we need to get before we can wade?"

Rogers shrugged, "Maybe three or four meters from the shore."

"Well it's better than risking the larger boat."

Rogers made his decision, "Better get started then."

One of the recruits glanced worriedly across the water, "Will the boat be safe here? Won't it drift away?"

"We have an anchor we can throw down, but for the moment I don't think we can risk leaving it without anyone on it. We'll have to take turns on guard."

Mason spoke for the first time since his outburst. "I can stay on board for now, keep watch."

I wondered about his reasons for staying. He definitely seemed to be avoiding the company of others since we'd left The Beck.

"Thank you, Mason. Anyone else?"

The same sandy haired recruit spoke up, "I will."

"That's great." Tyler took charge. "What's your name?"

"Shaw. Used to work in the Repair Sector before I volunteered for the recent Patrol trials." He made a hammering motion, "My building skills might just come in handy here."

"Great." Rogers smiled approvingly, "You two stay here for now then. We'll make sure that someone else comes out here later on and relieves you of the duty. Keep two of the guns. If there's an issue, fire one shot into the air and we'll get to you as soon as we can."

Both men nodded and retreated to the rear of the boat, beginning to open lockers and lift out their contents for transport to shore. Rogers beckoned Harper's dark-haired male friend over.

"What's your name?"

"Walker." The tall, broad-shouldered man's voice was deep.

"Give me a hand with these will you?" Rogers motioned to the canoes.

The two men busied themselves lifting the small boats from their fixings and testing their size. They were strictly meant to carry two people, but I wondered if they might fit three of the smaller citizens in. The shore might not be that far away, but we were all exhausted, and anything that could speed up the process would be a bonus.

Rogers had soon supervised the lowering of the two canoes into the water and appointed himself and Allen, another of the new recruits, as rowers. He beckoned to Tyler, who climbed down into the recruit's canoe without issue, and they assisted a pale but determined Price into the other craft beside Rogers. We watched anxiously as they set off, Roger's rowing smooth and steady, and the recruit's strokes a little jerky, but both managing to head more or less straight for the land.

The rest of us stood watching, as the canoes delivered Price and Tyler to shore. When the canoes pulled alongside for a second time, Rogers motioned to me. Cautiously, I began to shimmy down the rope they had fastened to the cleats on the side of the boat, trying to remember what my Patrol training had taught me about handling ropes. As my feet touched the canoe, I glanced to my right, where Harper was mimicking my movements. Suddenly, her hands slipped and she tumbled backwards and landed in the freezing water with a strangled cry.

Without thinking, I leapt in beside her. Gripping the side of the small craft tightly, I attempted to grab Harper's arm at the same time. I wasn't a swimmer, but was far stronger than she was, and hoped I'd be able to hold her up long enough for Rogers to haul her out. I tried to secure my arm around her torso, but without releasing my hold on the canoe, it was difficult.

She thrashed about in the water wildly, her wet limbs sliding from my grip. Taking a deep breath, I let go of the canoe momentarily and used both hands to grasp her writhing torso, trying desperately to calm her. But as I tightened my grip on her shoulders, she echoed my movement and wrapped her own arms around me. With the added weight, I felt myself being pulled underwater. Fighting for breath, I managed to wrench my arms free, but lost hold of her in the process. I panicked, kicking out and managing to break the surface for a moment, where I gasped a short breath and tried to orient myself between the shore and the two boats.

As I did, I felt a force plunge into the water beside me. Something shot past, heading in Harper's direction, swimming with strength and confidence. I desperately hoped it was someone who would be able to do what I had failed to. For now, I kicked my tiring legs once more and tried to get my bearings, hoping that I hadn't travelled too far from the canoe. Thankfully, the small vessel was only floating few metres away, and Rogers was already leaning out of it, a length of wooden pole held out to me. I managed to reach it and found myself being pulled in rapidly.

"Are you stupid?" Rogers' words as he hauled me out of the icy water were harsh.

For the moment I chose not to answer him, instead focusing on righting myself in the canoe and staring at the water, where the desperate thrashing had stopped. Rogers sighed and threw his own overall jacket around my shoulders. Glancing around, I worked out that the other figure in the water was Walker. I thought back to Harper's refusal to leave him in Clearance. It made sense. Obviously, they were close. I jerked my eyes back to the dark waters below, which remained ominously still.

And then from underneath the water, a large, dark shape emerged. Walker, with Harper closely gathered in his arms. They broke the surface together, gasping for breath. Rogers used the same pole to reach them, and they struggled together to the second canoe. They were hauled up into it: Harper first, followed by Walker, who did not really fit but seemed unwilling to leave her side. The collective sigh of relief was almost audible.

To lose more people before we had even reached our destination would have been devastating. We already had one body to bury. The thought of two or three was inconceivable. But as Rogers and Allen transported us to the shore, I thought about our narrow escape. I considered Harper and Walker's potential fate in Clearance—the Drownings—and how close they had both come to the same end in their attempt to escape. Clearly there were dangers ahead, new dangers, which we would have to adjust to and prepare for.

Chapter Four

Once safely on dry land, I settled myself next to Cass, shivering. She put a comforting arm around my shoulder, but the expression on her face was still troubled. Rogers and Allen brought across the remaining passengers without further issue and returned to the larger boat one last time. On their final trip, they set about bringing ashore the minimal equipment we had managed to take from The Beck. There were several backpacks which were filled with a small amount of medicine and food supplies, and finally the remaining guns from the Clearance boat itself. Once unloaded, the pile of belongings was pitifully small.

Eventually, they went back to one of the canoes and gently lifted out something much larger. Struggling slightly, they carried it across to an outcrop of rocks and laid it down. Davis. I thought of Mason, and looked back at the boat we had left. He had barely spoken since we left The Beck, and I was concerned about him. Once Rogers and Allen had dragged the two canoes out of the water, they stored them behind some of the rocks at the rear of the cove. Tyler set about distributing blankets to myself, Harper and Walker, as we were still soaking wet.

After standing to accept the blanket and wrapping it closely around her body, Harper made her way over to us.

"Hey, Quin." A shy smile stole across her face. "I wanted to say thanks. What you did meant a lot."

I shrugged, embarrassed. "That's alright. It was kind of instinctive. I was in the water before I knew what I was doing."

"Well it's a good thing you were."

"It's not like it was me who saved you." I gestured across the fire to the male Clearance citizen.

"Maybe not, but you got there before Walker did. You tried to keep me afloat."

"Old habits die hard, I guess." I smiled.

She turned her attention to Cass. "Hey, Cass. Long time, no see."

Cass stared at Harper, a number of different expressions flitting across her face. The three of us had not been together properly since we had been reassigned from Agric at the last assessment. For a long moment there was an awkward silence, and then Harper swept Cass and I into a shared embrace.

When she let go, Cass seemed to have found her voice. "Good to see you, Har. Thought for a while there we'd seen the last of you."

Harper grinned, and I marvelled at the change in her from the ailing girl I had known. She still looked pale, but was calm and well. I had always anticipated that Cass would be the one of us to succeed in her new position as Super, but she was the one who had struggled with our separation the most, and had since worked hard to find a way to join me in Patrol. Harper had clearly made new allies and forged some kind of a life for herself in Clearance. She and her new friends had survived somehow, against all the odds, and were managing on what I knew to be extremely meagre rations in a place where no one was treated well.

But they had been unaware of the ultimate consequence for those citizens living in Clearance: mass drowning. I myself had witnessed the last occurrence of this, which had taken place a few days after the previous Assessment Day. Boatloads of the weakest Clearance citizens were simply herded down to the harbour, taken out to sea, and dumped overboard. This had been my main reason for rescuing Harper, and she in turn had insisted on bringing her friends along with her, showing a determination I had not known her capable of.

"Can't get rid of me that easily," she joked, "Want to come and meet the others?" She jerked her head at the rest of the Clearance citizens.

We followed Harper to where her small group of friends was sitting on some rocks at the side of the stony beach. Harper perched next to Walker, who took her hand. The other two women looked at me curiously. I lowered myself into a seated position next to the older of the two, feeling slightly awkward. Cass remained standing, looking as though she might flee at any moment.

There was an uncomfortable pause, and then Harper smiled encouragingly at me.

Swallowing hard, I began. "Hi. I'm Quin. Known Harper since Minors. We worked together in Agric for three years before we were separated."

The man who had leaped into the water to rescue Harper stuck out his hand. His skin was quite tanned, suggesting a lot of time outdoors, and the beginnings of a beard showed on his chin with the absence of the usual Beck razors. "Walker. Friend of Harper's since we were assigned to Clearance together. Heard a lot about you."

I put out my hand cautiously, and found it was enveloped in

both his large hands, which were incredibly warm considering how exposed we were. He squeezed mine hard, as if trying to convey something vitally important, before continuing to speak.

"Wanted you to know how much we appreciate you coming for us. Sorry I didn't seem keen to begin with. I was surprised, that's all."

I found myself immediately liking him, yet at the same time wondering what had led such a strong, capable man to be assigned to Clearance. "It's understandable. Nice to meet you Walker. Happy to know someone was supporting Harper while I couldn't."

Harper cleared her throat loudly, "I can hear you, you know! Anyway, moving on." She motioned to the first woman, who was painfully thin. "This is Price." The woman smiled shyly. "We were transferred over to Clearance together. She's ex-Sustenance."

"Hey," I responded, "I'm glad you're here."

"And also from Sustenance," Harper turned to the other woman, who was far younger and had a distinctive scar just below her eye, "is Marley."

I started at the familiar name, wondering why I knew it. Marley was definitely a name I'd heard before. I thought back over the different citizens I had come into contact with, trying to remember. It wasn't a name I could put a face to, which suggested that I had never actually met her.

And then it hit me.

When the new recruits had moved up from the Lower Beck in the last few days we were there, there had been a recruit from Sustenance called Wade. From the moment she had entered Patrol, she had begun to cause trouble. She was placed in the same training group as Cass, and the two of them had begun to forge a close friendship. Wade was from Sustenance, and had applied for the transfer to Patrol to get close to one of our more fearsome Supers, Donnelly. He had been directly responsible for the death of Wade's closest friend, and she wanted him to pay for it.

I glanced at Cass, who had turned pale, and knew that she had made the same connection. She, if anything, seemed even more disturbed by the news than I was. Staring down at the ground, her hands were shaking and she seemed to be holding her breath.

In the end, Wade had managed to steal a weapon and sneak into Donnelly's pod, stabbing him fatally. When her crime was discovered, Governance sent Shadow Patrols searching for her. When she was found, she had been subject to a violent public execution, used as an example to others. Wade had died fighting for justice, succeeding in getting rid of her friend's killer, but losing her own life in the process. Despite the pain she had suffered, she had clearly felt that life was not worth living without her friend.

And her friend, I remembered with horror, was called Marley.

I stared hard at the Clearance citizen in front of me. The ugly scar she wore, which emblazoned her cheek underneath her eye, fit with Wade's description of Donnelly's attack. I had never known there to be any two citizens with the same name in the Beck. My heart sank. If Marley was still alive, Wade's sacrifice had been for nothing. And I could well imagine that Donnelly was cruel enough to lie about Marley's death, knowing the terrible effect it would have on Wade, just to punish a young woman who had tried to stand up to him.

The Clearance recruits were staring hard at me, and I realised that I had yet to greet Marley in the same way I had the rest of Harper's friends.

"You ok, Quin?" Harper's eyes were clouded with concern.

I hesitated, knowing if I was right the knowledge would hurt her. But how could I keep it from her? Cass still refused to look at me, and was clearly going to be of no help. I took a deep breath.

"Marley, you say?"

She nodded, a concerned look in her eyes.

"From Sustenance?"

"Yes. Is something wrong?"

"Do you know someone called Wade?"

A broad smile lit up her face. "Yes! She's a close friend of mine. I was waiting for the chance to speak to Rogers about when we might go back over to The Beck to rescue others." She paused for a millisecond before ploughing on. "I know I probably don't take priority, but I know Wade would jump at the chance to escape from The Beck, especially once she knew I was here..."

There was a sudden sob from my left, and Cass buried her face in her arms. Marley's voice trailed off as she took in Cass' devastated posture and my own serious expression.

"What? What is it?" Marley's voice quivered, as though she didn't want to continue speaking, to hear the truth. "Is it Wade? Have you seen her?"

Not knowing what else to do, I took her hand in mine. "I'm so sorry. She believed you were dead. Donnelly told her... he lied to her."

"And...? What else?" I could see her eyes welling up. She knew I did not have good news.

31

"She got herself transferred to Patrol with Cass here." I looked at my friend, expecting her to contribute, but she remained still. "They were friends, for a while, weren't you Cass?"

There was still no response. After a moment's silence, I continued.

"Anyway, it turned out that she got herself transferred for a specific reason."

Next to me, Cass jerked into action, thrusting herself into a standing position and rapidly stalking away, her head down. I wanted to follow her but knew I couldn't leave Marley halfway through my confession. I turned reluctantly to continue.

"She wanted to–"

"Donnelly. She wanted to get back at him." The dam broke and tears began to course down her cheeks. "She never could let anything go."

"Yes. She stole a knife and stabbed him." I hesitated before continuing. "He died."

Now her head was buried in Harper's shoulder and she was sobbing.

"I'm sorry. When Governance caught her, they executed her. Said they couldn't let her live, knowing what she'd done."

"Of course they did," Walker's voice was cold. "Can't have citizens thinking they can disobey their precious rules and get away with it, can they?"

Harper took a hand from where it rested on Marley's back and stroked it gently down Walker's leg. "Hey, you're right of course, but remember we're not there anymore. We've escaped."

He grimaced, "But we're still dealing with what they did to all of us, aren't we?"

"I suspect we'll be dealing with it for the next few years, Walker. Maybe forever," I replied. "But Harper's right. We need to try and move on, the best way we can."

He turned away, laying a hand on Marley's shoulder. "Ok Mar?"

She raised her face to meet his gaze, shaking her head. He shuffled closer to her and enclosed both women in his hug, exchanging glances with Harper. Their joint concern for Marley was clear from the look in their eyes as they crowded over her, as though they could physically shield her from the hurt. Feeling like I was intruding, I stood and quietly moved away, leaving them to try and offer what comfort they could. She knew the truth, but it would certainly take her a long time to get over what The Beck had done to her friend.

Chapter Five

I followed in Cass' wake, joining her at the shore, where she was staring out at the dark expanse of water.

"Cass?"

She refused to look at me.

"Cass, I know that was a shock, but . . ." I hesitated for a minute. "Well your reaction was a little extreme. Is something else wrong?"

I waited for a moment, hoping she would volunteer some kind of explanation. When it became obvious that she wouldn't I pressed her.

"What's the matter, Cass? Tell me, please."

She was silent for a while. When she finally spoke, her voice had a tone of desperation, a loneliness which sent a chill through me. "I said I had something to tell you, but I don't... I haven't..." she didn't seem able to get the words out.

I waited, knowing the words would come eventually. I could feel her body, tense and rigid beside me.

"That night when Wade escaped... I was asleep when she left. I honestly didn't know that she'd gone, or what she was trying to do. Didn't know how far she would go, or I'd have tried to..." she trailed off for a second but seemed to gather her thoughts and managed to continue. "Well everything after that happened really fast. We weren't allowed to leave our pods that day. They didn't tell us what had happened initially. Kept us in our own area. Didn't let anyone else near us. They had Shadow Patrol guard us, instead of our usual training Supers. And then... and then..."

I squeezed her arm ever so slightly in a move which I hoped would be reassuring and allow her to continue.

"And then they took our whole pod to the Lower Beck, to the Assessment Buildings. Marched us down there, didn't allow us breakfast, or contact with anyone else. When we got there, they took us into the Kennedy Building. They sat us at separate desks, well away from each other, in silence. Then they started to take us out, one by one. We'd no idea where they were taking us. But the group in the room started getting smaller and smaller. No one came back. We had no idea where they were being taken. But they left me until last."

I almost knew what was coming, but waited to hear my friend say it.

"When it was my turn, they marched me into the Lincoln Building. It was empty. Weird. I've never seen it like that before. During the assessments it's always filled with people, you know?"

She began twisting her hands in her overalls as she contin-ued.

"Well they took me into one of the curtained-off cubicles, right? And, sitting at one of the tables with an empty chair opposite her, was Carter."

My heart sank at her words and I braced myself for what was to come.

"She told me Wade had committed the worst crime possible and they knew that I was in on it. If I didn't tell her everything

I knew, she would make life–" Cass paused and shuddered, "difficult for me. She had a whip... a cattle prod..."

I recalled a previous injury to Cass' leg, a gift from a cruel Super who didn't feel Cass had done enough work one day, when we had only just been transferred to Agric. "I'm so sorry."

"You knew something was wrong, didn't you Quin? The day I saw you afterwards in the canteen? I could see it in your eyes."

I nodded. "Yes. You were moving strangely. Looked like you'd had some kind of injury. I know how they operate." I thought back to Mason's whipping. "I suspected it was linked to Wade somehow."

She closed her eyes and shook her head. "Quin," her voice was barely more than a whisper, "it's my fault she's dead. And now..." She gestured helplessly at Marley.

I tightened my arm around her, all the other citizens surrounding us fading away as I focused on trying to absorb my friend's pain. "It's not your fault, Cass."

"But it is! You don't understand. Carter wouldn't stop. She kept asking me, over and over, where Wade was. Saying how they knew I was in on what happened to Donnelly and I would find myself paying for the crime if I didn't help them... tell them where she was."

"Cass, they're the ones who executed her."

"Quin, it hurt so much. The wounds... they're still painful."

"You aren't to blame. They whipped you. Tortured you."

"But she was my friend. I should've... I should've been braver."

I hesitated before asking, but felt Cass needed to confess the whole thing to help her move on. "What happened?"

"I tried to... tried not to tell them..." She choked back a sob, "Wade and I sneaked out together at night once... like you and I used to."

I felt the stab of guilt again, realising how much Cass had craved company after losing both her best friends in the Transfer. I had assumed that Harper would be the one to crumble, but in the end, it had been Cass. The strong, proud young woman, desperate for the Super promotion which she eventually received, was the one who had struggled to manage without her friends.

"We sneaked out to a cave, hidden deep in the woods. Close to the Clearance guard post. She had been going there with Marley for a while I think, before she died..." She paused and visibly gathered her thoughts as the lie about Marley almost derailed her again. "And she took me there. Just for an hour or so one night. We both appreciated the time away... with the stress of the sudden move to Patrol... And, well I knew that was probably where she would be hiding out."

I felt my heart pounding as I anticipated the conclusion of Cass' tale.

"I managed for around an hour, I think... Carter questioned me, then whipped me. I managed... for a while at least... but eventually, l, I told her..." Her head was down, her voice breaking, "I was the one Wade trusted and... I gave her away."

"They'd have found her eventually. She'd never have never been able to hide from them indefinitely. The most you did was speed the process." I dropped my voice lower, "They were never going to let her live once she killed a Super."

I knew she wasn't listening. That the words I was speaking were not getting through. The scars of the whipping would fade, but the guilt of abandoning a friend could not be erased so easily. Placing an arm around her more firmly this time, I pulled her close. Laying her head on my shoulder, she allowed herself a brief moment of comfort. I shifted slightly to tighten my grip and was startled back into reality as I spotted Harper and Marley standing a few feet away.

Feeling me stiffen, Cass looked to see what had caused my reaction. Her eyes locked with Marley's for a moment and she hung her head.

"You gave her away?" Marley's voice was barely more than a whisper, but I could feel her words slicing into Cass.

The silence around us grew thick with tension. Harper and I exchanged concerned glances. Cass refused to look up, and Marley continued to stare, her eyes burning into my other friend, one third of our original trio. I hated how much she was hurting, but was helpless to relieve her pain.

"Have the decency to look me in the eye," Marley's voice was cold now, and bitter.

Cass remained still. I knew that guilt was raging through her, but also that she would never show it to Marley if she could help it. Suddenly Marley leapt forward, her hands reaching out, tearing at Cass' hair. Harper reacted quickly, both arms braced around her friend's skinny frame, and I leapt between the two women, but Marley was surprisingly strong.

From nowhere, a large, masculine frame thrust itself in front of me. Rogers.

"Stop." His voice was not loud, but the words were spoken with some force. "Have some respect."

He gestured to Davis's body, lying further up the beach. All eyes travelled to the blanketed figure and I could feel shame creeping over us all.

"We've all lost someone." He turned away abruptly and

went back to sifting through the piles of equipment.

The situation diffused, Marley allowed Harper to lead her away, and Cass, breathing heavily, wandered to another group of rocks, separating herself from the main group. Refusing to let her be alone, I joined her, placing my hand on her shoulder in a vain attempt at comfort which she did not respond to. Glancing over at Harper, who was once again huddled together with her Clearance allies, I wondered if the three of us would ever manage to renew the close friendship we had once shared.

We sat around in groups waiting for Rogers' next command, glancing uncertainly at the water and the cliffs behind us. I became aware of the sound of footsteps, at first faint, but increasing in volume, until they were thundering from somewhere close by. Several of us leapt to our feet, grabbing hold of guns or sticks. Rogers was the only one who seemed unconcerned, turning towards the sound and smiling broadly. A figure emerged at the foot of the cliffs, slowing only slightly before spotting Rogers and heading straight for him. For a moment I anticipated some kind of attack, but as the now clearly female figure reached him, she flung herself into his arms and he swept her up into the air and swung her round.

When he finally put the woman down, she embraced him fully, planting lingering kisses on his lips, which had the rest of the group staring hard at them. Such public displays of affection simply didn't exist in The Beck. Any embraces were furtive, taking place well out of the sight of Governance. From the reactions of those around us, I could tell that the other Beck citizens were just as uncomfortable as I was.

When they broke apart, Rogers grinned around at the rest of us, amused by the shock on our faces. He regarded the woman with an affection I had not witnessed in him before. Stepping away from her, he made a small, mock-bow at the rest of the group as he spoke.

"This, my friends," he declared loudly, "is Green. She was one of the escapees who came over the water at the same time as me. She's... um... missed me."

"Missed you!" The woman gave a short laugh, "You were gone so long I thought you were never coming back."

Her words were clearly intended to be light-hearted, but the worry lines carved into her face told another story. I considered the length of time Rogers had been away and understood her concern. Still smiling, Green crossed to Tyler, eying her closely.

"Long time, old friend." The two women embraced, their tight hold on one another lingering for several seconds before they let go. "How's Cam? I see you didn't bring him."

I started at his name, but was not surprised to see Tyler's gaze unwillingly flicker across to my own for a millisecond. She jerked it away the moment her eyes met mine, shrugging before she answered.

"He stayed behind. Someone had to keep the Resistance going."

Green's expression remained neutral, but she had followed Tyler's gaze to mine and stared at me for a moment. She was, like Rogers, older than most of us, and must have been an experienced Patrol citizen at the time she left. I wondered why she had been selected by the Resistance as one of the pioneers leaving The Beck. Perhaps Rogers had persuaded her, their relationship existing back in The Beck and continuing over here. Or maybe they had fallen in love later, when they reached safety.

She fascinated me: her hair hung long and dark to her

shoulders, curling wildly. Her eyes were bright and intelligent, and once they had left mine, roamed curiously over the rest of the group one by one. They came to rest on Blythe and Perry, and for a moment she looked puzzled, as if working something out. Eventually the light of understanding dawned in her eyes. For a minute her brow furrowed, and I feared that she, like Thomas and the other recruits, might have a negative reaction to Perry, but she took hold of herself and, dragging her eyes away from mother and child, faced the rest of us.

"Welcome! Let's get you all up to the centre, make sure you're warm and fed." She glanced at Harper and Walker, "and dry."

She jerked her head in the direction she had originally appeared from, and began walking away rapidly.

"Everyone up for a short climb I hope?" Her laughter rang back over her shoulder as she disappeared between the rocks.

Rogers motioned for us to follow her, and one by one, the group made their way to the path. I hoped desperately that the climb she had referred to simply meant walking uphill, rather than actually scrambling up the cliff face. I was still wet and cold, and hours with only a single oatcake to eat had taken their toll. It was a relief when we rounded the corner to discover a steep, but traversable path which, though covered with loose stones and narrow in places, was accessible without actual climbing.

I glanced behind me and saw Rogers and Walker struggling to carry Davis' body. Shivering, I forced my eyes away from the distressing sight as I started trudging up the path in Green's wake. My last glimpse of the water for the time being was of the lone Clearance boat, which I knew contained a desperately unhappy Mason. I could only hope that he would not find reasons to separate himself from the group for too long.

Chapter Six

It was a half hour hike, most of it through difficult, rocky terrain which sloped steeply upwards. Eventually the land flattened out and a group of buildings came into view. They were taller than the ones I was used to, and built from a greyish stone. I found myself fascinated by their construction, which seemed so solid in comparison to the wooden structures we had back in The Beck. And the thought that we might be able to sleep inside them was definitely a welcome one. The only time we had ever slept inside a building in The Beck was in The Annexe in Patrol, for the first week or so while we were in training.

Green led us towards one of the largest buildings, and we passed through its main door and along a hallway into a canteen not unlike the ones we had in The Beck. Within minutes, most of us were gathered around one of the large trestle tables waiting for Green to speak.

"Hello," she began, "and welcome to Brecon Crags."

"Did you name this place, Green?" Tyler sounded more relaxed and amused now that she had been reunited with her friend.

Green shook her head, "Nope. That's what the place is called. Was called. Before."

"Before?" This came from one of the Patrol recruits. "Before what?"

Green laughed softly, "I forget how little they teach you in The Beck about the origins of our society. There's a small library here, filled with the kind of books they don't allow you to read in The Beck. I've spent a lot of time this year reading them all. History books, geography books, different accounts of the way life used to be. In the past, before all the flooding, all of the islands you see were one large mountain range, as in attached to one another. It was only when sea levels rose and covered the land that the mountains were divided and were separated."

"Fortunately!" Rogers interjected as he entered, seating himself beside her and slinging an arm around her shoulder. "We'd have been in trouble if this island wasn't separated by water from the next one along."

"Trouble?" A shadow crossed Green's face momentarily.

He shrugged, "Maybe. They took a few shots at us as we passed, but gave up once we sailed out of range. Strange though."

"What?"

"They fired arrows at us. Not guns."

Green frowned, "I wonder why."

She looked thoughtful as she turned back to us and continued her speech. "Look, when we arrived, we attempted to land on the larger island over there. As I'm sure Rogers' told you, the people living there were not so friendly and we were forced to retreat and land over here. This whole area was an army base before the flooding set in. There were soldiers stationed for training up here all the time. It means that the base is well provided for and makes quite a decent camp."

Rogers took over, nodding in the direction of the enemy island. "The base station is over there. It's called Brecon Ridge, or just 'The Ridge,' and was where the main buildings and resources of the base were kept. We think it has numerous dorms, barns, training and storage facilities, and as you witnessed, weapons and ammunition."

"Which you didn't see fit to tell us about," snarled Thomas.

Rogers clenched his fists slightly at his sides. "No, Thomas. I didn't. And I'm sorry. But we're all still here, aren't we? And—"

Green interrupted him. "Aside from their attack as we passed them a year ago, we have had no contact with them. Rogers' just didn't want to frighten you all."

"Didn't want to give us any reason to refuse him, more likely," Thomas continued, "couldn't risk us saying no."

Rogers' drew himself up to his full height, "Listen, Thomas, I got you here, didn't I? Whose life was most at risk when we passed The Ridge?"

Thomas bristled, "Not the point, you—"

"Look," Green soothed, "the people on The Ridge know we're here, obviously, but, presumably because there are only a few of us, they've left us alone. We're not a threat to them."

"And now they know there are more of us?" Thomas raised an eyebrow.

"Well," she paused, taking her to time answer, "I suppose we'll have to wait and see."

Tyler chimed in, seemingly eager to change the subject, "So where do we sleep?"

Thomas sank back into his seat, clearly frustrated, while Green brightened visibly. "Brecon Crags, usually referred to as 'The Crags,' used to be the part of the base where they trained the young army cadets. They came to live up here between the ages of sixteen and eighteen, to prepare for army life. There are bunks here, and some facilities. We don't think they're as extensive as the ones over on The Ridge, but they do us nicely."

"There are only a few weapons here, however. Unfortunately, it seems that they were mostly stored at the main base on The Ridge, so we are more than a little under-defended." Rogers sighed, "But I'm hoping we can improve our defences with the added manpower we now have. We'll have more citizens available to ensure a round-the-clock guard on the boat at least, which is now one of our most valuable assets. We could still do with more guns, though and–"

He stopped speaking as the external door banged open. A moment later, two figures came through the door of the canteen. One was male, a tall, slim figure with a shock of red hair which made me think immediately of Jackson. The woman who stood beside him was older. In The Beck we didn't have a large number of elderly people, as most of us outlived our use long before we grew old. Occasionally there were citizens who stayed fit enough to cope with the rigours of Beck life for longer than usual. Those citizens who did live that long were rarities, though. Certainly I had never seen any in Agric, though I knew Sustenance had a couple of older women, like Price, and I had heard tell that they were held in high regard by their fellow citizens.

I estimated that the woman was in her mid-thirties, and her hair was a lighter colour than I had previously seen, and cut quite short. Not shaven, like The Beck citizens were, but certainly not long and flowing, like Green's. She was tall and wiry, and she did not smile in welcome like Green, or the man beside her. I wondered why. Both of the others seemed excited to greet a new group of people, and after so long with nothing but the company of three others I could understand why. But this woman's face was wary, thoughtful, cautious.

Rogers strode ahead, grabbing the red-haired man in a huge bear hug, the kind which I had begun to associate with him. Once he had released the man, he turned to the older woman. With her he was less enthusiastic, more respectful perhaps of her age and stature. He grasped her hands in his own and smiled warmly into her face. Her own expression softened slightly at the gesture.

"Still turning up like a bad penny, eh Rogers?" Her voice was surprisingly deep and gravelly.

He laughed heartily. "Thanks for the warm reception, Baker. You'll never change, will you?"

She didn't reply. As Rogers turned to the group once more and began the introductions, I noticed Tyler coming from the rear of the group and greeting the two ex-Beck citizens in a similar way.

"This is Baker, ex-Patrol. You wouldn't believe it to look at her, but she was one of our best guards. Amazing skills with knife, bow, and baton. Don't mess with her. She's faster than she looks."

I was surprised by Rogers' high praise of her fighting abilities. She didn't look particularly formidable. I wondered if part of her strength lay in the fact that assailants underestimated her. Rogers turned to the man.

"And this is Nelson. Old buddy of mine, Tyler's, and Cam's from Patrol. He, Lee, and I were quite a team when we first came up from the Lower Beck."

A pained expression crossed Nelson's face at Lee's name,

but Rogers didn't dwell on the negative, moving on quickly.

"Nelson, Baker, these are all Beck citizens, eager, as you can well imagine, to begin a new life away from the terrors of Governance. There are too many to introduce now, but I'm sure that later on today we can begin–"

He was interrupted in his speech by a plaintive cry from Perry, who was close to Barnes' chest underneath his overalls. As her cry grew louder, Barnes slipped her out and passed her over to Blythe, who attempted to calm her, an awkward look on her face as she contemplated the already thunderous looks she was being shot by some of the group. It was Baker, however, who had the most extreme reaction.

"A baby? A baby! Rogers, you have got to be kidding." A look of horror marred her features.

For a moment Rogers looked as though he was being chastised by Reed, and I wondered at the power Baker seemed to hold here. In the end, he laid a hand on her arm. "Look, I understand how you feel about this, Baker. But it was our chance to save one. To bring her here with her own mother. Can't you see that's a good thing?"

"But how are we going to feed her? Keep her safe? Difficult enough you bringing Clearance citizens," she gestured at Price and Marley, still dressed in their ragged overalls, "they're hardly strong and capable. But a baby? A tiny, helpless baby?" Her expression thunderous, she backed away, shaking her head furiously.

Turning, she stalked off to the kitchen without a backward glance. I noted the satisfied expression on Thomas' face, as well as Blythe's stricken look and the protective stance that Barnes had adopted in front of her. Rogers cleared his throat, attempting to take charge again.

"I know we need to feed you and show you where you'll be sleeping tonight, but there's something we need to deal with first." He turned to Nelson, "We lost one citizen in our escape. He was untying us from the jetty so we could leave when he was hit by a Shadow Patrol bullet."

Green's sunny expression had gone and was replaced by a sadness which conveyed great understanding. "We'll bury him alongside Lee." Noting a few puzzled expressions, she clarified, "It's how they used to do it. Who were his closest friends?"

Tyler looked around the group. "Mason. He's still guarding the boat though. Quin was with him for training." She beckoned to me. "Barnes and I were his training Supers."

Green elbowed Rogers. "Someone needs to relieve this Mason of his guard duties and bring him ashore. Quin, Tyler? Will you come with me?"

A few minutes later I was standing with Tyler and Green at a small site on the other side of the buildings. Barnes had elected to remain behind with Blythe and Perry, who were attracting a lot of attention, both positive and negative, from the others in the group. It was clear he felt protective over them both. The grassy area we stood in was small, not large enough to be a field, but surrounded by a low wall built of the same material as the buildings. Green led us to one corner, where a small pile of stones created a kind of pyramid shape on the ground.

"Lee." Green pointed at the stones. "He's buried here. I constructed the cairn when I read about it in one of the books inside. They used to call this kind of place a graveyard. It commemorates the dead. Helps those left behind remember."

I considered the pile of stones. They rested against one another, each one depending on the others for strength and stability. Despite their sadness, they struck me as a clear symbol for those of us who had managed to escape The Beck: the delicate nature of our dependence on one another, now we were free to live under our own rules. If one of us failed, we would threaten the security of the rest. We needed one another now, more than ever. I resolved to be as strong as I could be to make sure that I supported the others in our little camp, in the hopes that they would prop me up in a similar way when I needed it.

Tyler knelt down, touching the pile of the stones lightly, her eyes closed. A silence descended on the three of us, lost in our silent thoughts. I wondered how well Tyler had known Lee.

"Were you and Davis close?" Green's voice startled me. Her eyes, I noticed, were a vivid shade of emerald, and their intelligent gaze was currently piercing mine, as though trying to understand me.

"Um, yes I suppose so. I've only known him for a few months, but training alongside someone in Patrol makes you pretty close."

"It does." She stared at me hard, before turning to Tyler. "Don't mind Baker. She'll come round. It's just, well things aren't easy here. We're happy to expand our community, it's what we've been working for, but life here isn't without its challenges. Having a baby around won't make things any easier."

"I honestly don't think Blythe—that's the mother—would have survived much longer without her child." Tyler shrugged, "Surely Baker understands that more than anyone."

Green nodded thoughtfully. Before I had the time to ask why, she moved on. "Need to get back. Settle everyone in. I'll make sure someone is allocated to do the digging while we get the rest of you fed and warmed up. We can hold a service for him later on today. Maybe at sundown?"

Tyler seemed to agree. "We need to get Quin into some dry clothes. She fell into the water on the journey across from the boat... The last thing we want is anyone with a fever."

Green frowned. "You're right. We don't want to be digging another one of these." With a brief, macabre gesture at Lee's resting place, she set off briskly in the opposite direction, clearly expecting us to follow.

"Don't mind her, she has quite a dark sense of humour sometimes," Tyler's words were comforting, yet she still wouldn't meet my gaze for very long. "She's ok though. I'd trust her with my life."

She moved after Green abruptly, leaving me with little choice but to follow, my bones aching with exhaustion.

Chapter Seven

A few hours later I was still tired but had regained a little strength at least. We had been shown around the buildings, most of which had been largely unused up until now. There were four in total, three of which were dormitories, set up with numerous wooden bunks. There were two floors in each of these dorms, with a set of stairs at one end of the building leading to the upper floor. There was a bathroom at one end of each floor, small storage cubbies next to each bed, and a couple of separate rooms adjacent to the main space which contained extra beds. Green told us that the trainees' adult supervisors would have occupied these.

The final building was the one we had already visited. As well as the dining area, it housed a large kitchen; the small library that Green had spoken of; a common room, which we were told had been used during free time; and various storage spaces and offices. There were several additional storage huts close by as well. Higher up the hillside were a number of tall, spiky-looking constructions that Rogers informed me were wind turbines. When the wind blew, they were able to harness its power and convert it into electricity, and since poor weather was something we seemed able to depend on, they had served The Crags community well up to now.

After we had stored the few provisions we had brought with us, our hosts set about providing a meal for us. We sat to eat it in the canteen. There was a slight tension surrounding us as we entered, but once we had settled to eat, a comfortable chatter rose in the air. The meal was delicious, consisting of a thick stew of some kind of vegetable, topped with a mashed potato crust. It did a lot to restore our spirits, and was eagerly consumed by all.

Mason was still guarding the boat with Shaw, although two of the other recruits had been dispatched to replace them. I sat beside Cass again, still feeling a little protective. I realised I was unsure where I belonged in this new community, and found myself missing Jackson terribly. She had been a constant in my life over the past three months and to be suddenly without her was more difficult than I had imagined. I considered this bleakly amusing: if things had gone to plan, I would have been without her anyway. But at least, in that scenario, I would have had Cam by my side.

The separation from him was not the same. We had only really admitted our feelings to each other just prior to the escape, so there had been no chance to test the relationship. But I had wanted to. It had been the main reason for my decision to stay behind. Remembering the kisses we had shared, I felt a hollow ache in my chest which I suspected would stay with me until we were together again. *If* we were together again. I was trying hard not to think about what might have happened to him, and to Jackson, back in The Beck. The idea that we had put them in danger was too painful to bear.

Sighing, I shoved the last few forkfuls of my meal into my mouth. I was stuffed, but felt like I deserved the sustenance, and years of going hungry and being underfed meant old habits died hard. Food was too precious to waste.

Rogers had also finished his meal and rose to speak to us all. As he did so, Mason and Shaw entered the canteen and sat down. Nelson hurried over with two steaming bowls of stew for them before Rogers began to speak.

"Hi all. Hope the food has gone down well. You all seemed..." he paused, grinning round at the empty plates, "to enjoy it. I think you'll agree that Baker is something of a genius in the kitchen."

There were general nods and murmurs of appreciation. I wondered privately if Rogers was trying to extol Baker's virtues to excuse her earlier outburst.

Green came and stood with Rogers, a serious expression on her face. "Now although this is partly a celebration to welcome you here, sadly it can't be entirely positive. Tonight, we must pay tribute to a man who gave his life so the rest of you stood a chance of this new life. Now that Mason has returned, let's make our way outside."

Moments later I was back in the small grassy space behind the centre. The area had been lit with a few candles, and a hole had been dug in the earth close to Lee's cairn. Next to it lay Davis' body, still covered with the blanket. In the darkness, he seemed so much smaller than he had been in life. I stood to the rear of the group, wondering what was about to happen. Beck citizens who were close to death were simply sent to Clearance. There was never any kind of goodbye. I noticed Mason also hovered at the back, looking distinctly uncomfortable.

Once we had all gathered, Green began. "We're here this evening to commemorate the life of Davis, our fellow Beck citizen, who died last night during the escape." She paused for a second, looking around at the group. "Before the flooding, people who lived in our world used to celebrate the life of a loved one who had passed away with a service a little like this. It allowed them to bid a proper goodbye, as well as remembering the good things about the person's life."

Rogers cleared his throat noisily, and then looked a little embarrassed at the sound. "I did not know Davis well. But I knew Lee, who we lost in very similar circumstances. Escaping from The Beck, running from the people who controlled and threatened us." He heaved a visible sigh. "It seems that we're not destined to escape The Beck without losses, and for that I am sorry. But we won't let it stop us from returning to free more citizens. Meanwhile, we will remember Davis for who he was: a hero who gave his life to help his friends escape from the tyranny of The Beck. He was given one of the riskiest jobs: to secure the boat which would bring us all safely away, and he did that admirably, along with his friend Mason, who I am certain will miss him terribly."

Green continued, "Would those who knew Davis best like to step forward?"

Tyler and Barnes went to stand beside Rogers and Green. I glanced across at Mason, who had yet to move. Those at the front waited expectantly. I thought of Jackson, and how she would have dealt with this, and remembered a time when she had gently treated Mason's horrific injuries after a severe whipping. If she were here now, I knew she would make sure that Mason faced what had happened and didn't regret his actions later.

Acting with a confidence I did not feel, I moved closer to Mason and grasped his hand firmly, attempting to pull him to the front of the group. After a momentary resistance, he followed reluctantly. The rest of the citizens parted, forming a kind of path to the spot where Davis lay. At the front, Green smiled at us sadly and Tyler motioned for us to stand right next to the covered figure.

"It's customary for things to be said about the dead, by those who knew him," Green continued, "to pay tribute to his life and celebrate his passing. Would any of you like to say a few words?"

Mason's grip on my hand tightened, and I knew he was fighting to keep control. He would not be able to speak. Tyler noticed this too, and gave a small nod at me. Desperately wishing for the second time that Jackson was here instead of me, I took a deep breath.

"Davis was... that is, I hadn't known Davis very long," I began, hearing my voice shake as the words left my mouth. "Just three months. But as you know, often it doesn't take long to find an ally in The Beck, and once you do, well... you hang on to them. Davis was kind. He loved his friends and would have done anything for them. He and Mason had been friends for far longer... since Minors, and I know Mason will really feel his loss, but I will too. He was never anything but gentle and generous with me... with everyone, in fact, and he always did the right thing. Even when it led to... to this."

I stepped back abruptly, knowing I couldn't continue any longer without breaking down. Sensing my distress, Green took over.

"Thank you, Quin. I'm certain that as we get to know all of you over the coming weeks and months, we will appreciate Davis' effort all the more. Now, we'll place his body in the ground. Tomorrow, my first job will be to construct a second cairn to mark the spot, so anyone can come here and remember him."

Rogers stepped closer to the front, motioning to Mason and Barnes to help him. Together, they lifted Davis' covered body up and into the grave, lowering it as gently as they could. When it was done, Rogers clasped Mason by the hand, and whispered in his ear. He stepped back while Rogers and Barnes began to shovel the earth back into place. For a moment, I watched, but eventually I closed my eyes, finding it too painful.

Green's voice spoke softly one more time. "Thank you for participating in this ceremony, in witnessing the commemoration of our friend Davis. We'll now ensure that his body is properly laid to rest. If you'd like to stay while the burial continues, please do so, but if you'd rather return to the dorms for some much-deserved rest, we'll meet again in the morning."

I remained where I was, listening until the sound of retreating footsteps had died away and the only noise left was the rhythmic sound of the shovels. When I opened my eyes, the only people left in the field were Rogers and Barnes, who were filling in the grave with earth; Tyler and Green, who stood close to the burial site talking in muted voices; and Mason, who was off to one side, his shoulders hunched against the cold night air. I approached him cautiously, unsure of how he might react.

He didn't seem to notice me at all until I reached out to touch his arm. He jumped.

"Sorry. Wanted to make sure you were ok."

He stared at me, uncomprehending.

"Mason?"

"What?" His tone sent a shiver down my spine.

"Are you ok?"

He shook his head fiercely. "No, not really."

"Want to walk back to the dorms with me?"

"No. Sorry, Quin. Can't." His hands were shaking as he pushed mine away. "Not now. I need to—"

His voice had risen in volume and taken on an odd tone. Rogers and Barnes had stopped digging, clearly concerned. As I watched him, Mason glanced desperately around, seeming to see the others for the first time. Rogers approached cautiously, laying a gentle hand on Mason's shoulder.

"Look, Mason, we've all—"

But he stopped as Mason recoiled from his hand as though it was a poisonous snake. Shaking his head at us all, he took off at a run, heading away from the centre. He was out of the small graveyard and heading further into the hills before anyone could stop him. I started to follow, but found Rogers' hand on my arm now.

"Leave him." His voice was surprisingly gentle. "He needs to be on his own. He'll come around."

He nodded at Green, who joined me and began steering me back to the dorms. Tyler followed at a distance, and I heard the sound of the shovels in the background start up again. Covering Davis' body, so it couldn't be dug up by any passing creatures, was essential. The harsh reality of dealing with your own dead. Our first night free of Governance, and the responsibility of freedom had never weighed more heavily.

Chapter Eight

I woke with a start the next morning, alarmed by a loud, drumming sound. Sitting bolt upright, I tried to make sense of it, wondering if we were again under attack. It took a few moments for me to realise that it was just the rain hitting the roof of the dorm. I was used to it falling on the tarpaulin of the pods, but that made an entirely different sound. Regaining my breath, I looked around, noting that most of the dorm was already awake, our body clocks conditioned to getting up early for work in our Beck sector.

Pushing myself into a sitting position, I checked on Cass, who I had made sure slept right next to me the previous night. She looked pale and was still not her usual self, but managed to nod in response to my enquiring look. Slightly placated, I studied each bed in turn. Marley was nowhere to be seen, which was a relief. I also realised that Mason was not present. He had clearly not returned to sleep in the dorm with everyone else. He could, of course, have gone to sleep in one of the others, wanting some space, but I had my doubts. Davis' death had clearly hit him hard, and his distress the previous night only added to my worries.

My train of thought was interrupted as Green emerged from a separate room at the far end of the dorm, a purposeful smile on her face. I considered her perspective: a woman who had been limited to the company of three others for more than a year. Of course she was happy. We represented a better chance for her little society to thrive. But with Davis' death and Mason's disappearance dominating my thoughts, all I wanted to do was bury my head back under the blankets and go back to sleep. Green clearly had other ideas.

"Morning all! Can we get up and meet in the canteen in ten minutes please?" Her voice rang out across the entire bunk, "There's a lot to discuss."

The outer door to the dorm opened and Rogers walked in, running a distracted hand through his hair. Spotting Green, he slid alongside her, sweeping her into a massive bear hug and kissing her full on the lips. They had clearly missed one another during the days they had been apart. I looked away, partly still unused to such public demonstrations of affection, but also, if I was totally honest, fighting an uncomfortable feeling of jealousy. I considered the prospect of Cam coming to the island and moving into one of these rooms alongside him, having him be completely free to kiss me whenever he liked. The idea, while thrilling, seemed impossible. I pushed it out of my mind.

"Hi all!" Rogers boomed when he had put Green down. "Get up now. Lots to do. I've been awake and working for an hour already."

He motioned to Green, stooping to whisper something in her ear. She grinned, and the two of them left the bunkhouse, arms wrapped loosely round one another's waists. Once they were gone, the beds in the dorm began to empty. People gathered their overalls and boots, pausing to grab a quick wash as they exited the dorm and headed for the main building, hoping for breakfast. When I arrived, my eyes searched the room, hoping that Mason would be there, but I was disappointed. I hesitated, trying to decide who I felt comfortable sitting with. Noting Thomas was standing over an uncomfortable-looking Blythe, I headed over.

"...hard work building a new life here. Think you'll be able to do your part, with a baby in tow? Do you honestly—"

"Morning Blythe." I made sure my voice was loud and cheerful, and ignored the flash of annoyance on Thomas' face as I slid into the bench next to her. "Ready for the new day, Thomas?"

He looked slightly less sure of himself now there were two of us. "I was just saying to Blythe here—"

"I heard."

He stopped, glancing back and forth between the two of us before stomping back off to the other recruits. We watched him go and I felt the tension dissipate.

"Ok?"

She didn't reply.

"He's a bully. Likes to get people on their own. Knows they're more vulnerable."

She busied herself with Perry, shifting her position and refusing to look at me for a moment. When she did, there were tears shining in her eyes.

"Thanks, Quin." Her voice was no more than a whisper.

"Hey, don't let him get to you so much!" I laid a hand on her arm. "He doesn't know what he's talking about. You have friends who will defend you—you're not alone."

She sighed, "It's not just him." She wrestled briefly with a wriggling Perry, attempting to secure the almost-empty bottle of milk in her daughter's tiny mouth. "She's hungry. I can't seem to fill her. I've counted up the supplies Tyler brought. There isn't much."

"How long will it last?"

She shrugged. "Honestly, I've no idea. I always fed her my own milk. I don't know how much she's used to drinking. Plus, she's much bigger now, she needs more."

"Did you ask Tyler?"

"Yes." Blythe's gaze travelled to her friend, who had joined Green at another table. "She said not to worry, we'd sort something out."

"Can she eat other things?"

"Maybe. Babies aren't supposed to be on solid food this early though. Tyler suggested mashing up some oatcakes in a little milk but... I tried it and it didn't go so well." She looked down at her child, "I don't think she's ready for it yet."

As if she knew we were discussing her, Perry drained the remainder of the bottle and paused for a moment, her green eyes gazing up at us. Then, realising that the milk was gone, her face creased up and she began wailing loudly. Blythe held her closer, rocking her gently, but she didn't stop.

"I've split what remains into rations, with enough for a little while, but it's not much," Blythe raised her voice above her baby's wailing. "I daren't give her any more or it won't last at all."

Perry's cry grew in volume and I could see Thomas and the other recruits shooting dark glances at us. Clearly, they were no happier with the disturbance than they had been on the boat over. At that moment, Baker entered from the kitchen, a look of disgust on her own face.

Before I could stop her, Blythe nodded a brief good bye and stood rapidly, heading for the door. Halfway there, she met

Price, who stopped her. For a second, I worried that she was also going to confront the pair, but then she began conversing with Blythe and stroking Perry's head gently, a wide smile on her face. They moved out of the room together, Blythe looking a little more confident now she had at least one supporter. I was glad that not everyone on The Crags was so set against the child's presence.

It didn't take long for those around to begin muttering in undertones. Everyone was hungry and this only added to the general air of discontent. Baker set about serving up the breakfast, moving between the tables with plates, mugs and pitchers of water. Although it wasn't quite the hearty stew of the previous night, the hunk of bread and small portion of cold meat each was gratefully received. I thought back to the conversation the night before about rationing and wondered how much food there was here, and how well it might sustain us. Once breakfast was served, the room fell silent. I watched Barnes take a plate out, presumably for Blythe, and felt sad that she hadn't been able to stay.

The meal was over quickly and our leaders stood at the front, serious expressions on their faces. Green began, her trademark grin absent as she talked business.

"Good morning. Welcome to your first full day here. As I said last night, we're glad to have you, but the fact that there are so many more of you means there will be a lot of hard work involved to ensure that we can thrive here. There's enough food to sustain us long-term, but to ensure variety and volume we need to consider our food sources a little more carefully and begin growing more crops. We've a small vegetable garden here, which has served us well until now, but it's nothing like the fields you have in The Beck. Any of you who have knowledge of the Agric Sector will be extremely helpful here."

Rogers took over. "In addition, we hunt for meat and also fish, but will need to do so in larger quantities now there are so many of us. Nelson and I will be training some of you, especially those with weapons' experience, for this purpose. Others can be taught to make and mend additional fishing rods. Finally, we need to consider our security. We'll need round-the-clock surveillance over the boat at the very least, so each of you will be assigned a time of day to be on watch over that area."

Nelson chipped in, "Communication throughout The Crags is via walkie-talkie, much like The Beck. I'm responsible for them. We usually have enough energy from the turbines to keep four or five fully charged and ready to use. We don't have enough for everyone, but those of you on duty in key locations can have one. This being an old army base, we also have binoculars, which allow those of us on duty to see any threat approaching from quite a distance. Extremely useful."

"It's how I knew you were coming yesterday," Green's smile was back, and I understood her sudden appearance so soon after we had arrived.

Nelson continued, "Come to me if you're leading a group further out on the island and I can supply you with what you need."

"If you can see me in a moment," Green added, "and let me know what your Beck training is, we can assign you to a project which should allow you to work to your strengths. Until we can get more vegetables growing, we may need to endure a little rationing, but Baker can do wonders with small amounts, and we planted some extra vegetables in anticipation of your arrival which are almost ready to harvest, so we should be alright for a while."

"Are there any questions?" Rogers asked, eyebrows raised.

For a moment the room was silent, and then Allen stood up. "I wanted to ask when we would be considering going back to The Beck."

Rogers looked startled, then recovered himself. "Back? You only just got here."

Allen continued, after glancing around at the other Patrol recruits, "I know, but now we know more about Beck life… about the drugs they're going to give to the recruits—"

Never one to stay out of a conflict, Thomas butted in, "Lots of us left people behind. People we cared about."

"Look, I know that many of you want to go back for people you left over in The Beck, that you're concerned about them," Nelson's voice was soothing, "but you need to understand that this will take time. And planning."

But Thomas was not to be pacified. "Gov won't just stop because some of us got away. They'll go on experimenting with the drugs, just on other citizens."

Allen chimed in, "Friends of ours."

"We can't just waltz back up with the boat you stole from them and grab more of their people," Baker's tone was scathing.

Rogers agreed, "They're right though. And there are other, vital reasons to go back to—"

Green shot a dark look at him and he stopped abruptly. There was a brief pause, where they stared at one another. Finally, Rogers continued.

"—our severe lack of meds, for example. Believe me, we want to make a return trip just as much as you. But we'll have to be more cautious, plan carefully, see if we can communicate with those in the Resistance. We never dared to try this previously, but Tyler spoke to Cam before we left and he is going to be listening out for radio calls from us. We're hopeful that we will be able to establish some kind of contact, but there are no guarantees."

"And we really don't have the weapons to stage any kind of attack at the moment." Baker interrupted, clearly less patient, "That's why Rogers' return was quiet, stealthy."

Green resumed her speech, "Look, we promise you, there will be a discussion about returning to The Beck. We really want you to be able to have your say. But for now, can we ask that you all focus on getting settled in at Brecon Crags? That way, when we do bring people over, we'll have systems firmly in place and be able to welcome and incorporate new citizens swiftly."

Allen gave up and sat down, pulling an unwilling Thomas with him. People began making their way to the front of the room, crowding around Green who was busy jotting things down on a clipboard. People were clearly interested in seeing more of the island and volunteering to work in the various teams which would allow us to sustain life here for a larger group of people. It made me happy to see us pulling together for a change.

"Shall we go and volunteer our services then?" The quiet voice at my side belonged to Cass.

"Ready to rejoin Agric?" I joked, "Never thought I'd be going back to a life of–"

But as we stood to join the queue in front of Green, two other figures approached. Harper and, close behind her, Marley. Instinctively I moved slightly in front of Cass, but Harper held out her hands in a gesture of reconciliation.

"Hey."

"Hey yourself," I responded cautiously. "Look, we were going to volunteer for Agric, but if that's going to cause a problem," I looked pointedly at Marley, "then we can sign up for the hunting party instead. We both have some weapons' training."

Harper shook her head and moved aside so that Marley could see us. Her head was down and her slight figure seemed more vulnerable than ever. I could understand Wade's desire to protect her friend, this tiny girl who looked like a gust of wind could blow her over. She took a single step towards us and time stood still. Then, slowly, she raised her eyes to meet mine. They were filled with pain, and I could see her earlier anger had faded, replaced with the same grief I had witnessed in Mason the previous night.

"I... I wanted to say... sorry," she began, "to both of you."

She turned her head now and I could see her steeling herself to look at Cass.

"I know it wasn't your fault. I know what they did to you. And I understand they would have caught her eventually, whatever happened." She inhaled slowly and deeply. "I'm not sure I'll find it easy to talk to you, but I want you to know that I'm trying not to blame you. It was... it was just such a shock." She fought back a sob. "I still can't believe she's gone."

Harper moved closer to her friend placing an arm around her. I knew she had been the one to calm Marley, to help her understand that she was wrong to blame Cass. I smiled gratefully. Harper had always been able to judge people's moods and exert a calming influence.

"Tell Green our old Sectors, will you?" Harper's voice was

soft. "We'll be back in a few minutes."

She led Marley to the door of the canteen. Once they had exited, I turned to Cass, concerned to see the effect of Marley's words. She was still pale, still sad, still insecure. But there was a tiny spark in her eyes which had not been there before. As we moved to speak to Green, I began to believe that she might get over this, given time, and regain some of her old confidence.

I could only hope.

Chapter Nine

Within half an hour, Green had organised teams and assigned various tasks to people. One group of citizens was creating rods to enable a larger catch of fish than had previously been necessary. The group on The Crags had always fished from the rocks close to the shore, but they only had three rods in current use. Now there were more mouths to feed, there was also a larger number of people who could do the actual fishing, thus the first job was to create the extra equipment.

Baker had come up with another idea. Now we had the canoes, we would be able to fish further from shore, with rods, but she had read a book which told of fishermen bringing in large catches using nets. She had taken the morning away from the kitchen to look at possible plant matter and grasses available on the island which could be woven into some kind of mesh for this purpose. Rogers and Green had allowed her to take one of the Patrol recruits with her on her scouting mission, believing the nets could make a big difference to the food stores at The Crags, as fish were plentiful in the waters surrounding the island, and could sustain us indefinitely.

Other citizens were going to be further trained in hunting skills with knives and bows, with Rogers, who was self-taught, but apparently a crack shot with a bow and a genius at setting traps. Again, it was hoped this would allow us to catch larger numbers of the small creatures that lived in the few wooded areas on The Crags. I found myself assigned to Green, who was going to show the ex-Agric staff the existing vegetable plot. She had spoken of a potential site she had found where we could plant a larger quantity of crops, which we would require to feed the increased number of people.

As we left the centre and walked out through the courtyard, we passed Rogers' group, who were taking various weapons from a storage shed and stowing them in backpacks. He smiled at Green as we passed by. Among his group were Shaw and Thomas, who scowled at us.

"Where's your friend, Quin?" His posture was openly hostile.

I was one of the last in my own party. I stopped, motioning for the others to go ahead, before turning to meet his gaze. "Friend?"

"Yeah. Your friend. Mason, is it?"

My heart sank. I'd been hoping that no one would notice his absence, especially on a day when we needed all the manpower we had to get set up.

"You don't know, do you?" he sneered. "Did you lose him?"

I moved to leave, not wanting to reward his remarks with any kind of response. He took a step in front of me, forcing me to stop again.

"He should be here. Working hard. That's what you said, wasn't it? That we all needed to pitch in, help to make sure our little community runs smoothly?"

I recoiled, feeling his sour breath on the side of my face. Shaw moved over.

"Leave it, Thomas, alright?" He put a firm hand on Thomas'

shoulder. "She doesn't know where he is. And he was in a bad way last night—his friend just died."

"Well we've all lost people, haven't we?"

"Just don't take it out on her." Shaw remained still, a barrier between Thomas' rigid figure and my own. "It's not her fault he isn't here."

Thomas continued to stare at me for a moment, his eyes glittering. Then, without warning, he stepped away and returned to what he had been doing, turning his back on us. Shaw smiled apologetically.

I hurried to catch the others, who had headed around the side of the centre and a little further up the hillside. I shot a sideways glance at the field where we had spent the previous evening. There was now a second cairn standing at the head of the newly dug mound of earth. Green had been true to her word. I found myself warming to her even more.

"Well what do you think?" she asked us as we reached the vegetable garden.

Harper frowned. "You don't have nearly enough to feed lots of us. Not long term anyway."

"I know. That's why I had planned the secondary site for planting."

Harper bent down and took some of the soil between her fingers. "The earth's not as good here as in The Beck, but you've managed to get some kind of a harvest, so it should be possible to extend." She glanced up, clearly in her element considering the potential for planting and taking a lead role effortlessly. "Can you show us the area you were planning to develop?"

"Follow me." Green looked enthused at Harper's knowledge and the two of them led the way to the alternative site.

We walked for around twenty minutes, the ground sloping slightly upwards as we travelled, each step taking us closer to the distant hills. These slopes were different than those we had in The Beck, mostly scrubby, and bare of trees in many places. Here and there the wind turbines jutted up out of the hillside, spinning in the breeze today. At least the island had some kind of power, and we would be able to keep warm and cook food. When we were perhaps half way up the hill, the land flattened out into a plateau, and was backed on two sides by the hillside which rose steeply again behind it.

"I wondered about here," Green continued, pointing ahead, "Would this work? Sheltered, fairly flat, we could maybe dig irrigation ditches out along the sides of the fields. There's a stream close by, so we'd have access to water if we needed it, though I suspect we'll have sufficient rain to ensure we don't need to bring it from elsewhere."

Harper nodded enthusiastically, "This place is great."

Hurrying forward, she knelt on the ground, busily scooping soil samples into a small pot she had brought along with her. I could see her eyes roving over the field, beginning to divide up the space in her head, planning where she might plant each of the seed types she had brought over from The Beck, deciding which crops would grow better in which area. I knew she would be in her element here.

"She knows what she's doing, doesn't she?" Green smiled as she backed away, clearly recognising Harper's expertise.

The others watched Harper, awaiting her instruction. I marvelled at my friend's new-found strength and spirit, loving the way that others seemed keen to take instruction from her. She had certainly changed.

"Harper always was an excellent asset to Agric," I said. "Far better at it than I ever was."

Green looked intrigued, "Why was she sent to Clearance then?"

"She was ill. Weakened. We were never really sure what was wrong with her, but she wasn't recovering well and failed the last assessment."

Green shook her head, a look of total understanding on her features. "I lost a few friends like that. And when you think–"

"What?"

"Look, I've read almost every book in the library here." She smiled. "It's not very big. When I first got here my reading wasn't amazing, but I found the more I read—and the more I used the dictionary to look stuff up which I didn't know—the better I got. I got quite addicted in the end."

I waited for her to return to her original point. "So there are lots of factual books here—instruction manuals, that kind of thing. And at least one book on medicine. There are lots of ways The Beck could be helping citizens who are sick to get better, to stay healthy. That way they'd lose far less of us."

"But they don't care?"

"Not really. Adams doesn't consider us as people, but as assets. He and his associates have perfected a system where they can feed the Lower Beck citizens the minimum and allow them just enough sleep to function and work to keep the society running smoothly. It's not until we make it to the more elevated positions in the Upper Beck that we get treated any better. You can bet he treats himself and the others in Governance the best. I know he has access to some medicines, but he only chooses to give them to the people he deems worthy." She stared at me curiously. "Is Harper ok now though?"

"Sorry?"

"She doesn't seem ill now. A little thin, perhaps. Did she manage to recover in Clearance?" Her tone suggested disbelief.

I shook my head.

"So how did she—?"

"She was actually given some medicine."

She looked shocked. "What?"

I grinned wryly. "Not by the Clearance Supers. It was sneaked over to her. By a... by a friend."

Now it was Green's turn to wait. Her eyes were wide as she leaned closer.

I sighed. "It was Cam. Long story. But he took her some meds. He has access to Dev, is sort of friendly with one of the Supers there." I shuddered when I thought of the terrifying Montgomery. "And he wanted to help her."

Green paused a moment, clearly mulling over the information. "That's very like Cam. But how did he know Harper? She's your age, right? And he was never an Agric citizen. Their paths shouldn't have crossed, unless he was guarding her at some point. If she went from Agric to Clearance he wouldn't have—"

I interrupted, trying not to seem rude. "Like I said, long story."

I found I was struggling with the total freedom we now had to speak to one another. In The Beck, though we had talked, it had always been in secret, away from the prying eyes of the Supers. To be able to say whatever I wanted to anyone was something I knew I would need to get used to. And talking to Green about Cam when he was so out of reach was painful. Green seemed to appreciate how difficult I was finding the conversation and stopped pressing me. For a moment we simply watched, as Harper began to direct our small group with total confidence.

"I take it Mason didn't come back yet?" Green changed the subject.

This was one I felt more comfortable with. "No. I'm worried. And this morning Thomas was—"

"Oh, ignore Thomas. He's a fool."

"But he did seem angry. And I get it. We all should be here working."

"Mason was upset. I can't tell you how Lee's death affected us all. Nelson was in a really bad way for a while, but he came round."

"You think he's—"

She placed a hand on my arm. "He'll be fine. He can't go that far, it's a small island."

"But—"

"If he's not back by this time tomorrow, we'll send someone out to look for him."

Feeling comforted, I allowed her to lead me back to the field to rejoin the others.

"And Quin?" I turned to her again, seeing the kindness in her eyes. "If you want to tell me that story about Cam at some point... well I'd be happy to listen. Back in The Beck he was a good friend of mine."

After several hours in the field area, my back was aching. We had turned over the dirt in a large part of it, sectioned it off into smaller segments for the different crops, and Harper had even managed to get some of the faster growing crop seeds planted. We returned to the centre feeling satisfied that we had really achieved something. As we stumbled into the courtyard, the rain began to fall again and we hurried inside. Baker had returned from her mission armed with a large number of strong reeds and grasses she felt could be turned into nets, and since her return to base, had even managed to provide some oatcakes and a little more of the cold meat for us to share.

The fishing crew were back before us. Whilst those who had been out on the canoes had yet to catch anything, the rest boasted of managing to make six new rods. The afternoon was going to be spent training more people to use them, and Nelson seemed hopeful that, between them, they might catch enough for us all to have a fresh and decent evening meal. After gathering our share of the food, Cass and I joined Blythe, noting that she was alone with her daughter. Despite Thomas' current absence, I felt the need to protect her. She looked up as we sat down.

"How was your morning?"

"Good thanks, the fields are coming along well, though it's hard work." I rubbed the back of my neck tiredly. "Do you know Cass?"

She nodded, "Not officially, but I've seen her around. Hey."

Cass paused mid-chew and smiled her own greeting. Perry yowled softly in Blythe's arms and Cass and I turned to look at her.

"She's so tiny."

Blythe shifted her so she was more upright and we could see her better. "But she's so much bigger than she was when she was born. Already."

"How does it feel?" Cass flushed as she asked the question.

Blythe frowned, "How does what feel?"

"Having a baby?"

"Well it hurts. A lot." Blythe grimaced at the memory. "But

that pain was nothing compared to the pain of having her taken away."

I watched her face and remembered the pale, shell of a woman I had first encountered. She seemed so different now.

"Can I... can I hold her?"

I stared at my old friend. Cass had never seemed especially maternal. She was always so tough. But we weren't ever exposed to babies, and even children were out of reach once we left the confines of Minors at fourteen and were considered adults. I watched as Blythe handed over her daughter, being careful to support her head. She lay gurgling in Cass' arms, her little feet stretching out and her eyes struggling to focus on the things around her. I could see the attraction.

"Thanks. You're actually helping me out." Blythe leaned over to take one of the oatcakes and began to break it up, crumbling it into a bowl in front of her. "I need to try more solid food with her."

"Solid food?" Cass queried.

"There isn't a lot of the baby milk left over," I explained, as Blythe blended the oatcake with milk. "If Blythe can't get Perry eating this mush then she might run out."

Cass looked horrified. "Run out?"

Blythe's face darkened. "But babies aren't supposed to eat this kind of thing yet, so..."

She leaned closer, a little of the mixture on the end of a spoon. Perry flailed her arms around, catching the implement and flinging its contents over herself and Cass. Then she let out a loud shriek. I watched with concern as others round the room began to notice. There were a few disgruntled murmurs, but I noticed that some of the faces watching were more curious and less hostile. It seemed Perry was softening a few hearts, although I doubted that we would ever convince Thomas.

Patiently, Blythe wiped the goop from the baby's face and attempted to clean up a chuckling Cass too. Then she loaded the spoon again, and leaned across for a second time.

"Sit her up a little, will you? That might help."

Cass shifted position and held the wriggling bundle more firmly and upright. This time, the spoon made it to Perry's mouth, but as the food went in, her face altered, she screwed up her nose and stuck out a tiny tongue in distaste. Most of the food squeezed out between her lips and ran down her chin. A few spoons later, she began to cry, and struggle more determinedly to escape the metal instrument that kept invading her mouth.

"See, she's not ready!" Blythe whispered, her words tormented.

"You can try again tomorrow," I tried, "we can help again, if you like?"

"Thanks," she managed to mutter, but I could see how devastated she was as she took the squirming infant back from Cass.

"Hey," a voice came from behind us. "How is she?"

We turned to find Barnes, returned from the hunting crew, standing behind us. His tone was soft, gentle. One I had never heard from him before. As my toughest and most impatient training Super, he had been extremely hard on us as Patrol recruits, but here he was showing a completely different side.

Blythe had been holding it together until he approached, but as he sat down on the other side of her, she fell apart.

"She can't... she won't take the food!" Her tone was desperate. "And I don't know what to do."

He put both arms around her and began whispering words

of comfort into her ear. I exchanged glances with Cass, im-mediately feeling like we were invading their privacy. Blythe looked more comforted now that he had arrived, so we backed away, leaving them to talk.

As we joined another table, I realised how the noise level in the room had grown. It appeared that most of the hunters were even happier with their own performance than the fishing crew, having brought back three squirrels and a small hare. Baker disappeared into the kitchen with their prizes, but most of them continued to brag, forming a tight circle around one of the central tables in the room. Only Thomas hovered on the edges of the group, his face the usual mask of frustration and anger. I didn't like to think what was bothering him now.

Rogers had joined Green at the rear of the canteen, and they were deep in conference about something. Cass and I sat together and finished our own share of the food. I was pleased when she struck up a conversation with one of the other female Patrol recruits who had been part of the fishing detail. Perhaps Marley's apology had done some good then, allowing her to let go of some of her guilt over Wade's death. They were discussing the pros and cons of line and net fishing and I had tuned out altogether when I heard the door at the rear of the room open again. I turned.

In the doorway, soaked to the skin and covered in mud, was Mason.

Chapter Ten

His eyes travelled the room until he spotted me. The expression on his face told me nothing. All I knew was, it was me he was looking for. When his eyes met mine, he jerked his head in the direction of the hallway and was gone. Slipping outside as quietly as I could, I shut the door to the canteen and looked around. The corridor was empty, but the door to one of the offices was ajar, and I made my way towards it. As I stepped into the room he was sitting on the edge of the desk, a sheepish look on his face.

"Hey." He dropped his eyes to the floor.

"Hey."

There was an awkward pause, then, "I'm sorry, Quin."

I regarded him closely, unsure whether I should go to him.

"I shouldn't have run off." He continued to stare at the ground, "It's just..."

"I know."

He finally managed to look up and make eye contact, "I had to leave... wasn't sure what I'd do otherwise."

"Are you ok? I was worried."

"I'm sorry." He sighed, "Again."

I made my decision and closed the distance between us, putting a hand on his arm. "I'm just glad you're alright."

"I wasn't. But I am now." He looked away. "At least I think so."

Noise spilled from outside as people left the canteen. The meal was clearly over. We remained silent as the chattering voices passed by, fading away as they left the building. I waited until he spoke again. When he did, I could hear the pain in his voice.

"I thought I wanted this, Quin. I wanted to escape. From the very beginning, you know that. But, but—now I've done it, I feel like I'd give anything to go back to The Beck," his voice caught. "That's ridiculous isn't it?"

I shook my head. "No. It's not. You don't want The Beck. You want the people you're missing. And you know you can't have them."

I moved closer, sliding an arm around his shoulders, feeling like he needed the physical contact. He was shaking, and I knew I had done the right thing. He was wet, and cold, and grieving for the losses he had suffered. I put my other arm around him, and hugged him tightly, realising that we were mirrors of one another. We had both lost a friend, and left someone behind. We stood together for a long time, until he managed to control his breathing and pulled away.

I tried to smile. "Where've you been?"

"Everywhere. Once I left you yesterday, I walked and walked, until I was exhausted. I think I wanted to tire myself out so much that I could just fall asleep and stop feeling so... so...." He winced, "I finally collapsed in what I thought was a cave. An entrance in between the rocks at least. It was dark, so I couldn't really see what it was like until this morning."

"And was it a cave?"

"Sort of. When I woke up, I felt a bit better, but I still wasn't ready to come back. I did a bit of exploring instead."

"Ok." I settled myself into the chair in front of him, letting him tell me at his own pace.

"I wondered how far the cave went back, whether there were others behind it, places to hide, to keep stuff." He settled more comfortably on the desk as he continued. "I started to realise that it was manmade. Or at least parts of it were."

"Manmade? As in, human beings carved a cave out of the rock?"

"I'm not sure. Perhaps not originally, perhaps they widened an existing crack in the rock face. Anyway, the section behind had a ton of rubble in it, rocks which had fallen in, you know? I spent a bit of time hauling some of them out of the way."

"And?"

"And," he paused, "there was a tunnel behind them."

"Really?"

"There's more. Once I'd found the tunnel, I spent more time clearing a section of it, and eventually found a shaft. Again, it's partially blocked by some kind of rockfall, but I wondered if Rogers knew about it."

"Not sure. Green mentioned caves when she was talking about the island, but not tunnels or a shaft. Where do you think it leads?"

"I don't think. I know."

"You went down there?"

He grinned, and I could see a little of the old Mason. "Not all the way, but I managed to clear a good section and slid behind it."

I slapped his arm, "You could have been injured."

He waved my concern away, his eyes brightening, "I didn't get very far, but look what I found."

He held out his hand triumphantly. It contained some small metal pellets which I recognised instantly.

"Bullets?"

He nodded enthusiastically.

"And that's good because...?"

"Don't you see the possibilities? They're worried about the people from that other island, right?"

"The Ridge?"

"Is that what it's called?" He peered at the humped shape of the other island in the distance. "Well they were pretty fierce at defending themselves when we passed yesterday. Rogers and the others are concerned that we can't defend ourselves, aren't they? That we don't have enough weapons or ammunition?"

I stared at him, still unsure where he was going with this.

"What if the shaft leads to some underground storage?"

"Storage? Of what?"

"Who knows? But don't you think it's worth exploring? Who knows what they were keeping down there. Might be something useful." He proffered the bullet again.

"You mean—"

"If we can clear the shaft, who knows what we might find. Bullets are made from metal. Metal is mined from underground. This was an army camp, wasn't it?"

I wasn't sure I shared Mason's excitement, but did not want to discourage him. I hadn't seen him so enthusiastic about anything since we had left The Beck. I decided it was a good sign.

"You need to tell Rogers."

"I know. Just wanted to speak to you first. Hoped you might have my back when I explain this to them."

I tried to look dismissive of his concerns, despite secretly feeling he was right that the others might not buy the idea. "You think they won't be supportive?"

"They might not. It's going to be dangerous, removing all that rubble, and time consuming."

"And it might not lead anywhere." It dawned on me that they could be totally against the plan. "But we have to try, surely?"

"I think we should."

He stood up, looking expectantly at me.

"You mean now?"

"No time like the present. I want to apologise as well. Thank them."

"Which way did you come back?" I thought of the freshly built cairn, "Did you see the stones at Davis' grave?"

"I did. Was that Green's handiwork?"

"Yes. It's called a cairn. It marks the place where Davis lies."

"It's... I like it. I need to thank her." He passed me and pulled open the door, "Coming?"

I followed him into the hallway. The building seemed quiet, but we made our way back to the canteen first, to see if our unofficial leaders were still inside. The door was standing slightly ajar, and as we approached, we could hear voices coming from inside. Peering into the room, I could see Rogers and Green standing off to one side, while Baker faced them, her hands on her hips and a puzzling expression on her face.

"...not sure I can be around them," she was saying, "I don't know why you thought it was a good idea to bring them."

"I didn't exactly have a choice," Rogers sounded annoyed, "We left in a hurry, and Tyler insisted."

"You had to know Baker would find it difficult," Green's

voice, for the first time sounding annoyed with her partner.

"Look, Cam agreed to the people on the list. I trusted him to make the choices."

"But couldn't you have—"

"No. I couldn't." There was a shifting of feet, as though Rogers had moved away from the others. "In the end we were hiding, waiting for the others. Then Shadow Patrol turned up. It was chaos. If I'd have turned them off the boat at that point, they'd have been shot dead on the beach. That what you'd have preferred, Baker?"

"Obviously not." Another movement, this time in the direction of the door.

Mason and I shrank back into the office we had come from, fearful that we would be caught listening by anyone leaving the room. As we ducked inside, the last sentence of the conversation drifted to us from behind the canteen door. Baker's voice.

"You always have to play the hero, Rogers."

Her footsteps echoed down the hallway as she left the building. Mason and I stared at one another, unsure what to do next.

"Shall we risk talking to them now?"

He shrugged, "At least they're alone. And I did want to apologise before I see them again with other people around."

I hesitated.

"Will you come? Please Quin?"

I followed him across the hall and into the canteen again. Rogers and Green looked up, startled by our unexpected entrance.

Green exchanged a relieved glance with Rogers as she spotted Mason, "Everything ok?"

"Um... yes," he replied, hesitant now he was faced with the two of them. "I'm... well... that is I wanted to tell you I was back, and that I was sorry. For running off like that. I–"

Green crossed the room, took Mason by the arm and guided him to a seat on one of the benches. "It's fine. We understand."

"But I was..."

Rogers begrudgingly joined her, "She's right. It's ok. We were the same when Lee died."

There was an awkward pause for a moment before Mason spoke again. "I wanted to say thank you, for the burial. And the... cairn, is it called? I saw it just now."

Green smiled tiredly. "No problem."

"No really– it's very... fitting. It's kind of... comforting, that we... well that we have somewhere to go, if we, when we..."

"That's the point of it. I'm glad you agree."

"Anyway, I wanted to speak to you about something else, if it's ok."

He paused for a moment, and continued when they didn't argue, "I slept in a cave last night. You know the ones close to the top of the hill?"

Rogers nodded. "Yes, there are a few up there. Most of them only small. Not large enough for any kind of storage, if that's what you're thinking. Mostly full of rubble from small landfalls. Inaccessible."

"I disagree."

Rogers looked surprised at Mason's tone. "You do?"

"Yes. There is quite a lot of rubble, but I did some investigating. Found a tunnel behind the cave... and even a shaft going underground."

"How much of the rubble did you manage to move?" Rogers

seemed impressed.

"And why did you decide to move it?" Green echoed Rogers' surprise.

"Not sure." Mason grinned wryly. "If I'm honest I was still really mad, and I began moving the rocks to give me something to do, take my mind off Davis. It was pretty mindless at first. I thought maybe I could make some kind of a shelter, be useful, instead of people thinking I'm someone who runs off at the first sign of trouble."

I nudged him, "Show them what you found."

He pulled the bullets out of his pocket and held them out.

Rogers took one and examined it closely, "Where were these?"

"After I had moved a good portion of the rubble I managed to slip through into some kind of tunnel. I kept finding these here and there on the ground. Took me a while to realise what they were. And then I found the shaft. I think it goes fairly deep underground."

I remembered my promise to support him, "We think they might have stored things down there, or—"

"—or maybe there was a mine!" Green sounded excited, "It was an army base—mining metal to make their own ammunition makes sense, doesn't it?"

"Worth a look isn't it?" Mason beamed, "You said we were short on weapons and ammunition."

Rogers looked thoughtful. "We are. You think—?"

"At the very least we might find boxes of bullets stored down there."

"Maybe. It'll take some clearing though. And we might find nothing."

"Think you could show me where the cave was on a map

Mason?" Rogers said. "There's one on the wall in the office."

"Sure."

The two men hurried out of the door. Green turned to me and smiled. "I'm glad he has something which can take his mind off Davis. He needs a project which allows him to be useful."

"I agree." I stood up, still curious about Baker's earlier comments, but unsure whether or not I dared ask.

"Something else, Quin?"

I paused, and took a deep breath before asking the question, "Was Baker alright before?"

"Baker?" Green sounded surprised at my question.

"Sorry—we overheard some of the conversation before we came in. She seemed—upset."

Green's smile was strained as she turned back to me. "Come with me a minute?"

She stood up and gathered a small stack of books from the table in front of her. Walking to the door, she opened it and beckoned for me to follow. At the end of the hallway, she entered a room I had not yet seen. Assuming it was another office, I hurried into it after her. The room smelled a little musty, but inside the walls were filled with shelving from floor to ceiling, and every shelf was crammed with books.

"The library," Green proclaimed, placing the books on a small table inside the door. She took the top volume from the pile and slotted it back on one of the shelves.

Turning to me, she continued, "Look, don't mind Baker. She's had a difficult life, experiences we can't understand, so we have to make allowances sometimes."

"What's she got against Blythe and Perry though?" I fought to keep my tone calm. "They've done nothing to her."

"You're right of course, but don't judge her." She returned to the pile of books, moving with grace and fluidity, and selected another to return to the shelf. She seemed to know the exact position of every volume. Clearly this was her domain. "She's finding it hard to cope with a baby around, that's all. Please. Give her a chance. She's done more than you can imagine for us here at Brecon Crags."

I wasn't in the mood for being tolerant today. "Such as?"

"Never mind." Green was firm. "Look, the one thing I will confide is that her rejection of Blythe and Perry is not for the same reason as Thomas. She doesn't feel they're a burden. Well, not really. It's just she hasn't had any experience with babies since—well let's just say she has more in common with Blythe than you realise."

Something clicked. "She was assigned to Meds? Had to give up a baby?"

Green nodded. "Yes. And she survived the experience by hardening herself to the world. Many mothers—"

"I know. Many mothers don't survive the grief."

"No, they don't. Baker has looked forward to us building a new kind of life here just like the rest of us, but as you've witnessed, she's more nervous. She wants us to open our doors to more Beck citizens, but she's concerned about what it will lead to. A society where children are born normally and get to stay with their mothers, be brought up by them. We're a long way from that at the moment," she finished her task and came to sit beside me, "but in the future we'd like to be able to bring up children the way they used to be, in the old world before the flooding. And Baker knew she would have to deal with that when the time came, just not so soon."

"So, when we brought over a citizen with her own child…"

"...she found it extremely difficult, as Blythe has what Baker would have killed for, and can never have. Just try and give her a break, ok?"

I stared at her silently, my mind spinning with the revelation. After a moment, I realised she was waiting for confirmation that I would go easier on Baker.

"Sure," I managed to stammer. "I can see why she's the way she is now. I'll... try to be more understanding."

"Thanks. She needs friends more than she cares to admit." Green turned to me and smiled. "Quin, I like you. I can see why Cam likes you. I think you could have a great influence on the group we're building here." I felt myself blushing at her words as she backed away, "Look, I hope you can keep that piece of information to yourself please? Baker would hate to think people knew and pitied her. She's very proud."

"Of course. And I'd never pity her."

"Thanks Quin. I know she'd –"

At that moment, Green's radio spluttered into life for a second time.

"Rogers. Baker. Green!" The voice was Nelson's, his tone urgent.

"Yes?" Green's reply was instant.

"Some trouble. On the path down to the boats. Can one of you get here now please? And bring Blythe, or Quin."

"Copy that. On my way." Green was all business. "Quin's with me now."

Exchanging worried glances with each other, we headed outside.

Chapter Eleven

When we reached the cliff path, there appeared to be no immediate crisis. On the way down, Green had been silent, but I knew she was fretting about a possible invasion of The Crags from the people on The Ridge army base. Since there were now so many of us here, and a larger boat to boot, it seemed a fairly obvious conclusion that the closest encampment to us would want to investigate any threat we might pose.

But the waters around the island seemed clear, and the few people standing close to the shore were attempting to launch fishing rods into the water. Though she hadn't answered the radio call, Baker had got there before us, and we found her standing with Nelson close to the shore, involved in some kind of altercation with Barnes, who held an oar in one hand and had one foot in the bottom of a canoe. From a distance, the scene looked almost comical, the two men gesturing wildly at one another, Barnes' balance offset slightly by the rocking of the small craft.

Raised voices greeted us as we reached the small knot of people arguing on the shoreline. Other citizens had paused their work to listen.

"...can't stop me," Barnes's usual belligerent tone was even more forceful than usual.

"...ridiculous!" Nelson's arms flew skywards in frustration, "... you think you'll make it ashore without being seen? And for what? ...can't risk it!"

Barnes took a step towards Nelson, his hand on the oar thrusting closer to the other man. With a courage I certainly didn't feel, and wishing more than anything that Tyler would appear at any moment and take charge, I attempted to diffuse the situation.

"Barnes, what are you doing?"

He didn't even glance my way. The two men continued to glare at one another.

"Barnes!" This time his gaze flickered over to mine, but his expression remained mutinous. "What's going on?"

Nelson and Baker turned to Green. "Can you believe this? He's decided he needs to pay our friends on The Ridge a visit."

Green turned an icy gaze on Barnes. "Are you mad?"

"Mad, no. But I need to get over there."

Green stepped closer and took hold of the arm which held the oar. For a moment Barnes struggled against her, but considering there were now four citizens surrounding him, he seemed to reconsider. Eventually his grip went loose and he relinquished the paddle.

"Why, Barnes?" Green's voice was calm, reasonable. "Why the sudden desperation to reach an island which has attacked us?"

"He believes they have something he needs." Nelson had relaxed somewhat now that Barnes had dropped the oar, but still regarded Barnes' foot in the canoe warily, as though he might push off from the shore at any moment and try to paddle all the way to The Ridge with his bare hands. I had to admit he looked fierce enough to try it.

"I don't want to go there to cause trouble." Barnes' tone was thoroughly disgusted. "I'm going because I have to."

Green looked perplexed. "But why? What do they have that you need?"

I felt a presence behind me and turned to see Blythe, who had approached from the path, presumably also having heard Nelson's radio call. "He's worried about Perry."

Baker had been standing close to Barnes on one side, flanking him with Nelson and Green. I watched her face blanch at Blythe's approach and she backed away a little as the young mother continued.

"He wants to get supplies for Perry. There isn't much of the milk Tyler brought with us left." Her face was shadowed with concern again, but she attempted to mask it as she stepped closer to Barnes. "I told you it would be fine, didn't I?" She reached out a hand as if to calm him, and to my surprise, he allowed her to lead him away from the canoe.

"Look," she murmured to him, "things aren't that bad yet. I shared a concern, that's all. It doesn't mean you have to go off all fired up and save the day for me, alright?"

Barnes slumped down a little, "But you said–"

"I know you're trying hard to protect me and Perry. But our friends have welcomed us here and you're about to endanger their lives. They're concerned. You must see why."

Green and Nelson relaxed a little, watching the positive effect that Blythe had on Barnes. Baker remained a few feet away, reluctant to be anywhere near Blythe. It made sense now, and I found myself beginning to feel some sympathy.

Blythe guided Barnes away from the group, further diffusing the situation. "I know what I said, but I hadn't realised you'd act quite so... quickly. I'm worried, but things aren't desperate.

93

Not yet. Maybe we should be asking the people who've lived here the longest... handle this together... try to..." her voice faded as she moved out of earshot.

I had never heard her speak so rationally. She sounded like Tyler. I wondered whether this was more like the old Blythe, the capable Super she had been before she was sent to Meds. Perhaps having Perry back with her had begun to heal some of the wounds caused by their separation. She sat Barnes on a rock a little further along the shoreline and kissed the top of his head, before turning and walking back to us.

"I'm sorry. He has no idea how to deal with what's been thrown at him over the past few days. He's trying really hard to support me and... he just goes about it in the wrong way."

I turned to her. "You're worried about Perry though, aren't you?"

She frowned. "A little. I'm getting low on the supplies that Tyler brought with us. You saw yourself how the solid food isn't really working. Not yet anyway."

Green stared at Blythe, a thoughtful look on her face. "How old is she?"

"Five months."

"She should take a little solid food at least. What have you tried her with?"

"Just milk and oatcakes."

"I think there are other things she might find a bit more appetising. There's a book or two in the library here which might tell you more," Green blushed slightly. "Not that I've any experience of my own, of course."

"Would you show me later please?" Blythe laid a gentle hand on the other woman's arm.

"Of course." Green returned to the rest of us, keeping her

voice low, "Look, if Barnes is worried enough to try and take a canoe over there, we need to take him seriously. Perhaps we should have a meeting. Let everyone discuss their concerns. It's no good if people here aren't happy with the way things are." She shot a pointed look at Nelson. "We said we'd make sure things were run differently here. Not like The Beck. We need to follow through."

"Sounds good." Nelson moved back to his fishing team, returning to adjusting rods and demonstrating casting styles. This was a role he seemed more comfortable with.

Glancing around, I caught sight of Baker retreating up the path to the dorms, presumably returning to the kitchen. She had not really participated in the debate either, and it was clear that she wanted nothing to do with Blythe and Perry's situation unless it directly endangered others.

Green interrupted my thoughts, "Where are you scheduled to work this afternoon, Quin?"

"The fields again."

"Would you mind showing Blythe the library on your way up there? She can collect Perry on her way back and spend the afternoon there." She glanced at Barnes and I knew she was eager to get him away from the water. "She should be able to locate the appropriate books without me."

"Sure."

"Barnes. With me please." She paused for a moment by his side and waited for him to get up from the rock. "Let's go and see Rogers, shall we?"

They set off at a jog up the path. I hoped that a session hunting with Rogers might take Barnes' mind off The Ridge and the issues with Perry's food supply.

Once they were out of sight, I turned to Blythe. "Where's

Perry?"

"I left her with Tyler back up at the centre. Ty's great with babies. Perry's almost as happy with her as she is with me." She paused for a moment. "Can we give it a minute? I don't want to follow too closely. He already thinks I'm keeping too close an eye on him."

I nodded. Having allowed Green and Barnes a decent head start, we set off a safe distance after them, taking our time up the path. Blythe seemed preoccupied, and didn't speak until we were almost in sight of the centre.

"What kind of books do you think I'm looking for, Quin?" Her face was clouded with concern. "I was never much of a reader, to be honest."

I glanced around at the shelves. "I don't know. I'm not sure in an army base there will be books specifically aimed at motherhood. Perhaps a biology book?"

She looked doubtful.

"Want me to come in and help you look for a minute?"

Relief washed over her face. "Please!"

Wanting to support Blythe, I waited while she dodged into the dorms to collect Perry, and then led her inside the main building to the room at the end of the hallway. Inside, she giggled at the groaning shelves of books.

"Wow. Not like The Beck library is it?"

The only source of books in The Beck had been a very limited store of well-vetted texts which citizens were allowed to read in their minimal free time. There weren't that many, and most citizens who enjoyed reading had worked their way through the interesting ones within the first year of their life in the adult community.

Now I had a little more time, I wandered around the shelves, running my fingers along the spines of the books. There were ones similar to the stories I had seen in The Beck, but also a range of factual books which I could see would be useful. I selected an encyclopaedia and pointed Blythe to the section on infant development, as well as a book about food and health, which was filled with pictures I hoped would help her out if she struggled with the words.

"I'd better go and find my team," I said hesitantly, "Don't want people thinking I'm slacking!"

She looked up from settling Perry on a blanket on the floor. The baby kicked her legs up in front of her, gurgling happily.

"She seems more content now, at least," I ventured, wanting to seem encouraging.

"Tyler has just this minute given her a bottle. She'll be hungry again soon, and I can't risk giving her another until this evening."

"I'm sorry. I wish there were something more I could do."

She motioned at the books I had left out for her. "You are doing something. These should help me with a few more ideas. Thanks Quin."

"No trouble. I can come and help you look through a few more this evening if you like."

She smiled her thanks as I headed outside.

I felt a little guilty when I reached the vegetable plot to find the others had been hard at work for a while. Even Mason was there, having agreed to visit the cave site later with Rogers to further investigate, and he was hard at work, seemingly desperate to make up for his absence in the previous session. Sharing his guilt, I fell into rhythm beside him and tried to match his fervour. The rest of the day passed quickly, and by the end of it, my arms ached in the familiar way they used to when I worked in Agric.

As we walked back to the dorms, the wind picked up. The sky was darkening with clouds which clearly foretold rain. I shivered a little. Mason had gone on ahead and had struck up a conversation with Walker. Harper caught up with me and took my hand in hers. It felt strange after so long without her, yet the contact was still so familiar. She gestured at the two men ahead of us.

"Good to see people getting to know one another," she peered into my face closely, "Is Mason ok now?"

I shrugged, "Better than he was. I'm glad he's starting to make an effort to connect to others. How's Marley?"

"I'm not sure really. She's quiet. Sad. But she doesn't seem angry any more, not with Cass, at least. I tried to make her understand that–"

"I know."

There was a pause filled only with the sound of our footsteps tramping rhythmically down the path.

"How about you?" Her voice was quiet and calm.

I rubbed my tired eyes with my free hand. "It's been... an adjustment."

"I know. But I'm starting to really see the possibilities here, aren't you?"

"Harper, I–"

"It's not difficult to imagine, I mean... how we could make a better kind of life here. Our skills transfer. Between us we have every type of person we could possibly need."

"Yes, we do, but–"

She stopped walking and put a hand on my arm, turning me to face her.

"What I really wanted to say, Quin, was I'm sorry. For

hesitating when you came for me. I guess I was just shocked when you appeared in Clearance that night." Her voice dropped even lower, "And I know that you weren't supposed to take four of us, but you did, so thank you." She paused, a haunted look in her eyes. "You don't really understand what it's like over there. If it hadn't been for Walker and the others, and Cam of course, I honestly wouldn't have survived. I couldn't have left without them. But I'm really glad we came along, and–"

Her words were a torrent, cascading out one after another, and I realised that she had been waiting a while to say all this. In the end, I let her keep talking, enjoying the fact that someone here was happy, and able to see the positives of our new life. As she chattered on, the first drops of rain began to fall, and we hurried to continue our journey before it soaked us through.

"The other thing I need to tell you is... I don't know if you've guessed, you probably have, but Walker and I... well, I met him the day we were both transferred to Clearance." She paused, her eyes fixed on the muddy path beneath us, "He was so lovely to me while I was recovering. Helped me with the plants I grew... they supplemented the Clearance rations, which we badly needed. And I know... I know that Walker seemed reluctant to leave... at first..." As the dorms came into sight ahead, she continued hastily, "Anyway, he and I are... well we're kind of... together. You understand?"

She peered anxiously into my face, as though she were worried I might disapprove, and I had to smile.

"I understand Har. Cam and I..." I bit back tears at the mention of his name, "well we're kind of together too. It's just..." I trailed off.

"Just what?" Her words were kindly, but it didn't help.

"Just hard to keep it going when he's back in The Beck and I'm... well, here."

"Oh Quin... was he supposed to be on the boat with us?" She stopped again, despite the heavy rain which was now falling fast. "I'm so sorry."

"Actually," I hesitated, knowing that Cass had not been thrilled to find out the truth, but feeling like I owed it to both my oldest friends. I forced myself to meet her sympathetic gaze. "Look, I was supposed to be staying behind."

"Staying? But you... you came to get me... to take me..." she trailed off.

"I did. I knew they were going to drown you. I wanted to rescue you. But I knew Cass was going to be on the boat and... well I thought once I'd rescued you, you'd be able to look after each other." I dropped my gaze at her bewildered stare. "I wanted to... I needed to stay with him."

A range of different expressions flitted across her face. Confusion turned to surprise, then disappointment, and finally a deep sadness.

"I see." She wouldn't look at me. "Well that makes sense, I suppose."

"Harper, honestly, I didn't–"

She held up a hand to stop me. "No, of course not. I understand."

But her face told another story. Clearly, she was as hurt by my plans as Cass had been. I struggled to find words which might smooth things over, take away the look of pain which cast a deep shadow across her face. Nothing came to mind. And before I could say any more, she hurried ahead of me into the courtyard, disappearing into the dorms without another word as the rain continued to pour.

Chapter Twelve

The meeting that Green had promised took place after dinner that evening. Having spent the day working hard, most of the group was tired but feeling encouraged about the days and weeks to come. Even the rain which continued to fall, hammering on the roof of the building throughout the meal, didn't dampen their spirits. I tried in vain to share their optimism.

Harper had been polite to me on the couple of occasions I had approached her since our earlier conversation, but she was keeping her distance and clearly still upset. She was currently eating at a table with her Clearance friends, their heads bent close together, their conversation seeming to flow easily. I felt an unfamiliar stab of jealousy. She had her own friends now; she didn't need me. I was hugely glad that I at least had Cass to sit with, but found myself missing Jackson and Cam badly.

Eventually, Rogers stood up to speak. "We've had a good first day, on the whole, however, a few... small issues have come to light. We decided to call this meeting to discuss any issues any of you might have. Try to nip them in the bud, if you like."

Green smiled and added, "We don't want The Crags to be

like The Beck, a place we were all desperate to escape from, so we'd be very interested to hear your thoughts and want to make sure that we as a community are voting on issues which will affect us all."

"Voting?" The question came from one of the recruits, but I was glad someone had asked, as I wasn't sure myself what it meant.

"If we have any issue which we are not agreed on, we all get a say in the outcome. We vote... we all get to say which of the suggested options we prefer and the one with the most people in favour of it wins."

"And what if the choice you want doesn't make it?" Thomas challenged. I was again grateful that I had mostly managed to avoid him since our confrontation about Perry.

"Well there's nothing you can do about it. You accept it because you had your say and the majority rules." Rogers's voice was calm, but there was an undertone of steel beneath his words.

"It's called democracy," Green added.

Thomas fell silent, but the defiant look on his face worried me.

Rogers continued, "Here's where we stand at the moment. The positives: we have sufficient living space for now. Plenty of beds, a working kitchen, bathrooms, lots of storage. Moving forward, if we rescue more citizens from The Beck, we may need to consider the use of pods, like those in The Beck, to house newcomers, until we are able to create additional buildings for them. There are already some wind turbines up on the hill which supply us with electricity for several hours each day."

He looked at Green, who smiled warmly at him before

continuing with the list.

"We have our own clothes from The Beck, as well as some army uniforms which were already here, but we might need to look at making additional clothing and blankets as we gain more citizens, the younger ones among us outgrow their clothing, and the stock we already have wears out." A shadow crossed her face as she continued. "Now for the negatives, which we can't ignore. We don't have any kind of medicines, or ways of developing them, and although we have a small amount of first aid supplies, with more than twenty of us, they won't last long. Ultimately if anyone gets ill or injured, there will be little we can do for them, which is a huge issue. We also have no one with any knowledge of medicine or treatments."

Nelson took over, "We have no livestock, but there is limited space for any kind of herd to graze, and actually transporting any cattle or sheep here to begin a breeding programme seems impossible, to be honest. That's a massive advantage The Beck has over The Crags. Fish are in plentiful supply, and we are making the most of that by expanding our supply of rods and trying to create nets. The addition of the larger boat is great, but using it regularly risks being noticed by The Ridge. Fishing from the canoes might be a better plan to begin with."

"Finally," Rogers nodded at Mason, "We're concerned about our lack of defence. Mason found something today which we want to investigate further. There are caves close to the top of the hillside, and last night he found a partially-blocked tunnel behind them. We want to investigate where it leads. There is the possibility that we might find stores of ammunition underground, or even some kind of disused mine. If we had the materials and the ability to make bullets, it would make our existing store of weapons infinitely more useful. The downside is, the tunnels will need a lot of clearing, which may well be a large project."

"Aren't we better off focusing on securing our food supply at the moment?"

The voice came from the rear of the group, but I knew instantly who it belonged to.

Thomas pushed to the front, until he had the eyes of the entire group on him. "Look, I've spent all day hunting animals to come home with a couple of rabbits which won't even feed the whole group for a single night. That's a bigger problem, in my mind, than going on some wild goose chase underground."

"I take your point about the food, Thomas. I understand that everyone's concerned about our long-term sustenance, but things aren't that bad. Remember you're all new to hunting and fishing. It might take a while until we're bringing more food in, but we'll get there. Baker's great at preserving things these days: drying out meats and vegetables, storing them carefully for emergency use, that kind of thing. Plus, there are so many more of us to share the workload now. I don't think we need to worry too much. I promise the underground exploration won't take much manpower from the food resourcing, but I do feel that it's worth exploring, even just a little."

"In the future maybe, but now? We only just got here!" He looked at the people standing around him and, alarmingly, some of them began to murmur in agreement. "Bad enough we have citizens out of action..."

Green jumped in, "What do you mean, 'out of action'?"

He jerked a thumb at Blythe, who shrank away from him. "The mother here can't hunt for her own food, 'cos she's looking after the infant. Both of them are taking food from the mouths of those of us who are working to actually gather it."

"Perry's only drinking milk at the moment." Barnes' voice was low and threatening.

He snorted, "I saw you at dinner, trying to feed it mashed potato!"

All eyes turned to Blythe and she murmured, "It was just a little. I'm worried she's not gaining weight. The books said babies might take a little mashed vegetables."

"It was a tiny bit, Thomas! Hardly enough to feed a grown man." Barnes' words were a growl.

Thomas flushed and took a step towards Barnes, "And you weren't exactly working hard all day, were you? You only arrived half way through this afternoon's shift. I heard about your performance down on the shore." He turned to the Patrol recruits either side of him, "We all know your absence was to do with *them*."

Barnes had to be stopped from lunging at Thomas. Rogers stepped in front of him, facing the angry recruit.

"Look, Thomas, we get that you're all new to this. When you lived in The Beck there was a sense of routine. Food, no matter how small the portion, was doled out regularly. You slept, bathed, worked alongside the same people each day and were used to it. Coming here, having all this freedom, the lack of routine, it's an adjustment. But it's vital that we establish new routines here, and work together as part of a team. Otherwise..."

"Otherwise we risk failure." Green's tone was firm, "If we can't manage twenty people here, how can we expand the community any further?" She softened her tone. "Look, those of us who've been here a while are used to living with a very small group of people. It will take us a while to adjust too, but we hope that everyone will be able to adapt to our expanding society and be able to function as equals in the end. No one here is used to being around children, but I think some of us are getting used to it, and even quite enjoying it."

I glanced around the room, and could see from the expressions on the faces that Perry had won a few of our community over. No longer did everyone look aghast at the sight of her, and a few were even smiling affectionately. There was a silence for a moment when I believed that Thomas was satisfied with Green's words, but my heart sank as he continued.

"Look, you all keep saying how things are going to be fair here, but so far you're the ones doing all the talking. How come you automatically get to be in charge?"

This time it was Rogers who started forward, clearly angered by the open challenge, but Green placed a hand on his chest.

"Someone needs to be standing at the front managing the meetings, giving everyone a fair chance to speak. That's all we're trying to do."

"Ok. Why does it automatically get to be you two though?"

Green was unable to contain Rogers this time. He launched himself at Thomas, stopping just short of him and glaring fiercely. "Why? Because we were the ones who had the guts to leave The Beck in the first place! Because we've survived here all this time with nothing!" Thomas shrank back a little. "Were you ever once welcomed to a meeting like this in The Beck, where you were given a choice about how things would be run? Asked for your opinion? Ever see Governor Adams approach an Agric citizen and ask how fair they felt the crop rations were?" His speech grew in volume, and he was shouting by the time he had finished.

Thomas looked almost excited by the reaction he had pro-voked. Green stepped in front of Rogers again. "Thomas. Like I said, we want to make sure everyone gets a say. And you're right, you should have a choice in who leads you. But we had assumed that, to begin with, most of you would be happy to allow those of us with a little more experience to handle things from the front, until you all had found your feet."

Tyler joined her old friend, speaking for the first time. "Look Thomas, I've known Green and Rogers for a long time. They were among the first members of the Resistance. Brave enough to be the first to leave The Beck. If Rogers hadn't returned, we'd still be there now. Show some respect."

Green smiled at Tyler gratefully, "Thomas, do you feel there needs to be an election of leaders right away? Are you suggesting that you'd stand against us?"

For a moment he looked taken aback, but he rallied quickly, looking around, clearly adding up the number of votes he could count on if we were to vote now.

"Maybe you're right—now isn't the time." He backed up and leaned against the table behind him but was unable to resist a parting shot, "But I still think stumbling about underground will be a dangerous waste of time."

"Point taken." Green took a breath as she waited to see if Thomas was finished, before continuing. "Ok then, I return to my earlier question: What are other people's concerns? What do we think need to be our priorities at the moment?"

This time there was a cacophony of chatter as everyone tried to speak at once. Rogers held up a hand for silence and eventually got it. "One at a time, please. Maybe we should raise our hands if we want to be heard."

He selected one of the Patrol recruits first, a young woman

who I had never spoken to before.

"I'm frightened that the people who attacked us on the way over might come here and try again."

Green took this on immediately, "I totally understand. We will have a round-the-clock guard on the shoreline and do our very best to prepare for that. But, to reassure you a little, in a whole year here, the only time they have ever bothered us is when we approached their territory." She motioned to another of the recruits who had raised a hand.

"What about medicines? I mean, I know we never had them in The Beck, but is it something we might get our hands on, just in case?"

"Yes. We have some first aid supplies here, but it would be worth considering taking some meds from The Beck once we manage a return trip. For now, there are several books on medicine in the library here, and certain treatments can be produced from plants which we could look into. I'm pretty sure at least some of them grow on The Crags."

I raised my hand, and stood up when Green called on me, "I know there was a lot of research into plants and their role in medicines in the Dev sector of The Beck. Perhaps when we do go back, we could focus on bringing a Dev citizen with us. They would be a real asset, wouldn't they?"

Tyler nodded sagely. "She's right. There are a lot of Meds staff who have that kind of knowledge as well." She gestured to Perry, "Not to mention their experience with the birth process and infant care."

"And doesn't that bring us to another issue?" I continued, getting to the real point I wanted to make, "How soon are we going to go back to rescue more Beck citizens?"

There were murmurs of agreement from others in the room

and I knew I had hit on a key issue. Almost everyone had left somebody behind.

"We talked about this yesterday," Rogers seemed calmer now. "We're finding it difficult to function well with twenty people here, let alone increasing the number. I think we need to get things in order before we start to bring more citizens over."

"But the people we left behind might well be suffering because of our absence! We've no idea what Gov is doing back there. If we wait too long those people might..." I faltered as I spoke the words, "they might never get here."

Rogers's face darkened. "Look Quin, believe me, I'd like nothing better than to travel back there tomorrow. And we could, of course do that. But for the time being, there is no immediate need to do so. We would be much better served spending at least a little time making sure that we are set up here with the means to provide for more people before we go back."

"I know it's hard Quin," Tyler took over, her voice level and calm as always, "but we need to consider how we would approach The Beck a second time. Make sure we could sneak in quietly, somehow, or that we had the weapons to defend ourselves if we came face to face with Shadow Patrol. Cam is clever. Resourceful. He knows how Adams works. We have to presume he managed to get those left on the beach back to Patrol safely."

Rogers's face was sympathetic as he continued. "Quin, I promise that we take your point. Yes, there would be much we could gain from stealing supplies and bringing certain expert citizens here from The Beck. Obviously, our end goal is to return to The Beck to rescue as many people as possible." He moved his gaze pointedly over the entire group. "And if we work together, and work hard, we'll be able to go back for more people much sooner. Which is what we all want. To be honest," he paused for a moment and glanced at Green, "we've been trying to contact Cam via the walkie-talkies, as agreed before we left, since we landed here. So far, we've had no luck."

My heart sank when I thought about what this news might mean. No contact with Cam meant no reassurance that he, or Jackson, were safe. I was not the only one discouraged by the news. A chorus of discontented groans echoed around the room. Rogers held up a hand to quell it.

"Look, we'll keep trying. Our whole plan for the future depends on us having some way to contact the Resistance. We're looking into reasons why the radio hasn't worked, and," he continued quickly, "there are many things that could be interfering. Cam is not stupid. Most likely he's just fine and attempting to contact us in the same way as we speak. We know how important revisiting The Beck is, to all of you, but until we can contact them, be reassured of how things stand over there, we can't risk another trip. It would be stupid." He turned back to me, his expression softening, "Look Quin, we could lose everything we have gained, understand?"

Swallowing hard, I backed away. The discussion continued, people bringing up various issues with defences, sustenance, and rotas to guard our assets. I stopped listening, finding it difficult to drag my thoughts away from Cam's chestnut eyes. I considered the failure of Rogers' communication attempts so far and wondered how long it might be before I was able to see him again. With no radio contact, we had no idea what had happened once our boat left The Beck, and despite Rogers' attempts at reassurance, my biggest fear was that he might find himself another of Carter's torture subjects. I breathed hard, trying my hardest to picture those eyes filled with warmth and love rather than pain.

I did not succeed.

Chapter Thirteen

The next few days passed quickly. Most of us tried a shift in each of the different teams, learning new skills and finding out which tasks suited us best. Just having the freedom to choose was exciting. I was not particularly good at fishing, which was dull and required a lot of patience, but I could use a knife well enough, and learned how to set various animal traps with Rogers' team. Harper reported that the field project was coming along well, and the majority of the seeds she had brought from The Beck had now been planted. That meant fewer citizens were required to work in the fields, leaving more people free to hunt, fish, or assist Mason with clearing out the underground shaft.

I arrived for breakfast early one morning and found myself alone in the canteen with Barnes, Blythe, and Perry. The little family was fascinating to me. Barnes held Perry on his lap as Blythe attempted to shovel what looked like orange mush into her daughter's mouth. The baby was squirming, twisting her head this way and that and sticking out her tiny tongue. Her face was screwed up tightly, as though the new tastes were not at all to her liking, and she frequently knocked the spoon with her fist, splattering the goo all over herself and the table. I wondered how much of it was actually getting into her mouth.

Blythe's face clearly reflected her concern, and I could see her fighting to be patient with the tiny girl's struggles. I glanced at Barnes, expecting to see her frustration mirrored in his features. In contrast, he held Perry gently, his gaze resting on the small child in his arms. He didn't seem able to tear it away. I was shocked by the sudden gentleness of this man, a man who had mocked us during training sessions, bawled us out many times, and had never shown an ounce of sensitivity. And here he was, smiling down at Perry with such warmth in his eyes. This baby was not his own. Yet Barnes was captivated.

I wondered how much of this stemmed from his love for Blythe. Since he had brought her from The Beck, rescuing her at a time when she was utterly desperate, he had changed. But she had changed too. Now that she had her child back, she had embraced the role of mother, despite the worries it brought with it. Barnes, in turn, seemed to have signed up for fatherhood as a simple extension of his role as Blythe's partner. I wondered if this was the way things were supposed to be.

I caught Blythe's eye as I moved my gaze and she smiled and beckoned me over. I wandered over, embarrassed at being caught staring.

"Morning," she said, "How's it going, Quin?"

I shifted slightly as Barnes became aware of my presence. He immediately lost his look of adoration and frowned slightly. This was a more familiar Barnes.

"Ok thanks."

"You look... well, a little sad." Blythe's tone was concerned and I was amazed at how thoughtful she was in the light of her own worries.

Barnes sniggered under his breath, "Missing a certain Patrol

Super, are we?"

She slapped his arm lightly, "Don't tease. You know what it's like to be separated from someone."

"I suppose." Shamefaced, he shifted Perry so she was more able to sit upright, then looked at me directly. "Sorry, Quin."

I smiled at his apology and turned my attention back to Blythe, "How are things this morning?"

Her face clouded over. "Ok, I suppose. She's managing to take the mashed carrot and potato a little better than the oatcakes, but..."

"What?"

Barnes took over, his voice gruff. "We're down to the last of the milk Tyler brought."

"Almost. We're looking at watering down the formula we have left, making it last longer. After that I suppose we'll have to feed her entirely on solids, but I'm worried she won't cope with that yet." Blythe sighed. "She's so young. I don't think she's gaining as much weight as she should be. And she's thrown the food back up a few times. I'm worried that we've started her on solids too early. But if she can't keep enough of it down, she'll..."

Blythe's voice cracked a little and she couldn't finish her sentence. Barnes shifted closer to her and squeezed her hand. Perry squealed a little at finding herself squashed between them.

"We'll work it out." Barnes' tone was reassuring. Again, I found myself shocked at the change in him, at least when he was dealing with Blythe.

She turned, directing her words at Barnes now. "What if we came all this way... managed to escape, saved Perry from... and then she..."

Barnes handed Perry to me and wrapped both his arms around Blythe. Now that she was thinking about the dangers facing her child, I recognised the fog which descended over her. She looked like she had when I first met her. Barnes was whispering urgently in her ear. I tightened my hold on the child in my arms, embarrassed at the unfamiliar intimacy.

Perry's eyes gazed up at me inquisitively, as though her little brain was trying to work out who the new person holding her was. Blinking a couple of times, she yawned widely and lost interest in me, seeming instead content to lie in my arms and drift off to sleep. I found that I couldn't take my eyes off her. It was easy to see how Barnes had fallen in love with this child, but I worried at how far he might go to keep the pair safe.

Having momentarily accepted his comfort, Blythe now turned her attention back to her daughter. The brief hurt on Barnes' face as she pushed him away was quickly masked, but not before I noticed. Realising I had observed his pain, he scowled. A second later he clambered to his feet and headed out of the dining hall. I turned back to Blythe.

"I'm so sorry. What can we do?" I racked my brain for a solution but came up with nothing. "Did the books help?"

Blythe nodded pulling herself together visibly. "A little. I'm going to try her with a few different vegetables, mashed up, see if the varied flavours help. Otherwise, I'm at a loss. Returning to The Beck for supplies isn't an option at the moment, obviously."

"But what will…?" I allowed the thought to trail off, afraid of the answer, and of Blythe's reaction to it. She confirmed my fears with her response.

"If we don't get her eating more solids before the infant milk runs out, she'll continue to lose weight and, eventually, she'll... starve."

I blinked, disturbed to hear the truth. In The Beck we had known hunger, starvation almost, but we were old enough to survive at least a short period of time with little or no sustenance. Basic common sense told me that a baby with such a small body had minimal stores of fat to live off when food was scarce.

"Then there are those here who wish she would just hurry up and die," Blythe stared hard at the other side of the dining hall, where Thomas and the other recruits had just entered. "They resent sharing their food, and they hate the fact that I haven't been able to work with Perry around. In fact, they'd rather we weren't here at all."

"That's not true!"

She smiled tiredly. "Yes Quin, it is."

A thought occurred to me. "Well we can fix part of that today at least." I stood up and grasped her by the hand firmly, pulling her with me.

Startled, she pulled away. "Quin, I'm too tired for another argument. He'll never agree that we're worth providing for."

"That's not what I mean." I grinned, "Trust me?"

She followed me out of the dining hall and back to the dorms, where I confided my plan. Within fifteen minutes we were ready to go, but as we walked out into the courtyard, Blythe seemed hesitant, shifting from one foot to the other and glancing around anxiously.

"What's wrong?"

"I haven't seen Barnes since he left the canteen," she bit her lip, "I wanted to say goodbye, tell him where I'll be today."

"Can't you give someone a message to pass on?"

"I suppose so," she mumbled, still staring at the door to the main building. "Ready then?"

"Hold on," I cautioned her, "just a minute."

We waited outside the entrance to the dorm. Moments later, the door to the main building burst open and the rest of the group spilled out. We were early for our shift, having left the hall before most of the others, and I wanted to make sure that they saw us. Nodding to Blythe, we started walking. The path took us directly past the other citizens.

The first person we passed was Rogers. He looked at Blythe, the sheet wrapped firmly around her body securing Perry to the front of her body, and smiled widely.

"Great idea."

"It was Quin's." I smiled at his approval as she continued, "Can you tell Barnes I'm going to the fields with Tyler and Quin, and I'll be back later?"

He shook his head, "Not seen him. He must be on fishing duty today. I'll pass it on to Nelson though, if you like?"

Blythe shyly smiled her thanks as we continued on our way. Behind Rogers came Walker, Harper, and Price. They were chatting and laughing as they passed by, and although Harper smiled at me, she did not stop to speak. The closeness she shared with her new friends was obvious, and the envious ache I felt when I saw them together was becoming all-too familiar. She simply didn't need me. Next came Mason, who looked puzzled at Blythe's unfamiliar shape. He stopped and looked more closely, and I was touched when he leaned across and tickled Perry's cheek with his finger before continuing on his way.

Tyler passed us next, taking a moment to stop and touch the sleeping child gently, before calling over her shoulder in the least tender voice possible.

"Hey Thomas! Look at how our workforce has increased today."

Thomas, who had been deep in whispered conversation with some of the other recruits, hurried over to see what she meant. At the sight of Perry trussed up against Blythe's chest, he sneered.

"How long do you think that's going to last? You're planning on, what… digging…? With her strapped to you that way?"

I stepped in front of her, "No. She's going to be finishing the planting with Harper. And she has the means to lay Perry down safely on the ground when and if necessary."

Thomas smirked. "Think she's going to be a great asset to our workforce, do you?"

"She'll make it a little stronger than it was yesterday," Tyler countered, "and that's better than nothing. On your way Thomas, or you'll be late for your own shift."

He passed us, his face thunderous. The rest of the recruits surrounded him, resuming their noisy conversation as they returned to the dorms.

Blythe glanced at me, frowning slightly. "Are you sure I'm going to be able to manage this? I mean, all day?"

I shrugged, "We'll see. Like Tyler said, any work you manage to complete is more than you would have done sitting down here on your own with Perry. We just need to find the easiest job for you to manage while still taking care of her. The important thing was to make sure that people saw you. So they know you aren't slacking off and draining resources. We achieved that nicely, I'd say."

I was surprised to feel her hand creeping into my own. "Thank you." Her voice was quiet, almost a whisper. "It's good to have people on my side."

As I smiled my acceptance of her thanks, a voice called from behind us.

"Quin!"

We all turned. It was Green, waving me back to the centre.

"You go ahead with Tyler," I squeezed her hand as I let it go. "She'll keep an eye on you. See you later."

Tyler dropped back a little so she could walk side by side with her old friend while I headed back to Green.

"Could you come with me, Quin?"

I followed her into the building where she retraced her steps to the library at the end of the hall. Once inside, she motioned to several books which were laid out on the table.

"I have a project I thought you might work on for me, kind of, under the radar."

"What is it?"

"Remember the books on herbal medicine I mentioned?" She reached over and opened the first book on the pile. "These are the ones I meant."

I scanned the page she had placed in front of me. It named a plant, had a small picture alongside, and then a description of its properties. I turned the pages, to find each one an echo of the last, with a different plant on each page.

"Some of these plants grow here on The Crags. If we can identify and collect them, these other books," she scrambled through the pile on the desk in front of her, "give various recipes for herbal treatments which might just help us with medicines in the interim, until we have access to the drugs they have in The Beck."

"And you want my help?"

"I thought of you, yes."

I thought fondly of my old friend, "Wouldn't Harper be a

better option?"

She frowned, "She would, but I don't really want to divert her attention from her work with the crops. She's done well with it so far, and I don't want to slow the progress she's making. I agree with Thomas on one point," she rolled her eyes, "and that is the importance of ensuring we have enough food to keep us all going. I'd hate to divert Harper from that role. It would look like I had other priorities. No, it's better if you do it. You know enough about plants from your time in Agric. I hope I can trust you to be discreet about this, keep it to yourself, at least until we see where it leads."

"Thomas?" I rolled my eyes.

"Exactly."

Over the past few days, Thomas had made his disapproval clear on almost every issue. I could see how Green wanted to keep the medicine-seeking plan to ourselves, until it yielded something of value.

"Look Quin, with things the way they are, it might be a while 'til we get back to The Beck. We've managed here so far, but I think we've been lucky not to have any serious illnesses or injuries. It's only a matter of time."

I continued to turn the pages as she talked, trying to distract myself from her lengthy estimate of our return date to The Beck by running my finger over each new picture.

"The more people we bring here, the higher the chance of people getting sick, and passing the illness on. If we can collect ingredients which have healing properties, perhaps put together a few simple mixtures which ease pain, surely we'll be better off?"

"I agree."

She heaved a sigh of relief. "I was hoping you'd say that.

Think you could do a little bit of reading today? Try to figure out which plant types you need, and then tomorrow go and search for some of them? I'd do it myself, but I figure I need to stay more visible while people are just getting settled."

"Sure." Although I didn't relish spending the entire day indoors, I could see how much the project meant to her, and knew that its impact on our settlement could be as important as the discovery of a storage space packed full of bullets underneath us. She handed me a notepad and pencil, and I settled back in the chair to begin my research, hoping the task would prove more fruitful than it felt.

Chapter Fourteen

When I emerged from the library what seemed like hours later, I was starving and headed straight for the canteen. As I reached it, I could hear hushed voices in conversation. Entering cautiously, I spotted Nelson and Rogers at the far end. From their body language, I knew that something was wrong. I let the door bang closed behind me, alerting them to my presence. Both men jumped guiltily, darting almost frightened glances at the entrance.

"Quin!" Rogers' voice was filled with relief, "I thought you were—"

"Have you seen Barnes anywhere?" Nelson's tone remained urgent.

"Not since breakfast."

He scowled, "There was some confusion over the work schedule this morning. Rogers thought he was supposed to be on duty with me. I thought he was hunting."

"And...?"

"And he wasn't with either of us," Rogers finished abruptly.

The news sank in and I realised its significance. "So, no one knows where he is?"

Nelson shook his head. "And the rest of the teams will be back any minute. Thomas was insufferable all morning, asking questions about Perry, Blythe, the work rota, demanding to know what we were going to do about various situations. He wanted to know where Barnes was, thought he should have been with us this morning. I told him he was wrong, that Barnes was with the hunting team."

"But he wasn't." My heart sank.

"And when he gets here and realises Barnes is missing, there'll be questions."

"Ones we can't answer."

"Maybe he went with Blythe to the fields. To check she was ok up there?" I knew that this was the only plausible option, aside from the one we feared.

Rogers raised his eyebrows, "Hope so. They're due back any minute, so I guess we'll see."

Nelson frowned, "I can't wait to hear what Thomas says when he realises that we've been a man down all morning unnecessarily."

"If he was up in the crop fields he must have been working though?" I protested weakly, "He wouldn't have gone up there and done nothing."

Rogers laughed without any mirth. "No. But Thomas will accuse him of going with Blythe to make things easier for her—to do the job she went up there to do, so in fact, your argument about our work force being stronger today because of Blythe will fall down completely."

Nelson was quick to echo Rogers' depressing thoughts, "And Thomas won't let that pass without comment."

The door to the canteen thudded open again and we all jumped. A mixture of the fishing and hunting teams spilled into the room, chattering and laughing together. It was so different from life in The Beck. In other circumstances, I would have sat down to enjoy the pleasant atmosphere, but I feared Thomas' reaction if Barnes returned with Blythe, or not at all. He was one of the last to enter, and as usual wore a dark expression. I watched as his eyes roamed the room, assessing who was present.

The door opened again and Harper entered, followed as usual by her own small team. Blythe was nowhere to be seen, and I hurried across to find out what I could. She turned as I approached, her expression friendly, but distant.

"Harper, is Blythe with you?"

"She'll be here in a moment." She waved a vague hand at the door to the canteen. "She's just changing Perry."

She started after the rest of her group, but I put out an arm to stop her, dropping my voice lower. "Look, was Barnes with you this morning at all?"

She looked momentarily surprised, and then a flicker of curiosity crossed her face. "No. Why would he be?"

I frowned. "Keep it to yourself, but if he's not with your team, he's missing."

"Missing?"

I nodded my head.

Her eyes went wider as she considered the information, and she glanced around the room. "Do people know?"

"Not yet."

"Well I hope they find him soon." She looked like she might say more, but Walker called her over and she hurried to join him, looking concerned.

I hurried back to Rogers with the bad news, knowing I could trust Harper to keep it to herself. My expression must have conveyed my fear, because his face fell before I spoke.

"Sorry. Barnes isn't with the field team."

He closed his eyes. "Then I hope he somehow ended up with Mason at the caves. Or else—"

I shuddered. "Do we need to start searching?"

"Not yet. Let's give it a few more minutes. If he's not with Mason, we'll start to panic."

I left Rogers feeling very uneasy, and waited next to Green to collect my food. Her face reflected my own concern, and I knew Rogers had filled her in. As we reached the counter where Baker was doling out today's rations, her walkie-talkie crackled into life.

"Green? Rogers?"

She put her plate down and unhooked the device from her belt. "Yes?"

"It's Shaw. On the boat… got a problem."

Rogers chipped in, "What is it?"

"Barnes was just here. He…" his voice cut out for a second, "gone."

Green had turned pale. "Can you repeat please, Shaw?"

"Barnes took one of the canoes. He left. I tried to stop him, but…"

"Don't say any more over the air. We're on our way." Rogers cut off communication abruptly and headed across the room to us.

Before he reached us, Green pointed to the bread and meat Baker was serving. "Can you wrap some of that up for us?"

Baker frowned, "This is about that baby isn't it?"

"Probably. But whatever it is, we need to deal with it. Now."

Baker began wrapping some of the food up in a cloth. At Rogers' approach she thrust the parcel of food in Green's direction, shooting a filthy look at them both.

"What did I say? I said it would cause problems, didn't I?"

She stomped off to the far side of the kitchen so no one had the chance to answer.

The walkie-talkie call had not been particularly loud, and so far people seemed far too focused on eating to worry about the situation in the corner, but it wouldn't be long before they discovered what had happened. Mason entered, an uncharacteristically large smile emblazoned on his face. He hurried over to our little group, a sheaf of papers clasped in his hand.

"Hey, you'll never guess—" He stopped abruptly as the looks on our faces registered with him. "What's wrong?"

Before we could respond, a worried-looking Blythe arrived, Perry balanced awkwardly on one hip. She hurried over to our group immediately, concern flooding her face.

"Has anyone seen Barnes?"

I shook my head, unsure of what she should be told, but Green spoke up immediately, "When's the last time you saw him, Blythe?"

"Breakfast. Why?"

"He's gone."

Blythe's face fell, "This is what I was afraid of."

Mason's gaze darted from Blythe's to my own, "Do we think he's trying to...?"

"We all know exactly what he's trying to do," Baker had returned from the other side of the kitchen, and although the words were muttered under her breath, they were clearly audible to those of us close to the hatch.

"What's that supposed to mean?"

"Well he's threatened to take drastic action before, and now it seems he's followed through. All because of... that!" she motioned to Perry, disgusted.

A look of panic crossed Blythe's face as she struggled with Barnes' actions, but she rallied in defence of her daughter, "Her name is Perry."

Baker ignored her and turned to Green. "He threatened to go to The Ridge a few days ago. That's where he's gone."

Blythe hesitated a little before speaking. "I told him not to, but... well we're so low on milk now, and he's been worried about Perry."

Baker turned to the others. "He's gone to The Ridge. And that's a huge problem. If we start to steal their supplies, attempt to sneak past their security, who knows what'll happen? You know damn well they've only left us alone so far because we don't interfere with them."

"Let's keep calm, Baker. We don't know if that's what happened yet."

"We don't?" She almost spat her reply. "I think we do. We all know he's trying to play the hero, but he's acting without thinking. Without consulting the rest of us. And if he does this, he won't be saving a child, he'll be risking the lives of every single person here."

She turned and stalked away, shoulders hunched. I wanted to hate her for her harsh words, but something about them rang true. While I was just as desperate to work out a way to save Perry, I knew Barnes wasn't the most rational of people. By going off across the water, he was putting the entire camp in danger. Mason and I exchanged concerned glances and turned to the more experienced Crags residents.

Rogers reacted first, "We need to get down to the shore." His voice was low and serious. "Preferably without being noticed."

Green laid a hand on his arm. "I'll go. You stay here, attempt to keep Thomas in the dark. Nelson and Mason can help. If necessary, stop him from leaving this room. I have my walkie-talkie. I'll take Quin with me."

Rogers nodded tersely. We left him talking in low, curt tones to Mason. Making our way outside, we headed quickly for the cliffs, passing no one.

A pale shaft of sunlight was filtering down through the clouds as we reached the base of the path and rounded the corner to the little stretch of rocky shore. The scene looked peaceful, undisturbed, the comforting shape of the Clearance boat floated a safe distance out to sea.

"At least he didn't take that," Green murmured as we slowed to a halt.

A single canoe was approaching the shore. We hurried quickly to it and helped Shaw out. He was breathing hard.

"Barnes... he's gone..." he managed as he reached us. "Tried to stop him but he was... it was too late."

Green took hold of the panicked man's shoulders. "Slow down and tell us what happened."

I pulled the small craft a safe distance from the waterline as Shaw caught his breath. He leaned against one of the rocks, exhausted. The other canoe was nowhere in sight. Eventually, he managed to speak again.

"Look, I've been on watch with Allen since dawn."

Green interrupted, worried, "Where is he?"

"Still on the boat. Figured we shouldn't leave it unattended."

"Good man. Go on then."

"We were attempting to cast some of the new rods over the side of the boat. Nelson had told us to see what we could catch while on guard. Save us wasting time and manpower. Was quite tricky at first, but in the end, we got the hang of it. For a while nothing happened, but then Allen's line got a bite... we were both hauling it in, and... well I guess we were excited about the catch. We weren't watching like we should have been. Next thing we knew, one of the canoes was floating past. I could see it was Barnes, even though he was a fair distance away."

"Did you speak to him?" Green inquired.

"I tried to. Shouted at him several times. He turned back—I was close enough still to see his expression. He looked so determined." He shook his head. "He yelled back. Said not to try and stop him."

"Did you?"

Shaw's face flushed. "How could I? He was too far away to reach without me diving into the water. And... well, he had a gun."

Green made a face. "Did he say anything else?"

Shaw shook his head. "Sorry, Green. Should've tried harder to... do something." He looked totally crestfallen, "I failed."

I couldn't stop myself from interrupting. "Look Shaw, there was no way of stopping Barnes. Not when he was in that kind of a mood at least. Even Rogers would have had a job on his hands, and he knows Barnes well."

"But where was he going?" Shaw looked stricken. "To The Ridge?"

"Where else?" Green's expression only grew more severe. "And we've no idea what he'll find when he gets there."

"We need to work out what to do next then." I laid a hand on Green's arm. "At least now we know where he is."

Green snapped into action. "Shaw, row back to the boat and finish your shift. The replacement guard will be here soon. We'll deal with this."

Shaw nodded, looking a little pale. I helped him return the canoe to the water and pushed him off. The tense expression as he rowed away reflected the fear in my own eyes. As I turned back to Green, I tried to stay focused.

"Should someone go after him? Try to stop him before he reaches The Ridge?"

"No point. We'll never catch him unless we use the large boat, and it would be stupid to risk that to save a single citizen." Green sighed. "I can't believe he did this."

"What does it mean for us?" I wasn't sure I wanted to know the answer.

"Well it'll certainly stir up trouble. Depends what he does when he gets there. They'll almost certainly catch him. My guess is they'll question him, see what they can find out about us."

"You think they'll come here?"

"Maybe." She raised an eyebrow, "We have to consider it."

"Maybe he'll make it there and back without being caught?" I knew I was being naïve.

"I doubt it. Even if he does, they'll surely discover things are missing. That's when they'll come asking questions. I guess we'll have to wait and see. But in the meantime, we need to consider the group as a whole."

"What do you mean?"

"I'm extremely concerned about Thomas. At the moment he doesn't have a lot of support—most of those who are on his side are the Patrol recruits and two of them are currently down here, so he doesn't have enough people to create any real impact, but... when he finds out about this, it will only add fuel to his argument, and..." she trailed off, looking worried.

"Do you really think he'd try to take over?" I was appalled.

Green's reply was instant. "He might. And if it comes to it, and he has all the Patrol recruits on his side, he has the largest single group of all." She rubbed the back of her neck tiredly. "Look, we need to get back, Quin." She rubbed a tired hand across her forehead as she continued, "Work out what on earth to do about Barnes."

"Stupid fool."

Green managed a humourless laugh. "I'd call him worse than that. Still, no point standing around here any longer. Let's get going."

She took off back up the path, easily as fast as Tyler. As I turned to follow, I glanced back at the water, a feeling of dread creeping over me as I watched Shaw's figure rowing into the distance.

Chapter Fifteen

As we reached the camp, we could already hear angry voices ringing out across the central courtyard. Our hopes of keeping Barnes' absence from the rest of the group quickly faded. Blythe was standing outside the doors to the dorm, Perry clutched to her chest. Thomas was barring her entry, a nasty expression on his face. Several other citizens were standing in the middle of the space, Rogers at their head.

"Thomas, calm down."

Thomas slammed a hand against the wooden door frame and I saw Blythe wince. "Where is he?"

"I told you, he's—"

"Shut up, Rogers. I'm asking *her*." He leaned closer, spitting the word into Blythe's face.

She seemed to draw herself up a little taller, "And I told you, I don't know any more than you do. He was here this morning. As far as I know, he went off to work like the rest of us."

"Except he didn't. He isn't here. He hasn't returned from any of the shifts."

Rogers tried again, stepping a little closer this time, "He's on guard duty. On the boat."

"Liar." Thomas didn't look at Rogers, but there was venom in his voice. "I looked at the rota. Shaw and Allen are down there. Not due back for an hour yet."

Green hurried forward, placing an arm between Thomas and Blythe. "Thomas. Get out of her way."

"Not until I get some answers. Something's going on. No one knows where Barnes is. I've asked everyone, and he hasn't been seen since breakfast." He sneered, "Instead of having an extra citizen working today, we've had one less. And worse still, I don't think he's just slacking off." He paused for dramatic effect, "I think he's putting us all in danger."

The group had all exited the canteen now, and the crowd in the courtyard was larger, all eyes focused on the spectacle by the dorm room door. Thomas warmed to his audience, seizing the chance to gather support.

"You all know I think bringing a baby over here, when we're just starting out, was a stupid decision. It wastes resources, reduces the number of people working, puts us all at risk. She'd have been better left over in The Beck. Safer. They wouldn't have hurt her. If our purpose is to set The Crags up so that it's habitable for a large number of people, then we should have done it slowly, sensibly, bringing over the strongest people first."

Rogers could barely contain his anger. "If we agree with your way of thinking, we'd be almost as bad as The Beck themselves." Thomas' face darkened, but Rogers went on. "You're suggesting that we make selections. Choose only the fittest people to come over here. Make the society here from good, healthy stock. Leave behind the weak and feeble."

"I only meant to begin with—" Thomas spluttered.

Green took up her partner's argument. "We need to construct a fair and equal society. And that means accepting people, no matter how weak or strong they are. Yes, we need strong, able people to help us build, but those you suggest are weak can be made strong, if given the chance. We can care for them, provide them with good food, sufficient rest and comfort, and build them up to be the kind of citizens that we are."

"But at what cost? What's the point of attempting to set up a new society which is better than the Beck if we destroy it within the first few weeks?" Thomas drew himself up to his full height as he delivered his next line with triumph, "I come back to my original question. Where's Barnes? Why are you lying to us?"

There were murmurs from the rest of the crowd, taking up the question, curiosity on all their faces. A few of the Patrol recruits moved towards Thomas, gathering behind him in support. I braced myself for the truth to come out.

"We don't mean to lie to anyone." Rogers glanced at Green briefly before he spoke, "We were just trying to work out the situation for ourselves before causing general panic."

"So not quite lying. Just keeping information from us." Thomas' words were scathing.

Rogers gave Green a pointed look. She took over, delivering the words like bullets. "Barnes is gone."

There was a pause while the group took the news in. Thomas finally stepped away from Blythe and focused his attention on Green, his supporters following.

"Gone?" His eyes flashed dangerously as he spoke, "Gone where?"

Green continued. "He took a canoe. We think he's gone to The Ridge."

"A canoe!" Thomas' tone was disgusted. "And his disappearance is linked to the baby, right?"

"Yes. He's probably trying to find food for her."

"She's hungry." The voice was quiet, but firm. The entire group turned back to Blythe. She continued, her voice shaking only slightly. "He only wants to make sure she is fed. He loves her."

"Well now we're a man down. Not to mention the loss of one of our boats." Thomas almost exploded, and I inwardly cursed Barnes for leaving us in this position. "All for a helpless child who will probably die of starvation soon, when The Beck would have fed her well. Still call yourself a loving mother?"

Blythe attempted to hide her look of horror, but the damage was done. Thomas drove his point home cruelly. "Two lives lost. And for what?"

"Look," the voice came from the rear of the group, and I was surprised to see Baker move in Thomas' direction, wiping her hands on a cloth as she came. "Bringing a baby was perhaps not the best move. The child is currently a burden and her emotional ties to her mother and others have led to these unfortunate circumstances."

I could see Thomas smirking, and for a moment I was terrified, considering what would happen if the balance of power tipped and people began to side with him. It wouldn't take many to give him a majority, and if he had a majority, I didn't know what he would do. But now Baker turned to him, pointing a finger as she continued.

"But we have to consider the future. If we're to build a society here, we have to include the concept of birthing. Without children, our new society will fall apart pretty quickly. And while, at the moment, things are difficult, we cannot expect to create an effective society where there is no room for our offspring."

Thomas opened his mouth to speak, but Baker had reached him now and put a hand on his chest to silence him. He looked immediately furious, grabbing her arm and twisting it behind her back. Several of the group leapt to her defence, but as they did, she ducked to ground level, shifted to the side, jabbed an elbow into Thomas' stomach, and suddenly he lay sprawled on his back in the dust.

I glanced across at Rogers and Green, noticing that they hadn't moved. Clearly, they were aware of Baker's capacity to take care of herself, and had known that she needed no assistance in dealing with Thomas. Most people around them looked shocked, and Thomas' own face contained a mixture of terror and fury I had not witnessed before. Baker, however, continued with her sentence as if nothing had happened.

"Today, we have a problem. The biggest we have faced so far. And there are, at the moment, only twenty of us to try and solve it. If we dilute that number further, by fighting amongst ourselves, we stand no chance of averting disaster. Look Thomas, you need to swallow whatever personal vendetta you have and work with us. Or there's no place for you here. Got it?"

She stepped back and straightened up, relinquishing her grip on the recruit. For a moment, he lay motionless, staring up at Baker like she had gone mad. Then he scrambled to his feet, the recruits behind him scattering as he slammed into the dorm, a look of hatred scrawled across his features.

The silence that followed stretched out for several minutes. Eventually Rogers began again, a serious expression on his face.

"Look. We don't want to use force against any of you. We regard everyone here as part of the same team, but at the moment we can't permit people to be going off on their own, forming separate factions, when essentially that means rebelling against the good of the group as a whole."

Green continued. "We've told you we want to live in a democracy, but we're human beings. We will have disagreements, and we want to solve them peacefully. But at the moment, the issue with Barnes has to be dealt with. We have to face the fact that his leaving might cause us all sorts of problems."

I watched as the group of Patrol recruits melted back into the general group at large, clearly uneasy without their leader. It looked like Baker's actions, no matter that they were more violent than Green and Rogers might have wanted, had worked, reuniting the majority of the group with a common goal. How Thomas acted later was a different matter.

Green went on. "Barnes will reach The Ridge soon, it's not that far. We've no idea what will happen after that."

"Like we said, we're presuming that he has gone to get supplies for Perry," Rogers went on, "but he isn't entirely stupid. Tyler, you know him best. What do you think he'll do?"

Tyler had until now been standing at the side of the group, not participating at all in the heated debate. Now, she paused for a moment before starting to speak, calm and measured as always.

"He'll try to sneak onto the island without them noticing. Attempt to steal the resources for Perry without detection, return to the canoe, and row back to The Ridge."

Baker snorted, "He won't succeed."

Tyler's eyes flashed. "I didn't say he would. I just said that would be his plan. He won't want to cause a confrontation—he knows he doesn't stand a chance. The likelihood is that they're heavily armed. His Patrol training will help him work this out." She paused for a moment, her expression clouding as she took in the consequences of her friend's actions. She pulled herself together before continuing, her voice just a little shaky, "He'll want to make the least impact possible."

"I'm not sure there's any way of approaching The Ridge without being caught." This was from Rogers. "You saw how effectively they defended themselves the other day. I'd love to think Barnes will succeed, but I think it's extremely unlikely. They're so well guarded."

I was concerned for Barnes despite my feelings of frustration. Clearly his intentions here had been good. I remembered watching his affectionate treatment of Blythe's child the previous day and knew I had to voice my thoughts. "What will they do if they catch him?"

"I should think they'll shoot him on sight," Baker didn't mince her words. "And I'd say that he deserved it and be done with it, except for the trouble it might cause for The Crags."

I scowled at her openly, hating her unforgiving attitude. "Well, if they do kill him, surely he's been dealt with. Why would that cause problems for us?"

"Because, you silly girl, they're unlikely to leave it at that. They'll know where he's come from and they might well follow up. They're aware that there weren't any of us living here until recently. The attack which cost Lee his life told them we were in a small craft. They're not stupid. We've spent the entire last year keeping our heads down. They've never seen us as any kind of threat. So up until now, they've left us alone." She massaged her fists which had been clenched tightly by her sides. "Now one of us has actively threatened them, they might decide they need to deal with us."

139

Rogers stepped in again. "Look, they saw us go by in the boat the other day. They have to know that something has changed over here from that alone. They fired at us as we went past, but we can't be certain that they don't just defend themselves when they are under attack. So they'll deal with Barnes because he's turned up on their turf, but why should we assume that means they'll come here?"

She turned away, "It's just my opinion. They might not. But it's a possibility we have to consider."

"Ok, I take your point."

I glanced at Blythe, whose face had drained of all colour, and tried again, "What about Barnes though? Is there really no way we can help him? He's one of us."

"You're being very understanding, Quin. Are you forgetting that he stole one of our canoes? Our fish stocks will be affected without it. And even if he's lucky enough to make it onto the island, he's going to *steal* from The Ridge people too!" Baker was still furious, and I took a precautionary step back as she turned back to Rogers. "How do you think that will go down if he succeeds? When they discover they have supplies missing? You don't think they'll let that go, do you Rogers? We *have* to consider they might retaliate. And how will we defend ourselves?"

Rogers held up both hands in surrender. "Obviously, it would be difficult. But that's a worst-case scenario. Look, let's leave the recriminations for now and consider what we need to do." I admired Rogers' calm, and hoped it would diffuse the situation with Baker, who seemed to me to be causing just as much conflict as Thomas.

Green was similarly cool-headed, "I think we need to carry on as we were, keep things as normal as possible. Wait to see what their response is. Sending a boat-load of people after Barnes will only make the situation worse."

I cleared my throat and spoke up, as the seed of an idea came to me. "What if, that is if they do come, we give them the impression there are more of us here than there actually are."

Baker frowned in my direction, but I ignored her and forged on. "Look, if we keep a lookout, see them coming, and make sure we have as many bodies as possible on the shore when they arrive..."

Rogers looked doubtful, but was listening. "Go on."

"If we have everyone visible. Armed. They might be persuaded that we're more of a threat. If we can talk a good talk, maybe..." I trailed off, doubting myself.

"She's right." I was grateful when Mason stepped from the back of the group and joined me. "In fact, if we can keep them from getting to the shore altogether, they'll never know how many of us there are."

"You mean..." Green was thinking aloud, "Position some of us on the boat to talk to them?"

Rogers began to smile. "We don't let them past the boat. Not to start with. Make sure the biggest and strongest of us are the first to meet them."

"Convince them to be wary of us." Mason added. "Take us seriously."

"Those who are less impressive-looking can stay on the shore. Holding guns." This was from Walker, who had yet to speak. "From a distance they'll look formidable enough."

Harper chimed in. "He's right. They won't be able to tell from a distance. As long as we stand tall." I found myself feeling intensely grateful for her support. "We could bulk ourselves up, wear additional clothing. You have plenty here at the base, right?"

Rogers nodded. "Yes. That's a good idea. So you're saying we plan for the possibility of their arrival. Have set positions we go to on a given signal?" Rogers seemed to be warming to the idea.

"Yes." Nelson spoke for the first time. "I'd be happy to draw up a plan of the positions, make sure everyone can be seen clearly. I'll check everyone knows their places and make sure we have a clear signal to get to them as soon as any approach is spotted."

Rogers straightened up. "Alright. So the rest of you continue with your shifts as normal, but Nelson and I will work out an emergency plan. That way, if they do turn up, we stand a chance of defending ourselves."

He waved a hand to dismiss the crowd and the majority of them wandered away, setting off for their usual shifts, though the expressions on their faces reflected their shared concern at the thought of a possible attack. Rogers, Green, and Nelson huddled closer to continue the discussion. Baker remained behind, but kept herself apart from the others, her face still thunderous.

Once most people had left, Mason stepped closer to Rogers. He looked happier than the rest of us, and I remembered noticing a similar expression on his face earlier. I had forgotten in all the chaos of Barnes' departure. He waited a moment before beginning to speak, checking most people were out of earshot.

"Look, I wanted to tell you earlier, but with all the confusion about Barnes, well... it didn't seem like the time," he paused for a moment, his eyes gleaming. "But now I feel like it might be... well you might want to hear this. We found something. This morning. Clearing the tunnels behind the cave."

"What?"

"We managed to break past the first rock-fall completely and I squeezed through to see what was behind it. It's some kind of store room. Well a store-cave, anyway." He paused again, breathless with his discovery. "There were several boxes. Filled with bullets. Like the one I first showed you."

Green's face brightened, "How many?"

He beamed, "Three boxes so far. Two full, one half full. There's more of a blockage at the other side of the cave so I can't say for certain how many there'll be in total. In terms of defence, we have additional bullets, which I think will fit at least some of our guns." His grin broadened, "But there's more."

"Go on!" Mason's slow responses were clearly frustrating Nelson.

"Manuals." His arms stretched wide, "Shelves full of them. And records. Of how the shaft I found is only one of several. And they lead to a mine."

Rogers face brightened, "What kind of mine?"

"According to the documents I found," he gestured behind him to the dining hall, where he had presumably left the papers, "a lead mine."

"And the bullets you found... they're made from lead?"

"They are. But the documents explain how this base was originally stocked with ammunition. The mine provided the lead, which was taken to a smelting works to be made into bullets."

Green looked puzzled, "But we're been all over this island. There's no smelting works."

For the first time, Mason looked crestfallen. "That's the only issue. But maybe we just haven't found it yet."

"So you mean…" Rogers was almost breathless as he worked it out. "We have the materials to create bullets, we just have to work out how?"

The murmurs around me were more positive now. Rogers slapped Mason on the back.

"Well done, Mason. I'm glad all that digging led to something positive. Keep it up. See what else you can find. And can you bring down the boxes of bullets next time you go up there? I'd rather store them somewhere safe where we can get them if we need them."

"Will do." Mason rubbed a calloused hand across his chin before continuing. "But Rogers, surely now we have the bullets, it puts us in a stronger position with The Ridge."

"What do you mean?"

"Quin's idea depends on us acting like we're a stronger force than we are. It might well work. But if it doesn't, if they come closer to shore, then we'll be more able to defend ourselves with the extra ammunition. Plus," Mason paused, as if what he was suggesting was obvious, "if they come here looking to talk, now we have something to trade."

Rogers stared at him. "You think we should give bullets to the people who fired arrows at us?"

Mason flushed a little, but pressed on. "Well it depends on their approach. If they believe we're a force to be reckoned with, they might be interested in communicating with us." He drew himself up to his full height. "We have to consider every possibility. And what else do we have to offer?"

Rogers frowned. "I'll bear it in mind. Thanks again for your hard work Mason." He turned to Nelson, "Shall we head indoors and work out some kind of emergency plan?"

Nelson ran a hand through his reddish hair, seeming to

agree. He was far worse than Rogers at hiding his feelings, and looked pretty anxious to get started. The threat of invasion was frightening.

Rogers placed a hand on his friend's shoulder. "Look, Quin's idea is a good one. It might just be enough to convince The Ridge that we're strong enough to take them on. Try not to worry." He turned to Baker now. "But we'll need everyone we have to convince them. Are you with us?"

She nodded begrudgingly, casting a sideways look at me which I couldn't interpret.

"And Thomas?" Green turned to the rest of the recruits for assistance. "Someone needs to talk to him. We need him on our side and not working against us. We could at least do with another body to stand on the beach and look fierce."

"I'll ask Cass." I volunteered, hoping that being given a task would help my friend feel more useful. "She was part of his recruit group, knows him quite well. Hopefully he'll see this is our best chance."

As I left to find Cass before heading to my shift, I wondered what type of people lived on The Ridge. So far our experience of them had been a frightening one, but I wondered whether their fierce attack was merely an attempt to defend their community from outsiders they perceived as enemies. Could it be that they were just another group of people trying to cope in a difficult world? I considered how many of them there might be, and whether or not their society was similar to The Beck. I had to admit, a little part of me was curious to find out more about them.

I thought of Barnes, how desperate he must have felt to risk everything in an attempt to save Perry and, by association, Blythe. I wondered for a moment whether Cam would be prepared to do the same for me. I knew in a heartbeat I would do whatever it took to rescue him, and hoped he would feel the same way. But what was Barnes' plan? I presumed that he would try to sneak in and out unnoticed, but a part of me also believed he was pig-headed enough to threaten the Ridge people with his gun, and try to frighten them into giving him what he wanted. I wondered how they would react to his sudden appearance. Not well, I was certain.

As I reached the dorm entrance, the enormity of Barnes' actions hit me. We had no idea whether or not The Ridge would launch an attack. At least we had a plan now, in case the worst happened. And I had a sinking feeling that it might.

Chapter Sixteen

The next few hours passed in a blur. Most citizens continued with their normal tasks, but just in case, a larger group than usual were fishing, to ensure their close proximity to the shoreline, should The Ridge attack. The hunting group had gone out as usual, but were working in an area within fairly easy reach of the cliffs. Mason had returned to the mine with Allen. The guards on the boat had binoculars and were keeping a keen lookout in the direction of the Ridge, ready to warn us of an approach in plenty of time. Nelson had taken me off the field duty rota and roped me into ferrying weapons to the shore.

It took a while, but eventually we had our entire stock piled at the base of the cliff path. A box of bullets lay next to them, and Nelson had put aside the explosives and was now sorting the pile of guns into those to be used for show, which would not be loaded, and those which the new bullets discovered by Mason would fit into.

Like everyone else, I had been assigned a defensive position in case of attack. Mine was at the base of the cliffs, where I would hold a weapon I hoped I wouldn't have to fire. Nelson had done a good job of making sure that everyone was aware of their stations when the time came. Blythe and Perry were the only ones not assigned a position on the cliffs. As our most vulnerable citizens, they would stay away up in the fields in the case of any confrontation. As soon as the rest of us received an alert that The Ridge were approaching, we would head straight for the shore, collect our weapons, and wait.

Nelson was half way through sorting out the guns when he paused and gestured to a long thin rifle, "Will you be ok with this one, Quin? It's loaded."

"Fine," I said, with more confidence than I felt.

"You alright with weapons?"

I mustered what I hoped was a confident expression, "Of course."

He cocked his head to one side and frowned.

"Ok, not really. I've never liked guns much," I admitted. "But don't worry. I can fake it from a distance. Just as long as I don't need to use it."

"Well hopefully you won't. But I can't guarantee it."

I peered out at the water. Part of me was desperately hoping that, instead of a large boat filled with hostile citizens from The Ridge, we would see a small canoe making its way to shore from the same direction, containing Barnes with a large supply of food for Perry. But even if this miracle occurred, I had to admit Rogers was right: they would discover the theft and come for revenge.

"Try not to worry. There should be enough time for everyone to get into position," Nelson's gaze darted to the Clearance boat. "Those binoculars have a great range. Allen will see them coming and be able to give us sufficient warning."

I shrugged, "I know, it's just..."

He stopped and looked me in the eye, "Just what?"

"I'm not sure why you've put me here. So close to the shore I mean." I hesitated, "Not that I don't want to play my part. It's just that, apart from being tall, I'm not exactly an intimidating figure."

"It's not all about being intimidating. We want you down here because you talk sense. You're rational. You don't panic. Whose idea was this?" Nelson gestured to the neatly drawn out diagram of positions and smiled. "Look, we have the bigger men in conspicuous enough places, to give the impression of strength. But if we're forced to bring them to shore, we also need to show intellect. The ability to reason." He patted my arm reassuringly. "Green was particularly insistent that we have you close by. Try not to worry."

I attempted a smile, flattered by his words, but still unable to quell the fluttering in my stomach. "It's just the not knowing that's hard."

"I know." He shifted slightly, his own expression reflecting a similar concern. "But we've done everything we can to prepare, haven't we?"

I nodded and he went back to his task, sorting the remaining guns into two piles. I turned my gaze to the rolling grey water and shivered. There were so many unknowns that we had no idea whether our plan would work. How long would we need to be on alert? What if they never came? And if they did come, could we convince them to talk to us, work something out? We had no idea how many of them there were. If we were hugely outnumbered, we didn't stand a chance.

Trying to shut out the continuous rattle of the weapons as Nelson sorted through them, I rested against the rock and closed my eyes, exhaustion flooding over me. From the moment Barnes had gone missing, I had been on red alert, terrified of what lay ahead. For one crazy moment I wished myself back in The Beck, with a dull shift in the Solar Fields followed by the promise of a walk in the woods with Cam. I knew I'd feel so much better with him here. But as my thoughts turned to him, a further panic struck me.

The possible consequences for those we had left behind in The Beck had not escaped me. At the very least, Governance would have tightened up on the rules. There would be fewer citizens to perform the usual tasks, so shifts would be longer and harder. But with Cass' torture uppermost in my mind, I feared worse. Jackson had been injured on her way to the boat. If she was unable to carry out her usual duties, she would end up in Clearance. Cam would try to protect her, but there were limits to what he could do. Once more, the thought of either of them being whipped or beaten made my stomach heave.

The sudden sound of Nelson's walkie-talkie snapping into life startled me. Walker's disembodied voice echoed from it, "Boat approaching from the direction of The Ridge."

Nelson reacted quickly, grasping the walkie-talkie and giving the instruction I had hoped might prove unnecessary. "Emergency positions everyone!"

As he lowered the walkie-talkie, I could see his hand shaking slightly. We waited, until various replies confirmed people were on their way to the beach.

Within a few minutes people began arriving, the fishing crew first, followed by the hunters. They collected weapons and went quickly to their assigned placements on the shore or cliff side. Those in the fields and the mines would take longer to reach us, and I hoped that they would be here in time to give the show of force we needed.

Not wanting to pick up my own weapon just yet, I noticed Rogers and Green making their way to the beach and wandered closer. They were deep in conversation, but Green turned at my approach.

"We were just debating the possibility of using the explosives. What do you think Quin?"

"You mean, convince them of our firepower?"

"Yes," Rogers' expression was frustrated, "if we had them set up, ready, we could have..."

"Is there enough time?" Green interrupted, placing a cautionary hand on his arm. "And we don't want to waste them. We might need them later."

"How long would it take to prepare them?" I glanced from one concerned face to the other, unused to seeing the couple at odds.

"They don't take a lot of setting up. It will just be a case of placing them in a prime position." Rogers countered, shooting a look at Green, "And I wasn't suggesting we use them all."

"No, but even detonating one or two when we might need them in the future..." Her voice was calm, but Green's back was ramrod straight and her fists bunched at her sides.

"How about we get one or two ready just in case, on either side of the shoreline?" I pointed, "We don't have to use them, but they'll be there if we need to."

"I suppose not," Rogers seemed appeased by the suggestion, "There's no need to actually prime them. As long as we have someone stationed with each one ready to set them off at a specific signal, there's no cause for them to be used at all unless we absolutely have to."

"Ok, that sounds sensible," Green managed a smile as Nelson and Shaw joined us. "Ready?"

"As we'll ever be." He failed to return it. "I've given out most of the weapons. Just waiting on those who were further away to get here now."

"They can collect them as they pass Quin. We can't wait any longer." Rogers took a weapon from Shaw's hand and shouldered it, "We've survived worse." He turned to Green, his eyes still flashing with anger, "Here goes then."

She clutched his arm for a moment, as though trying to prevent him from leaving, "Be careful."

"Aren't I always?" He removed her hand more gently and jogged with Nelson to the waiting canoe to join Walker on the Clearance boat. It was hoped that the three men would make a definitive first impression on the Ridge.

For a moment Green looked devastated, but then she seemed to shake herself and tore her eyes away from his retreating figure. She glanced at the mouth of the path, where Thomas and Cass had just appeared. "Uh-oh. Here comes our next challenge."

They paused for a moment, taking in the scene on the beach, and then headed in our direction.

"Shaw, want to get the explosives in place either side of the beach? Just place them somewhere secure and be ready to prime them if necessary," Green whispered urgently, "I'll go talk to Thomas."

Looking relieved, Shaw hurried off, beckoning one of the other Patrol recruits over to assist him with the explosive devices. I started back to my own position, but Green placed a hand on my arm. "Wait please, Quin. Cass is your friend, and we might need another person on our side."

I paused and stepped back so I was standing a little behind Green. Thomas' face was unreadable, and Cass seemed to be deliberately staring at the ground as they approached. An uneasy silence descended over our little group as the two figures came to a standstill in front of us.

After a moment, Green attempted a smile. "Thomas, I know you currently disagree with certain decisions we have made here, but I wondered if, for now at least, you'd be able to put them aside and help us."

He looked thoughtful, "What Barnes did put us all at risk." He paused for a moment before continuing. "That hasn't changed. But these people are a danger to us all, so I'll do what you ask for now. When this is over though, don't think I won't suggest we put the leadership of The Crags to a vote. Not everyone thinks this place is being well run."

I watched Green force a smile. "Ok. Well we can worry about that later. Come with me. I'll find you a weapon, explain where you need to be."

I watched as Cass and Thomas were guided into place by Green, before racing back to my own position, collecting my assigned rifle from the pile. As the team from the field arrived, I directed them to the dwindling pile of weapons and was satisfied eventually that the majority of people were now in position. After wiping my sweating palms on the legs of my trousers, I clutched the gun tightly and waited.

Within ten minutes we were able to see them. Two motor-boats, far smaller than the Clearance boat but large enough to hold several people in each one, headed our way. As they neared, I felt someone else approach from behind. Startled, I turned to find Mason standing there, a large box in his hands. He was followed closely by Allen.

"You made it!"

"Are we too late?" His face was stricken.

I put a hand on his arm to steady him. "No, you're ok." I pointed at the approaching boats. "They're almost here though. Grab a weapon and take your positions."

Without a word, Allen picked up a rifle and strode off down the beach to join Thomas. Beside me, Mason visibly relaxed and I could see how hard he was breathing. "Took us longer than we thought to get back from the mines. Some more of the tunnel had collapsed, where we were working this morning. It's a bit precarious."

Noting the bruise on his cheek, I frowned. "Did you get hurt?"

"Not today no." He shrugged me off. "I just had to shift a few more of the rocks to get to these." He indicated the box of bullets in his hands as he placed them on the ground behind the rocks.

"Be careful please Mase, I don't know what I'd do if..."

He turned to face me. "Me neither. I mean... the same goes for you." He paused, as if the words were difficult for him.

I waited until he was able to speak again. "Look, I didn't get to say this to Davis. Or Jackson." He stopped, and visibly took a deep breath. "If this goes wrong, and it might, I just wanted to say... Well I'm glad you're here. I'm glad we left. I wish Jac was here, but... despite what I said, I don't regret leaving. And don't... don't..." He seemed to struggle again, finishing quietly, "Well just be careful today, won't you?"

Unsure what to say in return, I took his hand in my own. It was freezing, and I could feel him shaking.

"Mason, we have to... you have to believe that we'll be able to bring Jac here... one day soon." I knew that I understood his sentiments more than anyone. "I'm happy we left too. But that doesn't mean I'm not missing them like mad. It'll be worth it, in the end."

"I hope so." He managed a small smile.

The walkie-talkie in Mason's hand hissed suddenly, Rogers's disembodied voice floating out across the beach. "They're almost here. Signalling for them to halt and talk to us rather than approach."

Green's voice called back from the shore. "Can you leave the radio channel on so we're able to hear the conversation? Give us some warning if things go wrong?"

"I'll hand the radio to Nelson while we talk. He'll keep the channel open as best he can. I'll be the one doing the talking."

"Ok."

The radio went dead. I stood as tall as I could, stretching my body to breaking point, hoping the three pairs of overalls I was wearing made me look bulkier than I was in reality. At least I had the advantage of height. It seemed to take forever, but eventually the boats came to a stop close to our own. One was hidden behind it, but the other floated to one side and plainly contained the person responsible for opening the negotiations. The radio came to life again and we could hear Rogers' voice.

"What... purpose here?"

The response from the motorboat was more difficult to hear. We could only catch the odd word every now and again. "Ridge... theft... missing."

"We are aware that a man from our own camp travelled to yours this morning." Rogers went on, his voice so calm I couldn't help but admire him. "He did this without our knowledge, and only out of desperation."

"...unacceptable...actions taken against..."

Rogers' voice took on a more urgent tone. "We accept that, but you must know that he wasn't–"

There was a buzzing sound as the radio cut out for a moment. When it came back, Rogers was still speaking. "Our aim...

peaceful... do not wish to–"

The radio cut in and out a few times. What we could hear was unclear at best. Just the odd word from Rogers, and barely anything from the people in the motorboats.

"...prepared to fight... no way we can just..."

There were eight people stationed across the pebbled beach. Every one of us was frozen to the spot, desperate to understand what was happening out on the water. The radio continued to taunt us with tiny snippets of information.

"...don't think that... how can you say...?"

I exchanged a concerned glance with Mason. He jerked his head at Green, whose face had turned pale as she strained to hear the exchange.

"...something we need... The Beck..."

There was silence for several seconds, nothing from either side. And then, from the direction of the boats, a single gunshot rang out.

Chapter Seventeen

A scream echoed across the beach. Green. In times of crisis, I had never seen her be anything but calm and rational, but now she rushed to the shoreline, trying to see what was happening out on the boats, her eyes desperately searching the shoreline.

The radio clutched in her hand, she jabbed at the button over and over. "Rogers? Come in! Rogers?" She called his name several times before her hand dropped to her side, the radio clutched uselessly in her fingers.

I felt a movement beside me and when I looked, Mason was gone. He reached her before anyone else, bending to retrieve the radio before it hit the floor. Sliding an arm under her shoulders, he guided her back to her post, whispering quietly into her ear. Eventually he had her back in position and stood next to her, hoisting the gun she had abandoned and aiming it in the direction of the boats. The rest of us echoed his movements, remaining in place but raising our weapons.

"Rogers, come in!" Mason took over on the radio, "Nelson! Ready to fire on your signal."

All was silent again for a moment. We stood, guns useless in our hands, knowing there was no point firing until they were within range. I had never felt so helpless.

And then the radio a voice boomed from the walkie-talkie,

"Hold your fire."

Rogers. Green jumped slightly at the sound, but held her position. We waited.

"Lower your weapons. No one's hurt. We're coming ashore."

We were all aware that the instruction from Rogers could have been given under duress. If this was a trick, designed to put us off guard, we had to be ready. Mason was again the first to react. He lowered his gun, but kept it by his side. A decent compromise. Green motioned to Shaw and the other recruit who were manning the explosives, signalling they needed to be primed. She also moved to a position behind the rocks, to ensure the majority of her body was protected.

Mason followed suit, and eventually everyone on the beach crouched behind some kind of protection with their guns at their side, ready for use, but not overtly hostile. We watched, our eyes glued to the water, as the motorboats headed to shore, seemingly following the canoe containing Rogers and Nelson. As they travelled closer, the indistinct shadows on the boats sharpened into focus.

There were sixteen people in total, split between the two crafts. A similar number to us, and so far they were unaware that we had the majority of our community here on the cliff side. Not far from shore, the motorboats stopped and dropped anchor. Four representatives made their way towards the land in a smaller rowboat.

Rogers and Nelson waded to shore just ahead of them. Green raced to meet them, but Rogers put out a hand to stop her.

"Stay where you are," he muttered.

"But–"

"Stay. Where. You. Are."

The repetition was ominous. Green froze, but was clearly not going to be silenced.

"The gunshot," she glared at him. "What was...?"

"There was some... disagreement about what we wanted them to do," Nelson answered for him. "Rogers fired into the air, that's all. Just a warning. A show of force."

"It worked, didn't it?" Rogers glowered at us.

"Well I wish you'd told us the plan," Green muttered, but she seemed to finally accept the explanation and fell silent, turning to watch the newcomers arrive.

Of the four, three of them were male. They all wore camouflage-style clothing, large bulky jackets over trousers not unlike our own overalls in style. They each carried a gun, which they had slung over their back, and I could also pick out the shapes of other weapons: a knife in each boot, and perhaps a second gun or ammunition in a large leather belt which strapped around their waists. Their expressions were unreadable.

Once on land, they stood in a line facing Rogers and Nelson. I felt lucky that my own position was close enough to overhear the exchange. There was an uneasy silence, and I saw them glance along the shoreline and across the face of the cliff behind us, taking in the number of people they were dealing with. I was thankful that we were all partially concealed, and that they couldn't see how many weapons we might have. I hoped Rogers could bluff convincingly.

Finally, one man stepped forward. His jet-black hair was closely cropped and he was almost as tall as Rogers.

"You seem well defended." He gestured up at the people on the cliff side. "How many are there of you here?" His voice was low and gruff.

"I could ask you the same question."

"Enough." The man smiled, "Enough that you should be careful around us. I repeat, how many people are there on this island now?"

"Enough." Rogers echoed the man's frustrating response, his voice steady. I thanked heaven that he was so cool under pressure.

"You won't tell me?"

"Not at the moment, no." Rogers kept his gaze steady on the newcomer's face. "Can you tell us more about why you're here?"

The other man barked a short, curt laugh. "As I said on the boat, we find ourselves... frustrated by the actions of one of your men."

Rogers didn't comment, letting the silence spool out between them.

Eventually the other man continued. "What's your name?"

"Rogers."

The man inclined his head, "Hughes."

Rogers nodded in response.

"Like I said, we're here because your... one of you arrived uninvited at our camp earlier today. But you already know this."

It was a statement rather than a question, but Rogers gave a brief nod in response.

"He was clearly trying to steal from us. Possibly, he was trying to spy. I'm not sure which we would consider worse."

Again, Rogers held his nerve, saying nothing. Behind the rocks I kept quiet, my eyes fixed on the newcomers, attempting to stop my heart from leaping out of my chest. I was surprised no one else could hear its thunderous beat.

"Either way, we're not happy." The man paused again, looking annoyed by the lack of reaction from Rogers. "We have him captive back at our camp."

Rogers, unable to stay silent at this piece of news, blurted, "He's alive?"

"He is."

"We'd like him back then."

This time it was Hughes who stayed quiet.

Rogers paused for a moment, but curiosity got the better of him, "I have to ask. Why didn't you just kill him?"

"We thought he might be... useful," the man shifted, "you know, leverage."

This time Rogers' reply was instant, "Leverage? For what?"

"Well..." the man deliberately glanced up and down the beach again, taking in the number of people. "I'll ask again. How many of you are there?"

"Like I said," Rogers raised an eyebrow, "there are enough of us. Don't you worry."

Hughes gave no indication whether he believed Rogers or not. "We were planning on paying you a visit anyway. Noticed that you had... additional resources." He pointed to the Clearance boat. "Look, for the past year, we've left you alone." He waved a hand at the people on the beach. "There weren't enough of you to be a threat to us. And this island... well, let's just say we haven't needed anything from you."

Rogers regarded him steadfastly, his face betraying nothing.

"But suddenly there are far more of you. We're quite curious where your new recruits came from."

The retort was instant. "That's not your concern."

"It is if there are more to come." Hughes' tone was steely now. He was losing patience, "If your numbers are going to grow to a level where you start to cause a problem for us."

"And what if we do?"

"We'll be forced to do something about it." The man glanced at his companions and back at Rogers warily, "But we hope it won't come to that."

"That's something we can agree on," Rogers had softened his tone slightly.

The man nodded as though he had made some kind of decision. "Look, we want to enter into discussions with you. There has been a recent—change of leadership—over on The Ridge. We're trying to do things... differently."

Rogers did not respond, waiting instead for Hughes to finish.

"With that in mind, we thought we might attempt to talk about... making exchanges."

"Exchanges?" This time Rogers answered, cautiously. "What did you have in mind?"

"For starters, I presume you want your man Barnes back?"

"Of course. But what would you ask in return?"

Hughes retained eye contact with Rogers, looking like he was trying to work him out, "Various things. Once we establish what you have here. How useful you might prove to us."

Rogers frowned.

"I repeat, how many of you are there? It would be good to know. Also, what kind of weapons do you have? Where have you all come from?"

"I'm not confirming anything at the moment," I noticed Rogers also kept his gaze steady, "until I know exactly what it is you want."

"Look, we believe your new people came from the walled community across the water. We're quite interested in finding out more about it. Can you confirm that's where you came from?"

"I confirm nothing."

Hughes sighed audibly, "Do you want your colleague re-turned safely?"

"Of course."

The reply came quickly, Hughes' tone tougher, "Then you need to start answering some of our questions."

Rogers' face flashed with a sudden anger which I could see he tried to quash. He took a breath, "Look, I first came here a year ago. We tried to land on The Ridge and you fired at us. I've seen what you're capable of. It doesn't make me keen to trust you."

Hughes' face remained calm. "I told you, things have changed recently. The leadership at The Ridge will not act the way it used to."

Rogers stood his ground, "Sorry, I'm not convinced. That day we tried to land and you fired at us? There were only five citizens in our boat, and we were barely armed. We meant you no harm." He paused and I wondered if talking about Lee's death would break his composure, but he rallied, "When we fled here to The Crags, there were only four of us left alive. More recently, your people fired upon us only a few days ago. Don't come here expecting me to trust you. Looks to me like you're acting the way you always have."

Hughes' face softened very slightly, "I'm sorry about your friend's death, but you have to understand, we were only protecting ourselves."

Rogers raised his eyebrows, "From five barely armed people in a small rowboat?"

"From anyone who might prove a threat."

Rogers changed tack, "Why don't *you* tell us more about The

Ridge? How many of you are there over there? What kind of weapons and ammunition do you have?"

Hughes blanched suddenly, dropping his eyes to his gun briefly, "That's not your concern."

"But you'd have me answer the same questions, wouldn't you?" Rogers let his words hang in the air.

Hughes glanced from his own gun to that of the blond woman on his right. Rogers followed his gaze, a look of recognition dawning in his eyes. A strange, almost triumphant smile broke out on his face. "You need ammunition, don't you?"

For the first time, Hughes' assurance wavered. He blanched visibly. Close beside me, I felt Mason sharpen at the mention of bullets.

"I'm right aren't I?" I could hear the excitement in Rogers' voice. "You want access to The Beck's resources because you're running low on ammo. Perhaps you've even run out altogether!"

"And why would you think that?"

Rogers darted a quick look at Mason. "I'm only just making the connection. When we passed the other day, in the boat," he gestured behind him, "you fired at us with arrows, not guns. We thought it was odd at the time. And now you seem strangely nervous about the weapons you're carrying. Are there even any bullets in them?" Rogers pointed at Hughes' weapon. "Or are they just for show?"

Hughes jerked it away rapidly, "Careful."

Rogers gave a low chuckle, "Touchy subject?"

Hughes glared at him. The blond woman let out a long, audible breath and spoke for the first time, "Look, if we guarantee your colleague's safe return, are you willing to talk about a trade?"

"Perhaps." Rogers looked at her with interest. "Do you admit you're after bullets?"

Hughes glared at the woman, but hurried to answer, "Yes. Yes, we are. How much ammo do you have here?"

Before I could stop him, Mason took a few swaggering steps down the beach, "We have plenty, thank you. Boxes of the stuff, *and* a mine full of lead to make more."

Hughes' eyes gleamed at the revelation, and he exchanged a telling glance with the woman.

A brief, but searing, fury flitted across Rogers' face. He darted a look at Mason before he continued, "But why would we give our ammo to you?"

"I'm not sure you have much choice if you want Barnes back." This was from the woman, whose voice was steely, threatening.

Rogers held up a hand, "Let's not get ahead of ourselves here. *If* we decide to give you a small amount of ammunition, and it would be small, what guarantees can we have about Barnes' safety?"

"Look," Hughes continued, jerking his head at the woman, "Don't mind McGrath here. We're not here to cause trouble. We honestly want to talk to you. About trading. Now, and perhaps also later, once we build some trust, more regularly. Especially if you have a mine here."

Rogers shot another look at Mason and I felt my friend shrink back into place next to me.

"As long as you don't try anything," Hughes glanced pointedly at the gun which was still in Rogers' hand, "Your man Barnes will be brought back safely." He pointed at Mason, "Now, I'm very interested in your colleague's claims. Is he telling the truth?"

This time Mason wisely remained quiet, allowing Rogers to answer. "He is. But what kind of assurances do we have that you're on the level?"

Hughes motioned to McGrath again. At his signal, she swung the backpack off her back, bending slowly to access its contents. Her movements were lithe and graceful, and she reminded me of Cass in many ways. At the sudden threat, Rogers and Nelson went immediately for their guns, but Hughes moved in front of her, his hands outstretched.

"Like I said, we don't mean you any harm. We have something for you." Rogers lowered the gun a fraction and waited. "Look, I apologise for firing at you. Both times. It's a standard defence strategy. We've used it for a long time. Means we don't get unwelcome visitors."

He remained stolidly in front of the woman, despite the two guns pointed directly at his chest. I had to conclude he was brave. "Look, your man didn't tell us much, but we did get out of him that he was searching for food for a baby. That right?"

Rogers remained silent, his eyes fixed on the woman bending over the backpack. Eventually she straightened up and waited for Hughes to continue.

"You want proof that you can trust us," Hughes gestured to the woman, who handed a packet of some kind to Rogers, her eyes still flashing with unspoken anger.

Checking that Nelson's gun was still trained on the people in front of him, Rogers took it and turned it over in his hands.

"Powered milk." Hughes smiled. "Not exactly baby food, but we use it with our own infants with good results."

There was a movement to my left and Green was suddenly at Rogers' side, "You have children at The Ridge?"

"Of course," Hughes looked slightly startled at the sudden movement, his hand also reaching instinctively for his gun.

Rogers shot her a look. She stopped speaking, but stayed where she was.

Leaving his hand to rest lightly on the weapon fixed to his belt, Hughes continued, "There's a large stock of dried food stuffs over at The Ridge, in a couple of underground bunkers. Left from the days when it was an army base. We've a good amount of the stuff."

"A single packet won't last long," Green countered.

"No, it won't," McGrath's voice dripped with sarcasm. "That was the idea."

"We want assurances too." Hughes pointed at the milk. "This will help the child, until we can return with Barnes, and maybe bring you some more. You need things. We need things. We can trade." He paused for a moment, looking expectantly at Rogers. "Now, where are our assurances?"

Mason cleared his throat, and when Rogers looked across, jerked his head at the rocks which hid the box of bullets. After a moment of silence, Rogers seemed to understand, and gestured to Mason, who bent to retrieve them.

"It's working!" he whispered as he lifted the box.

I shot him a look to silence him as he straightened up. He grinned back triumphantly, but the smile disappeared as he turned to join the knot of people closer to the shore.

Rogers took the box carefully. Opening it, he held it out for inspection. For a moment, Hughes' face was unreadable. Eventually, he reached out, as if to take hold of the box, but Rogers snatched it back, snapping it shut.

"You can have these when Barnes is safely returned."

"Ok, it's a start, I suppose." Hughes nodded, but he

167

seemed unable to prevent himself from querying, "But I'd be interested in talking some more about the mines. Are they totally accessible?"

Rogers returned his gaze but didn't speak.

"If so, then you have metal for making many more bullets." Hughes continued, "How would you react to the news that The Ridge has a smelting works?" He grinned at Roger's startled expression. "You see, I think maybe we have more to discuss than you first thought. Agreed?"

"Perhaps." Rogers regained his composure, "When you return our friend, unharmed, we can talk more. Got it?"

There was a silence as the two men regarded each other. Finally, Hughes dropped his gaze. "Tomorrow then? Same time?"

"We'll be expecting you."

Hughes and his colleagues backed away, returning to their boats. Our entire group watched as they rowed back to the rest of their crew and fired up the engines of the more powerful crafts. My plan had worked, to a point. And Barnes, if they were telling the truth, was alive.

But there was no telling what might happen when they returned. Especially if they realised there were so few of us. If their biggest need was bullets, and they had discovered The Crags had a lead mine, I dreaded what they might do.

Chapter Eighteen

Once the boats were out of sight, Green was the first to move. Rushing to Rogers' side, she flung her arms around him. As they continued to hold on to one another, the citizens who had been stationed at different places on the pebbled beach and higher up the cliff side began to arrive. I noticed Harper and Marley among them, huddled together, Harper's eyes searching for the boat, where she knew Walker was still on guard. I felt for my friend, knowing all too well how she must be feeling. Allen and Thomas were among the first to arrive yet huddled close to the rear of the group, their expressions thunderous.

Finally, Rogers and Green let go of one another. The group converged around them, bursting into sudden conversation now that the need for the imposed silence was over. Rogers held up a hand for quiet, and the group simmered down slowly.

"How do we think that went then?" Rogers began.

"You did well. You know—keeping your cool," Nelson commented.

"Definitely," Mason chimed in, "Not sure I'd have been able to."

"No. Clearly you don't know when to keep your thoughts to yourself Mason," Rogers' eyes reflected his fury at Mason's revelation. "Information is power, and you just gave some away for nothing."

Mason shuffled his feet, "Sorry about that. I was trying to help."

"Think you had him convinced of our strength though Rogers," I added quickly, "and he was definitely interested in the ammunition."

"Too interested." Thomas' tone was steely. "And they're coming back."

"Yes. To bring Barnes."

"And discuss further trading. What happens when they find out there are only twenty of us? They appear to have more manpower than us." Thomas frowned, "The moment you allow them any further on shore than the beach, they'll see how few of us there are. What's going to happen then?"

"I suppose we'll find out." Rogers looked annoyed. "What did you want me to do?"

"I don't know. Fire at them? Set off these explosives, make a show of our weaponry? Make them realise they shouldn't mess with us?"

"You think that would have worked, Thomas?" Rogers was scathing, "No. Hughes is intelligent. Better to try and make some kind of deal. For now, we focus on getting Barnes back. Later, perhaps we talk again. They have a smelting works. We have the lead. He's right. We have things we could offer each other, and, if they were being straight with us, they don't want violence."

Green chimed in, "He said their leadership had changed. They might be willing to co-operate. And anyway, they don't have to find out how many we are. Not yet anyway. If they bring back Barnes alive, as promised, that's a start."

Thomas snorted, "Really?"

"Really." Green glared at him, "We just need to take things slowly, work out if we can trust them."

"How can we ever know that?"

"Look Thomas," Mason's fists were clenched by his sides, "we have something they want. If they're running out of ammo, and we have bullets, and lead, then we're in a more powerful position already."

"But for how long? And what about us needing ammo?" Thomas countered. "We can't just give it all away. They'll use it against us!"

Mason placed a hand on Thomas' arm. "We don't just have a few boxes of ammo. We have an entire lead mine, once we clear it out. And if they have a works where the bullets can be made, don't we stand at least a chance of trading regularly with them?"

"A slim chance."

Mason frowned at Thomas, "Well that's better than no chance."

I took a breath before voicing my own concerns, "They mentioned The Beck, too. That's a bit worrying, isn't it? What do they want over there?"

"They're probably just looking for another place to get their hands on bullets." Nelson argued, "If we come up with a solution to their ammo problem, I'll bet they forget all about The Beck."

"What if it's more than that?"

"I think it's unlikely, Quin," Nelson mused. "But I suppose it's worth considering. If they wanted to plan a raid, for example, information we could give them would be invaluable. You think that's one of the things they're after?"

"Maybe." Rogers looked thoughtful, "Any kind of attack on The Beck would be far more successful if they knew everything we know."

"Which is why we have to be careful what we tell them," I pressed my point home. "We can't reveal too much before we know we can trust them."

"Agreed." Rogers soothed, placing a calming hand on my shoulder, "But if we're clever, take things slowly like Green suggests, perhaps we can work with them."

I wished I felt as confident. But there was still a nagging concern in the back of my mind that their interest in The Beck was more than just stealing bullets.

"They're coming back tomorrow then. What's the plan?" Allen asked. "We assume the same positions, and they continue to believe there are more of us than there are?"

"I think that's a sensible idea," Rogers said. "At least until we have Barnes back safely. Once we know he's alive, maybe we can start to talk about trading."

Green spoke up. "Look, it's getting late. Let's leave sentries on duty here and convene back at the dorms. We can have something to eat. Hold a meeting where everyone can have their say, then formulate a plan for tomorrow."

The murmurs around me showed that we were all in agreement, at least with the suggestion of food. Most of the group began to shuffle in the direction of the path which led up to the main buildings. Mason and I remained behind, taking in what had happened. Green came over before she left the beach. She seemed to have regained most of her usual composure, and smiled with understanding at us both.

"You have people back in The Beck who mean a lot to you, yes?"

We nodded in unison.

"Look, I can see how you're concerned about The Ridge's interest in our old community. And honestly, I understand." She took a deep breath. "When that gun went off... Well when I thought Rogers might be— Let's just say if you feel that way about the people left behind, then I get it. I promise we won't put anyone at risk unnecessarily."

"You'd better not," Mason spoke through gritted teeth.

The conversation came to an end as Rogers returned from securing the canoe. He wrapped his arms around Green and they walked away, their earlier disagreement forgotten. Within moments, we were left alone on the beach.

I struggled to voice my fears, "They can't... we can't let them hurt The Beck citizens, Mase."

"No. We can't. And we won't." He squeezed my hand reassuringly, then tugged me in the same direction as Green and Rogers, "Come on, let's go."

Shrugging my shoulders, I trudged away from the rocky shore and began the climb upwards to the main dorms. We spoke very little on the way up, exhaustion overwhelming us. It had been a tiring and stressful day. When we reached the courtyard, it was quiet.

"They must all be inside already."

"Think you're right. I'm just going to put these somewhere safe." Mason motioned to the box of bullets in his hand and moved off to the storage sheds.

I didn't feel like facing the others just yet. As I stood in the growing dusk of the space, I noticed large clouds looming in the sky above, and wondered if we were in for our first major storm on The Crags. A figure emerged from the dorms and headed for the dining hall. I recognised her slight but graceful figure as she crossed the courtyard. It was Harper.

I stepped out in front of her as she passed me. "Hey Har, how are you?"

She stopped. "Quin! You startled me."

"Sorry." I stared down at the ground. The distance between us since I had confided that I had not intended on coming to The Crags had been bothering me and this seemed like a good time to mention it. "Look Harper, I want to apologise."

"Apologise?" She looked surprised.

I pressed on, determined to set my mind at ease. "I know things have been a little distant between us since I told you I wasn't supposed to be here on The Crags, but..."

"It's fine, Quin." Her voice was soothing, the same calm and understanding girl I had known. "I get it. I mean, I was hurt at first, but... when I thought about how I made you bring Walker along with us... it kind of put things into perspective."

I paused, unsure what else to say.

"Like I was acting exactly the same way. Putting my feelings for him above everything. So you don't need to worry Quin." She peered at me more closely. "Did you think I was mad at you?"

I shook my head, not wanting her to see how much her words had affected me.

"Well I'm not. Ok?" She backed away a little, turning to go. "Don't worry Quin, I'm fine with it."

She walked away, and although I knew her words were truthful, I also knew that her bond with the Clearance citizens was stronger than the one she had once had with Cass and me. That she wasn't angry, but she didn't really need me anymore. She had them. The ache of sadness returned as strong as ever.

"You ready?" The voice came out of the darkness.

Now it was my turn to be startled. I spun around to find Mason looking curiously at me. I muttered something about being fine, and set off into the canteen, swallowing my disappointment.

Once inside, I forced myself to finish my food, despite not feeling hungry. The meal was modest, consisting of some potatoes and a small amount of roasted meat caught by the hunters, who had managed to catch something, despite their disrupted day. The room was quieter than usual, the conversation hushed. Mason and I sat down at a table close to Thomas and the Patrol recruits, who were muttering in disgruntled undertones to one another. Harper, Price, and Marley were eating together quietly on the other side of the room. I wondered whether Walker had been relieved in his shift guarding the boat yet, and found myself hoping he would get back in time for our discussion.

Blythe sat alone cradling Perry, her concern for Barnes' welfare clear in the tired lines around her eyes. As I watched, Baker approached her, a full bottle of the powdered milk in her hand. Blythe's face lit up at the sight, and she grasped the older woman's hand tightly in gratitude, before beginning to feed her daughter. To my surprise, Baker took a seat alongside her, watching with a half-smile on her face as Perry guzzled every drop.

I considered the difficult situation: being around a baby when you had never known your own child couldn't be easy. But maybe Baker was beginning to manage it. I smiled at the tiny ray of light in an otherwise terrifying day. Despite her hot temper and constant mood changes, I could see that Baker clearly cared about others. She just didn't like to show it.

After she was seated, Rogers, who had clearly been waiting

for Baker to finish in the kitchen, stood to address us all. "Look, I know it's been a bit unsettling for everyone today. I realise that not everyone is present, but we feel like things need to be said before we turn in for the night. We knew that settling here wouldn't be easy, and today's encounter with the people from The Ridge has proved that. But it looks like we might get Barnes back, and maybe even to work out a way of co-operating, maybe even trading, with The Ridge.

"Look, I know people here care about Barnes. He's one of us, and we have to hope that the people from The Ridge will be as good as their word and return him to us. We have some things in our favour. We know they need ammunition, and I'd say they're pretty desperate for it. We have bullets, and the mine. If we're clever, give them a small amount of the bullets they need tomorrow, and make sure that we don't promise them too much, maybe we can gain some kind of control. But for this to work, we all need to be on the same page."

Green joined the discussion, "Today we convinced them that we are not going to be a pushover. And they have promised to return tomorrow to bring Barnes. This is the first step in seeing whether they keep their word. If they do, perhaps we can discuss what we might have to offer them. Mason's discovery, the disused mine on the hilltop, is a huge asset."

Mason beamed, but his smile died with Green's next few words.

"But they have the smelting works and we don't. We can't make the bullets, but they don't have the raw materials. It will require a lot of trust, but maybe, if we start small, we can work to help one another out. I'm also not convinced that ammo is the only thing they're after." Her gaze came to rest on mine for a moment, "As some of you have already said, they seem very interested in The Beck for some reason, which might be a concern. No matter how much we despise Governance, we all have people over there that we care about, and we do not want to put them at risk."

"No, we don't." I was surprised how long it had taken Thomas to join the debate. "Not to mention, if we provide them with the ammo they want, what's to stop them from using it against us? Or going straight over to The Beck and invading?"

I found myself begrudgingly agreeing with Thomas, "That worries me too. What do they want with The Beck?"

Rogers took this up. "They want to steal from them. What else?"

"You're suggesting they want to steal supplies? Weapons? Surely they have plenty on an old army base. Ammunition? Well we've already provided a possible solution which doesn't require them bothering going to The Beck. And they've told us they have food stores, so that seems unlikely."

He nodded. "What are you getting at, Quin?"

I shook my head, "I'm not sure. But I just think there's a lot at stake here. Doesn't The Beck have even more desirable assets?"

"Like what?"

"The solar fields? The hydro plant? The livestock? The Dev labs?"

Rogers didn't seem to understand what I was getting at. But I could see from the looks on the faces around me that a few of my fellow citizens were starting to get it.

I took a deep breath before I continued. "What if the people on The Ridge want to *move* to The Beck? What if they want to take it over?"

To my horror, it was Thomas who voiced my biggest fear. "What if their ultimate plan is to attack?"

Chapter Nineteen

The room was silent for several minutes while Thomas' words sank in. Green was the first to speak.

"You mean The Ridge might want to live there?" She looked shocked. "Why?"

"I don't know... because The Beck has better land than The Ridge? Is better supplied with power and food? More secure and large enough to house greater numbers of people? None of us have ever seen The Ridge close up. We don't know what problems they may be having."

"She's right." I couldn't believe that Thomas and I were still in agreement. "We've no idea what it's like at The Ridge. Aside from the fact that they're running out of ammo, we're totally in the dark. What if they have bigger problems we don't know about?"

I could see the faces of those around me taking in what we said. I could see people were taking my suggestion seriously. It was entirely possible that the Ridge had sinister plans for The Beck. Whether or not they would be truthful about them was another matter.

I pressed on, seizing the opportunity now that people were listening to me and determined to make them understand, "Just think about it. I know it seems quite a radical claim, but if I'm correct, and they do want to take over The Beck, what are they going to do with the people who currently live there?"

A silence followed my words. Eventually, Tyler spoke, "Look, for now we have to take this one step at a time. First, get Barnes back. Give them a small number of bullets, as promised. Consider how the first exchange goes, and move on from there." She glanced at me, "Quin, you might be right. We can't know what it is they want. And we shouldn't give them anything unless we can be sure of the consequences."

A quiet voice came from the rear of the group, "Is it too much to hope they might be allies?"

It was Blythe. Perry was now contentedly asleep on her knee. "I mean, they brought Perry the milk, didn't they? They didn't have to do that. And they said they'd bring more. If they bring Barnes back tomorrow like they promised, doesn't that say something about them?"

Tyler sat beside her friend, carefully making sure she didn't jolt the sleeping infant. "You're right, Blythe. We shouldn't automatically think the worst. But we have to be practical. Quin also has a point, we know very little about them. And they could well be lying to us. They need ammunition, and believe that we can solve their problem, or they might not have been so peaceable with us today."

Thomas, ever the pessimist, latched on to Tyler's more negative viewpoint, "What's to stop them from storming the island, killing us all, and taking over the mine for themselves?"

"Well, I suppose that's a possibility," Tyler's words were, as ever, calm and rational. I realised how much I missed her being in charge. "But I don't think it's going to happen, not tomorrow anyway: they don't know how large a force we are. They need us. They won't risk an attack with so little in the way of operational weaponry."

She placed an arm around her friend, and Blythe managed a smile. "Small steps hey? Your child is well fed tonight. You should get some rest."

Thomas stared around at the others in the group, seeking more fuel for his tirade. His eyes came to rest on mine last, and I purposefully looked away. His eyes flashed with sudden anger.

"I hope you're right," he muttered, turning away.

"He must be tired," chuckled Mason in my ear, "he doesn't usually give up so easily."

"I suppose all we can do is wait and see what tomorrow brings," Green concluded. "Are we all fairly happy with that? We'll make sure we retain a strong presence on the Cliffside, shift around a little, perhaps convince them it's not all the same people on duty."

Rogers thrust a sudden finger in our direction, "Mason, can you get some of the mine plans to us by the time they arrive? You know, maps, the layout, that sort of thing?"

Mason nodded eagerly, "Sure. I'll set off first thing."

"That ought to convince them we know what we're talking about," Rogers glanced around the group. "So tomorrow we give them a single box of bullets, and they return Barnes. After that, we can consider our next move. Take things slowly at first, wait and see whether or not they keep their promises before we offer to do anything drastic. If trading is a possibility, we could do with more of that milk for Perry. Let's start with something small, before we discuss exchanging some of the lead from our mines for bullets made in their smelting works."

"I think that's probably a good idea." Tyler slipped away from Blythe and stood up. "And in the meantime, ask them what they want with The Beck. Barnes might know more. He'll have kept his eyes and ears open. He's the only one of us who's ever set foot over there."

"Alright. We have a plan, but we can see you're all exhausted." Green placed a gentle hand on her old friend's arm. "It's been a long day. How about we call it a night, get on with our usual chores tomorrow, maybe start a little earlier so the interruption doesn't affect progress through the day too much? Then gather on the cliff side a half hour before they're due to arrive. That suit everyone?"

There were various tired nods, and no one tried to argue. I had to admit Mason was right, even Thomas didn't seem to have the energy to start a fight this evening. As the room began to empty out slowly, I caught sight of Harper and Price gathering their things and heading out of the room, laughing together. They looked relaxed, happy even, and I felt the same sense of sadness. I took a deep breath and joined Cass on her way to the dorm, hoping a good night's sleep might clear my head and bring a more positive day tomorrow. Outside, my earlier fears were founded as the rain had become far heavier, lashing down in sheets as we hurried across to the dorms.

Despite the sound of the thundering rain on the dorm roof, sleep came easily enough. I found myself again plagued by nightmares containing shadowy figures thrashing in dark water, the sound of a single gunshot, and the plaintive howl of a baby who I searched for, but could never reach. I had found myself tortured by such dreams for a while after I had witnessed the drownings taking place in Clearance. They had eased off lately, but the confusion of the day and my distress at Harper's anger had clearly caused them to resurface. When I came to, it was still dark. I was sweating profusely, and could not stop my heart from hammering. I eased myself into a sitting position and looked around, wondering what had woken me.

The blinding flash of lightning a moment later solved the mystery. For a brief moment, I could clearly make out the humped shapes of the sleeping figures around me. The storm continued to rage outside, but unlike those I had experienced in The Beck, the more solid building I slept in felt stronger, more protective. I doubted my ability to get back to sleep though. Sighing, I grabbed a blanket and wrapped it around myself before making my way to the bathroom. Once inside, I fumbled with the taps until a gush of ice-cold water came flooding from them. Bending over the sink, I sluiced my heated face with water before greedily scooping handfuls into my mouth. The water felt blissful as it travelled down my burning throat, cooling my body from within. My thirst slaked, I turned around and leaned against the sink heavily.

With a start, I realised that there was a shadowy figure blocking the doorway. Strange, as I had not been aware of anyone else being awake when I passed through. The dim light was not sufficient to see who it was, and wearing only my vest beneath the thin blanket, I felt exposed.

"Who's there?" I tried to keep my tone confident, but wasn't convinced that I managed it.

A low chuckle came from the figure. Definitely male.

Giving up on discovering who this person was, I tried to push past him. There were others in the dorm, and a single scream from my lips would bring several of them running, I was certain of it. I had nothing to fear. But the figure remained in my way.

"Excuse me?" I tried, forcing my voice to remain calm.

The man shifted sideways slightly, forcing me to brush against him as I passed. His breath was slightly sour and I resented having to get so close. Once I was through the doorway, I tried to hurry away, but he caught hold of my arm.

"Thanks for your support today, Quin."

Thomas.

"Support is quite a strong a word for it."

"No, I mean it. Was good to have you on my side."

"Just because," I wrenched my arm out of his grasp and leaned closer so he could hear my words, "I agreed with *one* point you made, does not mean that I am," I made sure that my final words punctuated by clear pauses, so he would not misunderstand, "On. Your. Side. Got it?"

He laughed again. Backing away, I hurried through the darkened dorm. Why he was out of bed in the middle of the night harassing me I had no idea, but I knew I wanted to be as far as possible from this man, and the thought that he believed I might be an ally made me shudder.

When I reached my bed, Mason was awake. He too, caught hold of my arm as I passed. In contrast, his touch was reassuring and gentle.

"Ok?"

I deliberated whether to tell him about Thomas. Suspecting his reaction would be less than calm, I decided against it, for now at least.

"Fine. Well... just finding it a little hard to sleep."

"Storm's pretty loud, isn't it?" He shifted in his bunk. "Want to get in here with me?"

Suddenly my heart was beating rapidly again. I didn't want to offend him, but instantly felt awkward about his offer. He saved me from my embarrassment, clearing his throat quietly.

"Not like that. Jac's the only one I... well, you know." He sighed. "Look, bring your own blanket over here if it'll make you feel better about it."

Hesitating for a moment, I considered, and decided he was genuinely only offering comfort. I trusted him. Making sure that my own blanket was wrapped tightly around me, I tentatively perched on the edge of his bed. He slid across to the other side, so there was space for me next to him, and I lay down cautiously. We lay side by side for several moments, without speaking. Eventually I relaxed a little, easing myself a little closer, and he placed a protective arm around me.

"See?" he whispered. "Nothing to worry about, is there?"

In the darkness, I shook my head. I remembered being this close to Davis once, when we had been sheltering from a huge storm in The Beck. He hadn't been there when I fell asleep, and upon waking, I had felt hugely uncomfortable at how close together we lay. It was made worse by the fact that I knew he had feelings for me, which I did not return. But this was different. Innocent. We were both missing the people we had left behind. And I knew that the experience would have been totally different if I had been lying here next to Cam.

Mason's voice came out of the darkness, "Remember the night of the storm when we sheltered in the Agric barns?"

Startled, that Mason was thinking of the exact same moment, I was unable to do anything but nod and wait for him to continue.

"It was the night after Reed whipped me. I was in agony—Jackson looked after me, remember?" I could feel his smile even in the darkness. "Nothing happened, not really... it hurt too much to move, but I remember lying there next to her being so glad we needed to share that blanket."

We fell silent for a few moments, and I thought perhaps he had gone to sleep, but then he spoke again. "You know, I think Davis was hoping... that night..."

I shrugged, knowing he couldn't see, but would feel the gesture.

"I guess you only had eyes for Cam from the start, right?"

I felt tears pricking at my eyes at Mason's understanding. And that was why, I realised, lying next to Mason was comforting. We were in the same situation. Having to endure a forced separation from the very person we wanted to lie close to every night. Mason's arms tightened around my torso and I knew he understood. I returned the squeeze, hoping that he felt just as comforted as I did. When his arms loosened their grip, I shifted away slightly, knowing that I didn't want to spend the entire night in his bed. He let me go immediately, understanding that the moment had passed.

"Night Mason. And thank you."

"Right back atcha," he muttered, already half asleep.

My own bed was cold, but I wrapped the blanket more tightly around myself, knowing that I would soon warm up. The sleep I managed this time was filled with the comforting darkness of oblivion.

Chapter Twenty

The next morning we awoke to a washed-out landscape. Although the storm was over, and had not done too much structural damage, Rogers and Green were concerned about the newly planted crops. There was no sign of Harper, and I suspected that she had gone off to the fields to assess the damage before anyone else was up.

After a hurried breakfast, Mason and I were leaving to prepare for our shift when a determined-looking Baker strode over. She looked as fearsome as usual, and after the incident with Thomas the day before, I was more wary of her than ever. She made a direct beeline for me. Motioning for Mason to go ahead, I stopped and waited to see what she wanted.

"Morning."

She ignored my greeting. "Green tells me you have the books on plant life and herbal medicines."

"I do, yes." I hesitated, "Do you need them?"

She shook her head, "I need some plants finding and fetching from up on the hillside. Some greenery and some fungi. We've almost run out of our stock. They're all in the books. Can you get them for me?"

"Sure, I mean, I'm supposed to be on fishing duty today though–"

"Already sorted. Nelson knows you're needed elsewhere." Her response was abrupt, "Go and get the book and bring it back here. I'll show you what it is I need."

She turned her back and was halfway to the kitchen before I could think to ask anything more specific. I hurried to the dorm and gathered the smaller of the two books, a bottle of water and an extra overall jacket, in case the rain decided to return. Letting Mason and Cass know where I would be, I returned to the dining hall and found Baker in the kitchen, yelling at Collins, one of the Patrol recruits, who was not chopping up the meat for that night's stew finely enough. She caught my eye and motioned for me to wait outside. Moments later she stomped out through the kitchen door and glanced impatiently around the room.

"There you are." She spoke as she moved towards me, giving the impression that she had far more important things to do than teach me which plants to hunt. "Do you have the right book? The little one?"

I waved it in the air. She took it from me and sat at the closest table, leafing through it and muttering under her breath.

"Wanted Harper."

"I'm sorry?"

She looked up at me, her eyes suggesting that she had not been addressing me. "Harper. She would know what I needed straight away. She's the plant expert, isn't she?"

"Um, yes, she's excellent with all types of crops. Shall I–"

"No." Her look was scathing. "She's checking the status of the new crops. They might well need some attending to today after last night's deluge. You'll have to do."

I waited as she thumbed through the pages, running her eyes down the contents of each one as she did so. Eventually she stopped, jabbing a finger at a particular item.

"This," she thrust the book at me, "I need some of these fungi. Look closely at the picture. And I also need to stock up on greens." She leafed through the book to another section, pointing at a number of plants in a chapter called 'Edible Leaves'. "Any in this section will do: burdock, chicory, even clover. We've found all of those up on the hillside in the past and been able to use them. Understand?"

I took the book from her. "Sure. How many?"

"The mushrooms are quite large, but try to get at least twenty. Just bring what you can find and carry really. I usually dry them out so I can use them for longer." she motioned to the backpack, "You need to pack them carefully between pieces of cloth. I'll get you some in a minute. The leaves can just be thrown in on the top, as many as you can manage. Don't worry about crushing them, they mostly get boiled up in soups or stews to supplement our vitamin intake."

"Where am I most likely to find them?"

"You know where the caves are? Mason's mine?" Her gaze was piercing and I wondered how far she trusted me with what she clearly considered a vital task.

"Of course."

"Just beyond the entrance is a large, flatter area of land. There are more trees up there. The fungi grow underneath them, in the damp areas close to the tree roots. You might have to hunt around a bit to find the right kind of trees. The greens are everywhere up there, you'll find bunches of them. Focus on the mushrooms first, then see what time you have left to gather the greens. You'll need to be back down here in plenty of time to get down to the shore for The Ridge visit this afternoon."

"Right. I'll get going then."

"See that you do. And don't eat any." Her tone was as sharp as ever, and I wondered how long you had to know her before she went any easier on you. Turning to go, she called back over her shoulder, "Don't bother me when you get back. Take them straight to Collins. She'll unpack and store them. She knows how."

And she was gone, letting the kitchen door slam in her wake.

Half an hour later I reached the entrance to the caves. I paused and grabbed a drink from my water bottle while assessing the landscape. Sounds of shifting rubble and a cloud of dust emanating from the cave betrayed the presence of Mason's crew, but there was no one to be seen. Stowing my canteen, I walked a direct path to the largest section of trees I could see. They were far shorter than the ones that towered over our heads in The Beck, but there were definitely more of them here than down on the shoreline, and underneath their cover I shivered slightly, wondering whether I should don the extra overalls to keep me warm.

I scouted the area around the edge of the woods to begin with. The ground was soft due to the overnight rains, littered with leaves and twigs which had blown from the trees in the wind, and there were several branches which slowed my search. Along the way, I located lots of the greens which Baker had identified as edible, and made a mental note of where they were for my return journey. They seemed to grow in clumps and were mostly found on the borders of the wooded area, where more light could reach them. After consulting the guidebook further, I delved further into the trees, knowing the fungi were far more likely to be found in wetter, darker areas.

I had been searching for around an hour, finding no sign of the elusive mushrooms, when I began to worry about when I might get back to the centre. The ground underneath the trees was soggy and it took far longer to move around the woods. I knew I still had to harvest sufficient greens, hike back with my findings, and make it down to the cliffs in plenty of time for The Ridge visit. It didn't give me long. I also found myself perversely wanting to impress the intimidating Baker, although I wasn't sure why. Picking up the pace, I used one of the larger tree branches I had found lying on the ground to clear some of the debris from under the canopy of trees. This made the going a little easier, and I found myself making more progress.

A while later I heard a rustling coming from the trees behind me. Startled, I spun round, my hand reaching instinctively for the knife I carried at my belt.

"Who's there?" I called, forcing my voice to remain steady.

The rustling grew in volume, and a head appeared from between two trees to my left. It was Marley, out of breath and sweating profusely, despite the chilly day.

"Quin! Been sent to help you," she panted. "Been... been looking for you for a while now."

I smiled at the expression on her face, "Sorry. Been hacking my way through these trees looking for mushrooms," my smile faded, "with no luck as yet."

"That's why Harper told me to come."

I was surprised. "Harper told you?"

"Yup. I was supposed to be with her up in the fields, but the damage wasn't as bad as she'd first thought. She said she could do without me, sent me up here."

"She did?"

"M-hmm." Marley looked around. "So, what am I looking for?"

I couldn't help but smile. This offer of assistance was just like the generous Harper I knew. It showed she had been concerned about me, and was proof of her continuing friendship. The weight of my sadness eased slightly as I welcomed the thoughtful gesture. Showing Marley the picture, we continued with the hunt, sweeping the woods in a parallel line now that there were two of us, which made it easier to cover more ground. It was only a few minutes later when I stumbled across a small clump of fungi under a particularly thick-trunked tree, and I showed it to Marley eagerly.

"That's it!" she fingered the root, regarding it closely before looking up at the tree is was growing under, "There have to be more close by."

I spent the next few minutes carefully gathering the heads from the fungi I had found. Marley located a second, smaller clump not far away and stored the heads in her own backpack. We didn't have quite the amount that Baker had wanted, but we were running low on time. For now, at least, we would have something to show for our hunt, and now I knew where to look I could easily return another day. Within half an hour we had topped off our packs with as many of the different greens as we could find, and headed out of the woods. As we passed the caves, Mason and two of the Patrol recruits were exiting, carrying three boxes of bullets between them. The five of us made our way down the path in good spirits, hopeful that the trade with The Ridge would go well and we would soon have Barnes back in our midst.

After dropping the supplies we had gathered with Collins, who seemed much happier now that Baker was nowhere to be seen, we headed down to the cliff side. She promised to follow close behind once she had stored our finds.

"More than my job's worth to let them spoil," she remarked, with a good-humoured grin.

As we reached the shore, the fishing group was bringing in a catch. Nelson dispatched some of the citizens to carry it up to the kitchens before our visitors arrived, and I feared that Collins would be even longer getting down here. Rogers and Green had already been busy positioning our weapons stock, and were deep in conversation with one another.

"Anything we can do down here at the moment?" I asked as we reached them.

Green shook her head. "I think we're all set. The Ridge should be here fairly soon. Just get into position and wait. Know where you should be?"

"Sure."

Despite some shifting round of the citizens on the cliff side, my own position had remained the same, and I settled there to wait. Cass had been placed on the cliff path just above me, and we shared a nervous smile as we took our places. It wasn't long before we got the radio call from the clifftop that The Ridge boats were headed our way again. I felt my stomach tense as they drew closer, still fearing a confrontation, despite yesterday's reassurances. Mason was again stationed not far from me, the box of bullets by his side. He kept shooting me reassuring glances, as though he shared or understood my concerns.

This time there was no waiting for them on the Clearance boat. They headed closer to shore immediately, and although there was the same number of citizens in each boat, one of the larger figures was definitely Barnes. As they transferred into the smaller rowing crafts, towing our second canoe behind them, it was clear that his hands were tied. Clearly, the mistrust went both ways, and they weren't taking any chances.

As they pulled up close to the shore, Hughes helped their prisoner out, while McGrath untied our stolen canoe and pulled it up on to the beach. I regarded Barnes closely. There was dark bruising on his face and when he moved, he seemed to be limping slightly. I was glad that Blythe was again up in the fields with Harper and Perry, and couldn't see him.

Rogers and Green stayed closer to the shore this time, which meant I was not privy to their conversation. I watched in frustration, trying to interpret what was going on. As they talked, their faces remained calm and the conversation appeared to be going well. The only time anyone's expression changed was when Green motioned to Barnes' face. Hughes seemed only to shrug in response. A familiar flash of anger lit Rogers's face for a moment, but he managed to stifle it and the rest of the exchange appeared to be relatively peaceful. Eventually, Rogers beckoned Mason over with the box of bullets, which Hughes and his female companion examined.

Satisfied, they returned to the rowboat which Barnes had vacated and placed the boxes inside, testing the weight carefully. Finally, they freed their prisoner from the ropes which held him captive. He stood for a moment, swaying slightly, as the conversation went on around him. Eventually he wandered unsteadily back up the beach and settled himself on some rocks, waiting for the interlopers to leave. The female Ridge citizen handed over a few more packets of the milk, while Hughes gestured to his walkie-talkie, conversing with Rogers animatedly.

We had agreed that it would be worth arranging to contact

them via the radio in the future, to ensure ease of arrangements without the need to meet face to face. I hoped that Hughes would agree to this, heaving an inward sigh of relief that our pretence of strength might not be a regular necessity. I watched as Rogers brought Mason forward to show Hughes the layout plans for the mine, proving its existence and, as discussed, hinting that we might be prepared to begin tentative trading if they continued to keep their word. Hughes seemed fascinated with the maps though, and I feared that he would insist on coming ashore to see the mine for himself at some point.

A few minutes later, with a curt nod, Hughes and his crew returned to the rowboats and departed. Green had been shooting concerned looks at Barnes, and now she hurried to the top end of the beach. She approached Barnes with care, stopping a few feet away from him. His expression was blank and his face paler than I'd ever seen it.

"Hey Barnes," her voice was gentle, "how are you?"

He seemed to shiver, but didn't speak.

"Shall we go back up to the centre? Get you some food? Let you rest?"

He tried to push himself into a standing position but after a moment of struggling, sat back down heavily.

"Sorry." His voice was gruff, and sounded like it came from far away, "Might need a bit of help, Blythe."

"Green. It's Green, Barnes."

He raised his face and peered at her, a sheen of sweat on his forehead. "Green? Yes. Right. Green." He dropped his head again.

Alarmed, Green turned back to Rogers, "What have they done to him?"

"They insist that the mistreatment only happened when they first came across him. He fought them, tried to run."

"That sounds like Barnes."

"I suppose." Rogers' tone was doubtful. "They say they had to use force to get him under control, which I can believe. They swear that once they had him locked up, he was treated fairly."

Green gestured to the marks on his face, "But look at his wounds! And he seems exhausted."

"He doesn't look good." Rogers admitted, "Not a good way to begin a positive relationship with them, is it?"

"Well never mind that for now. We need to get him up to the dorms quickly." Green glanced around, spotting Cass a little further up the path, "Hey Cass, think you can help Barnes out? We need to gather up the weapons and organise getting them back to base. Quin, can you help us with that?"

We nodded. Green handed the powdered milk to Cass, who stowed it in her backpack, and we began to collect the weapons left on the beach as the others returned to their usual shifts. I watched as Cass helped Barnes to his feet. He seemed a little more able to walk now. With a nod at me, she directed him back up the path, making slow but steady progress. I hoped she would make the summit without needing assistance. Because I in all the time I had known him, I had never seen him like this.

There was no denying it: Barnes was in bad shape.

Chapter Twenty One

It was late before we managed to store the weapons away and get back to base. Green was pleased that we had made the initial trade without issue, feeling it meant we might begin to trust them, but Rogers was still furious about Barnes' treatment. There had been no further arrangements made to meet as yet. As planned, our two groups had arranged to communicate using the walkie-talkies for now. Hughes had been happy to receive the first box of bullets, and was clearly eager for more, but seeing Rogers' anger, had sensibly backed off for now. Worryingly though, Green said he had mentioned The Beck again, hinting that he was still interested in knowing more about it.

Mason was also concerned that if we were to begin trading with Hughes, he would ask for some lead samples from the mines. They were a long way from being fully cleared, and Mason still had to work out how the metal could be best retrieved. The mine was his project, and I knew he was still bent on proving himself to Rogers, after his initial reaction to Davis' death and the mistake yesterday when he had accidentally revealed the existence of the mines. Knowing this, he had returned to the site alone straight after The Ridge visit, leaving a message with Cass that he would be back later.

I worried that he would totally exhaust himself after two consecutive shifts down there, but Cass had mentioned how determined he seemed, and I knew better than to follow him and attempt to talk him out of it.

With Blythe still up at the planting site and everyone else busy, Green had instructed Cass to keep an eye on Barnes, who had gone straight to bed. She was concerned, as he seemed weak and unstable, and there were several cuts and bruises on his face which had needed attention. Baker had given Cass a solution of salt water to apply to them, ensuring that they were clean. Cass had stuck her head out of the door only once, to report Mason's whereabouts, and let us know she had applied the salt solution successfully and now Barnes was sleeping. After this, she retreated inside to watch over him until Blythe's return.

As I wandered back to the main building, I considered how much she had changed in the last few months, from the ambitious girl who found it difficult to express her feelings and was determined to progress to Patrol. I decided I liked this new, more caring side of Cass. The dining hall was quiet, most people still on shifts which they had resumed after The Ridge meeting. I helped an exhausted Collins prepare for dinner while we waited for the others to return. Baker came in a few times, barking instructions at us, but was mostly elsewhere, dealing with the catch of fish that had been brought back that morning.

Despite her fatigue, Collins was quiet and focused, and working with her was a calming experience after the stress of the day. I didn't have a lot of knowledge about food preparation, but Collins was ex-Sustenance, and fairly patient with my lack of skill. Things were quiet until Blythe, recently returned from the fields, dashed into the kitchen breathlessly.

"Is he...?" Her face was almost as pale as Barnes'.

"He's back. Sleeping. In the dorm." I kept my voice as reassuring as possible. "Hasn't said much. Cass has been taking care of him, waiting for him to wake."

She hurried out of the room before I could ask where Perry was. Turning back to Collins, I shrugged. "I hope he's ok. He hasn't said a word about what happened to him over there yet."

"Can't blame him. Maybe he just wants to forget about it." She looked thoughtful, "Were there plenty of those mushrooms you brought down from the hillside?"

"Yes. Once I figured out where to find them, there were plenty. Why?"

"I'm wondering whether I can make a broth from the ones you gathered this morning and then we can replace them tomorrow without Baker knowing. Sounds like he needs it, but she might not approve."

"That's nice of you." I tried to keep the surprise out of my voice. "Most people are furious with Barnes for what he did."

She stared intently at the shelves above the counter in front of her. "He's always been nice to me. And I've seen the way he treats Perry. I kind of get why he went to The Ridge."

As she finished speaking, she stretched across and pulled down a book of some kind.

"What's that?" I motioned to the book.

"Recipes. Baker's bible. She hardly lets it out of her sight, but because I'm ex-Sustenance, she occasionally allows me to consult it." She pushed it over so I could read the page. "There are lots of soups in here, and helpful ideas about how to make sure they're filled with all the good stuff to build people up."

I skimmed the title on the page she indicated, "Mushroom soup?"

"Yes. Very filling. And I'll put in some of those greens you brought back too, they're full of vitamins, which will also help him recover." She frowned, "There's only one issue."

"What's that?"

"Baker wanted our supplies replenishing. I'm not criticising, but you didn't get that many really. If I use lots of them in a soup for Barnes, our stock will be low again."

"I can go out again later tonight or early tomorrow morning, find you some more. I know where they grow now. It wouldn't take me long."

She beamed, "As long as you don't mind. If we're lucky I can replace them before she even knows they're gone. I'd like to think she'd be supportive of us helping Barnes recover, but she was so angry when he left..."

"She was." I agreed, thinking of Baker's struggle with anything baby-related. "Let's just replace it and hope she doesn't notice, ok?"

Collins turned to begin chopping the mushrooms. I put a large pot of water on the stove to boil, before returning to the dorm to see how Cass was doing. I found her just leaving Barnes' room, and she beckoned me away.

"Think they want a little privacy," she motioned awkwardly to the closed door behind her, "He's just woken up. Blythe was so happy to see him."

"How did he seem?"

"A little better. He didn't say much. Apparently he made it on to The Ridge without being caught, but was discovered sneaking around their kitchen areas. The guys who found him were on guard and beat him up pretty badly. Once Hughes arrived, he stopped them and questioned Barnes. When he realised where he had come from..."

I needed no help to finish her sentence, "He knew we might have things The Ridge needed. And if there was a chance of him bargaining with us, he needed to make sure that Barnes was treated better."

"Yep. He was locked up, and not especially well fed, but I didn't get the impression that there was any more mistreatment after that point."

"Collins is making him soup. Said she'd bring it in soon. Might help to pep him up."

"I hope so."

As she spoke, the door opened and Harper wandered in, with Perry on her hip, followed by Marley.

I hurried over, eager to show my gratitude for her earlier support, "Thank you, for sending Marley up to help me out this morning."

She shifted Perry on to her other hip, "It was no trouble."

"She made the search a lot easier. I'd probably have been there for hours without her.

"I'm glad she was useful." The same gentle smile crossed my old friend's face. "Hey, we were just going to eat, want to come?"

I glanced over at Cass, thrilled with the invitation. She smiled shyly, and I knew the idea of the three of us sharing a meal was as appealing to her as it was to me. The four of us headed for the dining hall and sat down to eat together for the first time since we had come to The Crags. The atmosphere was pleasant, despite the situation. Perry cheered up once she had been fed another bottle of the powered milk, and began to gurgle and wave a tiny hand at people as they passed the table. It was a skill she had only just learned to master, and never failed to make people happy. The meal passed quickly, and most people began wandering off to bed. It had been a tiring day. Before we left, Green came across to our table.

"Everyone ok?" We nodded in response. "Look, I've spoken to Blythe and she thinks Barnes needs an undisturbed sleep tonight, so Rogers and I have offered to take Perry, save waking him." She glanced at the infant fondly, "I'm actually quite looking forward to it."

Harper handed her over carefully, "She's becoming so interested in everything now. Have you seen her latest trick?"

After a momentary demonstration of Perry's new-found skill, followed by much cooing and clapping, Harper and Marley headed off to the dorms and Cass went to check on Barnes. I kept Green company for a few minutes as she waited for Rogers, watching her face as she held the small child closely. We were quiet for a while, until she saw me staring at her and blushed.

"She's so adorable. I can't stop looking at her."

"Wait until the morning, when she's woken you up every other hour," I joked, "see how adorable she is then."

Green chuckled, "We'll just see about that, won't we?" She tickled Perry under the chin lightly, "You wouldn't keep us awake all night Perry, would you?"

Perry gurgled back at her, thrusting her little fist into the air. Green smiled even more broadly, but a moment later her face clouded with unmistakeable sadness.

"What's the matter?"

"Nothing." But she blinked hard and shifted Perry to her other shoulder.

"Look," I searched for the words, "you don't have to tell me, but you might feel a whole lot better if you do."

She stared at me for a moment before taking a deep breath, "Rogers and I have been together for a long while now. Even before we left The Beck. And being here, among such a small group, has brought us even closer."

I listened carefully, knowing she was sharing something she perhaps hadn't before. She stroked Perry's cheek as she continued, soothing the tiny child until her eyes began to droop.

"Well what we'd like more than anything is to be able to have a child. We want to settle here, begin to build a community, but the most important thing will always be missing, until we manage to get back to The Beck."

I shook my head, not understanding.

Look Quin, we're trying to build a new society, right? But we can't keep it going indefinitely until one vital thing changes."

"What vital thing?"

"Birthing. A society where no children are being born isn't going to last long. As we stand at the moment, there isn't a person on this island who could bring a baby into our community. The serum they inject us with as we enter The Beck at fourteen stays within us until we are given the appropriate antidote, the drug which will allow us to produce the eggs which we need to make babies. Blythe was given it, and Baker, but once the baby is born, unless they decide that the mother will continue on and birth another child, well the serum is re-administered." She sighed, "So the population growth is totally under The Beck's control. But Rogers and I," she blushed, "we'd like to be the first to conceive a child together in our new home... a new hope for the future, to spur us on to a society we can be proud to live in." She dropped her gaze to the ground.

"But to do that you need the drug to reverse the effects of the block, right? The one which stops us becoming pregnant?"

"Right. We all do, in the long run. Or none of us will ever be able to carry a child. We'll just become extinct."

It made sense, the fact that Rogers and Green would want to be among the first to bring a child into our new community. But achieving that meant getting to The Beck, and knowing what was required.

"If Rogers made it to the Beck again," I mused, "does he even know what he's looking for? I've been to Dev. They keep it pretty locked down at all times. How will he know which specific substance to take? Do you know its name? What it looks like?"

She stared at the ground. "No. That's the issue. We were hoping that Cam would know someone in Dev, he was supposed to be getting close to someone, forging a relationship with them..." I thought of Montgomery with a shudder. "But on Roger' last visit, there simply wasn't time." She cradled the now-sleeping Perry close to her body. "And there are other, more pressing issues..."

She stopped talking as Rogers entered the dining hall, looking exhausted. When he spotted Green with Perry, his eyes lit up. I took the hint.

"I'll head off to bed myself then Green, if there's nothing else to be done?"

"No. I think we're all good." She rose to meet Rogers, who lifted Perry from her arms and cradled her with surprising gentleness for a man of his size. "Let's get a peaceful night's sleep for a change, maybe have a normal day tomorrow, with no upheaval. We need to talk about contacting The Ridge again soon, but it can wait a couple of days."

We said our goodnights and I headed back to the dorm. As I entered the courtyard, Cass was coming across it. She carried a bowl in her hands, and smiled as she reached me.

"Is that the soup from Collins?"

She nodded, "Want some?" She proffered the spoon. There was a small amount left in the base of the bowl.

"No thanks, I'm ok."

"It's delicious. Barnes couldn't finish it, and I missed dinner so..." She looked at me, shamefaced.

"I'm sure it's ok that you had some, if he was done with it."

"He was." Her reply was instant.

"I'm off to bed now."

"Me too. I just want to get a glass of water for Barnes. Then I promise I'll come in."

"Ok." I turned to go, "You've been a real help to Barnes tonight, Cass. I'm sure Blythe appreciates it. Goodnight."

"Night Quin."

I passed Barnes and Blythe's room quietly, moving to the bathroom to wash up before bed. I found myself wary of coming across Thomas again, and shot a quick glance down the room. To my relief, he was already in bed at the far end of the dorm, talking quietly to Allen and Shaw. Entering the bathroom, I splashed water over my face and neck rapidly, glad of its soothing effect. As I turned off the water, I heard voices coming from just outside the bathroom.

"You're back." Rogers' voice, "Make any more progress?"

"A little." It was Mason who replied, "Cleared a few more feet behind the main rock fall. Found a kind of underground storage area, some tools. Axes, chisels and so on. They'll be useful for mining when the time comes."

"You ok?" This was Green, "You're sweating."

Mason's voice retreated, presumably making his way to bed. "I'm hot and tired, that's all. Be fine in the morning."

"Get some sleep then," I heard the door to Rogers' and Green's bedroom open. "We intend to."

The voices quieted and I heard the door close behind them. I finished washing and wandered down the dorm. Mason lay in the bed next to mine, snoring already.

"Must've been tired," I muttered, turning to Cass, who to my surprise was also asleep. "Talk to yourself."

Taking Green's advice, I settled down in bed. It wasn't long before I followed my two friends into a deep and, thankfully, dreamless sleep.

Chapter Twenty Two

The next day I spent a dull morning on guard duty aboard the Clearance boat. It was the first time I had done it and I found the lack of space totally frustrating. Since we had decided that the people from The Ridge did not pose an immediate threat and our manpower could be better used elsewhere, I was the only one stationed on the boat and was thrilled when Allen headed out in a canoe to take my place.

When I returned to the dining hall, most of the others had already eaten lunch and headed back to their afternoon shift. Only Tyler and Green were still sitting at one of the tables, talking quietly, some documents spread out in front of them. I collected my share of the leftover food and headed for a table to their left. Tyler looked up and tutted impatiently.

"You can sit with us Quin, we don't bite."

Green chuckled, "Don't be mean, Tyler."

"Sorry," I hurried to join them, "I didn't want to intrude."

"You aren't," Green pointed at one of the papers, "take a look at this."

I peered at the document, which on closer inspection was some kind of map.

"We're hoping to try again to contact Cam," she continued. "Now we're fairly sure The Ridge citizens won't shoot at us, especially if we warn them that we're coming, we think we might be able to sail to a point just the other side of The Ridge," she pointed to a spot on the map, "and be within reachable radio range."

My heart leapt at the possibility, but I tried to keep my voice calm. "You think the previous issue was because there was land in the way? The mountains?"

"We're here. The Beck is here." Tyler jabbed a finger at various points on the map as she spoke. "As you know, we've had no luck contacting Cam so far, but The Ridge has pretty high mountains, and we think that might be what's blocking the signal."

Steadying my voice, I contemplated the idea of hearing Cam's voice again. "Makes sense, I suppose."

Green cut in, "We might try to make contact with him in the next week or so, see how things are over there, keep him updated with our progress."

I felt a stab of guilt that my immediate thought had not been the welfare of my friends, but my excitement at being able to talk to him again. I remembered that he too would be worried about what had happened to all of us.

"He doesn't even know that we made it here yet," I was almost talking to myself.

"No, he doesn't. And after all he did to rescue everyone, well..." Tyler paused, looking thoughtful, "he deserves to know we're safe."

"Rogers will contact The Ridge first, check they're ok with it," Green began to fold the map, "Then a couple of us will head out on the boat sometime after that."

I didn't like to ask whether or not I could be one of those assigned to the mission. I suspected Rogers would want the people he trusted the most with him, and my own reasons for wanting to go were purely selfish. Still, I held on to a tiny scrap of hope that I might at least hear news of him in the near future.

"Can I ask, that is, if we do manage to make contact, would it be possible to find out what happened to Jackson?" My voice was hesitant, but I shot a pleading look at Tyler as I said it, knowing that she had trained Jackson and liked her.

"That's one of the questions on the list," Green pushed another piece of paper at me, "We just need to decide which questions have the highest priority. I don't suppose we'll be able to speak to him for very long."

"Of course," I dropped my gaze, "it's just I know she was injured, and, well..."

Green took hold of my hand, surprising me. "Don't give up on her yet, will you? Chances are she got back with nothing more than a few bruises."

"I hope so."

Tyler was also quick to reassure. "She has Cam over there, don't forget. He knows what she means to you. He'll be doing everything he can to help her out."

I had no time to consider the implications of her words, as the door banged open and a worried-looking Blythe burst in. She collected a couple of bowls of food from the counter and began scooping some stew into them.

Green frowned at her, "Everything ok, Blythe?"

"Barnes isn't very well."

"You have to remember he's been through a lot." Green's tone was sympathetic. "It might take him a few days to get back to normal, but the bruises will heal and, with enough rest, he should be just fine."

"No. He perked up last night, talked to me quite a bit, but this morning he's really gone downhill again." Blythe shook her head. "I think it's more than just the bruises and some tiredness. He's sick."

Tyler stood up and went to her friend, an arm out ready to comfort her. Blythe backed away, her hand out in front of her.

"Stay away. I don't know what he has, but it seems pretty nasty." She smoothed her hands anxiously down the front of her overalls. "I've been with him all night, so I might well have it too."

"Don't be silly," Tyler smiled and kept coming. "I just want to help. It can't be that bad."

Blythe shifted even further away. "Look, Harper has Perry right now, but would you get word to her that Barnes' is ill... perhaps keep hold of Perry for now please? I need to look after him. And I don't want her catching it."

Green moved quickly to Tyler, placing a cautionary hand on her arm. "Blythe's right. Let's be cautious Tyler, just in case." She turned to Blythe, "What are the symptoms?"

"He's sweating and I can't cool him down. And he's so pale. Been throwing up on and off since this morning. Doesn't seem able to keep anything down."

"What's he eaten?" This voice came from the kitchen. Baker, who had apparently been there the whole time, thrust her head through the hatch, her scowl even darker than usual.

Blythe turned to face her. "Since he got back he's had a little stew, part of a bread roll, and some water."

"And soup," I added my own contribution. "He had some of the soup that Collins made."

"Collins what?" Baker's tone was icy.

I turned to face her, wishing I hadn't said anything, "Collins.

She made him some soup last night... trying to build him up. Out of your recipe book, she said."

"What type of soup?"

"Mushroom. With the ones I brought back yesterday." I hurried on, fearful of her response, "I promise I was going to go out later today and collect some more. I know it might have left us low on supplies again, but we thought he needed the pick-me-up more than anyone else."

"It's not that," Baker cast a scathing look in my direction, "Did anyone else eat it?"

Blythe was paler still, "I tried a little, to test whether or not it was too hot, before he ate it."

"And Cass," my heart sank. "She brought the bowl out afterwards, and there was some left. She'd missed dinner, so she..."

Baker turned without a word and hurried back into the storeroom. Blythe stood uncertainly for a moment, before turning back to Tyler. "Will you make sure that Harper gets the message about keeping Perry away? Please?"

"No problem." Tyler looked again as though she wanted to comfort her friend, but this time stayed where she was. "How are you feeling Blythe?"

"Me?" Blythe looked a little blank, and then recovered herself, "Oh, I'm fine. Tired, that's all."

Green glanced at Tyler and back again at Blythe. "Look, take him the food, see if you can get him to keep some of it down. Let us know how he is in a couple of hours, ok?"

Blythe managed a tight smile and hurried out of the door with the two bowls. Green waited until she had gone before heading into the kitchen after Baker. Moments later they emerged, with matching concerned expressions.

211

"Quin, where are the mushrooms you collected yesterday?"

I passed her and went into the kitchen, crossing to the storage room at the rear. The shelf where Collins had placed the mushrooms the day before was empty.

"They were here. And now they're gone." My heart sank, "Collins must have used them all."

Tyler spoke from the doorway, "What's the problem?"

Baker responded quickly, "Mushrooms are very nutritious, and grow in good amounts here on The Crags, but there are quite a few different types. Some of them aren't meant for humans."

"Some of them are poisonous," Green added.

"And if there aren't any left, I can't check if they were safe to eat." Baker wiped a hand across her face, "Look, there's a type of mushroom which looks very similar to the type I sent Quin looking for, but it's not edible. I was going to check before we used them that they were all ok, but if Collins went ahead and used them without asking... fed them to Barnes and the others before I had checked, then..." she trailed off, her usual anger leaking away as worry took its place.

"You really think the soup could have caused this, Baker?" Tyler's tone was filled with concern.

"I do." She disappeared back into the kitchen.

Tyler seemed to shake herself, "Ok. Green, you need to go and find Rogers. Now."

Green didn't respond. Tyler took hold of her arm, pulling her to her feet.

"I'm serious. Go find him." She shook her friend, "Now. If Barnes, and maybe others, have taken some kind of poison, we need to act fast."

"She's right. You know we've no real medical supplies here

on The Crags." Baker added. "Our only options for getting hold of meds are The Ridge or The Beck."

"Right." Green blanched at our limited choices, but came to life at last. "He's hunting. I know the area where he'll be, but it might take me a little while to find him."

"Well get going then. No time to lose." Tyler was all business. "Bring him back so we can decide what, if anything, we can do."

Baker returned, thumbing quickly through a small notebook. She settled on a page and thrust it into Green's hand.

"These are the names of the fungi he may have consumed. If he has..." she paused for a moment, "...well, it's not good. We need to find out for sure."

Green nodded, "Can you take care of that while I find Rogers?"

"We can." Tyler ushered her friend out of the room. "Go find him. And bring him back here fast," she added, "or it might be too late."

Green paled as she hurried to the door and disappeared.

Tyler turned to me, "We need to find out for sure what Barnes took. And separate him from the rest of them."

"Why?"

"What do you think Thomas' reaction to this is going to be?" She sighed, "If we move him, tell the rest of the citizens he needs quiet recovery time..."

"Hopefully they'll buy it, at least for now," I mused.

"The last thing we need is to give Thomas something else to rage about," Baker agreed, her tone snappy again.

I touched Tyler's arm tentatively. "What can I do?"

"Help me get him moved into Dorm Two. Then find the source." Tyler turned to Baker, "Know any remedies we might try, in the meantime?"

The older woman looked thoughtful, "Maybe. There's some information in the books Quin has about medical treatments, though it may well be too late for them."

My blood ran cold, "What do you mean?"

"I mean that the key thing with ingesting something hazardous is to get rid of it as soon as possible, for example by making the patient sick. But they all had the soup last night. It's been in Barnes' system for several hours."

"And now he can't stop throwing up..." Tyler looked stricken.

"But we have to remember that other people also ate the soup, albeit in lesser quantities," Baker's words sent a chill down my spine.

"Cass."

Tyler and I exchanged glances, united by a shared concern for a good friend.

"Blythe."

Baker was now the voice of reason, "Chances are, they'll have slower reactions, less dramatic. It's vital we keep them hydrated and their temperatures down."

I tried to take in what she was saying, my mind racing over the possible consequences of the food source I had brought into our camp. My heart was pounding, and if my face reflected Tyler's, I knew I would find it hard to hide my fears.

"Go and move all three of them into the other dorm. Barnes, Blythe, and Cass." Baker continued, "Get them comfortable. I'll prepare some supplies for you to take in to them."

Tyler turned to go and I went to follow her, but found that Baker's hand was on my arm. I turned to her, surprised at this very human contact from the formidable woman.

"Once they're settled, you need to go back up to the hills, to the place where you found the mushrooms. Bring me another sample of the ones you picked the other day. That way I can check whether they're the poisonous kind. You're the only one who will know."

I felt my cheeks redden at her request, glad that Tyler was now out of earshot. "I-I- of course. Want me to go now?"

She shook her head, her expression less severe than I had expected under the circumstances. "No. It's not too urgent. We can't do anything much about it now they've eaten them. I'd just like to know. But prioritise moving them to the other dorm first, ok? And don't do anything stupid like eating any of them, will you?"

"I won't."

She turned back to the kitchen, but I stopped her, "Look, I-I'm so sorry. I didn't know... I didn't realise..."

She turned to face me, "Look Quin, you weren't to know. And it wasn't you who made the soup. It's just a combination of unfortunate happenings, that's all." She shook her head and turned back to the kitchen.

I would almost have felt better if she had screamed at me for my carelessness. I wanted to feel berated, challenged over what I had done. There was a ball of lead in my stomach which I feared would not leave me no matter what I did, and the thought of returning to the mountain to collect more of the poisonous fungi filled me with dread.

But not as much as the thought of what might happen to Barnes, and Blythe, and Cass in the next few days if we didn't get them some meds. Because then, I knew, I would never be able to forgive myself.

Chapter Twenty Three

When we reached the building, it was quiet. Most citizens were still at work, hunting or fishing, or guarding the boat, with no idea of what was going on back here. Tyler and I were silent, concerned for the friends on the other side of the dorm door and unsure of what comfort we could offer them. We both hesitated on the threshold.

"We need to tell them the truth," Tyler muttered.

"How d'you think they'll react?"

She shrugged helplessly, and pushed open the door in front of us. Inside, the beds were empty, but we could hear sounds coming from the bathroom, and the door to Barnes and Blythe's room was ajar. Inside, we could see an exhausted looking Cass, slumped in a chair by the bedside. She barely looked up at our approach. We hovered awkwardly in the doorway.

I cleared my throat, "Hey, Cass."

"Oh hi," she managed a tired smile.

"How are things?"

She rubbed a tired hand across her forehead, "He's worse. Sweating, pale, retching... There's honestly nothing more in his stomach to come up, but..."

There was a noise from the bathroom behind us and we

turned to see Blythe, supporting a ghostly-looking Barnes. He was wearing only a pair of undershorts, and his hair stuck up in different directions. Tyler pulled me away from the doorway and we watched as Blythe guided her patient back into the bedroom.

Barnes was shuffling, his feet barely able to leave the ground. As they passed, I could see the sheen of sweat glistening on his chest and back, and he was making an odd moaning sound which sounded almost inhuman. They staggered the last few feet to the bed and he collapsed onto it. Cass helped Blythe manoeuvre Barnes into a comfortable position, then turned to us.

"What's going on?"

Tyler and I exchanged glances.

"Green sent us. It seems," she hesitated, "like Baker said, that the soup Barnes ate last night is probably the cause of his illness."

"Soup?" Cass sounded confused. "But it was good."

"It was mushroom. And though many mushrooms are edible, tasty, good for you, some are…" she paused again, "well some are not so good for the human body."

"And that's definitely what's causing this? Poisonous fungi?" Blythe seemed more confused than angry.

"We think so yes." Tyler couldn't meet her gaze. I could sense her uncertainty.

Blythe was more practical. "What can we do?"

"There's a suggestion that we should be trying to make him sick, clear out his system, but he's already been throwing up, and since he ate the soup several hours ago… it's probably too late for that."

"You're telling me we can't do anything?"

"We didn't say that. What we can do is call for help. Green has already gone to find Rogers."

"What good is that?"

"We're hoping he can talk to The Ridge. See if they have anything that might help us. Failing that, sail the boat out to a point that is within radio range of The Beck and contact Cam."

Cass stared at me blankly. "I thought we weren't going to do any more trading with The Ridge until we trusted them?"

"Well ideally we wouldn't. But this is an emergency."

"And Cam?" Blythe's face reflected her confusion, "How can he help?"

"By providing meds, hopefully, if The Ridge don't have any. Cam has access to Dev, and knows a scientist who works there. She might well be able to get hold of some antidote which can help."

"And how would we get it to The Crags?"

"That's trickier. We're hoping that we could launch a mission and get there and back quickly."

She didn't look convinced, "How fast do you think you could manage it? Only a few days ago we were discussing how difficult and dangerous travelling to The Beck would be."

I thought back to our discussion. "Look, we said it was dangerous and while we were not certain what was going on back there, we wouldn't attempt it. I was the one who suggested returning, remember? But now we have a definite crisis." I gestured at Barnes. "One citizen seriously ill. Two others with the potential to end up the same way."

Tyler took over. "If we can make contact with Cam first, have more of a sense of what's going on back there, we think the trip could be worth it."

"It's just that..." Blythe fought to keep her voice steady,

"...well, look at him!"

Our eyes turned to the massive man sprawled across the bed. His eyes were closed, his face twisted in pain, and the moaning sound continued, quietly.

"Blythe, I promise we'll do our best. Find a solution as fast as we can." Tyler was fighting for control as she spoke, which scared me more than anything. "We know how serious this is."

"Blythe. Cass...." I paused, unsure how to phrase it without alarming them, "Look, you both had the soup too. Are you feeling ok?"

"I'm fine. Nothing wrong with me." Blythe's response came quickly and I knew the same thought had already crossed her mind, "But then I only had a couple of spoonfuls."

Cass' response was slower. ""I'm ok too, I think. I'm tired that's all. And wouldn't I already be showing symptoms if I had been affected? I ate it just after Barnes did."

"That is a little strange," Tyler said, "Are you sure you don't feel odd at all?"

She shook her head. "Nope. A little woozy, but not sick."

"You had less than Barnes though. And he's weaker." I wondered if I was kidding myself. "The effect on you might be less. Or slower."

"Maybe." Cass shrugged, "But we can't sit here worrying about that."

"No," Tyler's reply was rapid, her voice calm. "Green wants us to move you."

"Move us?" Blythe's eyes flew to Barnes.

"Yes. She's concerned about certain other citizens... their reaction."

"You mean Thomas," Cass' words were filled with bitter-

219

ness.

"Well, yes. If you're not in full view, she's hoping we can avoid any more trouble."

Blythe sighed, "I suppose you're right."

"Plan is to move you over into the second dorm," Tyler gestured to the door.

"What will you tell people?" Blythe frowned, "I don't want them blaming him any more than they already do."

"For now, that Barnes needs rest after his ordeal. We can keep them out, for a little while at least. Hopefully in that time we'll have something in the way of a plan." I tried to smile. "In the end, I guess we'll have to tell them. We just need to buy ourselves a little time to think. Present them with the most sensible solution."

"Perhaps he'll have improved by the time they start asking difficult questions." Blythe's voice was unconvincing.

An awkward silence fell, and we realised that the moans from the man on the bed had stopped. As one, we looked down at Barnes. His eyes were wide open, staring wildly ahead. After a moment, he shot a look at Cass. Panic flushed his face and he sat bolt upright and grasped her hand so forcefully that she winced.

"Lee!"

"What?"

"Lee. He needs me. Needs us. We have to... we have to go and check on him."

Cass tried in vain to release her hand from his vicelike grip. He continued to hold on, pulling her ever closer. His eyes roamed the room for a moment, desperate, feverish. Then he clutched Cass tighter, almost begging.

"Please? We need to go. Lee. He's in trouble. Someone's

after him. Wants to kill him. Needs..."

Tyler leaned towards me. "Hallucinations."

I shot her a glance of alarm. "What?"

"I've seen it before, in Meds. A young mother who became ill while giving birth. She had visions... saw things which weren't there. Things which couldn't be there."

"What? He really believes that Lee's alive? In trouble?"

She nodded and took a small, decisive step into the room. "Barnes."

Tyler's commanding tone stopped him and he looked directly at her. I waited for her to tell him that Lee was dead, that he was imagining things, that he should stop worrying and calm down.

"I'm going to check on Lee for you, ok? I will make sure that someone helps him. You need to stay here and look after Blythe and the others, ok?"

He seemed satisfied, and sank back on to the bed as she turned and left the room. The rest of us were quiet for a moment, but then Blythe took over the pretence. "She'll be back in a minute. Tyler's tough. She'll sort Lee out. You know she won't let anything happen to him."

Cass reached down and wrung out a cloth from a basin she had at the side of the bed. She handed it to Blythe, who ran it over Barnes' face and neck. It did seem to calm him, and a moment later he closed his eyes again.

"Tell me..." his voice was faint, so far from the angry, tough-guy I knew. "Tell me when she gets back."

When Tyler did return a few minutes later he appeared to be sleeping. There was no need for her to continue to pretend that she had checked on a long-deceased Lee. She looked relieved as she pressed on with the task at hand, "We need to get you all moved before the others get back."

"Ok. You help to carry the stuff across, get a room set up." Blythe glanced around the room, noting the items they might need. "Cass and I will bring Barnes over in a few minutes. You two shouldn't get too close, in case this isn't about the soup."

Nodding, Tyler swiftly moved into the room, scooping up some blankets and towels. I collected the bowl of water and the cloth and followed her out.

"Rinse that out now and take it next door. Then you can fill it with fresh water." Tyler spun on her heel and was gone before I could respond. I hurried to the bathroom and swilled out the greyish water, rinsing and wringing out the cloth several times. When I arrived at the next dorm, the door was propped open. Its layout was identical, except that the beds were unmade. Tyler was in one of the private rooms, an echo of Barnes and Blythe's home in the other dorm. She was already in the process of making up the bed with fresh sheets.

I filled the basin with fresh water from the bathroom and returned as quickly as I could. We spent the next few minutes trying to make sure that the room was as comfortable as possible, opening the window, smoothing down the sheets, closing the curtains so the light was soft and dim. I fetched several more glasses and filled them with water. I had just returned to the bedroom as Baker arrived. She cast a critical eye around the room and seemed satisfied.

"Brought some food." She proffered a box which contained some bread rolls and a small tub of stew. "Not sure Barnes will manage to eat, but the other two need to keep their strength up."

"They don't seem to be affected at the moment, at least."

"It doesn't really mean anything." Her tone was brusque.

"If they had less it will just affect them more slowly, that's all."

I turned away, busying myself with placing the cups on the table next to the bed.

"Sorry. Just trying to be practical." Baker's voice was softer than I had heard it before. "I know I'm too honest sometimes. Least that's what Green keeps telling me."

I wasn't able to reply.

"Are you worried about Cass? She's your friend, isn't she?"

I nodded.

"Look, get them settled, then head straight up to the hills, find those mushrooms. Bring them back and let me take a look at them. At least then we'll know. And if this is poisoning, we'll have to hope that we can get them some meds in time." She surprised me by placing a tentative hand on my arm. "Let's just see what the day brings. You'll feel better if you're keeping busy."

I took a deep breath to make sure I could speak without losing control. But when I turned back, the space where Baker had been standing was empty. She had disappeared as quickly as she had arrived.

"Baker's not one for long speeches. She does mean well." Tyler smiled. "There's a heart of gold in there somewhere."

We didn't have time to discuss the enigma that was Baker any further, because the door swung open and an odd-looking trio stumbled through it. Barnes, his eyes downcast, had one arm slung around Blythe and was shuffling across the threshold as Cass held the door. Again, I rushed to try and help, but this time was swatted away by Blythe.

"Stay back. Let Cass and I take care of him. You two sort everything else out, but leave Barnes to us."

Cass hurried from the door and hustled past me, her expression serious.

"Do you have everything you need?" Tyler was calm and practical again. "Baker just brought you some rations. I suggest you two try to eat. Even if Barnes can't manage anything."

Blythe turned from the bed where she was adjusting the pillows, "What do we do if some curious citizen wanders over to see why we're in here?"

"We'll make an announcement over dinner. Tell them that Barnes needs some rest and you're caring for him. That he's to be left alone."

"Don't you think that will make Thomas curious?" Again, it was Cass who was concerned about the Patrol recruit. "You know he'll be angry that Barnes isn't pulling his weight."

"I'm sure he will, but I think that's a lesser evil." Tyler ran a hand across her head wearily, "Look, we'll probably have to tell them the truth at some point. But until then, if we can keep them out of your way, figure out the plan with Green and Rogers, then we can make another announcement at breakfast, can't we?"

The two young women seemed satisfied with the response. They fussed over Barnes, getting him settled in the bed and again cooling him down with the damp cloth.

As we turned to go, Tyler had a final piece of advice. "You need to sleep. Do it in shifts, if you like, one of you take a nap while the other keeps an eye on the patient. Go into the other room next door if that's more peaceful. You need to keep your strength up."

"I wouldn't be able to sleep," Blythe's statement was sharp.

Tyler was sharper, "You need to try."

"How about Cass rests first? By the time she wakes, maybe Green will be back and we'll have some better news," I attempted to appease them both. "I'll bet you'll have more success sleeping if you know there is something we can do to help him."

"Fine." Blythe blinked and turned back to Barnes.

I wondered how I would feel about sleep if someone I loved was really ill. I shot a pleading look at Cass, who stood up and collected a cup of water for herself. She wandered to the door, her steps weary and slow. I followed her out, comforted that she was going to take our advice. She paused at the door of the second bedroom.

"Quin?"

"Yes?"

"Think Barnes will be ok?"

"Honestly, I don't know, Cass." I wished I had something more positive to say, but didn't want to lie to her.

"I don't feel bad. Ill, I mean." Her voice sounded like it was coming from far away. "I'm just so tired."

"Get some sleep then," I soothed, feeling better for being able to suggest something practical. I felt a stab of guilt as I realised that I wanted her to leave so I could escape the confines of this dorm, with its sick people and its stuffy air.

She managed a smile and disappeared. Moments later Tyler emerged from the other room and we went out into the courtyard together. I felt like I was actually able to breathe again for the first time in several minutes. Gulping great lungfuls of fresh air, I felt my eyes filling with tears and shot a look at Tyler, hoping she hadn't seen. With a jolt, I realised that her eyes were a mirror of my own. Unable to look at her any longer, I hurried into the first dorm to grab my pack and set off for the hills.

I could only hope that Barnes would not get worse while I was gone.

Chapter Twenty Four

I made it to the woods where we had collected the mushrooms and back in record time, desperate to do whatever I could to make up for my mistake. I managed to collect a decent sample of the fungi I believed we had gathered and brought it back to Baker, who I found in her usual spot in the kitchen with Tyler by her side. She grasped my pack and tipped its contents on to the counter. Tyler and I held our breath while she inspected the mushrooms, seeming to sort them into piles. Her face told us nothing about her feelings, and the process seemed to take forever.

When she finally looked up, her eyes were troubled. She held up one of the mushrooms and gestured to it, "See the speckled pattern on the top here?"

We nodded silently.

"That's common to two types." She grasped another from the second pile. "And this one?"

Tyler and I exchanged doubtful glances.

"They look the same, right?" Baker glared at me, "You have two different types of mushroom here, Quin. This one," she jabbed a finger at the pile to her right, "is nutritious and tasty. The other is deadly."

There was silence as we took in what she was saying.

Tyler leaned closer, "So you're saying they're different? How?"

Baker indicated the pattern again. "The speckling is a slightly different shade on this one."

"That's all?"

"That's all."

"Well there's no real way of telling, is there? Quin," Tyler turned to me, "no one could blame you for this."

I couldn't seem to find my voice.

Baker spoke again, "No. They're very similar. Which was why I was going to check them before using them." She turned to me, "Quin, is there any way you can be certain which ones you picked?"

I shook my head, "I'm so sorry."

"Not to worry." Her tone was brisk. "The fact that you brought two types back suggests you couldn't tell the difference in the first place. Nothing we can do about it now."

"Do we presume that Barnes has eaten the wrong type then?" Tyler queried.

"Yes, we'll have to."

"Then our only hope is getting hold of some meds which work against the poison?"

"I think so." Baker was serious, "And, like I said earlier, The Ridge and The Beck are the only places we might get hold of the right meds." She glanced at the door to the canteen. "I'm going to see if she's back yet."

She turned and headed for the exit, her brisk stride belying her concern. Tyler and I wandered back into the dining hall where the stew and bread for dinner had already been laid out. It felt strange that such normal routines continued while a crisis lurked in the background. We sat, dazed, waiting for the rest to return from their usual shifts. Green returned alone around the same time, hurrying over to sit down immediately.

Tyler began grilling her, "Where's Rogers?"

"He's just outside talking to Baker. He's going to try and contact The Ridge."

"Already?"

Green nodded. "No time to waste. He's going to ask if they have any kind of meds over there." She paused, biting her lip. "It's not ideal, but they're our closest option. We've already chanced one trade with them, so we're hoping..."

"They'll help us again?" Tyler frowned.

"Well, in short, yes. I guess we know they're interested in our ammo. And we could potentially barter with them if they have access to some kind of medicine. They're closer than The Beck at least." She shifted slightly, as though not sure of the course of action Rogers had taken. "If that's not an option, we're hoping they might allow us to pass by The Ridge safely so we could potentially return to The Beck–"

"But–"

She held up a hand. "I know we said it wasn't the right plan to go back yet. No one here was ill when we made that decision, and there was no certainty that anyone back at The Beck was in trouble. This is a definite emergency." She looked defeated for a moment. "We have to try something. Anyway, maybe it won't come to that." She turned to look around the canteen which was filling up slowly. "What's happening here then?"

Tyler glanced at me briefly, then began. "We managed to move Barnes and the others without any issues. They're all set up in the second dorm: they have blankets, and Baker has made sure they have sufficient food to keep them going for now."

"That's good."

Tyler nudged me. After a moment, I realised she wanted me to deliver the rest of the news.

"I hiked up to the site where I found the fungi yesterday and brought another sample back." I paused, unwilling for a moment to confide my naiveté. Green waited expectantly. "Apparently I can't tell the difference between two similar types of mushroom. One of them is fine to eat, the other pretty poisonous. I brought a mixture of the two."

Tyler finished off the thought, "So the upshot of it is that we can't be sure what went into the soup, but we can only assume that Barnes' illness and his consumption of the soup is no coincidence."

Green seemed to deflate in front of us. "So, we *are* dealing with poison."

"Looks like it." Tyler placed a hand on her friend's shoulder. "We need some type of medicine which might counteract it then."

"Ok." Green pushed the bench back and stood up. "I'll go and see what success he's had. If he's managed to get through to The Ridge, we might already have a solution. If not, we need to try and contact Cam. And fast."

"Do you think we'll be able to successfully reach him from the other side of The Ridge?" I voiced my doubts.

"Well we can only try."

Without another word, Green stalked off in the direction of the door, avoiding the questioning eyes of a few others on her way. Tyler and I stayed where we were, watching as Baker and her assistants handed out bowls of stew and bread to the hungry workers. For now, the food seemed to distract them, and we were able to postpone any awkward questions, for the moment at least.

Green returned a few minutes later and headed straight for our table again. "Ok. He's spoken to Hughes."

"And?"

"It's a no-go on the meds. According to Hughes, the supplies they have over there are as basic as what we have here. They're happy to allow us to take the boat past The Ridge though. They'll hold their fire now they're expecting us."

"Well that's something I suppose." Tyler sighed. "Guess we have to hope we can contact Cam now."

Green agreed. "Rogers has gone straight down to the boat. Might as well get going, not waste any more time. Shaw's on guard. Rogers will ask him to go along. Seemed easier than involving anyone else."

There was a pause as we took in how fast things were happening. I thought of Rogers and Shaw, about to set off to try and contact Cam, and found myself wishing for once that I had been the one on boat duty.

Tyler ploughed on, "When do you think he'll be back?"

"Not sure. It will take them around an hour to get past The Ridge, I think. Then, they have to try to contact Cam. Depends whether they manage to or not. If he doesn't reply straight away, Rogers might stay a while, keep trying."

I couldn't keep the alarm out of my voice, "So it might well be tomorrow morning before he's back?"

"Yes, it might." Green glanced around the canteen, her eyes anxious. "Look, we need to make some kind of announcement. Let them know that we've moved Barnes to the second dorm, play it off like he's just tired and needs rest, until we have a better idea of what the plan is."

"Should work for now at least," Tyler mused. "Tomorrow,

if he doesn't appear, they'll start to ask questions."

"Let's worry about that then. I can't think about it now. Too much going on."

A sudden thought struck me, "What about Perry?"

"I don't think she should go back to Blythe. She has too much going on looking after Barnes. Make sure she's ok with Harper for now, will you? Tell her that I can take her overnight if she's not happy to. We'll let the others finish eating, then make an announcement. They'll be in better spirits after the meal."

"I'll do the rounds of the team leaders, see how they all did today. Be good if one group did really well today, then we can sandwich the announcement about Barnes in amongst some positive news, distract them a bit." Tyler disappeared off across the dining hall. As usual, I found myself marvelling at her practicality.

Turning to survey the rapidly-filling room, I spotted Harper. She was talking to Walker and Marley, a broad smile on her face as I approached the table where they were sitting.

I tried to echo her smile. "Hey, how was your day?" The group turned and I was happy to see the happy expression on Harper's face did not falter. It finally seemed like I was forgiven.

"Not bad Most of the newly planted seeds survived the recent bad weather without too much damage. The area's quite sheltered—Green chose well. There was only one section at the very edge of the field that was damaged, but we even managed to rescue some of that. We dug some of the irrigation ditches a little deeper too, for added protection. Oh, and Perry here," she chucked the baby under her chin, "was very entertaining."

I stroked the top of the small girl's head and she gurgled happily, "She was?"

"You know she can wave now, and point?" I nodded. "Well today, she actually managed to roll over!"

I thought of Blythe missing this vital step in her daughter's life and my heart ached. "Roll?"

"Yup! While no one was even looking, she rolled herself over on the blanket. Then she got stuck on her front and wasn't sure what to do next. So she cried until Walker here turned her back over." She clapped her hands together, "Can't wait to tell Blythe."

I took a breath, knowing I had to tell them. "About that."

Harper's face clouded as she recognised the serious note in my voice. "Something wrong?"

"No. Well, not really." I hated lying to her, "It's just... Barnes is exhausted still, and... Green thinks it's better if they're left in peace again tonight. So he can recover. They've moved to dorm two for now. Do you mind keeping Perry for a little longer?"

"Mind?" Walker beamed. "We don't mind at all."

"Green says she's happy to take her again at bedtime."

"No need. We'll keep her," Walker continued. "She'll be good as gold, don't you worry. We'll take her to the far end, make sure she doesn't disturb anyone else."

Harper was gazing at Perry in the same way Green had. I was glad for now that it had distracted her from the Barnes situation, and hoped that she wouldn't ask many more questions.

"I'll tell Blythe about Perry... her turning over, I mean."

"No, don't." Harper seemed to realise the significance of the milestone at last, "Let's wait until she can leave Barnes.

It'll give her something to smile about."

I wasn't sure if Blythe would be smiling any time soon with the worry she had hanging over her, but I left it, happy that at least Perry would be well taken care of for now. Returning to Green, I forced myself to finish my own meal while we waited for Tyler to return. As yet, no one had questioned the absence of the three citizens who now inhabited the second dorm, but I knew it was bound to happen at some point soon.

Mason and his crew were last to return. They looked fatigued, but satisfied. Even Thomas, who had been in the mining team today, seemed to be smiling begrudgingly. I went across to greet Mason, realising I had missed him.

"Hey."

"Hey yourself." He eased himself down on a bench and ran a hand through his hair. His face seemed paler than usual. He began to eat slowly, each forkful seeming to be an effort.

"Did you have a good day?" I found myself hoping that he would have things to tell me which might distract me from my fears.

"Mm-hm," he seemed to swallow with difficulty, and paused for a second, staring into my face, "I know I need to eat, but I'm just not that hungry. How was your day?"

"Oh, fine."

He frowned at me, and ate another mouthful of the stew. When he had finished chewing, he continued. "We finished clearing the major part of the rockfall in the tunnels today. Spent most of the afternoon hauling stones back up to the surface."

"That's great."

He nodded wearily. "I think we'll be able to start working with the tools tomorrow, trying to extract the first lead deposits. That'll give us more to bargain with when we speak to The Ridge."

"It will. Well done, Mase." I thought of the grief-stricken man who had run away when we arrived at The Crags, "It's a real achievement."

"Thanks," he managed a smile. "What's up?"

"Huh?"

"What's wrong?" He regarded me suspiciously from underneath his eyelids, "I know you better than you think."

"It's nothing." I turned away. "Just worried about Barnes. He's still pretty exhausted. Green has moved him to the other dorm to give him a proper chance to rest."

"Well then he's being properly cared for. I'm sure once he gets a few hot meals inside him and has some decent sleep, he'll be just fine. That's what I told Thomas."

"Was he asking about him?" I tried to keep the concern from my voice.

"Sure. He's concerned, and when Thomas is concerned, well... you know how he likes to make his feelings clear. I set him straight though, don't you worry. Told him Barnes'd be back to work in a couple of days."

A thought struck me. "Would you go tell Green about your success today? She was asking for good news that she could pass on to the citizens, boost morale a bit, you know."

"Sure." He swallowed another mouthful of food and stopped, "Now?"

"If you could."

"Errm, ok." He pushed himself to his feet and, looking puzzled, wandered in Green's direction.

Again, I was struck by how tired he seemed and resolved to make sure he had a proper rest tonight, whatever happened.

I watched as he spent a few moments in conversation with our leader. Tyler, too, had returned, and it looked like she was pleased with what she had to report back. I hoped there was sufficient good news to mask the bad, and that Thomas would remain in a good mood.

Moments later, Green rapped sharply on her table to gain everyone's attention. "Thanks for all your hard work today. I think the visit with The Ridge went fairly well. We have Barnes back, and we know they kept their end of the bargain, which suggests in the future we could perhaps look into trading with them regularly."

There were murmurs of agreement around the room, but I also noticed people looking for Barnes before she continued. "I also hear that the work in the tunnels has gone really well today, and the team up there might need a larger workforce tomorrow, as they begin to extract the lead we're hoping to trade."

There was a small cheer from those around us.

"In other news, Barnes is taking a little longer than we expected to recover from his ordeal over on The Ridge. We have allowed him to move into a separate dorm for now, to try and ensure that he has total peace and can rest fully. We hope you'll all stay away until he is well again."

A few citizens exchanged puzzled looks, but no one spoke, and Green hurried on to her next item. "Finally, the hunters and fishing crew have also done well today and brought in a larger haul than previously. Baker has been working on extending our storage areas and methods, and we are now able to keep a larger amount of food in the kitchens. This means we can begin to slowly increase our rations, which we had kept cautiously low when you first arrived here. The amount of produce coming in each day has been closely monitored, and Baker feels it is a realistic prospect to give out larger portions from now on."

This announcement provoked a larger celebration from the citizens around me and I marvelled at how Tyler's tactics had worked. Green had managed to slot the worrying news about Barnes in the middle of a very positive speech about our successes, and managed to distract them as we had hoped. The information about the increased rations was a stroke of genius. No one was going to remember the earlier points Green had made in light of the fact that they would be getting more to eat each day. Even Thomas seemed unconcerned, as he was slapped on the back by his colleagues and accepted their praise for his part in the work at the mine.

It was late before I left the dining hall. Once citizens had listened to Green, they began disappearing off to the dorms, happy at the positive news and filled with satisfying food. I dreaded them discovering the dire truth of the matter. The thought that the pale, shaky man I had seen earlier would be back on duty in a matter of days was laughable, but at least Green had managed to keep the truth from them for the time being.

When I reached the courtyard it was empty, aside from a figure on the far side, who was peering down the path to the cliffs. I approached cautiously to find Green, a look of concern on her face.

"You ok?"

"Oh sure. But I'll feel better when Rogers gets back."

There was a silence, which I had no idea how to break. I waited, unsure whether or not she would continue.

Eventually, she began again, "I know he hasn't gone far this time. But I hate being separated from him. When he went to The Beck, I was terrified the entire time he was gone. I tried keeping busy, to take my mind off it..." she grimaced, "I almost drove Nelson and Baker crazy. But I wasn't sure if he'd ever come home you see? It was so hard being apart from him, not knowing whether he was alive or dead."

Her words struck a chord in me. I imagined that, right now, Rogers could be actually talking to Cam, and desperately hoped that he would come back with news that he was alright. I glanced back to find Green watching me closely.

"But I think you know what that's like, don't you?"

I could feel myself blushing and looked away. She left the topic for a moment, and continued with her own story, "And then he came back, and I was so relieved. But now he's gone again, and he'll go on other missions in the future, and I can't help feeling the same dread, the same sickness in my stomach, that maybe one of these days he won't return." She sighed, "But I know I can't stop him. It's in his nature."

She was quiet for a moment, and I felt able to voice, hesitantly, my own thoughts, "Think he'll manage to speak to Cam?"

"I certainly hope so. Without that, I don't know what we're going to do." She shook her head and turned to me, looking me straight in the eye. "And I hope, for all our sakes, but for yours in particular, that Cam is answering that radio call right now."

She reached across and squeezed my hand before heading back to the dorms. I waited a few minutes before following her, collecting my own thoughts before having to face others who I might have to lie to about Barnes' condition. As I crossed the courtyard, I glanced over at the second dorm, wondering what was happening inside. The main dorm was in darkness, but the bedroom at the end, the one facing out into the courtyard, had a small light burning. I felt something like guilt twist inside of me as I stared at the small patch of brightness.

At the window, her face a stark white against the darkness of the night, was Cass. She stared out into the darkness, and I wondered whether or not she could see me. I raised a hand to wave, but she did not respond. A moment later, she disappeared.

Chapter Twenty Five

It took me a while to get to sleep, and when I woke it was still not morning. I could hear voices at the far end of the dorm, whispers which conveyed a note of urgency. I stumbled out of bed and walked over to them. Tyler was standing in the doorway of Green's room. She turned at my approach. I could see Green inside, hurling herself around the room, collecting various items and throwing them into a backpack.

"Something wrong?" I whispered.

"Rogers just radioed. He's on his way back," Tyler muttered.

Green paused in her quest for a moment and turned to face me. "Cam's ok, you'll be glad to hear. He answered the radio call. Said he thinks he can help us. We need to get to The Beck as soon as possible. That means setting off as soon as Rogers gets back."

I ignored the jolting of my heart at the news, asking what I hoped was a practical question instead, "In the middle of the night?"

"Yes." She resumed her search, pulling things out of drawers and shoving them into the bag. "Hughes got in contact. Offered us the loan of one of their motorboats. It will get us to The Beck faster and be less conspicuous than the Clearance boat."

"What do they want in return?" I frowned, trying to clear the sleep from my head. "More ammo?"

"Apparently not. Hughes just asked that he and a couple of other Ridge citizens come along. Have the opportunity to look around."

I felt my heart lurch for a second time. "So, they *are* interested in The Beck?"

"Guess so."

"And Rogers agreed to this?" I couldn't keep the frustration from my voice.

"Well it makes sense." Green sounded defensive. "We get there much faster if we go with them. They came through on the deal with Barnes, didn't they?"

"Well, yes, but that's hardly concrete proof they can be trusted. What are the others going to say? I thought we made decisions as a group?"

Green shot me a look. "Not this one. There's no time. We'll deal with the fallout when the mission is complete. Hopefully it will be a success and people will understand."

Sensing my rising anger, Tyler wisely changed the subject. "Look Quin, I know you're not happy about the decision being taken out of your hands. But we could do with your support. Rogers and I are both going on the mission, as well as Mason. Think you can you help us out?"

"Sure, but can I–?"

Tyler shook her head. "Sorry, no. You can't come."

I glared at her, but Green laid a cautionary hand on my arm.

"Sorry Quin, but she's right. One of Cam's conditions was that you didn't go."

"But–"

She interrupted me, "Says he won't be able to keep his mind

on the mission if he knows you're there and potentially in danger. So no, Quin, you can't go."

"You can be helpful though, since you're here and already know the situation." Tyler was all business, "Wake Mason. Get him ready. Help us carry the equipment down to the shore to the boat. I'm going to get Baker, ask her to prepare some food supplies for us."

Tyler turned abruptly and left the dorm. I watched her go and was startled when I turned back to find Green standing right in front of me.

"Quin, I know you're frustrated that Rogers has made a decision without consulting everyone, and angry with Cam for excluding you. But can you put that aside for now please?"

"But I want to—"

"I'm sure you do, but now's not the time for heroics. The fate of several citizens depends on him getting hold of the right meds. Cam needs to concentrate on that, not worry about any danger you might be getting yourself into." She frowned. "Cam cares about you. Let him be protective."

In truth, I didn't know whether to be elated that Cam cared enough to ban me from going, or frustrated that I wouldn't be able to see him. And despite my annoyance with Rogers' quick about-face in terms of decisions being made as a group, it did seem like this was the only solution if we wanted to save Barnes. I took a deep breath, trying to steady my nerves. Green was staring at me pointedly now, and I realised she was waiting for me to act. Shaking myself mentally, I made up my mind to support the plan, and turned and walked as quietly as possible to Mason's bunk.

Thankful that Cass was absent and his bed was therefore separated from anyone else's by a good amount of space, I approached with caution. He slept very soundly, and I dreaded having to wake him. I shook him, gently at first, and then with more frustration, as he simply groaned and tried to turn over, clasping the blankets closer to his chest. I felt bad, knowing how tired he must be with all the extra work he had been putting in down in the mines, but dark thoughts of the consequences of Barnes' sickness for all of us drove me on.

"Mase!" I hissed, as loudly as I dared, bending down so that my voice was close to his ear. "You need to wake up!"

He groaned again, and opened one eye a crack. Seeing the expression on my face, he shook himself awake and blinked a couple of times.

"S'up Quin?" He rubbed an eye, "Something wrong?"

"Yes. We need you."

He struggled into a sitting position, "What for?"

"Look, we didn't tell the whole truth about Barnes earlier. He's really sick. Rogers radioed The Beck, to see if we can get hold of some meds. He managed to speak to Cam." I fought to keep my tone calm. "Apparently we're sending a rescue mission over there. We have to set off tonight. They want you to go with them."

"Ok." He groped underneath the bed for his overalls, and swung himself into a seated position on the edge of the bed. "Wow, I'm a little dizzy."

I touched my hand to his forehead. "You're quite warm. Sure you're ok?"

He shrugged me off, "Fine. Just a little tired, that's all. Stop fretting and leave me alone to get ready."

I could see Green emerging from her room at the end of the hallway with several packs in her hand. She beckoned me impatiently.

"Meet me outside in a few minutes, Mase? I'll go and ask what else I can do to help."

He merely grunted in reply. I made my way to Green, hoisting one of the bags she carried onto my own back. We headed to the courtyard, where Tyler and Baker were ready.

"Got everything?"

Tyler nodded. "Baker has packed some provisions. I have weapons. All we need now is Mason."

"He's coming. It took a while to wake him actually," I tried. "Look, he's been working long hours down the mines, and he's so tired. Are you sure that–"

"We're sure." Tyler's tone was firm and brooked no argument. "Look Quin, just help us down with the kit. Then stay here and help Green explain things to everyone in the morning, ok? It's just as important to keep everyone here calm."

"Sure." I felt like a sulky child, but the thought that contact with Cam was so close, yet being denied me, was torture.

Tyler sighed, "I'll tell him how much you wanted to come."

"You can go next time, Quin, when things are more settled, ok?" Green soothed.

As I considered my response, Mason appeared in the doorway.

"Ready to go?"

He seemed to sway a little, but grasped the doorframe and pasted a grin on his face. Tyler and Green might have put his disorientation down to being woken in the middle of the night, but I wasn't so sure. Yet I knew any attempt I made to convince them otherwise would be taken as me wanting to take his place, so I kept quiet.

Green smiled at Baker as she handed over the food she had carefully wrapped for the crew. "Coming down to the shore with us?"

Baker shook her head, "No. I need my sleep." She backed away, "You have all you need?"

"Yes. Thanks."

"Tell Rogers to watch himself, yes? One of these days he won't be so lucky."

Green's smile faded and I could see her struggling with the older woman's words. Baker noted the effect of her statement and stopped.

"Sorry. There I go again." She bit her lip, clearly struggling with how to fix the hurt she had caused. "Look, just tell him we're proud. Wish him luck." She moved a step forward and then stopped.

Green closed the gap between them and flung her arms around Baker. "I'll tell him. You care about him more than you like to admit, don't you?"

Baker frowned, "I'd just rather not lose him is all. And I'm used to him." She shot a look at Mason and I. "Not like all these newcomers."

And then she was gone, the dorm door swinging silently shut behind her. Now that Mason was here, we divided the supplies between us and set off for the cliff path in near silence. No one seemed to know what to say. There was so much at stake and so much secrecy. Green was no doubt worried about Rogers, I was frustrated that I couldn't go, and Tyler was certainly contemplating the journey ahead. Mason plodded along, his steps still seeming uneven.

When we reached the shore we could see the Clearance boat approaching. We unloaded our bags and sat down on the rocks to wait. Rogers and Shaw anchored the large craft and dropped into the canoe. As they began to row into shore, we heard the low humming of The Ridge motorboat. It was clearly faster than the larger vessel, and arrived in the cove before the canoe had reached us. Once it was close enough, it idled in the water, waiting for Rogers and Shaw to approach.

When they reached the shore, Rogers headed straight for Green and threw his arms around her. Shaw followed more slowly, giving us a slightly embarrassed smile as he hung back. Green buried her face in Rogers' shoulder, and for a moment I thought that she would cry, but she pulled herself together as she moved away from him.

"Hey Rogers," Tyler was more in control. "We have everything you requested. Not sure it'll all fit in the one canoe though."

He pulled his walkie-talkie from his belt. "Hughes?"

A second later, the response from The Ridge motorboat crackled through. "Yes?"

"We have equipment we're going to struggle with. Can you send a rowboat to assist?"

"On our way."

Rogers turned back to the group, his voice low and urgent even though The Ridge were not within earshot. "Cam says he thinks he can get us meds. It's Assessment Day tomorrow, which is the reason for the urgency."

Assessment Day at The Beck seemed like so long ago, yet I still felt alarmed at the thought.

Shaw chimed in, voicing the thought in everyone's head, "Means there'll be lots going on, and people not in the places they're supposed to be. Should make it easier to sneak around unnoticed."

"Good plan." Tyler peered through the darkness, "How many Ridge citizens?"

"Just two I hope." Rogers frowned. "That's what I told them anyway."

Tyler pressed him for more information, "And how are we going to deal with them. What do they want from the trip?"

"We'll discuss specifics on the way. I've asked Shaw to come along. He proved to be very helpful tonight. We should have enough with four of us. Two of us can look for Cam, while one of us supervises Hughes as he looks around The Beck. I'm not letting him roam around alone. That leaves one of us to stay behind with the other Ridge citizen and guard the motorboat."

Tyler seemed satisfied. She motioned behind Rogers, to where McGrath was steering a rowboat to the shore. She waved a hand in greeting.

"Need me to grab some provisions?"

"Sure. Thanks." Rogers directed her to some of the packs. "And can you take Tyler and Shaw too please?"

"Whatever you need." She wedged an oar in the shallows and began to climb out.

Tyler and Shaw busied themselves loading boxes into the craft with McGrath. Eventually, the only items left on the beach were a single pack and the small stock of guns and ammunition that we had brought, which Rogers was intent on keeping with him. Turning to Green, Tyler flung her arms briefly around the other woman and held on tightly for a few seconds before letting go and turning back to the rowboat. Ignoring the hand McGrath held out to her, Tyler stepped over and seated herself as far from her as was possible in the tiny craft. Once Shaw was also on board, they set off for the motorboat, Shaw's eyes on us, but Tyler's firmly focused on the horizon.

Rogers stooped to pick up the weapons and began loading

them into the canoe. Following suit, I picked up the final backpack and stowed them away, before turning back to Mason, also dreading the farewell. Last time the goodbyes had been non-existent, as we had left The Beck in such a hurry. Now I was surprised how difficult it was to actually say it. I took a step closer to my friend, grasping helplessly for the right words to say.

"Be careful out there, Mase."

He didn't answer. Not knowing what else to do, I simply stepped closer to him and mimicked Tyler's actions of a moment ago.

"Take care of yourself, won't you?"

There was still no response. Standing back, I studied him closely. His face was slightly flushed and his eyes did not seem able to focus on mine. When I let go of him, his entire body swayed as it had earlier, but this time I was afraid that he would fall. Rogers, realising that something was wrong, held out his arm, and Mason leaned heavily against it.

"Be alright in a minute," he said breathlessly, "Just need to... Just need..."

But he collapsed sideways and Rogers had to lower him to the ground, grunting at the effort as he took the majority of Mason's weight.

"Mason!"

I knelt on the sand beside him. He was still conscious, but his eyes had fluttered closed and his breathing seemed uneven.

"You were right Quin, he's exhausted." Green's voice was concerned. "He's been down in the mines pulling double shifts for several days now. He can't go."

"We'll just have to do without him then," Rogers shook his head.

"Can't I–" Green began, but Rogers cut her off.

"No, you can't. We need someone to stay back and keep everyone calm. They're used to you being in charge. Baker and Nelson will be no good. If you and I are both gone, things might start to fall apart."

I jumped in, "Then you'll have to take me."

He grimaced, "I promised Cam."

"I don't care what you promised. We all know The Beck is a dangerous place. Without Mason, you only have three people you know you can trust. Take me with you."

"But–"

"She's right," Green soothed. "Cam'll get over it." She stroked a hand down Rogers' arm. "I'd feel better letting you go if I knew there were three others who had your back."

He glanced down at Mason, pale and shaky, though his eyelids had begun to flutter open now, "How will you get him back up to the dorms?"

"I'll manage. I'll wait 'til he wakes properly, and we'll take it slowly. Or I'll stay with him until the next shift gets here, ask someone to help me bring him back. Don't worry. Just get going."

Rogers turned back to the water, watching as the rowboat reached the motorboat and began unloading its cargo.

"I think we'll have to." His tone was gruff, and he turned and embraced Green once more before he got into the boat.

I bent down close to Mason. He had come round slightly and was fighting to sit up. I soothed him with a gentle hand on his arm.

"Hey," I made sure my lips were close enough to his ear so that only he could hear me, "You're in no condition to travel."

"But... I need to..." his words were faint, but I knew what he

249

was trying to say.

"I'll try to find her," I dropped my voice even lower, "Jackson. Or what's happened to her, at least. I promise."

Hearing my words, he relaxed, allowing his whole body to sag. I was glad that I had given him some peace with my promise, and he might now actually rest and recover. With a final glance back at him, I rose and turned to follow Rogers.

"Don't worry, I'll look after him," Green said, smiling with a bravery I wasn't sure she felt.

I followed Rogers into the canoe and gazed back at the shore as the figures of Green and Mason grew smaller and smaller. A feeling of dread settled over me. Moments ago I had been desperate to be included in the mission and now I actually had the chance to return to The Beck.

And I wasn't sure I wanted to go at all.

Chapter Twenty Six

Rogers was quiet as we began rowing to the waiting motorboat. I knew he was thinking about the promise he had made to Cam and how quickly he had broken it. I didn't see what choice we had given that Mason had been in no state to travel, and resented the glowering looks he kept shooting my way.

"What's the plan then?" I ventured, wanting to speak to him before we reached the boat and joined Hughes and his crew.

There was no reply except for the low grunts as Rogers hauled on the oars.

"Look, Mason was in no state to come. Stop it with the silent treatment, Rogers, ok?" I sighed, "I promise I'll tell Cam it was my idea."

He shook his head, "He'll know it was. But he'll still blame me."

"Well I'm sorry. There's nothing either of us can do about it now. Look, what do we do when we get to The Beck?"

"Get the meds and get back as soon as possible."

"Does Cam know what kind of meds to look for? How's he going to get hold of them?"

"Not sure. Said he'd try and sound somebody out about it before we got there, work out what they have that could help us."

I thought instantly of Montgomery and had to force myself to continue. "You told him it was poison, right? From fungi?"

"I described it to him, yes. I have the book with the pictures of the specific type too, if that'll help."

There was another silence. Ahead, I could see Hughes eagerly awaiting our arrival. One of his colleagues held out a lantern, its light lending an eerie glow to the waters below. I shivered.

"How will he know what we need?"

Rogers' face was grim. "We're hoping he might use his influence with a citizen in Dev to help him out."

I hated the idea of Cam needing Montgomery again. Feeling a sudden pain, I looked down to see my fingernails had carved crescent shapes into my palms. I shook them free. We were close to the motorboat now, and I knew we didn't have much longer before we would have to stop talking. I pressed him once more.

"His contact will get him access to Dev?" I remembered a night where Cam and I had sneaked in. A Dev Super had been later blamed for the unauthorised access and packed off to Clearance. "It's just I know how difficult it is to get in there without authorisation."

Rogers' face was grim. "I have no idea. He just said he had a way of accessing the meds."

We had reached the boat now and we said nothing as we pulled alongside. Hughes secured the canoe and held out a hand to me. I took it for as short a time as possible, allowing him to help me over the side, and then moved across to sit beside Tyler. Rogers followed suit.

Hughes smiled broadly at us as we boarded. "Introductions

first. This is Howard," he indicated the current driver. "He's very reliable. And you've already met McGrath," he gestured at the same woman he had brought along each time he had visited.

The two other Ridge citizens nodded. Rogers seemed tense, barely acknowledging the introductions.

"We'll drop the canoe there." Hughes gestured at the Clearance boat.

Rogers stiffened, unused to being given orders by someone else, but quickly seemed to realise the sense in Hughes' suggestion. Straightening his back, he gave a terse nod of approval, "No point in carrying the extra weight."

"Ok. Shall we get going then?" Hughes waited for Rogers' agreement, which seemed to help in calming our leader down.

Rogers shrugged in agreement. "Sure."

Hughes exchanged a brief glance with McGrath, and I wondered if they were a couple or simply two key members of The Ridge leadership. Then he pointed at Howard, who gunned the engine and began to turn the boat. Hughes seated himself next to Rogers. After dropping the canoe at the Clearance boat, we sailed off into the darkness. The roar of the engine made it difficult to converse, so I was able to sit in silence and contemplate what might lie ahead.

Despite the difficulties, Hughes attempted a conversation with Rogers, who responded with reluctance. McGrath did nothing but stare out into the growing darkness as we sped across the water. Leaning closer to Tyler, I nudged her until she turned to face me.

"How will we get close enough without being spotted if the boat makes this much noise?"

It took her several attempts to understand me, but eventually she leaned in closer, "We'll go more slowly—the noise should reduce as our speed does. And then we can cut the engine altogether and just row the final distance."

Not for the first time, I was glad of Tyler's practical, reassuring presence. I backed away and tried to relax as the journey continued. The conversation between Rogers and Hughes went on throughout the journey, and I wondered what information was being exchanged. Shaw sat quietly, smiling at me the few times he caught my eye. From what I had seen of him so far, he was calm and rational. He had made practical suggestions, volunteered to support others, and as a recent Patrol recruit, he was certainly in good shape. I had never seen him operate a weapon, but since we were hoping it wouldn't come to that, perhaps he wouldn't need to. He looked a little nervous, but I was glad he had come along to even out the numbers.

I must have dozed off, but I woke as the boat engine was cut to find Rogers staring around at us all. Rubbing my eyes, I pushed myself into a more upright position so I could listen to what he had to say.

"Look."

He pointed off into the distance where the familiar hilltops crested the horizon in the moonlight. The Beck. I felt a sudden chill as I contemplated our return.

"We aren't far out now and will proceed with extreme caution. The boat will be quieter, but as a result will travel much more slowly. We will use this time to go over our plans. Howard and Shaw will remain here on the boat ready to pick us up and leave, at speed if necessary."

I remembered our last escape with a shudder as Rogers waited for agreement from the two citizens remaining on board before continuing. Shaw looked relieved.

"When we get there, we'll need to cross the beach while keeping a lookout for any Shadow Patrol. Once we're in the woods, we should head for the pass between Clearance and the rest of The Beck." He turned to Hughes, "You just follow us and keep quiet, ok?"

"No problem." Hughes was quick to respond.

"What do we do from there?" Tyler questioned, "There'll be guards on duty on the other side."

Rogers frowned. "We have a few options. We could incapacitate the guards, though I'd prefer not to, as it could result in one of us getting hurt and would also raise questions later when they're missed. We're trying to make as little impact here as possible."

"Maybe we could attempt a distraction. Or we could hide and wait until the guard changeover? Move during the switch, when they're less focused." Tyler was as practical as ever. "Alternatively, we could hope that the guards who take over are citizens we know. Unless things have changed, by the time we get there it shouldn't be long 'til the morning shift starts."

Rogers took the negative view. "I'd say there's a good chance that things might have changed since we left, don't you?"

"Maybe." Tyler bent to begin sorting through the equipment in the boat's lockers. "But if there's even a chance we might get past the guard post without a conflict, isn't it worth waiting to see who's on duty?"

I agreed with Tyler. "Surely there's a decent chance we'll still know them?"

"Fair enough." Rogers held up his hands. "We wait and see who's there, but be ready to adapt the plan if necessary. Once we're in the woods on the way to Patrol, we need to split up. Tyler: you will take Hughes and McGrath on a surreptitious tour of The Beck. Stay under the radar. If you come across others, keep a little distance from one another. Make it look like you're alone."

Tyler looked frustrated at being relegated to touring The Beck with our new associates, but I knew why Rogers had assigned her to the task. He still didn't fully trust our neighbours, and Tyler was an experienced Patrol guard with excellent strength and skill. While I could have shown them round, there were parts of The Beck she knew far better than I did, and I knew he trusted that she could defend herself, and others, if necessary. While Cam would be angry to discover that I had come on the mission, his wrath was less frightening than The Ridge citizens somehow going rogue.

Tyler would deal calmly with any situation which arose. She also knew better than to argue with Rogers in front of Hughes and managed a tight nod as Rogers continued with confidence. "Quin, between us, you and I need to find Cam. Talk to him about the meds as we discussed earlier. I'll begin searching in Patrol, you head for the Lower Beck, perhaps start with the Lincoln Building, ok?"

Hughes cleared his throat. "The meds. Do we get some of them?"

Rogers stared at him, his fists bunching by his sides. "Do you have citizens who are sick?"

"Not at the moment." Hughes shrugged calmly. "But in the future, who knows?"

"Look. We allowed you to come with us. That was the deal."

"But you're using our boat." Hughes countered.

Rogers took a deep breath. "Let's see what we come away

with. We can discuss it later." He turned back to me. "Ok, Quin?"

"Ok."

We all turned our attention to the Clearance harbour, peering ahead as it loomed into view. It seemed brighter than it had ever been, and we could see that lights of some kind had been rigged up on the jetty and at the guard hut which stood at the rear of the beach.

"A direct result of our escape, no doubt," murmured Tyler.

The extra precautions meant there had to be guards around somewhere, and I wasn't sure how we would manage an approach without being spotted. Clearly growing nervous, Rogers stood and joined Howard at the wheel, motioning to the shore ahead and talking agitatedly. The jetty appeared empty, and for a moment I thought we might get away with it, but then a figure emerged from the guard hut and I knew we had been spotted.

I looked at Rogers expectantly, wondering what his plan was. He was already busy, grasping one of the guns from where they had been stowed in the lockers at the side of the boat. The guard had stopped and was standing, hands on hips, staring out at us, the light from behind him outlining his tall frame. Although I knew he was Shadow Patrol, I was still horrified at the thought we would simply shoot him dead. I closed my eyes, bracing myself for the shot.

There was a slight disturbance at the front of the boat and when I opened my eyes, Hughes was leaning close to Rogers, pulling the gun out of his hand. Confused, I turned back to the guard on the beach, who was raising a hand which no doubt held a walkie talkie. Before it could reach his mouth though, he appeared to be struck by something and staggered to one side. I knew I hadn't heard a shot though. Looking back at the citizens sitting around me, I noticed McGrath for the first time. She stood in the centre of the motorboat, her stance tense, a bow stretched taut in her hands.

Following her gaze back to the shore, I watched as the guard fell to his knees, and then collapsed sideways, until his whole body hit the ground. He lay still, his walkie talkie lying a few feet from him, useless.

"A gunshot would have alerted anyone within several hundred metres," Hughes was saying, stepping away from Rogers now he could see there was no danger of him using the gun. "Use your brain, man."

Rogers replaced the gun in the locker quietly. McGrath stowed the bow and returned to her seat.

"We need to get there fast and hide the body." I marvelled at how Hughes' voice was still calm. "Someone will come looking sooner or later."

"You're right." Rogers sounded a little surprised that he was agreeing with Hughes, but there was no doubt that his words made sense. "That's where we're headed." He motioned around the side of the Clearance Sector to the far end of the harbour. "Better step on it."

It didn't take long for us to travel to the spot where Rogers had directed our pilot. When we reached our destination, Howard cut the engine and those of us going ashore used the oars from the rowboat to edge closer to the land. The sound of the water lapping around the base of the boat might have been soothing, were our position here not so dangerous. Once we were within wading distance, Rogers hopped out and motioned for us to follow, lifting the packs containing dry clothing above our heads.

The shore here consisted of a number of jagged rocks and an outcropping of trees. These were difficult to navigate, but meant that we approached from a direction which would not be expected. We struggled through, climbing up and over large, gnarled tree roots in many places, until we reached the other side, where we abandoned our soaked overalls in favour of dry ones in the familiar Patrol blue. Rogers crouched down on the ground at the edge of the trees, gazing out across the deserted beach as the rest of us concealed the wet clothing in the bushes.

From behind him, I recognised the area with a start, remembering the woods I had crouched in with Harper before our previous escape, and the last place I had seen Jackson, being carried by Cameron back under the cover of the trees rather than risk being caught by the Shadow Patrol. Glancing over at the jetty, I noted the presence of only three Clearance boats for the first time with a small sense of satisfaction. Forcing my attention back to the man at the head of our group, I was grateful for his usual practical attitude.

"Right, we need to get that guard out of sight." Rogers looked around the group.

"I'll help you." Hughes was the first to volunteer.

"It might be tricky. There are often two guards on duty. I've not seen anyone else yet, but they won't be far away. Maybe just up getting some food or taking a short rest break."

Hughes nodded. "Better get it done quickly then."

The rest of us watched as the two men checked the horizon once more before sprinting across the stretch of beach. None of us spoke, too focused on our colleagues' dangerous mission. They made it to the Shadow Patrol officer without issue, but their progress back was far slower, their burden weighing them down. When they eventually reached us, they were breathing hard.

They staggered through the outcroppings of bushes and lowered the guard to the ground as soon as they were concealed from the beach. McGrath leaned over him, her ear to his chest, listening for a heartbeat.

"Dead," she pronounced after a moment, not sounding like it mattered at all. "Best get him hidden."

Between us, we rolled the man's body to the rear of the clearing where a thickness of bushes would conceal him well. At first, I recoiled from touching him, but found when I did that his skin was still strangely warm. McGrath seemed unfazed by the incident, and I wondered how used to dealing with death she was.

"Pretty sure he didn't manage to use this." Rogers held up his walkie talkie. "And there was no evidence of another guard anywhere near."

"Perhaps they have less of a guard over here on days like today," Tyler suggested. I knew she referred to the Assessments.

"Let's hope so. It should give us more time before they notice he's missing." Rogers stood up and shot a quick glance along the beach again. "Anyway, we'd better get going. All clear, I think, but let's go in small groups, just as a precaution."

Several nods confirmed that we were all more comfortable with minimising the risk to ourselves by travelling a few at a time. It was still dark, but dawn was creeping up on the horizon and we wanted to be in the woods on the other side of the hill before it was light. Tyler went first, dashing quickly across the open beach with Hughes and McGrath following close behind. Within seconds they were in the woods on the other side.

Left with Rogers in the trees, I suddenly felt a little shy. He turned, his eyes boring into me. "Quin, you and I have an important job here. We can't come back until we find Cam."

I nodded warily.

"Like I said, he wasn't sure where he would be, so if I take Patrol and you check the Assessment Buildings, one of us will hopefully locate him. If not, you head to Agric and Sustenance, I'll cover Rep and LS. That way we are searching as methodically as possible. Whichever of us finds him first needs to get the meds and get back here fast. Nightfall at the latest."

I didn't like to ask what would happen if we didn't manage to get them.

"If you're back any earlier, make sure you're hidden well out of sight. Once everyone is here, we'll wait for dark and head straight back to The Crags." There was a look of determination on his face, "Be aware that he isn't expecting to see you, Quin."

He paused and took in my look of disappointment. "For what it's worth, I know you're desperate to see him and I suppose, in the end, he might well be more pleased to see you than me anyway." He smiled and then looked more serious. "If you can give him hope, well... that's good. And now that we might have The Ridge folk on our side... things might be looking up. I'm beginning to think, if we tread carefully, they could be really strong allies."

"Really?" I knew I sounded doubtful.

"Yes. From what Hughes said on the way over, they want a lot of the same things we do. Seems like he's on the level, though we shouldn't jump into anything too fast. But he's been helpful so far. And if we *can* work together... who knows

what could happen? We just need to get through this first."
He peered out from the trees on to the beach again. I noticed
Tyler beckoning to us from the woods on the other side. "You
ready?"

I had never felt less ready in my life.

Chapter Twenty Seven

We sped across the beach, heads down, and made it without incident, reuniting with the rest of the group. The path to the top of the hill was mostly wooded, and we reached the entrance to the passage without being spotted. Once there, we fought our way through to the other side, where we found ourselves peering out at the Clearance entrance guard post, which was currently housing two burly Shadow Patrol guards.

The pass was always guarded by Shadow Patrol at night, whereas in the daytime the job was often assigned to ordinary Patrol citizens. As planned, we settled in various positions in the thicket of trees which had a view of the guard hut to wait for the morning changeover. After an hour, I found myself having far more sympathy with Rogers, who had spent hours hiding in the Clearance passage on his last visit to The Beck. My muscles were extremely cramped and, no matter how often I shifted, there were always pins and needles in one foot or the other. I was afraid I wouldn't be able to stand when the time came.

Eventually, two figures made their way out of the woods, and the Shadow Patrol who were currently on duty came out of the hut.

Rogers leaned sideways, peering through the gaps in the

foliage, "Can you see who their replacements are?"

I strained my eyes, but couldn't make out the faces. As they came closer, one looked shorter and was definitely female. The other was a tall, slim male figure. I didn't think I recognised the man, but the woman seemed familiar. As she crossed the final gap between the forest and the guard post, I realised who she was.

"Will."

Rogers had recognised the female citizen at the exact same moment, and he was smiling broadly. Will was an old ally of ours, and a solid member of the Resistance. As she and her companion took over and the Shadow Patrol guards disappeared into the woods, I felt a little hopeful.

We waited until they were completely out of sight before we made any kind of move. None of the ex-Beck citizens recognised the man on duty with Will, but we knew if we could talk to her alone, she could distract him or send him elsewhere. It didn't take long until he went inside the guard hut, and Rogers took this opportunity to throw a well-aimed stone. It hit the ground right in front of Will, and she immediately stiffened.

Following the stone up with a sharp bird-call, Rogers attracted her attention to the Clearance passage entrance and I watched as she stared up at the woods in confusion. As she did, Rogers stepped a foot or two out from the trees and waved a hand at her, before disappearing back into the branches again. She immediately drew her gaze back down the hill and we could see her processing the situation. Moments later, she entered the guard hut. We waited. When she emerged, she began hiking up the hill.

She reached the forest quickly and concealed herself within

the branches before calling out softly.

"Rogers?"

"Hey, Will. Miss me?"

"What's going on?"

"Important mission. Need to collect some meds from Cam urgently. Then we'll be gone again."

"Oh." Her voice was small, and she sounded disappointed.

"I'm sorry, Will. But the meds are needed desperately. No time to explain, but we'll be back with more of a rescue plan soon, I promise."

"Who's sick?"

"Barnes."

"How bad?"

He hesitated, "Bad, Will. Really bad." I could hear her soft intake of breath as Rogers continued, "So glad it was you on duty today. Who's that with you?"

"Name's Hall. Don't know him all that well. Only recently promoted. He's very keen to impress those in charge." She raised her eyebrows. "He's not Resistance, if that's what you mean."

"We'll need him out of the way then. We have to access the rest of The Beck while it's... busy."

Will glanced down at the guard hut. "Ok. Give me five minutes and I'll send him over to Clearance with some equipment. When he's gone, you can get past without anyone knowing you're here."

"Thanks." I heard the bushes rustle slightly as someone shifted position before Rogers' continued. "Any idea where Cam will be this morning?"

"Not sure. Most likely somewhere in Patrol, Reed's been keeping quite a close eye on him since..." she trailed off for a second, as though she was thinking. "But with Assessment Day here, he'll be pretty busy. Cam might have been stationed somewhere in the Lower Beck, I guess."

"Right. We'll stick to the plan then."

"You're not alone?" Will sounded surprised.

"Nope. There are five of us."

I heard a low whistle of approval. "Anyone I know?"

"Hey, Will!"

"Tyler!" The pleasure in her voice at the familiar tone made me happy. "Anyone else?"

"Quin's here too," Rogers said.

"You ok, Quin?"

I murmured an agreement, keeping my voice as low as possible.

"Glad to hear it. There's a lot you should..." she trailed off and decided not to finish. "I'll let Cam tell you."

"The others you don't know." Rogers continued, "Better not to ask for now."

"Right. Well... good to know you're all still alive."

Her tone attempted humour, but there was a sadness behind it. I wondered what it was she had wanted to tell us. Before we could question her any further, she disappeared down the hillside and into the guard hut again.

We all shifted even further back, to make sure that Hall couldn't see us as he passed. Then we froze in silence until we heard his footsteps on the hill. He parted the fronds of overhanging leaves with confidence and moved smoothly into the forest, passing within inches of my own hiding place. I wondered for a second what I would do if he caught me, but I held my breath and within a few seconds he was gone.

Inching our way out of the cover of the trees, we made our

way swiftly down the hill, passing Will but not stopping, as we could not guarantee how long Hall would be gone. I was the last to pass her, she reached for my hand and squeezed it.

"So good to see you," she whispered. "You give me hope."

I paused for a brief moment, "Are things bad?"

She nodded gravely. "Yes. Cam's doing what he can, but well, since the escape it's been worse than usual."

I clutched at her hand, "I'm so sorry. I was meant to be here with you."

"I know." She smiled sadly. As I turned to leave, she did not let go of my hand. "He's missed you terribly you know."

I looked back at her, seeing nothing but honesty in her eyes. "Thank you. That means a lot."

She shook her head. "Just come back for us, won't you?"

I managed to nod in response, then hurried to join the rest of the group, hoping I would be able to keep my word.

When we reached the edge of the woods, we split up. Rogers was the first to leave, striding into the Patrol Compound as though he had only left it yesterday. I was to be the next to go. Tyler and the others would wait a few minutes after me before setting off, making sure that there was sufficient distance between us. The plan was for them to walk down to the Lower Beck and try to blend in with the general citizens as they went to and from their assessments. That way they could see the Hydro Plant, and the LS and Agric Compounds quite easily. We had agreed to meet them back at the boat later.

Crouching under cover of the trees, I tried to calm my racing heart. I had no idea who I would encounter at the Assessment Buildings, and whether or not Cam would be there. Still, the thought that I might be with him again in the next hour or so made my stomach churn. As I stood up to leave, my legs were like jelly.

To my surprise, Tyler also rose. "Look, if you see Cam, give him my—our best? Tell him we miss him."

"I will."

"And Quin?"

I stared at her, not sure what to expect next.

"Stay out of trouble, ok?" Her words were supported with a small smile that suggested forgiveness. I was glad to know she no longer held a grudge.

Taking a deep breath, I plunged deeper into the woods, heading for the Lower Beck. The route through the forest was familiar, and I jogged in an effort to push my body and distract my mind. When I broke through into the square on the other side, there were more citizens moving about: Lower Beck citizens making their way to the Assessments, Patrol staff beginning shifts, Sustenance staff clearing the first sitting away in the canteen. It felt strange to be back.

I did my best to blend in, my Patrol uniform at least allowing me more realistic freedom to roam in areas other citizens would not be found alone. I headed for the Assessment compound with as much confidence as I could muster, unsure what I would do when I got there. My heart pounded so loudly I thought it would explode from my chest, but no one seemed to be paying me any attention. As I moved past the Agric fields, I paused for a second to watch the few Supers who were manning them, and realised that I didn't recognise any of them.

Seeing a line of Agric citizens approaching, I picked up the pace and hurried past them with my head down. As the last one reached me, I noticed another figure up ahead. My heart sank as I took in the grey of his Governance suit. The man stood in the centre of the path, his head bent low over a clipboard. I froze. Since our escape, I had no idea what action had been taken, but I imagined that all Gov staff had been made aware of those who had escaped. I imagined being recognised, dragged off in handcuffs, and whipped. Wade's agonised face flashed into my mind and I could barely breathe.

Realising it would look odd for me to turn back now, I forced myself to continue in the same direction, keeping my stride as purposeful as possible and my eyes glued to the floor. As I reached the man, his grey legs were joined by another pair, clad in the blue of Patrol.

"How many through so far?" the first man was saying.

I was almost safely past when I heard the Patrol Officer's voice.

"We're making good progress. LS are done, and we're half way through Agric now."

Cam.

Consumed by blind panic, I lost concentration and my foot caught on an uneven section of the path. I pitched forward, unable to stop myself from tumbling to the ground. Until that point, they had not been paying me any attention, but I could hardly escape their notice now.

Endeavouring to keep my head low and face the opposite way, I pushed myself to my feet. I was aware of a figure, bending to help me. I had little choice but to take the proffered hand, knowing as I did that it was Cam's. As our skin made contact, a bolt of electricity shot through my body and I was unable to avoid his gaze. His eyes met mine and I felt rather than heard his sharp intake of breath. Fighting for control, he helped me to my feet before mumbling something about me being more careful and shoving me hastily in the direction I had been travelling.

It was then that the other man began speaking, "Where are you supposed to be right now, citizen?"

Cam stayed where he was, shielding me so I couldn't be recognised.

"She's very late if she's headed for a Patrol shift at the assessments," the Super clearly knew the shift patterns. "Changeover's not for several hours and the first one started a long while ago."

Cam's hand was hot against my back, and I could feel the sweat on my own palms. "Are you headed for the Assessments?"

"Yes," I muttered under my breath.

"This late for duty? Or do you have a message for someone?" Cam's voice was controlled, meaningful. "An officer in the Lincoln Building, perhaps?"

I understood what he wanted me to say, but not who I could safely say I was delivering a message to. I raised my eyes to meet his gaze, and watched as he mouthed something at me. After a second, I knew which name he had spoken.

"I've a message for Director Reed."

"I know where he is. I'll take you." He took hold of my arm and began guiding me in the direction of the Assessment buildings. Over his shoulder, he threw some final remarks at the Gov Super, who I desperately hoped was leaving, convinced by our charade, "I'll be back soon with more to report. Let me take care of this first. Must be important."

His voice trailed off as we continued up the path. His grip on my arm was tighter than it needed to be and he didn't loosen it, even when we were well out of the other official's sight. I remained silent, desperately hoping we had been convincing enough. We moved into the Lincoln Building, where the psych tests took place. Ignoring the citizens lined up outside the partitioned areas where the examiners worked, he guided me to the rear of the hall and into an empty cubicle. Once inside, he let go of my arm and stared at me for what seemed like an age, an indescribable expression on his handsome features. I stayed as still as I could, no idea whether he was angry, hurt, or overjoyed to see me.

Then he took a step and pulled me to him, almost crushing me in the process. I found myself being held so tightly I could barely breathe, his arms encircling me and his cheek pressed hard against the top of my head. After a moment I responded, putting my own arms around him and revelling in being close to him once more. We stood for several minutes, our breathing in time with one another's, our hearts racing. I felt his lips graze the side of my head gently as he planted a kiss tenderly. I wanted to stand there forever, despite the danger, but knew it couldn't last.

Chapter Twenty Eight

Eventually he released me slightly and backed away. I watched as his face darkened and he began to clench and unclench his fists. Fear crept into my heart as he turned his back on me and walked away, his jaw rigid.

"Cam, what's wrong?"

"What are you doing here?" He whirled to face me. "I told Rogers! I told him you weren't to come."

"Look Cam, there was no choice," I began, but he cut me off.

His face was like stone. "He promised he would leave you at The Crags, but here you are anyway."

"Look, Mason was exhausted. He was all set to come, and then he collapsed as they were about to leave." I paused, knowing I didn't have a lot of time to explain, "He's been..."

He closed his eyes, seeming not to hear me. Cautiously I moved closer to him, taking his hand and enclosing it in my own.

"Cam." I kept my voice low, aware of the possibility that we could be overheard. "Please listen. There's no time to explain. You just need to trust that there was no other way. It was the only option. I had to come, understand?"

He opened his eyes again, but his gaze was far from warm.

Releasing my grip on his hand, he twisted away from me. He moved instead behind the desk, and motioned to me to sit, as though this were an actual psych assessment. I obeyed, unsure what else to do. Once we were seated, I became aware of the tests going on around me, the hushed voices echoing eerily around the hall. I certainly didn't miss this.

Cam leaned closer so we couldn't be overheard. His face was still a mask of fury.

"I don't know how long we'll get away with being here." His voice was tense, urgent, "I know you need meds, and fast. I think I've found a way of getting hold of them for you, but right now I can't get away. It will have to wait a little while."

I stared hard at him, wanting him to relent, to smile, to give some sign that he had forgiven me. None came. Instead, he pressed me for answers.

"How did you get back?"

"Motorboat. With people from another community. Brecon Ridge."

"You trust them?"

I shrugged. "We hope we can. We didn't have much choice."

He was quiet for a long time, and I knew that behind the composed exterior, his mind was working overtime. I recognised the expression. I had seen it before, during Resistance meetings, when he was working on the wall defences, when he had been planning our previous escape. He wasn't even thinking about me now. And despite being glad to see me, he was also furious with me for coming. As I continued to wait for a response, something inside me snapped. I was angry too.

I fought to keep my voice low. "Cam, you have to believe me. I had no option but to come, Mason wasn't capable and there was no one else."

The silence continued, but something in his face twitched slightly, and I knew I had his attention. I continued, clasping my hands in front of me to keep them from shaking.

"I won't lie though. I wanted to come. And if you think I'm going to apologise, you're wrong. I've thought of you and Jackson every day since we got to The Crags. I felt so guilty about leaving. But it wasn't my fault! What happened that night was totally out of my control. Didn't stop me from worrying myself sick that you'd been blamed for our escape though. And then, when I saw the chance to come and find out for myself, I took it."

I reached out and grasped one of his hands.

"Why do you always get to be the one who worries about me? Don't you think I'm just as concerned for your safety?"

He looked away, staring down at the table and avoiding my eyes.

"Are we really back to this again? You being all protective, and keeping me in the dark, out of danger? Because I thought we were past that. And, if we are actually going to save Barnes and Blythe and Cass, we need to work together, don't we?"

There was a further pause, where he seemed to consider what I had said. Finally, he spoke. "Ok. Ok. I get it. You were as worried as I was." He raised his eyes to meet my gaze. "S'pose at least I know you're safe now. Until Rogers' radio call yesterday, I had no idea whether you'd even made it or not."

He reached across and placed a gentle hand on my cheek, "And it is good to see you."

My body shivered at his touch and, for a moment, I allowed my eyes to close. We sat quietly for a moment together. When I opened them he was looking directly at me again, his eyes warmer, kinder. Cautiously, I took his hand from my face and held it in mine, knowing the more intimate touch would distract me.

"Look Cam, I thought when we left... I knew... that you and Jackson would be in danger. What happened? How did you manage to escape that night? Did Gov suspect you were involved?"

A shadow crossed his face. He shifted to one side and pulled down the collar of his uniform. I could see the tell-tale welts on his back. I dug my nails into my palms, trying desperately not to gasp out loud. Somewhere at the back of my head, I had known this was likely, yet the confirmation still came as a shock. I had seen similar wounds before, but the sight of Cam's body carved up so violently felt like a knife slicing into my own skin.

"They whipped you."

He straightened his overalls, not needing to respond.

"And did you..."

For a moment I didn't think he would answer. When his voice came, he sounded far away, "I concocted a story. Said I was trying to prevent you all from leaving. They knew I was aware of the escape plan, but I think... eventually... they believed that I was attempting to stop you. They've said nothing to me since..." he gestured vaguely to his back, "...this. But I'm pretty sure they're keeping a close eye on me now."

I hated how much they had hurt him, wondering how long he had been tortured for. Fearful of his next answer, I made myself continue.

"And Jackson?"

"Well, she... she was hurt in the escape."

"I know. I could see her limping on to the beach as the

shooting started. I felt–" I broke off, unable to express my guilt, but hoping he would understand.

"I got her back to Patrol. That part wasn't too difficult. The Shadow Patrol were busy in the harbour, so we ran... well, I carried her mostly. There was no one around to catch us. They were all trying to stop the boat–"

He stopped and listened for a moment, ensuring that the usual bustle of the assessments outside carried on as normal. There was an agonising moment before he continued, and afterwards I wondered if he was simply delaying, trying to avoid delivering the next blow.

"She was in pain. I had to carry her the last part. I was hoping that, with a night's rest, she might improve, but..."

"What happened?"

He sighed. "She's in Clearance, Quin. I'm sorry."

"Her injury–" I paused, "–it wasn't fatal?"

He shook his head. "No, and I've been trying to help her, but it's harder than it used to be. Like I said, I'm sure they're watching me now. But I've had people keeping an eye on her. She's not in any immediate danger, as long as she keeps her head down. Her injury was just a sprain. She seems to have recovered. I think she's still quite strong."

"And after these next Assessments..." I dreaded his answer, terrifying nightmares of hundreds of souls being dragged under the water returning to haunt me.

He grimaced, "We'll have to wait and see. At the moment, I don't think they'll drown someone like Jackson. Not yet, anyway. There are far weaker people over there."

The thought didn't make me feel any better about my friend's position. For her to survive, others had to die. That was one of the many things that had appalled me about The

Beck since I had discovered the truth, and I knew Cam felt the same. We stared at one another for another moment before he tore his eyes away.

"Tell me more about what you need." I knew he was purposefully changing the subject, but let him continue. "Are you certain that you're dealing with some kind of mushroom-poisoning?"

"We think so. Several people are sick. Barnes is the most serious case, but Blythe and Cass probably also have it. We're pretty sure it came from them eating..." my voice almost failed me as I considered my role in the disaster, but I pressed on regardless, knowing at least I was trying to put it right, "fungi. They cook with it over there, but there are types which are safe and, well... this one probably wasn't."

"So, you're probably looking for something to combat the poison?"

I nodded, "If possible, or if not, maybe something to reduce or treat the symptoms of the illness."

"I see. And the symptoms are...?"

"Fever, sickness, dizziness, and disorientation."

"Ok, I know Montgomery has meds which treat all different kinds of things. The trick will be to work out which ones might be useful to you."

"She's going to give you access to them?" I was surprised that the fearsome Montgomery would commit such an act of treason, despite the feelings I knew she harboured for Cam.

"No. She and I... well let's just say we're not so close these days." He smiled, knowing the information would please me, "But I do have someone else who I think could be very helpful. He's been an ally since you left, to be honest. And his background is proving... useful, shall we say."

Curious to discover who else was working closely with Cam, I started to respond, but he held out a hand to stop me.

"Look, I have to go. They'll notice I'm not at my post. I think Reed has people watching me. And I need to get those meds for you. Soon, if the situation's as bad as you say."

I knew he was right, but was still reluctant to leave him. Despite his words, he didn't move and it seemed like he felt the same way. Sliding his chair back, he came around the table. I echoed his movements until we were standing mere inches from one another.

"I'll walk out first. Give me a few minutes, then follow. Walk like you're supposed to be here, and keep your head down. Perhaps wait until the next group of citizens leaves, then there'll be more going on and you're less likely to be noticed."

"What's the plan?"

"I have another half hour left on this shift before I can legitimately leave without anyone questioning me. Get back to the woods and walk up to Patrol. Wait for me at the hollow tree. Remember?"

"Of course I remember." I blushed, recalling the place where he had first kissed me, in an effort to distract some Patrol guards and hide Cass. Despite being unaware of his feelings for me and believing the kiss was purely a ruse, the embrace had demonstrated how I felt about him beyond a shadow of a doubt.

He took my hand again, his thumb tracing circles across the palm. I trembled at his touch and pulled away, unable to take the sensations it brought with it. There was a flash of hurt on his face which disappeared as rapidly as it had arrived. Then he was all business.

"I'll bring Anders with me and we can work out how we get the meds together."

"Anders?" I was startled by the familiar name, remembering a young man who had trained with me when I first reached Patrol, what felt like a thousand years ago now.

"Yes. He's ex-Dev. One of the only citizens ever to transfer over. Like I said, I don't see much of Montgomery anymore. She had started to get too…" he glanced at me, concern on his features, "close. And after the escape and…" he gestured to the scars on his back again, "she became a little suspicious. I backed off. And then I discovered Anders, who is almost as useful."

I felt a second surge of relief that Cam was spending less time with the very beautiful Montgomery, but didn't have time to dwell on the fact, as he was looking at me expectantly.

"I'll meet you there as soon as I can." He frowned, "Though I'd feel a lot better if it were Rogers I was dealing with."

Anger surged through me again, quashing all previous feelings of warmth. I backed away "Well it isn't."

His sigh was audible, "I have to go."

I was furious, my heart pounding in my head, my breathing short, yet I found myself wanting to stay with him anyway. And I suspected he felt the same.

He took a couple of steps towards the curtain which shielded us from view, then stopped and spun around, arriving at my side of the table without seeming to move, and pulling me to him. I found myself stumbling, my body slamming into his. He stopped me from falling and suddenly we were kissing greedily, our lips pressing hard against one another's, our breath coming in short gasps, our hands roaming over one another's bodies. I hadn't realised quite how much it had hurt to be without him until now, when I was finally with him again. And he seemed to feel the same way. This time there was no hesitation.

His tongue invaded my mouth hungrily, exploring, while his hands slid from my lower back to my waist, to my shoulders, where he moved them around to take hold of my face. I returned every part of the embrace with equal fervour, not caring, for the moment, that we might be caught, or how much trouble we would be in if we were. For now, all that mattered was the possibility that this might be the only time I was with him, alone, for a long time. And I was determined to make the most of it.

It was over long before either of us wanted it to be. We broke away simultaneously, some noise from outside of the curtain alerting us to the dangers of the outside world again. We stared into each other's eyes for one more moment before leaving.

"See you soon, Quin."

He turned once more, parting the curtain rapidly with a slash of his hands. Seconds later, the fabric was swaying gently back and forth, the movement causing a slight breeze to waft over me. The cubicle was empty. He was gone.

Chapter Twenty Nine

Once Cam had left, I waited a few minutes before peering around the curtain. The Lincoln Building had not changed: when Psych Assessments were going on, there was always a steady flow of citizens moving in and out. It wasn't difficult to attach myself to a line of Agric citizens and follow them outside. No one questioned me. As the group moved to the assault course for their physical, I slipped away and headed in the opposite direction. Agric was quiet as I passed, but LS was working normally, the men having finished their assessments.

I paused for a moment and watched the men working with the various animals. The barns echoed with the lowing of cows being milked and the clanking of buckets and tools. I realised I missed the taste of fresh milk, however rarely I had tasted it in The Beck. Access to livestock was something I had always taken for granted. Despite receiving small rations, the Beck food stocks were only ever in doubt if there was a large storm. After the uncertainty of hunting for food at The Crags, I could see how the Beck herds gave the community a huge advantage.

I was startled by a sudden movement close by. Shrinking back, I watched as another figure crept through the trees a few yards away. It was Tyler, on her exploratory circuit of the Beck with Hughes and McGrath. I searched the woods around her for a sign that the other two were close by, but could not see them anywhere. They were clearly keeping well out of sight. I decided to slip across and speak to them for a moment, feeling the need for reassurance. Just as I did, the cows thundered out of the barn behind me and galloped off into the fields beyond.

Momentarily distracted, I checked my position to make sure I couldn't be seen by the LS citizens who were driving the cattle. When I looked back, Tyler was gone. I waited for several moments, hoping I would spot her again, but she didn't reappear. Giving up, I moved off through the trees in the direction of the main square, where the main path exited the Lower Beck and wound through the woods to Patrol. It was deserted when I reached it, and I skirted the edges, trying not to attract attention.

Once I was safely under the cover of the trees again, I jogged through the woods until I reached the tree stump that Cam had mentioned. Concealing myself inside it, I settled down to wait. I realised I was hungry, and slid a hunk of bread out of my pack. Knowing I was well concealed, I didn't pay much attention to my surroundings as I ate, and heard several pairs of footsteps pass by over the next half an hour, presumably Patrol citizens making their way to various duties. Not one paused in its progress through the trees, until one set of footsteps halted close by. I froze.

If it was Cam, I was fine. But Cam had said he was bringing Anders, which would mean two sets of footsteps. My hands scrabbled in the dirt, searching for something I could use as a weapon. I had just armed myself with a small rock, when a voice from above startled me.

"Quin!"

Spinning to face the sky, I caught the side of my head on the trunk and winced. I could only see a dark shape above me, but the voice was familiar enough.

"Rogers!" I cursed and rubbed my head.

"Sorry," he dropped down beside me, half-in and half-outside the trunk. There wasn't enough room for his large frame. "Did you find Cam?

"I did."

My heart sank. If Rogers was here when Cam arrived, I knew he would be asked to accompany them instead of me.

"What's the plan?"

I considered sending Rogers away on some pretence, but quickly dismissed the idea, knowing how much was at stake.

"He's meeting me here. Any minute now. Has someone with him who can get access to the meds."

"Great." He shifted slightly, and motioned to his legs, which were cramped up underneath him, "Look, I'll hide somewhere else and come out once he gets here."

He moved away, finding a large tree close by and swinging himself into it with surprising dexterity for a man of his size. Once up in the branches, I couldn't see him at all, and I remembered how long he had managed to conceal himself in the Clearance passage. Rogers was a man built for this kind of mission.

We did not have long to wait before we heard the sound of footsteps again. With a better vantage point than me, Rogers dropped noiselessly to the ground and beckoned me out of my hiding place. Watching Cam approach brought back a flood of memories from the past. I knew I didn't want to be without him again, at least not for much longer. But I knew I could never come back to The Beck, at least not while Adams and Carter were still in charge.

Quashing any thoughts of revolution for now, I straightened up and attempted a smile. Anders was exactly the same, nodding his head shyly in way of a greeting. Cam's face lit up when he saw Rogers. The two of them clasped one another in a bearhug, and I resented the anger he had felt at my own appearance. When they broke apart, they were grinning. Watching their enthusiastic greeting, I waited for my inevitable dismissal.

"Like old times."

"Almost. Better get going though." Rogers warned, "We don't have time to spare."

"Better get going then."

Cam motioned to Anders, who began a rapid explanation which betrayed his nerves. "There's a storage base up in Gov. They keep things there which are strictly for their own use. I know there's a large number of meds up there. A variety, too. I'll give you a couple of different types, since I'm not sure exactly what will work. The base should be fairly easy to access as long as we can avoid detection. But with the Assessments going on all day, I'm sure there'll be fewer guards up there."

"Great." Cam looked relieved, "I was dreading having to access Dev again."

"The storage base does have security, but I think I can get us in."

"How can you get us in?" Rogers looked doubtful, "You're not even a Super!"

"He's ex-Dev," Cam explained.

Rogers looked shocked. Ignoring his reaction, Anders moved past him, heading in the opposite direction from Clearance. Rogers began to follow, but found himself stopped by Cam's arm.

"What is it?"

"Quin doesn't need to be here. Now we have you, I mean."

Rogers glanced at me and back at Cameron, who continued with his argument.

"She wasn't supposed to be here in the first place. I get that you had to bring her to make up the numbers, but now you're here. We have Anders, who can get us in, and me for back up. We don't need her."

I scowled at them both. Despite having anticipated this, it still hurt. Rogers again glanced between us, seemingly torn.

Cam pressed on, "Another body just makes us more visible. And I might find myself too concerned about protecting Quin to have my mind on the job."

I watched Rogers make his decision. The thought that Cam might not have his mind completely on the job worried him more than anything.

"I see your point." He turned to me, "Quin, you can head back to the Clearance guard post now. Get over to the other side if possible. Let Shaw and Howard know what's going on. Conceal yourself with them and wait for us to come back."

I glowered at him and he shrugged his shoulders, motioning to Cam. I knew there would be no changing his mind.

"We'll be..." he turned to Anders, "How long should this take?"

"No more than a couple of hours, as long as we don't run into any issues."

"Let Howard and Shaw know how long we'll be, help them get the boat ready to leave. Might need a quick getaway."

The task was unnecessary, created to make me feel more useful, but it didn't help. He set off after Anders, leaving me behind with Cam.

285

"Sorry, Quin." He didn't look in the least bit ashamed of his actions.

"You're not."

"I know how you feel... it's just... well seeing you, after so long apart, I can't... I won't..." He groaned in frustration, "If you're there I'll–"

"Fine." I turned to go, knowing I was punishing him for his feelings.

"Hey!"

He grabbed my arm and tried to swing me towards him again. At first I resisted, but seeing his hurt expression I gave in, allowing myself to be pulled into his arms. His kiss this time was different, sweeter, as though he wanted to dissolve my anger with it. I responded for a moment, pressing myself as close to his body as I could, but as I felt my head start to spin, I pulled back. I saw the flash of disappointment in his eyes before I spun away from him. I strode in the opposite direction, not wanting him to see my tears.

Once I was deeper in the trees, I kept going, heading for Clearance, trying hard to look as if I was supposed to be on my way there. My head was spinning, and I was finding it hard to slow my breathing. I tried to calm my racing pulse as I considered our success so far. I couldn't quite believe that we almost had the meds to help Barnes within our grasp. It felt like the mission should have been more difficult. We were almost there. But the fact that I had been excluded from the final stage was frustrating.

As I walked on, I realised that I would not see Cam again on this visit. Once we had the meds, we had to get straight back to The Crags. It was unlikely that he would accompany Rogers back over to Clearance. If Reed was keeping a close eye on him, the longer he was away from Patrol, the more chance there was that he would be missed. My tears continued to flow as I realised I wouldn't get to say goodbye again, and that I hadn't said any of the things I had promised myself I would.

As I reached the guard post, I paused to get hold of myself. To my relief, when I peered out from the trees, Will was there alone. Unable to believe my luck, I waited, to make certain that Hall wasn't merely inside the hut. When after ten minutes she hadn't moved or spoken to anyone, I felt it safe to assume that he wasn't there. Still, I approached with caution, skirting the edge of the area carefully and staying under the cover of the foliage until I was close enough to attract her attention.

"Will!"

She turned at my first call, and her eyes searched the leaves until she found me. A broad smile on her face, she crossed to me quickly, standing with her back to the bush I was crouched behind as she spoke.

"Hey Quin. You find Cam?"

"I did."

"I'm so glad." She glanced back at me for a second, frowning, "Hey you ok?"

I tried to smile, but suspected I didn't fool her. She sighed.

"Was he angry with you? Don't take it to heart, he's been under a lot of strain, worrying about everything. When I think of how long he's been waiting to see you," she rolled her eyes. "Where is he now?"

"With Rogers. They need to get the meds before we get back."

She placed a hand on my arm, "I get it. He sent you away to keep you safe, right?"

I nodded again.

287

"Typical. I'm sorry. If it helps at all, it shows he cares. Keeping you out of harm's way."

I knew this already. My mind had raced ahead, another thought striking me. We were nearing the end of the working day now, and I still had an hour or so before I knew the others would be back with the meds. I asked the question before I could think better of it.

"Will, what time does the shift end over in Clearance?"

She looked at me curiously, "Soon, I think. In twenty minutes maybe? Why?"

I didn't want to involve her in this any further, knowing how much she had helped us already.

"No reason. I just wondered."

She regarded me for longer, a puzzled expression on her face. Then, understanding dawned.

"I know why." She patted my shoulder, "Yes. The shift should finish in the next half an hour definitely. Then the workers will be let out. They usually have a little free time before their evening meal. For bathroom breaks and so on."

"Thanks."

"Look, none of the others in your group are back yet. You should have a little time. And we have a lot of equipment to transfer to and from Clearance today. Hall is over there at the moment. He didn't leave long ago, so if you get up into the trees now and hide, when he passes by and returns to me, I'll keep him distracted while you sneak away through the passage."

"Thanks," I squeezed her hand tightly before letting go.

I was immensely grateful for Will's support. She had always been reliable, and I was so glad she had been on duty today, of all days. Following her instructions, I headed up into the trees, concealing myself well until I heard Hall come striding by. Once he had returned to Will, I watched as she sent him inside the guard hut and stood, blocking the entrance as she talked to him. I wasted no more time, but pushed on through the passage, a plan forming in my head with every step I took.

Chapter Thirty

Once I reached the other side, I stared down into Clearance. It looked no different: the shabby-looking pods grouped in several areas up the hillside, the Warehouse at the bottom of the hill, the tiny building next door which passed for their canteen, and in the distance, the beach and the harbour with its three boats. I knew that the fourth boat was concealed around the rocks at the edge of the cove. That was where I was supposed to go. To sit. And wait.

But I didn't want to sit and wait.

Now I had spoken to Will, I knew what I was going to do. Jackson was here, in Clearance. Working in the Warehouse. If I could find her at the end of her shift, I would be able to do more than keep my promise to Mason to check on her. If I could get her to the motorboat without anyone noticing she was gone, and if the timing was right, we could take her back to The Crags with us. I'd done it with Harper. Admittedly under cover of darkness, but I had. If the others would be back soon, and I could time it so that I found her as she was leaving, it might just work.

I was suddenly overcome by an intense desire to see my friend. I ducked into the woods on the other side of Clearance and pushed my way through the branches, working my way around gnarled roots and ducking under tree limbs until I had made my way as close to the Warehouse as I dared. The space between my hiding place and the building which housed the Clearance workers was not vast, but enough that I would have to be careful when I tried to attract her attention. I considered borrowing a Clearance uniform and masquerading as a worker, but decided that if the shift was due to finish, the most sensible option was to sit here and watch as the citizens left.

It was at least another twenty minutes until anything happened. From my vantage point I had watched Hall travel down the hill with another load of equipment. I wondered if Tyler had made it back yet. I knew I could only wait for so long. And then a whistle sounded, jolting me out of my reverie. Immediately, I glued my eyes to the Warehouse doors. The citizens began to wander out in pairs and threes, all looking worryingly weak and exhausted. Most headed for the wash tents, a few going back to their pods for a moment's rest before the meal, which I knew would not provide them with sufficient energy after such a long day.

Finally, after most citizens had left the building and I had begun to give up hope, I saw her. She paused just outside the door, gazing at the sky. Once inside the Warehouse, Clearance citizens were deprived of natural light all day. There was a slight bruise on her left temple, and she was paler and thinner than I remembered, but still Jackson: the woman who had been my ally since the moment we began our Patrol training. As I tried to work out how I could grab her attention, she stretched her back, reaching her arms upwards, turning her body this way and that, as if unknotting the tension in her weary muscles.

I glanced back and forth. Currently there were no Shadow

Patrol visible, and few other Clearance citizens close enough to hear. I risked calling out her name, as loudly as I dared.

"Jac!"

She froze, having heard me, but clearly afraid to react. Slowly, under the guise of continuing to stretch, she worked her way closer to the foliage which concealed me.

I tried again. "It's Quin."

She bent down and touched her toes with some effort, and as she straightened up, whispered, "Washroom on the hill. Two minutes."

And then she was gone, continuing to stretch as she made her way slowly in the direction of the pods. I backed away as two Shadow Patrol made their way out of the Warehouse and began walking towards the dining hall. Studying the buildings on the hill, I worked out which washroom she meant. There were only two up there, and one was situated close to the sick-pods, which were separate from the rest. There was also a decent screen of trees behind it. Jackson had selected a meeting place which was as safe from Shadow Patrol as possible.

I skirted the path and kept under cover of the trees until I reached the right spot, then worked my way into position behind the washroom. For once I was grateful for the poor upkeep of the Clearance buildings. The pod was in bad repair and there was a large tear in the rear of the fabric. I watched Jackson approaching from the path. I glanced quickly back up the hill and spotted Rogers slipping in between the trees, heading for the harbour. Panic struck. I had to act now, or it would be too late. If Tyler was already back, I didn't know how long the group would wait.

Jackson was approaching the tent now. After checking that

it was unoccupied, she ducked inside. A moment later she emerged through the slit in the back of the small pod and suddenly, she was standing right in front of me.

We stared at one another for a few moments, frozen to the spot, and then a broad grin spread across her face and she covered the final distance between us with a few strides, enveloping me in a huge hug which almost knocked me off my feet. I returned her squeeze just as fervently. We stood welded together for a long time. When we broke apart, my shoulder was damp with her tears.

"Quin."

"Jac."

"Can't believe–"

"So sorry–"

"...actually here–"

"...couldn't wait–"

"...so worried."

Our speech overlapped for several seconds before we broke off and stared at one another again, grinning. Then I recovered myself.

"Look, Jackson, there isn't much time. I came by boat. But we're leaving. Now. If you want to come, you can, but we have to go now."

The look on her face told me all I needed to know. But I had to warn her.

"Look, we only have a small boat. There isn't much room. I promised Mason I'd find you, help you, but the others in the boat aren't expecting me to bring you back. We're only really here to get some meds. It's not supposed to be a rescue mission. What I'm saying is..." I paused, out of breath, "if you come with me, we might have to argue your case to be on the boat."

Her eyes flashed, "Oh I can argue. I was supposed to leave the first time, remember? And I risked my life to help the others escape." She broke off, her eyes pleading. "I don't think I can stand it here for much longer, Quin. Honestly, without you all, I can't do it. And the rations here are so small they wouldn't sustain a five-year-old Minor."

As she spoke, I remembered that she had yet to know about Davis, but decided that the news could wait until later. I beckoned her to follow me, and we made our way cautiously into the thick of the woods, heading in the direction of the harbour.

We began well enough, but soon I noticed Jackson had a slight limp and, although she tried to keep up with me, she was lagging behind. I slowed my pace as much as I dared, and soon we had reached the copse of trees closest to the beach. This was the difficult part. It was not quite dark yet, though dusk was falling, and there were now two Shadow Patrol officers guarding the beach. One was outside the guard hut, speaking into his walkie talkie. The other was walking the length of the beach, as if looking for something. Although there was no alarm currently, if they discovered the body of their colleague on the other side of the beach, I knew we'd all be in trouble. It was definitely time to leave.

Jackson's eyes roamed the open space, panic making them wild, "What do we do now?"

I put a hand on her arm, "Don't worry. We'll figure it out."

Her earlier bravery had disappeared, and I worried that her courage would fail at the last moment.

"Look, the boat's just the other side of those rocks. No one's noticed you're gone yet. We'll wait until the guard is as far away as possible and make a run for it." I glanced back at the hut and watched as the man disappeared inside it. "Look, that's one of them out of the way at least. And it's not far from here. I promise there's a boat waiting on the other side."

I could see her taking a deep breath, composing herself. I glanced across the space and was suddenly aware of another presence close by. My own breath quickening, I grasped the knife in my belt and prepared for a fight if necessary. A closer look revealed two pairs of eyes staring out at me from the bushes on the far side of the beach. Tyler. And Rogers. I heaved a sigh of relief, signalling to them and pointing at the guard on the beach so they would understand my plans. I couldn't see much of them, but Rogers signalled his understanding, and backed away. Tyler, on the other hand, remained, watching me closely, her eyes filled with suspicion.

We waited what seemed like an age, until the guard on the beach had made his way to the woods at the rear and disappeared, his flashlight beam lighting up the trees eerily. Our twin gazes travelled back to the second guard, who was thankfully still inside the hut. Knowing we didn't have long, I took Jackson's hand and together we raced silently across the small stretch of sand. Safe in the foliage on the other side, we glanced back. Neither guard had reappeared, and I fought back a sob of relief as I clasped Jackson's hand. We had made it. I could see the motorboat floating exactly where we had left it. Howard, Shaw, Hughes, and McGrath were already on board.

Next to us, Tyler's expression had morphed into one of fury. She turned her back and followed Rogers, who had already gone ahead to collect the wet clothes we had hidden earlier. I crossed the final distance to the water's edge with trepidation, knowing there would be consequences when it became clear what I had done. As we caught up with the others, Rogers turned to see us both and his face darkened.

"What do you think you're doing, Quin?" he hissed.

"I brought Jackson," my tone began as defiant, but ended in more of a squeak when I realised that he was as angry as Tyler. "Look, she'd been consigned to Clearance. She was supposed to be with us last time... I thought she—"

Rogers held out a hand which brooked no refusal. "Stop. We'll discuss it later. Right now we need to go, before her disappearance is discovered."

"I thought we were going to leave under cover of darkness?"

"We were. But that was when I thought we might manage to make the trip here and back undiscovered." He nodded at Jackson. "Now you've taken her, that's fairly unlikely. We might as well get out of here, before they realise she's missing. Don't want a firefight like last time. We all know how that ended, don't we?"

I realised there was no point in arguing and tried to be useful instead. There were several backpacks still on the shore, so I selected one and hoisted it on to my back. Jackson tried to follow suit, but recognising her weakness, Tyler relieved her of the burden, despite the pack she was already carrying.

"Just get yourself to the boat." Her words were not unkind. Clearly she blamed me and not Jackson for the transgression. "Ask Shaw for some food. You look like you need it more than anyone. Then try to rest."

We waded out to the boat with the remaining packs and Rogers handed them to Hughes, who was storing them in the various lockers underneath the seats. I noticed that Tyler attempted to keep hold of the one which she carried on her back, but eventually she had to allow Hughes to stow it away. We needed more space now we had an extra passenger, and the packs were full rather than empty. I realised that I hadn't fully considered the risk I had put the mission in, but I knew I couldn't have abandoned Jackson for a second time when she was in such a vulnerable position in Clearance. Once we had stowed the baggage, we began to clamber on board.

Shaw held out a hand to me, "You don't much like sticking to the plan, do you Quin?" he teased.

"It seems not." I accepted the gesture gratefully, noticing the colour in his cheeks, "You look good, Shaw."

"Howard and I managed to sleep in shifts while you were gone. There wasn't much else to do."

It made sense that our driver and guard should have rested. I only hoped the rest of us might manage a little on the return journey. It was hours since I had slept, and I was exhausted. The skyline showed dusk was fast approaching, and the cloudy sky meant it was darker than usual for this time of day. Rogers glanced across at the beach, calculating.

"Think now's as good a time as any to get going. We should row out in that direction," he pointed in the opposite direction from the one we had come, "as far as we can. When we're out of range, we start the engines and get out of here as fast as possible, ok?"

Howard began to hand out the oars, "I'll be ready."

As he leaned across to pass one to McGrath, there was a sudden cry of alarm from the beach. My blood ran cold. We turned as one to stare at the shore.

One of the Patrol guards stood at the water's edge, gazing out at us. He had clearly come out of the woods and made his way to the far end of the beach, in search of his missing colleague. His first shout had been one of surprise, but as he regained his composure, he bellowed into his walkie-talkie.

"Invaders at the far end of the Clearance beach. All Shadow Patrol head down here immediately!"

The words travelled across the water clearly, and I realised just how close we were to him. As the enormity of this hit me, Rogers gave a command of his own.

"Duck!" His voice seemed to scream inside my head. Disorientated, I was slow to react, until he followed it up. "Now!"

Chapter Thirty One

I laid myself flat against the floor of the motorboat, finding myself squashed almost nose to nose with Jackson. Her expression was one of pure terror, and she was breathing hard. Behind us, someone slammed the engine into gear and the boat began to throb, the vibrations rattling through our bodies. For a moment I was confused at the movement, but soon realised that, as we had been spotted, there was no further need for secrecy. Rowing would be a useless pursuit, slow and far more dangerous. The officer's shock had slowed his reaction, and this was our only advantage. With enough speed, we still stood a fair chance of getting away.

I twisted round to find Howard at the wheel, bent as low as he could manage and still control our rapid exit from the bay. The rest of us stayed down and waited, holding our breath. The boat lurched forward, but seconds later the engine cut out and we slowed again. As it did, we became aware of another sound, one which I had heard before. I felt sick with dread as I caught the unmistakeable slap of bullets hitting the water around us.

Howard turned the key once more, and the engine spluttered into life for a second before dying away again. "Come on. Come on!" I could hear the desperation in his voice.

"Take your time, man." The voice belonged to Hughes. "Don't panic."

"There are more of them coming," Tyler muttered, peering over the rim of the boat briefly. "We have to go."

"Get down, Ty!"

She let out a shrill scream as Rogers lunged across and thrust her on to the base of the boat. As he did, another bullet came slicing through the air, this time burying itself in the side of the boat.

"Howard," Hughes continued, still remarkably calm, "get us out of here, would you?"

I was comforted to find my hand tightly clasped in Jackson's, though I didn't remember either of us reaching out for the other. Our eyes met, and we shifted a little closer to one another. For the third time, Howard attempted to start the engine. It protested again, but instead of cutting out, this time it roared into life. The sound of the bullets was overpowered by the growl of the engine, and I heaved an inward sigh of relief. The boat leapt forward, once, twice, and began to make steady progress across the water.

As the boat travelled out of range, I curled up, my head in Jackson's shoulder to avoid anyone seeing the tears of relief which slid down my cheeks.

It was several minutes before anyone spoke. Once The Beck was a safe distance away, Hughes turned to the rest of us.

"Well that was close."

I marvelled at how composed he had remained throughout the entire attack. He seemed, if anything, to be invigorated by recent events. I wondered if he was truly unaffected, or whether he was simply good at hiding his feelings. Either way, I could see why he was a good leader. Howard had been panicking until his intervention, and panic led to mistakes. By calming him down, Hughes had ensured our getaway.

He straightened up and looked behind, "There are lots of them lined up on the shore now, all in black, but we're out of range. They can't reach us."

He settled himself back on the bench and waited for the rest of us to join him. I was slower to respond, cautiously rising to my feet and checking he was correct about the distance we had travelled from the shore, before lowering myself on to the bench again.

Once everyone was seated, he was back to business. "Well, The Beck's an amazing place. It's larger than The Ridge, and has far better resources."

For a moment, we didn't react, but eventually Rogers found his voice.

"How much of it did you manage to see?" he questioned, glancing at Tyler, who looked pointedly away.

"A fair amount. Most of the Sectors in the Lower Beck: Agric looks to have some extremely large fields cultivated. The fact that they have livestock is amazing. We also saw sections of the wall, a little of Patrol, the Solar fields, the Hydro Plant. And we didn't get into the Dev Sector of course, but all the meds they're working on developing sound amazing."

"Dev's definitely an interesting Sector." The words came from my left, McGrath joining the conversation, her face unreadable, "And certainly unlike anything we have at The Ridge."

I was startled by her sudden contribution, after she had been mostly silent throughout the journey. I stared at her curiously, wondering what her take on the Beck was. She gazed out to sea and said nothing more. The noise of the engine made it difficult to speak continuously, and perhaps sensing the tension, Hughes stopped talking and closed his eyes.

I leaned closer to Jackson, whose head leaned heavily against my shoulder. Placing a hand on her cheek, I realised that she was sound asleep already and hoped she would manage to rest for the remainder of the journey. The news about Davis would have to wait. Hopefully she would feel stronger when she woke. I shifted in my own seat, hoping to get some rest myself. But there was one question I needed answered before I allowed myself to shut off.

Leaning across Jackson's sleeping form, I tapped Rogers' arm. He turned to me, his eyes conveying less anger now we had put a good amount of distance between us and The Beck.

"Did you get them?"

"We did." He frowned, "You know how much danger you put us all in back there, don't you? It was a stupid thing to do."

I hung my head, unable to meet his gaze.

He continued, "Now they know we were there, they'll check things, make inquiries, question people. You might well have put others in danger."

I thought of Cam, and Will, and Anders with terror. Seeing the expression on my face, Rogers recognised he had got through to me and could see that I was already chastising myself enough. Ever practical, he turned away and pulled one of the bags from the lockers beneath him. He began to look through its contents as best he could in the cramped space, reading the sides of the different containers of pills. I shifted until Jackson's head rested more comfortably on my shoulder, his words continuing to plague my thoughts.

We travelled on as it grew dark, most of us managing to grab a little sleep. As the boat pulled up in The Crags bay at dawn, we hurried to unload our precious cargo into the rowboat. It took two trips to shore, with Hughes rowing the second time, but eventually we all stood on the rocky beach once more, ready to race the meds back to the dorms. There had been little radio contact with The Crags on the journey, aside from a brief message from Nelson in response to our own, stating they were eager for our return. But the beach was deserted as we arrived.

Rogers and Shaw hurried ahead, taking the two backpacks with the meds. Tyler, Jackson, and I were next, and had the remainder of the kit to carry back. Hughes helped us hoist the backpacks onto the rocks before turning to leave, but Tyler grasped hold of his arm. He turned, surprised.

"Thank you," Tyler's voice was uncharacteristically gruff.

"No problem. I hope that I didn't get you into trouble." He nodded up at Rogers, disappearing rapidly up the cliff side, "And that we've shown you we can be trusted."

"I think you have."

She stood awkwardly, staring back at him. Jackson and I shifted, eager to return to the others, but Tyler seemed unable to move.

Hughes reached out and squeezed her shoulder briefly, "I hope everything's ok when you get up there."

I wondered what had happened as they had navigated The Beck together. They certainly seemed to have grown closer. She shook herself, as though her thoughts had been elsewhere. "Me too." Almost as an afterthought, she added, "We'll be in touch soon."

"I'll be waiting."

Hughes moved swiftly back to the boat, and still Tyler remained where she was, almost frozen to the spot. We watched as he began to row back to the others.

"Ty? You ready?"

Abruptly she spun round and faced us, her face unreadable, "Sure. Let's go."

And with that she set off up the path at her usual breakneck speed, daring us to keep up.

In the end, we couldn't. Jackson was not strong, and I felt the guilt bite at me again when she couldn't keep pace with me. I slowed deliberately, not wanting to make her feel bad, and we watched Tyler disappear into the distance.

"I'm sorry," Jackson puffed, "I wish I could be faster."

I smiled, "Don't worry—we'll have you back to strength in no time. You should see Harper now."

She managed to return my smile weakly, "It's killing me I can't race up there. I can't wait to see Mase."

"You will soon, I promise." I stopped for a moment, my hand on her arm, "Jac, wait a second. There's something I need to tell you."

She stopped immediately, as if she understood the significance of my news.

"It's Davis." I began, and then didn't know how to go on.

She waited patiently, the same old Jackson. Her considerate nature made me so happy to have her back, but I wished I was able to protect her from my next statement.

"He was hit by a bullet as we left Clearance that night." I took a deep breath, "He didn't make it."

Her face paled, but she didn't cry. For a moment, I wondered if she had taken it in. I glanced away, unable to take the pained expression on her face, and noticed Nelson had appeared at the top of the path.

"Jac, I'm so very, very sorry."

I guided her onwards as Nelson approached. Even from several metres away, his face sent a cold chill through my body. When he reached us, he clutched my arm tightly and bent to catch his breath.

"What is it, Nelson?"

"The sickness."

"Did Rogers bring you the meds?"

He nodded, "Baker's looking at them now, working out who to give them to."

"Who to give them...? I don't understand."

"Quin, whatever this is has got steadily worse. Green came back with Mason in tow the night you left. It wasn't just fatigue. I had to carry him the final distance, he was so weak. We put him in the second dorm, like Barnes and the others. He started throwing up before morning and hasn't improved since."

I heard a sound to my left and remembered Jackson's presence. Turning, I saw the flash of fear in her eyes and slid a comforting arm around her neck.

"Wait, it's ok. The meds. We have the meds now."

Nelson looked enquiringly at us, momentarily distracted from his message.

"Nelson, this is Jackson," I began, "we brought her back from The Beck, she was in Clearance. She-"

"How is he?" Jackson's voice was desperate. "Mason? Is he really bad?"

Concerned about the impact of the news on Jackson so soon after learning of Davis' death, I took her hand and turned back to Nelson to quickly explain, "Mason and Jackson are... close. And they haven't seen one another since... well since we left the Beck. Jac was left behind, but she's here now, and..."

Nelson frowned, "Look, whatever this is, it isn't poison from the mushrooms. Like I said, Mason started with it, and he hadn't touched the soup. Barnes has been going steadily downhill. Cass and Blythe both have it too, but somehow not as badly. I guess it affects some people worse than others."

"So what is it?"

"Baker and Green think it's some kind of virus. They were reading up on it, until..."

My heart sank, "Until what?"

Nelson seemed paler than before, and I knew what he was going to say before he opened his mouth to deliver the blow.

"Until Green got sick."

Chapter Thirty Two

I took a deep breath, "How bad?"

For a moment, Nelson did not respond.

"Nelson!" He looked startled at my tone, "How bad is Green?"

"She's not great. Along with Cass, Mason, and Barnes. They're the worst affected so far."

I glanced at the dorms in the distance, dreading the scene that awaited us. I tried to stay calm and practical and continued with my questions. "How many people are sick?"

He frowned. "Around half."

I couldn't stop the gasp that escaped from my mouth. "Half?"

"It's weird though. Some people definitely have it worse than others. We have all those showing symptoms in dorm two, and those who are less sick trying to care for those who are very sick."

"Who's taken charge?"

This time, the reply was instantaneous, "Baker."

When I thought about it, I could imagine Baker delivering orders and responding without emotion in a crisis. I found myself feeling glad that she was the one delivering the orders and wondered what could be done to support her.

"What are the healthy people doing? How can we help??"

"We've abandoned the usual schedule. There are still people hunting, as food is obviously a priority, but we've had to let the watch lapse." He paused, as though he was trying to gather his scattered thoughts.

It was difficult to be patient and I couldn't help urging Nelson to continue. "What else do we need to know?"

"There are eight people in dorm two. Four of them are seriously ill." He seemed to pull himself together and continued with more conviction, "We've been passing food in to them. Soups and stews, which should be simple to eat, but hopefully build up their strength. The only work being done has been people hiking up to fetch supplies—vegetables and greens... and like I said, a couple of people have gone to try and shoot or snare some meat. And we have been trying to keep the healthy people away from the second dorm as much as possible."

As he paused again, I tried to think. My head was spinning. The repercussions of this were huge. If the sickness couldn't be stopped, would we all die here? A thought struck me.

"If this wasn't the mushrooms, where did it come from?"

He shuddered visibly, "I don't know. Green was hopeful that with the right kind of meds, ones which could ease the symptoms—cool the temperature, prevent the vomiting—most of us could get through it. And develop what she had read was called immunity... like we'd get used to it too, and it wouldn't be such a threat anymore?"

I began to understand. It made sense. "Anders gave us a selection of meds, because he wasn't sure what would work. Rogers took a look at them on the way back. I guess we have to figure out which we think will work, and administer them as fast as possible to those affected, then... then see who..." I struggled to finish the thought.

He nodded sombrely.

Beside me, Jackson took a deep breath. "Can I see Mason?"

"I'm sorry, you can't." Nelson said, not unkindly. "You're not affected by the virus. You haven't come into contact with it. We can't risk you getting it."

"But how do you know? How is it passed on?"

"We're not sure. Baker seems to think it's physical contact between people."

"Then how did Mason get it?" I demanded, thinking back to the events leading to the illness, starting with Barnes' arrival back on The Crags.

"It took us a while to work that out." Nelson took a deep breath, "Turned out he helped Cass bring Barnes up from the beach the day The Ridge brought him back."

I thought back to Barnes' lack of strength, which was due, no doubt, to the sickness, as well as the ill-treatment he had received from The Ridge guards. Cass had been close by, been asked to assist him in walking back up the path. I had stayed behind to help collect the weapons and store them away. When I got back to the dorms, Cass had already delivered Barnes to the dorm and begun taking care of him. She had never mentioned Mason.

Nelson read my mind, "When Green got Mason back up here and realised he was sick, the same kind of sick as Barnes, she questioned Cass. It turns out she was struggling with Barnes half way up the path, and stopped to rest. Mason came past, realised they were in trouble, and offered his support."

"Just like him to try and help," Jackson's comment was soft.

"Yes. But once he was sure that Cass could cope, he headed off to the mine, got back to work. No one saw him for a while, and when he collapsed on the beach we mistook it for exhaustion because he'd been working so many shifts."

"The mine?" Jackson was distracted for a moment.

"There's a lot to fill you in on, but for now I think we should get up there and see what we can do." I started walking in the direction of the dorms, but Nelson held out a hand to stop me.

"One last thing. Baker decided that we shouldn't tell Rogers about Green yet. He knows the illness is contagious, but that's all. She wants him to focus on looking at the meds, deciding which ones should be the most effective, before she tells him..." He looked desperately sad. "You can imagine how he'll react."

I could. We reassured him that we agreed Baker was taking sensible precautions with Rogers, and began the walk back. Our steps were hurried, but part of me wished it would take us forever to reach the centre. The buildings were quiet when we arrived, and we hurried after Nelson into the main building and the dining hall. Baker stood at the front with Rogers, Shaw, and Tyler, who were laying out the different meds on the table in front of them. She looked up as we arrived.

"Presume Nelson has filled you in?"

"Mostly, yes. What can we do?"

She gestured at the table, "We've done everything we can for them, aside from..." she gestured at the pills in front of her. "It'll be up to the meds now." She pointed at them. "Rogers is deciding where they can have the most impact. Anders gave him some guidance, and I've been reading up on some basic treatments too. I'm hoping that we can work out what we have here, and make a decision as to which are most likely to work, and who to give them to."

"Shouldn't everyone get them?"

"Not necessarily. There may not be enough for everyone.

And not everyone is sick yet. We need to give the meds to those who can actually benefit from them. I think some of these may help to reduce fever and relieve the symptoms of the sickness. Barnes is by far the worst, but there are others," she shot a rapid glance at Rogers which he thankfully didn't seem to notice, "who are also seriously affected."

Rogers looked up from the containers he had set out in front of him. "We're working on the premise that this is some kind of virus or bacteria from The Ridge. We've never come into contact with them before. And Barnes spent quite some time over there, so it makes sense that he would be the sickest, having been exposed to whatever this is for the longest."

"But that means that those who have had it for less time could get far worse over the next few hours." Baker's words were terrifying, but made sense. She glanced down at the meds on the table. "I doubt very much that there will be a cure-all here for an illness The Beck has never seen. I'm hoping that by relieving the symptoms, people's bodies will be more able to fight this on their own. The best we can do is distribute the suggested dose of meds to everyone affected."

There was a small sound from my side, and I looked to see Jackson stumble sideways. She was extremely pale and a sheen of sweat shone on her forehead.

"How long has she been like this?" Baker's tone was sharp.

"Not sure. We brought her from Clearance, so she wasn't in the best of health to begin with." I stammered a little, "I– I– I was sure that bringing her here would be the right thing to do... make her stronger..."

"Well I think it's fairly unlikely she has the same sickness as the rest of us, but you'd better isolate her just to be safe. Direct her into dorm two." Baker moved her gaze to Jackson, her eyes blazing. "Stay away from the private rooms, Jackson. Keep to the far end of the dorm, unless you want to get very sick."

Baker turned back to the table of meds. Her words seemed harsh, but I suspected she was right. Despite her formidable exterior, Baker had shown that she cared about people, but was also able to put aside her feelings when necessary. Suddenly I found myself glad that she had taken charge.

I turned to go but halted again at the sound of her voice, "Do not be tempted to take her in there yourself Quin. Just show her where it is. We don't need anyone else getting sick!"

Motioning to Jackson to follow, I headed out of the canteen. When we reached the relative privacy of the hallway, I turned to my friend.

"I'm so sorry to bring you back to this."

She shrugged. "I'd rather be here than back there. At least I'm closer to Mason, even if he is—"

She faltered, her bravado dissolving at the thought of the danger Mason was in. I found myself wishing I could comfort her but knowing I should steer clear of anyone who was showing symptoms of illness. I attempted a sympathetic look and jerked my head at the dorms.

She followed me out into the courtyard in the direction of the second dorm. Stopping a safe distance from the door, I stared at it, wishing I could see what was going on inside but knowing that Baker was right.

"That's it over there?" Jackson's voice sounded small.

"Yes. I'm sorry I can't come in with you." I paused, not knowing what else to say. "I wish I could. But the people in there are nice. They'll take care of you. And I'm sure this will be over soon."

"I hope so."

She started walking away from me, but Baker's words and my own desire to see how the people inside the dorm were doing came back to me. "Jackson!"

She stopped and turned. I tried to consider the effect I wanted my words to have. "I know you'll want to see Mason..." My eyes pleaded with her to listen to me. "But don't. Please. He's being looked after by people who have already been exposed to whatever this is. There's nothing you can do for him right now, d'you hear me?"

She stared at me for a moment, her face pale and her eyes haunted. She nodded. Just once, and barely long enough to confirm that she had understood what I was trying to say. And then I watched, as the friend I had just risked everything to rescue limped away from me, opened the door to the second dorm and slipped inside.

Chapter Thirty Three

As I watched her disappear, I found myself fighting a tide of fear which threatened to totally overwhelm me. We had managed to get the meds, escaped The Beck without injury, and I remembered only an hour ago feeling like we had managed to save the day. Now it all felt very long ago, a hollow victory, if those left at The Crags were so sick. I wasn't even sure which of The Crags citizens were inside the second dorm: the only ones confirmed sick at this point were Barnes, Mason, Blythe, and Cass. But Baker had mentioned others. I went cold at the thought.

The door to the building behind me banged open and jolted me from my stupor. I turned to see Rogers, closely followed by Baker. Their voices were raised and the older woman appeared to be racing to keep up with Rogers' long stride. As they got closer, Baker shot me a look that told me the worst had happened.

He knew.

"Rogers, no. I know you're frightened for her, but you can't go in there. We've worked hard to keep the sickness contained." She raised her voice as she delivered her final blow. "We have to keep the healthy people healthy."

"I don't care! I—"

"I said no! I've been running the show here since you left and Green fell ill, and I've been fighting hard to keep things going. You're not ruining that now."

She finally got ahead of him and stood directly in his way. He moved to get past her and she laid a warning hand on his chest. Again, I admired her boldness. I had seen her in action with Thomas, and though I doubted she could beat Rogers, I knew she would give him a run for his money. I could also see how torn he was between his respect for her and his concern for Green. He paused, and glanced left and right, as if deciding whether to barge past the older woman. Baker pressed on, using the softest voice I had ever heard from her.

"Rogers. You have to trust me. There's a system in place. Look, we've decided on the meds we think are best now, and how many we should give to each of the people in that building. By morning, we should see some improvement. Those who aren't too sick will pull through, I think. The four worst sufferers... well I'm not sure," she hurried on, "but we'll do our best. We'll give them a double dose... What harm can it do? I promise..." I could see how hard she was squeezing his arm, "I promise Green will be given the best care possible. It's only because we have her research that we can act so quickly and understand which of the drugs stand a chance of working. She wouldn't want you to get sick too and be unable to continue work here, would she? All we've achieved, all you've managed... Don't let it be over now, because of one stupid decision."

She stopped talking and stared at him, her eyes filled with concern, but her words seemed to have the right effect. Rogers had not moved any closer to the dorm and it seemed as though the fight had gone out of him. He took a step back and stared mournfully at the dorm ahead. Baker used the opportunity to steer him firmly to the first dorm.

"Look, rest, will you? You haven't slept. You've been awake for god knows how long now. Please understand Rogers, we all know you've done everything you can to help us. There's nothing more you can do for now, except get yourself rested and ready for whatever tomorrow brings. Ok?"

She glanced to the side and spotted me, "Quin. Go with Rogers. Take him into the dorm and make sure he gets some sleep. I need to get these meds to Marley and Price. When he's settled, come back to me. I'll need you."

"Got it." I moved closer to Rogers, taking his hand in mine.

As she turned to leave, Baker looked back to Rogers, "You've done all you can. Now rest. And don't think I'm above locking you in a room if that's what it takes!"

I had no doubt that she was serious. I escorted Rogers, who was slightly calmer now, into the dorm. It was empty. He glanced into his usual room and blanched visibly.

"Can't," he muttered, "not without..."

"That's fine," I reassured him, guiding him into an empty bunk and sitting him down. He seemed almost unable to function. He managed to slip off his boots and lie down.

"Rest up," I whispered, "I'll check on Green for you. I promise."

His eyes were open but he didn't respond. It was daylight, and I wondered if his mind would allow him to grab even the shortest of naps. I hoped for his own sake that he could. Still I feared the nightmarish quality of our current reality would prevent him from getting any kind of meaningful rest. I knew that I wouldn't manage to sleep at the moment, and with my mind racing, headed back outside to look for Baker and see what else could be done.

I could see Baker at the door to the second dorm, keeping back but gesturing with her hands and pointing at the containers of meds she had left on the porch. I strained my eyes, but couldn't make out who she was talking to on the other side of the door. Giving up, I leaned against the porch of the dorm, trying to calm my racing mind. It was clear Baker had done what she could to keep things going here, but if the meds didn't work, we were in real trouble. A weary-looking Nelson came out of the main building, rubbing a hand through his beard.

"You ok Nelson?" I took his arm, "Not feeling ill yourself?"

He paused for a minute and placed a hand on the back of his neck before replying, "Don't think so. No temperature at least. I'm just a little tired."

"I'm sure. So what needs doing?"

"Everything. Nothing." He sighed, "I don't even know any more. We were waiting for you to get back, but you're just as tired as we are. To be honest, I think all we can do is get the meds into as many citizens as possible. Wait for them to work. Or not."

"They'll work," I tried to sound reassuring, but wasn't sure I'd managed it. "They have to."

"I think we have food enough for today and tomorrow at least. Baker made sure everyone had a job and we were just focusing on the essentials. Those of us outside have been stocking up on food and helping out in the kitchen while the ones in the bunk looked after each other. It was working quite well until Thomas and his cronies walked out."

"Wait! Walked out?"

He grimaced, "You didn't hear? Thomas left with Allen

and Johnson this morning. Didn't even tell anyone they were going."

"Why?"

"Why d'you think?" he snorted. "Frightened for their lives and too cowardly to stay and help."

I stared at Nelson in horror, my mind wildly lurching through possibilities. "Where've they gone?"

"Only up into the hills, we think. Hiding out in the caves, probably." Nelson stretched as though it were painful to do so. "They've been on duty there enough times now. They know the mine."

"But how will they–?"

"Oh, they took supplies with them. Some food stores, guns, some clothes, and bedding. They planned quite well."

"Do you think they'll come back??"

He shrugged, "Not sure they know themselves. Perhaps they'll come back in a couple of days, thinking we'll all be dead? Then they'd have the place to themselves. I don't know. I'm not even sure Johnson wanted to leave. I think Thomas and Allen persuaded her—safety in numbers."

I forced myself to relax the fists my hands had unconsciously formed. Shaking them out, I tried to breathe more slowly. Hearing footsteps approaching from behind, I turned to see Harper walking across the courtyard towards me. I had never been so glad to see anyone in my entire life. She walked slowly across the courtyard, dumping a heavy-looking backpack onto the ground as she approached. I hurried to embrace her, but stopped short when I realised she also had a sleeping Perry strapped to her chest. She smiled apologetically and took hold of my hand instead as Nelson continued.

"Was just telling Quin about Thomas."

Her face clouded over, "The less said about him, the better. They'll have a hard job coming back once this is all under control."

I stared at her, "Under control?"

"Sure." Her voice was steady, calm, even. "You brought the meds back right?"

"We did."

"I knew you would. So now things will be alright." She held out a hand as Nelson went to argue, "I'm not saying they'll be perfect, but they have to be better than they've been for the last twenty-four hours."

There was silence for a moment. Perry snuffled in her sleep and Harper rubbed her lower back wearily. "She's getting heavy."

"Can you put her down now that she's asleep?"

"Hopefully. My job was to keep her out of the way." Harper gestured at the second dorm, "Blythe was the key to looking after Barnes and Cass, to start with, and then Mason and Green. She's the only one who's been around the worst affected, yet she doesn't seem to be as seriously ill as the others."

"She's been worried sick about Perry catching it. Made us all promise to keep Perry as far away from them as possible. Not that we would ever have put her at risk," Nelson added.

"Baker made me promise," Harper continued, gesturing to the older woman, who still stood on the dorm porch giving instructions about the meds. "Walker and I had her with us all last night and I took her up to the fields today." She turned to Nelson, "Speaking of Walker, seen anything of him?"

"Not yet," Nelson replied, "Been waiting for him to get back actually. I was going to store anything he'd caught before I went for a rest."

Harper glanced anxiously up at the hillside, "He won't come back til he's caught something. I know him."

I squeezed her hand, trying to reassure my friend, "There are more of us now we're back though."

"Sure, but you must be tired too. We'll all have to rest at some point."

I heard Baker's footsteps on the dorm porch and turned to see her making her way back to us. At the same time, Tyler came out of the main building. They headed from their respective directions across the courtyard, their faces serious.

Baker reached us first. "I've passed the meds to Marley and Blythe. Anders gave us a couple of different types. There's one which should help to ease the symptoms, hopefully allow people's bodies to fight off whatever this is, but he also gave Rogers a couple to combat infection. Since we're not sure what this is, we're going to try both. They have instructions to distribute them to everyone, and a double dose to the four worst affected." Baker looked around at our little group, "It can't do any harm."

She stared around at us, as if calculating who could be given which job next. Then she blinked a couple of times, and her expression softened, "We all did well today. Whatever we did, we tried our best. They have the meds. And we have enough food for the meanwhile, though we will have to get someone out hunting again later. We can give them another dose in a few hours, but for now we have to just wait and see how well they work."

"Baker, you've done wonders," Tyler put a hand on the older woman's arm. I expected her to shrug it off, but she let it remain.

"Not sure you could call it wonders, Tyler. I just stepped into

Green's shoes when she couldn't walk any further. Someone had to."

"But it was you who did... while others ran away."

"I suppose." She frowned. "Wait til I get my hands on those three. To leave was bad enough, but to steal food from the mouths of the sick? It's disgusting!"

The angry murmurs around the group confirmed we all felt the same way, we were all exhausted and Baker was right: without rest, none of us would be able to function for much longer. I longed for someone to suggest getting some sleep, but didn't want to be the one to do it, especially if there was more we could do.

Baker sighed, "Sorry, I'm just tired. Look, we've done everything we can for now. Let's get some rest."

I could feel the relief flooding across the little group. Harper set off in the direction of the dorms, eager to lay her tiny burden down. I looked around at those who were left.

"I'll take the first shift, wait for Walker to get back," Nelson volunteered.

I expected Baker to argue, knowing how tired Nelson was, but instead she reached for his hand and squeezed it tightly, "Thank you. I'm not sure I could stand for another second."

We all watched as she followed Harper to the first dorm and disappeared inside. Nelson motioned for us to follow and Tyler and I followed in his wake, in step with one another for once.

"You shouldn't have gone back for Jackson you know," she began, "but I understand why you did."

"Thanks," my voice was a whisper, but I hoped my gratitude for her forgiveness was clear.

She paused for a moment and shifted from one foot to another, seeming uncomfortable. "Quin, look, I did something stupid. And I figure what with your own actions, rescuing Jackson and all, you might just be the only one who understands."

Surprised at the admission, I waited for her to continue.

"While we were over in The Beck, I saw Harris."

I remembered the Gov Super who had been part of our rebellion.

"He was down in the Lower Beck, checking on the Assessments. I caught him in a quiet moment, managed to speak to him. He was happy that we were safe and said he had something to show us. On our way back up to Clearance he caught up with me and handed me some files. Told me to bring them back to The Crags. He wanted them kept safe."

"What was in them?"

"Not sure. I didn't have much time to look while we were over there. I managed to glance at them briefly while we were waiting for you to get back. Just saw the first page really. They looked like some kind of records, from when The Beck was first established. There were definitely names, and some figures. I stowed them in my backpack for safekeeping. When we got back to the boat though, and there was no room, Hughes took it off me and stowed it in one of the storage lockers and I didn't want to get it out and look at it with The Ridge folk around." She paused, a look of horror settling over her face, "But in all the chaos and panic over the sickness, I only just realised that it was the one bag we didn't come back with."

"You think Hughes kept it?"

"I don't know. Maybe it was just left behind accidentally. It's possible. But it means The Ridge might have access to some sensitive information." She grimaced. "Which was my whole reason for not looking at it in front of them in the first place!"

"You have to tell the others."

She paled and I realised how frightened she was. Tyler was always calm, always sensible, and I wondered if this was the first time she would have to admit any kind of failure.

"I know... I will, it's just... well with everything going on..." She grimaced, and took a breath. "You're right. I'll tell them, I promise."

There was a moment's silence before she changed the subject, clearly wanting to move on from her admission. "How was Cam?"

I found myself startled at the question. Seeing Cam felt like something which had happened days ago.

"Ok, I guess. He managed to get the meds for us anyway. It was... good to see him."

"But it must have been hard to leave."

"Yes." I suddenly felt a little dizzy, and blinked hard.

She peered at me, an unexpected look of concern crossing her face, "How are you feeling?"

"I'm ok. Just tired, that's all. Nothing a little sleep won't cure."

I was glad that Tyler was speaking to me again. Under the circumstances, our previous arguments seemed petty. We needed each other even more now. In the dorm I headed for my old bed, more conscious than ever that the beds either side of me were empty now that Mason and Cass were elsewhere. Lying down without even removing my overalls, I doubted my ability to sleep, despite my exhaustion.

In addition to all the stress and the worry of the past few hours, and the tiredness which had taken over my body, I also had another concern.

I felt sick.

Chapter Thirty Four

I did manage to sleep, but woke several hours later in the darkness, knowing that I had to get to the bathroom. I staggered up the centre of the room, only half awake, my legs propelling me instinctively in the right direction. When I reached my goal, I threw myself into a stall and emptied the contents of my stomach into the bowl. I retched until there was nothing left, and then sagged, panting, against the door. Wiping a hand across my forehead, I felt a sheen of sweat which had not been present when I went to bed.

After a few moments I was able to stand again and made my way shakily into the dorm. I felt better for throwing up, but knew it wasn't a good sign. Wrapping a towel around my face, I went to wake Tyler.

She sat up the instant I said her name, and I knew she had been sleeping on alert. She stared at me, her eyes wild, and clutched at my sleeve. I backed away, not wanting to get any closer than I already had, though I knew it was probably too late for that.

"I've just thrown up." I watched as the significance of the words sank in.

"What? You've..."

"Yes. I don't feel too bad, but I'm going to move next door

and get some meds just in case."

"Want me to–?"

I shook my head, "No. I'm fine. I just didn't want you wondering where I was."

"Ok." She sank back down on to the pillows, but didn't look like she would be getting any more sleep. Part of me was sorry I'd had to wake her.

When I reached the second dorm it was quiet. I reached out for the handle and opened the door with caution, trying not to wake people. The smell hit me as I slipped inside: an unpleasant scent of unwashed bodies, sweat, and the distinct odour of vomit. I collected a cloth from a pile by the door and fastened it across my face before glancing around me. The citizens in the main dorm appeared to be settled and mostly sleeping. The door to the first private room was firmly closed, however the second had a light burning. I paused at the entrance. A figure lay on the side of the bed closest to the door.

Mason.

He was pale and drenched in sweat, his matted hair plastered to his forehead. Clutching his stomach, he tossed and turned as though demons possessed him. Green sat on the bed beside him. She was pale and sweating, but was managing to mop his feverish chest with a cool wet rag. I couldn't tear my eyes away from my friend, who was now moaning much like Barnes had been doing the last time I saw him. I heard a cry before I realised it had come from my own mouth.

Green looked up with alarm. "Get out, Quin! You shouldn't be in here!"

I held out a hand to quiet her, "I'm sick too."

Her face fell. "Just when I thought we might be seeing some

improvement..."

"Really?"

She nodded weakly, "I haven't been able to sit up since early yesterday morning, but since I took the meds...." She motioned to the basin of water and her ability to tend to Mason, "...see what I can do?"

"Well that's good, but don't exhaust yourself. No offence, but you still don't look great." I tried to smile, "Look, I don't have a temperature. But I did throw up, So I figure I'd better take precautions. Know where the meds are?"

She pointed through the wall, "Blythe has them. She took charge of them earlier, once Marley had doled them out. If you knock, I'm sure she can get you what you need. Then get to bed and rest."

I began to back away, but glanced down at Mason, "He looks terrible. Did he take the meds?"

"He did." She frowned, "But he had it far worse than me, so I guess it might take longer for them to take effect." She looked down at the covers. "I'm not sure about Barnes, though. Blythe wasn't even sure she could get him to swallow the meds."

I could see the tears in her eyes. "I'll go and see." I managed to say before I backed away, trying not to look at Mason's pale, feverish torso.

The first door remained closed, and I leaned close to it in an effort to prepare myself for what I might discover on the other side. I could hear the same haunting moans and a second voice, pleading softly, the same indistinguishable sound over and over. I drew my hand back and knocked as softly as I could.

For a moment there was silence, but then I heard shuffling footsteps and a pale face appeared in the crack in the doorway.

I stepped back, shocked. Blythe looked the way she had when I'd first met her and she had been grieving Perry's loss. I didn't want to intrude, but after registering her surprise, her face became concerned.

"What are you doing in here, Quin?"

"I'm so sorry to disturb you... Do you have the meds please?"

The door opened a little further, "Who needs them?"

"Me, I'm afraid. I've just been sick... don't feel too bad, but..."

She seemed to pull herself together a little, "Wait a second."

She disappeared, leaving the door open a tiny crack. Unable to resist, I leaned on the heavy wood slightly, and the space widened. I could now see into the room. Blythe busied herself on the far side, sifting through the packages which Baker had brought in earlier until she found the pills I needed. Cass lay still on the opposite side of the bed, facing me this time. She was sleeping, and looked peaceful, despite the pallor of her face. I hoped that she was improving in a similar way to Green.

My gaze came to rest, finally, on Barnes. He lay far closer to the door than Cass, and I knew I had avoided looking at him for as long as possible. He seemed to be barely breathing. His form was shrunken and deathly-white. I was unable to prevent the rush of air that escaped as I took in what was, I knew for certain, a dying man. Hearing my distress, Blythe looked up and saw me in the doorway. I shrank back, afraid that she would be angry, but instead her face creased up and the tears began to fall.

Making sure that the cloth was still covering my mouth, I slid inside the room. Closing the door behind me softly, I made my way to Blythe. When I was standing next to her, I put a hand on her shoulder tentatively, unsure of her reaction. She flinched, but eventually turned to look at me, pain etched into every line of her fatigued face.

"I don't think he has long," her voice was a whisper.

"But the meds..."

"He's been ill the longest. I can't even get him to take the pills."

"Could we—?"

She put up a hand to cut me off, "I already tried. Crushed them up into a powder, mixed them with water. He drank a little of it, but..."

She stopped. The room seemed to be closing in on us as we stood there and I wondered how she, the woman who had been in here for days now, could stand it. I moved even closer, aiming to put my arms around her, but she recoiled from my offer of comfort, backing away with a look of alarm on her face.

"Take this." She proffered a small white pill and waved a vague hand at the pitcher of water and glasses set out on the side. "Make sure you take one of those—I washed them earlier." She glanced back at the pill. "For now, that single dose is probably all you need. But let me know if you get any worse."

Not knowing what else to do, I moved away and poured myself a clean glass full of water. Pulling the cloth aside, I put the small white tablet into my mouth. Then I downed it in a torrent of water, continuing to swallow until there was nothing left in the glass. Replacing the cloth over my face, I turned back to Blythe. She was sitting on the bed next to Barnes, his hand clasped between her own. She seemed to have forgotten I was there.

Moving to the opposite side of the bed, I laid a hand on Cass' cheek. She stirred, shifted slightly, and resettled. Her face still had the sheen of sweat, but she looked far healthier than Barnes.

"I think she's improving," I was startled by Blythe's voice. "I promise I'm taking care of her too. Her temp is down and she hasn't been sick in a while now."

"Thank you."

I walked around the bed again, leaving Cass to sleep peacefully. Gazing down at Barnes, I could barely see the rise and fall of his chest, and his face was twisted in a vague grimace, as though he felt pain but no longer had the strength or will to express it. Biting back tears of my own, I bent down and laid a hand on his forehead, which was raging with fever. I thought of the man who had bawled us out for not keeping up in training, whose constant impatience with his trainees had frustrated me on numerous occasions, but these images were quickly replaced by those of the father he had tried to become, the man who was so desperate to protect the ones he loved he would risk death for them.

I laid a useless hand on Blythe's shoulder, "Want me to stay?"

She shook her head. I waited for a second, wondering if there was anything else I could do. She remained silent, her head bowed over the body of the man who had risked it all to prove his love for her. Feeling like an intruder, I turned to go, closing the door gently behind me.

Back in the main dorm, I found an empty bed between Jackson and Marley, who I hadn't even known was ill. The others seemed mostly to be asleep now, or at least pretending to be. Jackson lay still, and I did not want to disturb her, but as I lay there, I became aware that she was awake. Months of sharing a pod with her back in Patrol meant I knew how she slept: her deep and even breathing, the occasional snore, the fact that she always lay on her back. Now she was curled up on her side, facing away from me. In the stillness of the dorm, I could see that her shoulders were shuddering ever so slightly, and hear the sudden, sharp intake of her breath. She was crying.

I crept across the gap between our beds, laying a hand on her arm gently. For a moment she was startled, but her face relaxed as she realised who it was. Seconds later the concern was back as she realised what my presence in the dorm meant.

"You're sick too, Quin?"

I nodded. "I'm not so bad though, and I've taken the meds."

She stared at me for a moment, her face tortured. "I didn't go in."

"What?"

"To see Mason." I could see her struggling to speak above a whisper. "I didn't go in. Like you said."

"Oh. Right. That's good." I didn't understand what she was trying to tell me. "You could have–"

"But I saw him." She dropped her gaze. "The door was open. He looked... he looked..."

"I know. I'm sorry." I had never felt so helpless. "But he's had the meds. We have to hope they start working soon. Wait 'til tomorrow, he'll..." I trailed off, knowing nothing I could say right now would help.

Her tears returned, and I gave up trying to comfort her with words. Instead, I slipped into the space next to her, a mirror of the way the man she now cried over had comforted me only a few nights ago. She allowed me to slide my arms around her and the sobs which she had been trying to conceal, though still silent, now racked her body completely. I held her as she cried for several minutes, until eventually she lay, spent.

In the darkness I wondered what I could say to make things better. I struggled to form some words of comfort, but none came.

After a lengthy silence, a whisper came out of the darkness, "I thought once we were together everything would be alright."

I held her tighter.

"I've waited… waited for this. Spent days and nights dreaming of the time when I'd be back with him, with you."

"I'm so sorry, Jac."

"All those nights in Clearance. You can't imagine what it's like Quin. Night after night, it's so hard to stay hopeful when you know what's in store for you. But I tried to be strong and believe you'd come back for me."

"I know."

"What will I do if–?" Her voice trailed off in a sob.

"Don't think like that. You can't. You hear me?"

But she had stopped listening. I held her until her breathing evened out and she fell into the exhausted sleep of one who no longer has the energy to carry on. Meanwhile, my own thoughts continued to torment me, until sheer exhaustion drew me into the temporary relief of a black and dreamless sleep.

Chapter Thirty Five

When I awoke, it was to a different world. The dorm, which by night had been hushed, filled with figures whose sleep was disturbed by worries about their survival, was now louder, brighter somehow. The majority of the people in the room were sitting upright, eating, conversing quietly. As I pushed myself onto my elbows, I realised I didn't feel too bad either. The meds seemed to be doing their job, at least on those of us who had not been hit hard by the illness.

I looked across to see the space next to me was empty, but barely had time to consider where Jackson might be when a shadow fell across the bed. Marley stood above me, smiling at me without the protective cloth.

"How are you? I heard you joined us during the night."

I tried to respond and failed, realising how dry my mouth was.

"Oh hey wait, let me get you a drink." She poured noisily from the pitcher next to the bed while she talked. "I need to give you a second pill, but we're hoping people won't need another dose after that. Most of us are much better today."

I gulped the water down and obediently took the small white tablet she handed me. Once I had swallowed it, I sank back on to the pillows, still exhausted by the effort.

"You're tired, I'm sure. Most of the people in here have had a decent night's rest, and the pills seem to have brought the fever down. We think that's the secret, see? Once the fever is gone, the body seems able to fight the sickness. Then things start to improve."

She waved a hand around the room, "Most people are out of bed now and Baker says she thinks we can be allowed outside again once we've been without temperature or sickness for a decent period of time."

"Can I see her? Baker? Talk to her, I mean?" I wanted to know what had happened during the night. "Where is she?"

"Um, she's outside in the courtyard." Marley regarded me with suspicion. "Sure you're up to walking?"

I forced a smile. "I am if you help me."

I sat up again, this time with more success. Marley offered me an arm and helped to hoist me off the bed. Then she supported me as we walked to the door of the dorm. I considered how the role of nurse had rejuvenated her, from the devastated woman who had struggled to deal with Wade's death. It seemed that sometimes the most negative circumstances could bring out the best in people, forcing them to dig deep and find strength they had not previously known.

As we passed the two private rooms at the head of the dorm, I noticed with trepidation that both doors were firmly closed. Seeing my expression, Marley guided me quickly outside on to the porch. Baker stood outside in the courtyard, moving closer as she spotted me. Her expression was unreadable.

"How are you, Quin?" Her voice was uncharacteristically concerned. "I'm not sure you should be out of bed yet."

"I'm ok... at least I think so," I managed.

"Glad to hear it. I heard you got sick in the night. Was

worried it would be worse than this, but it appears that you got off lightly... more lightly than some anyway." She frowned cryptically, and I thought immediately of Barnes and Mason.

"How are things now? Is everyone...?"

She looked sharply at me again, "Everyone...? No. The majority of people seem to be improving, for which we should be thankful. And we have enough meds left to deal with more illness, should it occur. Tyler has stored what's left safely. She and Rogers are working on a new temporary schedule to keep us going until people are properly recovered. She's trying to keep his mind off Green."

"And Barnes...?"

She shook her head sadly, "Blythe's done her best. But he's been ill so much longer than everyone else."

I blinked back tears.

"He's still with us. We just have to stay hopeful."

I felt selfish for asking, but had to know about the others, "What about Cass?"

"We're going to move her into the main part of the dorm. She isn't half as sick as she was, and we felt..." Baker stumbled over her words for a moment, "We felt it wasn't doing her any good being in the same room as Barnes, never mind the need for him and Blythe to have a little time alone." She pressed on, more positively, "Green's improving too. We're hoping to bring her out of the room she's been in with Mason."

"How is Mason, then?"

She held a hand up to stop my questions, "All in good time. He's had the meds. He's not quite as bad as Barnes, but he's still seriously ill." She made a face as she registered the effect her words had on me. "We're waiting to see how he does today. We're hopeful he'll pull through."

334

I tried to smile.

"I think we need some time to see that the meds haven't just given us a temporary reprieve. As long as temperatures don't start to spike again, and people stop throwing up, we think we might be ok." She turned to walk to the door, "Rest up now, Quin. We have enough people and supplies that we can manage for a few days until people are fully recovered."

I found myself following her out, "I don't feel too bad. Couldn't I–?"

"No Quin, you couldn't." She turned from the doorway. "You can sit in the porch area of the dorm if you want to get some fresh air. But no attempting to leave the area by dorm two, please."

Obediently, I went outside and took a seat on the porch, watching closely as Baker began to walk back to the first dorm, where she was met by a concerned-looking Harper.

"Any sign yet?"

"No." She chewed on her lip. "Baker, where is he?"

My mind was still clouded with sleep, and meds, but I considered who she had been looking for the last time I had spoken to her.

"You still looking for Walker?" I called over, "But it was hours ago when you..."

Her face was as white as a sheet. "No one's seen him Quin. We don't know where he is."

Before I could respond, the door to the main building opened and Tyler headed out into the courtyard. Rubbing her back tiredly, she headed our way.

"Hey Quin, are you feeling better?"

I nodded.

"Good. Rogers and I have been working out a duty schedule.

I think we're almost done. We've covered all the essentials, for now at least." She turned to Harper. "Any sign?"

"No." My old friend hurried off, her face still furrowed with worry. I turned back to Tyler now that she was out of earshot.

"Did you–?"

She shook her head, "Not yet. I was going to tell him, but with everything going on, well... I couldn't."

"You know you have to, don't you?"

"Yes. I'll–"

But before she could continue, Nelson's familiar voice echoed from behind the building.

"Can I get some help?"

Tyler was the first one to race around the dorms to see what was happening, swiftly followed by others, including Baker and Harper. Still barred from leaving bunk two, I inwardly cursed my helplessness. I heard Harper cry out and felt fear grip my heart. The small procession of people returned a moment later, supporting a figure between them. It was Walker. They brought him to the porch of the dorm and laid him down. His face was swollen and bloody, and the sleeves of his overalls were torn, as though he had been attacked.

Baker took his pulse and felt his forehead, "No temperature. He isn't sick."

Walker sat up with difficulty, Nelson supporting him from behind. "Not sick, no. Was hunting..."

Nelson finished his sentence, "I found him on the path. He'd been heading back, it was just taking him a while, what with his injuries."

"Was it an animal?" Harper's voice was soft, concealing her panic.

He shook his head, "I'd caught a couple of rabbits. Took me

a while, but I managed it. Was heading back, but..."

We waited for him to catch his breath again, knowing he would continue.

"It was Thomas." A collective gasp travelled the group.

"You were right. He, Johnson, and Allen are holed up in the caves. He asked me to hand over one of the rabbits I'd caught. Said they needed food. I told him no." He glanced around as various people reacted to his refusal. "Why should we help them? They abandoned us! Anyway, as I walked away he attacked me from behind. I tried to fight him off, but he hit me over the head with something hard. I think I blacked out for a while."

He rubbed his head absentmindedly, as though remembering the blow. His expression went from anger to guilt as he continued, "Anyway, when I woke up he'd taken both the rabbits. I didn't have the strength to go up there after him."

"Bastard!" Harper's voice was filled with a venom I had never heard before.

An audible hiss of air escaped Baker's mouth and I could see her trying to control her reaction, "He is. But there's nothing we can do for now. We'll deal with them once we have our strength back. For now, let's get on. Those of us who can manage to work need to get out on shift, make sure we start bringing some more food in again. Those who are still recovering," she directed a sharp glance at me, "get back into Dorm Two and rest up."

People began to shuffle off in various directions. I obeyed Baker's instructions and headed back into the bunk. As I passed the two private rooms, I noticed that the door to the second one was slightly ajar. Pausing for a moment, I peered inside, knowing before I did what I would find. Inside, Jackson lay on the bed next to Mason, her arm wound around his neck, her head on the pillow beside him, and her eyes closed.

Pulling my shirt up until it covered the lower half of my face, I slipped inside the room and knelt down next to the bedside close to my friends. Of course, in the end, Jackson had made her way to Mason. She must have waited until anyone who would have tried to stop her was asleep. I noted with some relief that at least she had covered her face with one of the cloths before lying down beside him. Her breathing was even and she looked peaceful, clearly resting easier now that she was with him. I smiled, even as I fought back tears.

"She snuck in here in the middle of the night." He kept his voice low, but the warmth in his voice was unmistakable. "I was still running a fever, but I knew it was her."

Startled, my eyes flew to the speaker. Mason's eyes were open and, although he looked weak, he was smiling.

"Thank you, Quin." His eyes shone as he gazed at Jackson, "You brought her back to me."

Now the tears were flowing down my face helplessly. I grasped my friend's hand as tightly as I dared without disturbing the woman sleeping beside him. His eyes glowed for a second before fluttering closed again. I backed out of the room, leaving them both to rest.

As I eased the door closed, I heard a noise from inside the room next door. Concerned, I knocked gently. There was no response. I pushed the door open a fraction, dreading what lay on the other side. Blythe sat next to the bed, her head bent low over the man who lay before her. Her shoulders were shaking, and before I even looked down at Barnes, I knew.

He lay on his back, his body still, his face at peace, all signs of pain and anguish gone. The weight of the pain had been passed to those he had left behind now.

Becoming aware of another presence in the room, Blythe raised her head to look at me. Her face was drawn and haggard, and she looked twice the age I knew her to be. Her eyes were red rimmed, and she looked totally defeated. I moved towards her in an attempt at comfort, but she leapt up and made for the door, turning her face away as she pushed past me in her haste to escape the space, which had now become a tomb.

Suddenly, I couldn't breathe. Blythe had overcome so much and fought so hard to save the man she loved, but in the end it hadn't been enough. I stifled a cry of my own before following in her wake.

Outside, there were still enough people milling about to provide an audience to Blythe's grief. As the group fell silent, she came to an abrupt standstill on the porch, her eyes searching the space until she found Baker's. When she did, she gave the tiniest shake of her head.

Baker's face fell. Blythe stumbled forward again, her gaze continuing to scan the group, until they finally came to light on Perry, who was still cradled closely in Harper's arms on the steps of the first dorm. Only then did her eyes fill with tears. It was too soon for Blythe to hold Perry: she might well still be infected, and there was no point in risking her daughter's health when she was still so young and vulnerable. But it was abundantly clear that all she wanted to do in the wake of her loss was hold her child.

Instead, she slipped down the dorm steps, skirting the edge of the group to avoid making contact with any of us. Once she had crossed the courtyard, she headed off up the path into the distance, craving, I was sure, a little privacy and time to grieve.

We let her go.

Chapter Thirty Six

A week later I sat on board the Clearance boat within range of The Ridge, anchored down and waiting. We had sent a boat out here three times since the people on The Crags had begun recovering from the terrible sickness. We all wanted to put Cam's mind at ease, to let him know that the meds he had provided to us had worked. On every trip so far, our messengers had sailed out here and waited for more than an hour, intermittently trying to contact him on the radio with no success.

Today I was finally well enough to make the trip, and I was hoping my presence on the boat might, by some twist of fate, bring Cam's voice over the airwaves. I sat next to Green, who was recovered enough now to make the trip, and had been desperate to escape the confines of The Crags after her illness. A weak sun was breaking through the clouds overhead, and aside from Barnes' death, things appeared to be improving. We had lost one man, but saved the rest of our community, and, without our trip to The Beck, this would never have been possible.

There now stood three cairns in the field behind the centre, and we had held a ceremony for Barnes a few days ago. It had been similar to the one Green had arranged for Davis when we had first arrived. This time though, we were prepared, and understood the significance of it. Many more people had spoken, and even Blythe had managed a few words. At the end, Marley had sung a sad, mournful song in a beautiful voice which few people had known she possessed. As we stood listening, it seemed a fitting goodbye.

Most other citizens had managed a full recovery. Mason was taking a little longer than the others to return to full health, but in the end, he had pulled through. The remaining meds had been stored away for future use, though I desperately hoped they would not be necessary. It seemed that Anders' knowledge had been solid and the meds he had sent over had been enough to combat the terrible sickness.

The Ridge had been in regular contact with us via the walkie-talkies, again enthusing about the wonderful facilities at The Beck: the large open spaces, the multiple energy sources, and the workforce. Hughes seemed to think we should plan another trip there soon, and had mentioned holding a meeting with Adams, to discuss trading with The Beck as well as with us. I had to admire his ambition. Those of us who had lived there knew the impossibility of holding a sensible discussion with our ex-leader, but in the wake of the dramatic events of the past week we had humoured him, promising to communicate with them further once things had settled down.

He had yet to mention the files which Tyler had accidentally left in his charge. She had spent a lot of time worrying about their content, and whether or not The Ridge leadership had read them. What they might contain for now remained a mystery. She had finally plucked up the courage to confide her mistake to Baker and Rogers. Baker had been furious, her natural mistrust of strangers evident yet again. She had been stomping around her kitchen for days, muttering about what Hughes might do with any sensitive information he had gleaned from the file, and was barely speaking to Tyler.

Rogers had been less severe. Every spare minute since his return had been spent with Green, ensuring she was fully recovered, and trying to make up for his absence. He seemed bent on proving that she was more important to him than anyone else now, and his focus on the community as a whole was lacking. Clearly the thought that he could have lost Green had shown him what she had been through every time he left. I wondered if he would be prepared to be parted from her ever again, after the events of the past week. And while I was glad for them as a couple, I wondered how we would fare without their leadership.

I looked out across the water at The Ridge. It seemed quite beautiful from this distance. Hughes was pushing to trade tours: he would allow Crags citizens to visit The Ridge, but in turn he would get to look around our community. This was something I knew we weren't prepared for. For one, we weren't quite ready to reveal how few of us there actually were living at The Crags. Despite Hughes' support on the mission to The Beck, no one felt able to trust him completely yet. If and when we did decide to trade with Hughes, Mason wanted to get the mines fully functional, but his illness, in addition to the continuing presence of Thomas and his fellow traitors, meant we were a long way from that at the moment. So despite Hughes's enthusiasm, Rogers had firmly put him off for the time being, explaining that we still required some assurances before taking our relationship any further.

We had sent several people up to the caves where Thomas and his friends were holed up. There had been no further sightings of them, but we were certain they were still there. Those of us on hunting duty were careful to travel in groups now, and carried weapons with which to defend ourselves, but since the attack on Walker, there had been no more trouble. Most of the Crags' citizens were furious with Thomas, and many wanted to charge up there and drive them out, but Tyler and Green had persuaded them to leave them alone. The simplest thing to do, they had argued, was just to wait the traitors out. Sooner or later they would have to come out in search of food, and we would deal with them when they did.

I felt heartsick. Too much had happened since we had arrived at The Crags and we needed time as a community to build and recover before we dived into new endeavours.

Green tried the walkie-talkie once more, on the expected channel, with the same call: "Cam, come in. Are you there Cam? Respond please."

Again, nothing. Green sighed.

"Haul up the anchor, will you? We'll have to try again tomorrow."

I walked to the side of the boat where the anchor's rope hung over into the water and began to pull on it. Green slid into position at the wheel, ready to start the engine.

And then the walkie-talkie crackled. Just faintly, not enough to even be heard at first, but growing in volume and length. Someone was trying to come through.

We rushed back to the tiny radio and fought to pick it up. Green got there first, and I hung on her elbow, excited, desperate to hear Cam's voice. She fiddled with the dial, adjusting it by tiny increments until the squealing grew louder and became more continuous.

"I told you!" I was unable to stop myself from crowing,

"Told you I'd bring us luck. That this would be the day."

Like sunlight through the clouds, a voice came though. But it did not belong to Cameron. I couldn't place it until he said his name. And then I knew.

"Hello? Is anyone there? This is Anders."

Green exchanged a glance with me as she raised the walkie-talkie to her lips, "Hello Anders, my name is Green."

There was a pause as he took in the information, and then, "Are you from The Crags?"

"I am. Quin is here with me."

"Hi Anders, is everything ok?"

"I..." the radio crackled, "I have a message. Sorry it's taken me so long, but..." The radio cut out for a minute. "...don't have long. Things are crazy here."

It cut out again.

"Anders? Are you there?"

"Yes. Yes, I'm here. Thought you needed to know. The Beck has some kind of sickness. Spreading... rapid... some meds but low on supplies... Gov acting, but not fast enough..."

Green tried to respond, "Anders. We've had it here too. The meds you sent, they work though..."

He didn't seem able to hear us properly, and ploughed on regardless, "Cam is sick."

My heart seemed to stop at the words.

But he hadn't finished. "Most of the Lower Beck too... quarantine... drastic measures... Need to−" his tone changed suddenly, "I have to go. Someone's coming."

And as Green and I exchanged terrified glances, the radio went dead.

Reeling from the news, we sat there for a few moments, neither of us able to move. The information ricocheted inside my head, repeating over and over, but not fully sinking in.

Cam was sick. With the same illness we had suffered. And *I* was the one who had given it to him.

My mind was racing. What proportion of the medicine had we taken from The Beck? Would they have enough to deal with the sickness? The possible scale of casualties if the illness swept through the entire Beck was unthinkable. How many more would die like Barnes?

Green backed away, her face ashen. There was nothing she could say to comfort or console me. I wondered if the expression of horror on her face came anywhere close to my own.

After holding my glance for several desolate moments, she tore her eyes away and moved back to the wheel. I barely heard the engine roar to life. The steady throbbing sound wasn't able to drown out the screams of guilt which echoed inside my head.

For as long as I could remember, I had dreamed of a life free of The Beck and its confines. As the boat began to chug slowly back to The Crags, I wondered what that freedom might cost.

And whether, in the end, it would be worth it.

Author's Note

Thank you for reading Drift. I hope that you enjoyed following Quin from The Beck to her new home at The Crags (and back). I love building relationships with my readers. If you enjoyed Drift, and would like to receive updates when I'm releasing a new book, sign up for my readers' club:

http://www.clarelittlemore.com/free-books/?signup= book-drift

If you sign up, you'll receive a regular newsletter with give-aways, book recommendations, special offers, the occasional free short story, and (of course) details of my all new releases. I promise there will be no spam.

Reviews

Liked this book? You can make a **big** difference. Reviews are really powerful. Being a self-published author, getting my books noticed can sometimes be a challenge. If you enjoyed reading Drift, please consider spending just a couple of minutes leaving an **honest review** (it can be as brief as you like) on the book's Amazon or Goodreads page. I'd be so grateful.

Thank you very much.

About the Author

Clare Littlemore is a young adult dystopian and sci-fi author who thrives on fictionally destroying the world in as many ways as she possibly can.

She was born in Durham, in the UK. Her parents were both teachers, and she grew up in a world surrounded by books. She has worked for most of her life as a teacher of English at various high schools in England, where she has shared her passion for books with hundreds of teenagers. In 2013 she began writing her own fiction, got totally hooked, and hasn't stopped since.

Clare lives in Warrington in the North West of England with her husband and two children.

You can connect with Clare:
- on Twitter at twitter.com/Clarelittlemore
- on Facebook at facebook.com/clarelittlemoreauthor
- Instagram: https://www.instagram.com/clarelittlemore
- in the Last Book Cafe on Earth Facebook group: https://www.facebook.com/groups/lastbookcafeonearth/
- or send her an email at clare@clarelittlemore.com

Acknowledgements

Getting this book finished is one of the hardest things I've ever had to do. I had heard that the third book in a series could prove a tricky one to write, but didn't realise quite how difficult it might be until I started on Drift. Since its first draft, it has gone through a MASSIVE rewrite, had huge numbers of words cut from it, had characters disappear or be renamed, and undergone too many minor alterations to count. The book is only here in front of you today thanks to the help and support of a number of very important people, to whom I owe a HUGE debt of gratitude.

Firstly, to my editor, Beth Dorward, who has come through hell and high water with this book with me! Thank you for always being honest. Thanks also for bearing with me, being patient while I struggled with the redrafting, answering my never-ending queries over this character and that plotline, and finally for extending and amending deadlines on several occasions so that I could take the time I needed to get it right.

Similarly, my cover designer, Jessica Bell, deserves huge praise for coming up with another amazing cover which both continues the motif for the series, yet stands out as a distinct and eye-catching design. Jessica also deserves credit for patiently waiting for me to complete the book. I'm often too ambitious, expecting more of myself than I can realistically manage, and she bore with me through a large number of deadline extensions. For this, I am extremely thankful.

This is a new one. I love meeting new writer-friends online, but some are truly gold. Alison Ingleby is a fellow-writer (and fellow-Brit) who happily read an earlier version of Drift and was hugely helpful on many occasions when I got myself into a tight spot with the plot or characters. She is a far better plotter than I am, and I have to thank her for her many amusing 'wild card' suggestions, some of which actually ended up in the final version of Drift! I'm also very grateful for her endless patience when talking through potential plotlines with me, usually when they were so mixed up in my head that I couldn't even think straight! (She also writes pretty great dystopian books herself. Check her out: https://alisoningleby.com/)

To Mum, who remains my most nifty proof-reader, spotting even the smallest of errors. To Dad, for reading the books despite not being a huge lover of the genre, and offering never-ending support and praise. To Linda, still my fastest pre-reader, whose comments on the books are always useful. And to Maria M, another fellow writer, whose encouragement and understanding has seen me through a couple of my darker moments. Thank you all.

To my lovely friend Lucy, who provides another eagle-eye on the grammar and general sense of my writing. Thank you so much for your numerous suggestions and comments, always couched in supportive terms, which often shape the early edits of every chapter I write.

To my other early readers (you know who you are): thanks, as always, for your comments. And to all those readers on my mailing list, who read my every newsletter, comment on my progress, eagerly await my next book, and snatch up a copy the moment it is released: thank you so much. Without you, the word about my books would not get out the way it has done: your support is so important to me.

To my husband Marc, as always. You are my most stalwart supporter, and even when I lose confidence in my ability to write another word, you're there with more encouragement, a hug and another cup of tea. And to my children, Daniel and Amy, who are always interested in finding out when Mum's next book is coming out (and not afraid to tell me that it has been far too long between instalments!)

Lastly, to you, my readers. Without you, there would be no point me continuing to write. So thanks for taking a chance on this book. I hope to write many more for you.

CPSIA information can be obtained
at www.ICGtesting.com
Printed in the USA
BVHW081818290721
613187BV00009B/693